Betty Radford Turcott, [illegible] immediately into the story [illegible] *of Hope* is a beautifully crafted [illegible] teaching us not only the biblical story but also the times and customs of the day. How I wanted to linger in the women's tent and take part in all their activities.

Pat Gilmore, Grand River Book Store

As a former protestant minister, I often struggled with the female biblical characters. Their stories were written by men, where women made cameo appearances in support roles. Turcott remedies this and brings a sense of wholeness and equality to this patriarchal period. It is an enjoyable page-turner as the immersive experience intensifies during the course of the novel.

Historical fiction has been my preferred way for expanding my sense of the past and escaping to another time and place. Betty Turcott's *Rebekah* does this well, as she engages the reader in this biblical matriarch's world. Through skillful character development and keen imagination, this strong and knowledgeable author brings her subjects alive.

Paul Irwin, Retired Minister

This story of Rebekah is a thoroughly enjoyable read. It works well as a standalone novel even though it is part of a series. This story develops familiar biblical characters into fully developed people with a complete life story. The details not included in the bible have been developed in an engaging way and makes this a rewarding experience. The characters are biblical, but this is a story of the strength and frailties of real women from long ago. If I were working in a public library instead of being retired, I would definitely add this to the collection.

Kathy Baskey, Retired, Ottawa, Canada

Rebekah comes alive in Radford Turcott's book, *Rebekah, The Valley of Hope*. The reader is transported back in time to walk with Rebekah in the desert, to feel the heat of the day, and the refreshing evening breeze through the open flap of her tent. It is a brilliant portrayal of the day to day life of a strong and most interesting woman. Ms. Radford Turcott's vivid writing pulls you in and doesn't let go until the last page. A great read for women of all faiths or no faith. And for men too of course.

Gloria Nye, Author of the Dragonfly Novels.

Other books by Betty Radford Turcott

And She Said: Monologues on Biblical Women

A Circle of Stones: Sarah's Story

Rebekah
The Valley of Hope

Betty Radford Turcott

Betty R. Turcott

Cover Design by Erin Samson
Cover Photo by istock.com
Photo of Author by Jim Ellis

Published by

Kentisbeare Press
1088 Maritime Way, Unit 316,
Kanata, ON K2K 0L9

ISBN 978-0-9959905-2-4

Rebekah
The Valley of Hope

Betty Radford Turcott

Dedication

This story of a woman's life is dedicated to three exceptional women who have been my mentors and teachers four decades of my life.

Sr. Dody Donnelly, 1926-2013. The first woman professor at a major theological college in California.

Dr. Marion Logan. 1929-2022. A passionate advocate for women in all areas of their lives, and a leader in the United Church of Canada.

Dr. Anne Squire 1920-2017. The first lay woman moderator of the United Church of Canada. A gentle, dynamic trailblazer.

Thank you, my friends, your spirit of hope, inspires me still.

Author's Foreword

Our women forebears have been a life-long interest of mine; women of secular history, but especially the women of the bible. One purpose of scripture was to tell the story of the people's understanding of God. Men told the story, and men were the main characters. The lives of the women were of minor interest to the writers. They were present as wives, mothers, daughters, sisters, queens, and slaves. Their contribution was always secondary to the males. Considering the society at the time this is to be expected. Misogyny continued to impact translators and teachers of the material for centuries. It is primarily in my lifetime that women have brought their voices to the telling of these ancient stories.

Where women are included in the story, we learn little about them and hear their voices only in the background. I have always been fascinated by the untold story. Who were these women? How did they live? What did they understand about the events of their day? How did they react to or contribute to the incidents that were related in the story?

In my imagination I have answered these questions. And this series of fictional books is my answer; this ancient story imagined and told, in a woman's voice, my voice. The Bible is my starting point, and the main characters come from the pages of scripture. The others are fictional, and they came to life as the story unfolded at my computer.

This is the second book in the series Women of the Bible, and the third is beginning to take shape in my heart and mind.

There is a list of the characters at the back of the book, and some questions. The reader can consider them alone or use them as a starting point for group discussion.

Chapter One

They stood together, watching the sun go to its rest behind the distant hill; their arms linked, their bodies almost touching. A gentle summer wind blew their head scarfs like hands waving in joy. Two women joined in a lifelong friendship.

"You are quiet tonight, Rebekah. Where are your thoughts taking you?"

"Back to my days as a baby. You were always there, Debba."

"Not always. My parents sent me to your mother when I had seen about fifteen winters. You gave me my new name the first time you saw me. Deborah was too big a word and so from that first time I held you, I have been Debba."

"Would you prefer your proper name now? I am sure a can learn to always call you Deborah."

"No, Debba is fine. I like it. It usually means that all is well, and you are feeling playful. You are the only one who calls me that, and it gives me a warm feeling. I was surprised that your mother trusted me to be your nurse and companion. You were a child, not a baby, but you were totally in my care. Your mother was always watching, and I was severely punished when she thought I neglected you. I soon learned how important you were."

"I never thought mother cared what happened to me. She always favoured Laban. I know he is the first-born son, but surely her daughter deserved some affection."

"It's true Ruth favoured Laban, but Bethuel worshipped you, his only daughter. He carried you everywhere even after you could walk. He lifted you on his shoulders, or you clung to his back. He talked to you about anything and everything."

Rebekah smiled. "I remember the stories of our people, their journeys, troubles, and the tall tales about Father Abraham. He and his wife, Sarah, seemed too good to be true. I always thought they were legends. I was much older before I realized they were real people and my ancestors."

"At times, I agreed with your mother that your father filled your head with useless things for a girl."

Rebekah shook her head. "No Deborah. Knowledge is never useless. I know who I am, and that I can take care of myself if I ever need to. Father taught me that I am a worthwhile person and what I want, and need is important. He often told me I would need courage to live a life that mattered, and I could be someone when I was older. Not just someone's daughter, wife, or mother, but a person with her own story and dreams and hopes. A person to be respected and listened to."

Deborah shook her head but did not reply.

The sun had almost disappeared, and the hills flamed crimson and gold. The two women turned and walked back to the house where they lived.

Deborah chuckled. "Is that why you have rejected every man who has been put before you as a possible husband?"

"It is too beautiful a night to worry about a husband for me. What about you? Don't you want to marry and have babies?"

"I am a servant. I have no dreams of anything but being your friend and companion for the rest of my days."

"Then we will grow old and wise together."

They continued on the path, enjoying each other's companionship.

"Remembering younger days, did you have a ceremony when you bled for the first time?"

"No Debba. Not really. Mother wasn't interested in rites or ceremonies. She explained what was happening and that I was now ready to be married. She said that for some reason she didn't understand, I was supposed to choose a spirit symbol to guide me. I asked what her symbol was, and she said, 'if I ever chose one, I don't remember.' She didn't make it seem very important, but Zera, my grandmother, told me it was wise to choose a symbol. If chosen wisely, it could be a source of comfort and strength in troubles. I trusted my grandmother more than my mother."

"And what did you choose?"

"I chose the cedar tree."

"I love the earthy smell of cedar wood, but why did you choose it? There are many lovely trees, the flowering almond for one."

"Cedars grow strong and beautiful along the river, and I loved to sit under the shade of their feathery branches and smell the earthy scent. It lives a long time and is very useful. Its wonderful aroma keeps bugs away and we drink cedar tea for different ailments. It bends but does not break. I want to be like that, strong and resilient. Mother said it was a foolish symbol as the tree dies. Well, I will die too, but I can be strong, useful, and beautiful all my life. Zera stitched berries and fronds on my tunics and capes. They remind me of my symbol and my grandmother whenever I see them."

"I think it is a wonderful symbol for you. You are wise and sensible."

"Do you have a spirit symbol?"

"I do. But there was no ceremony for me. I just decided if other women had a symbol, I would too. I chose a honeybee. I felt that they lived a life like mine. Always working, dressed in plain clothes, driven by the needs of others. Fragile and always at risk. I wonder still how they survive the rainy season. And that too is the life of slaves and servants. We survive, somehow. I am not unhappy as your servant. You are kind and more of a friend than a master. But I think of others who live day to day, never sure of the future."

"The bee is perfect for you. You are an uncomplicated woman. Why must life be so difficult? We all seem to think that someone else has a better life that we do. But we each must find our own way."

Deborah yawned as they reached the house and Rebekah smiled. "You go to bed. Sleep well, my friend. I will sit by the fire for a little while longer."

Deborah touched Rebekah's arm in blessing and went to her room. It was a small one beside the larger one where Rebekah lived in the house of her father.

Rebekah crouched by the fire and watched the glowing coals. She stirred the embers with a stick and wrapped her shawl around her to keep off the evening chill. Once the sun disappeared and the sky turned dark, it quickly felt cold and damp.

She thought of her mother and spoke softly to the night air. "I wonder what made her the way she was and still is. I envied girls I saw laughing, running, and playing with their mothers. Pleasant times we shared are not easy to recall. She doted on Laban, and they spent all her spare time together. While I missed having a mother, my father made me feel important. He loves me and shows it in so many ways."

Rebekah stood to go to her room, and she touched the small, embroidered cedar frond on the corner of her shawl. As she walked she fondly remember the sprig of cedar attached. to the curtain over her window. It was the first thing she saw in the morning, and the last thing before sleep closed her eyes.

The night breeze carried its scent into the room, and she breathed deeply of the calming aroma. She walked to her small window and as she closed the curtain, she touched the cedar branch. *Zera was always there, teaching me so many things and helping me grow up. I haven't thought of that ceremony for a long time. Zera was the only caring mother I knew. She loved me and taught me, praised me, and encouraged me. I miss her smile and her wonderful laugh. Even though she died many years ago, she is with me every day.*

Chapter Two

Abraham stood and stretched his arms wide. He grimaced in pain. "My old bones are stiff as sticks and my eyes are cloudy like a rainy sky. The days are long and empty. The fire offers little warmth, and memories fill the long, aimless hours. Whenever I am alone by my fire, my wife of many years, Sarah, dwells in my thoughts. How many years has it been since her death? More years than I can count."

Abraham reached for a stick and stirred the embers of the fire. He mumbled to himself, lost in the mist of memories.

"I remember her on our wedding day. So young. So beautiful. So trusting. Life was good with her by my side. Not always easy." He chuckled. "She had a mind of her own and a strong will. But we were happy. Thinking of marriage reminds me that I must find a wife for our son, Isaac. He needs to marry and have sons, or else my life has little meaning.

Abraham stood and looked to the distant mountain, the dwelling place of the god of his people. Its twin peaks reached high into a cloudless azure sky. This morning, the mountain slept. There was no smoke or fire and no thunder rumbling deep within its hidden centre.

"Here in Canaan, we live amid idol worshippers, but we obey the great god of the mountain, El Shaddai, the mighty one. Isaac seems only to care about goats and sheep. Lately, he only goes to the altar to worship when I beg him for his help. Before his mother died, he was faithful to our worship and recited the prayers. Her death changed him. He spends too many hours alone in his tent. I have asked what he does, but he shrugs and talks about the goats."

He stirred the fire again, and it sent up a shower of sparks.

"Sarah coddled him. In her eyes, he could do no wrong. I can understand since he came long after we gave up hope of having a child. He spent most of his time with her, and I had little influence on him. I worry about the future when I am gone. How he can be a leader for this large tribe since he can hardly read or make neat marks to keep track of numbers? He has little backbone and no interest in the law or the sacred stories. I must arrange his marriage to a strong woman who can keep him in line, and she must be a follower of the one god of my people. Isaac cannot marry a woman from this land. Sarah said I would need to go back to my homeland and find a wife for my spineless son. And she was right. There are many of our family still living there. The children of my brother Nahor must remember their old uncle."

He chuckled.

"Foolish thoughts. Travel back to the land of my birth when I can barely hobble to my vineyard. I can't even begin to think of a trip to the land from which my father and I came, and there is no way that Isaac can go. I can't trust him to make a sound choice. He would return with…" He scratched his beard. "I don't know who he would bring, but she would not be a helper to him. That leaves Eliezar. My wise, faithful, obedient, and trustworthy servant. What a friend he has been to me all these years."

The old man scanned the hillside, looking for his servant.

He has been by my side through every trial and every joy. Never questioning my decisions, even when I am sure he knew I was being stubborn or just plain wrong. He rubbed the aching bones in his back. *I can trust him with my life, and I can trust him with Isaac's future and the future of my people.*

Abraham waved as he spotted Eliezar bringing a bowl of figs and a cup of cool water for him.

"Sit here with me, old friend. I need to ask a favour of you."

"Whatever you need, I will do at once."

"Careful what you promise. Today, my need is a lot more complex than a few figs. I need you to undertake a journey that I can no longer do myself."

"Where would you like me to go? Do you need something in Hebron?"

"Isaac needs a wife and I want you to go back to my homeland and choose a bride for my son."

"Me? Find a wife for your son! That is not an easy task. A man wants to choose his own wife, or at least have his father do it. Better I help you with the journey. We could take a cart and you could ride the whole way, then make your own choice of Isaac's wife. Much better, I think."

Abraham smiled, took a drink, and offered Eliezar some figs.

"I cannot travel so far anymore. It is a journey of many weeks. Besides, with my poor sight, I might bring back the ugliest women in the land, and you know Isaac is very fussy." They both hooted. "No, this is a job for you. You are many seasons younger than I am. I will explain it all to you and give you, my instructions."

Abraham made it clear to Eliezar that the girl must be young, beautiful, strong, and clever. She had to be a woman who could manage Isaac and support him, giving him advice and shaping him into a leader. She must be a believer in El Shaddai and worship him only.

Eliezar groaned and shook his head.

"Of course, you remember when my father, Terah and I moved to this land, my brother stayed in our homeland, Ur. Later I learned that Nahor had moved to the north to Haran. We lived in a valley near there for a while and that is where Terah sleeps the long sleep of death. Return to that place and perhaps you can find my brother if he lives, or his son Bethuel. I have heard stories of Bethuel's daughter, a woman of great beauty and determination. She might be the woman Isaac needs. But you will find the right one."

"I will do your bidding as always, but this task fills me with dread. I do not want to fail you and destroy your trust."

"Eliezar. There is no one else who would understand. Trust in the mountain god and remember my instructions. All will be well."

"I have one request."

"What do you want?"

"I ask to take Benjamin, the camel drover, with me. He is a good man, strong, young, and he knows camels. He has travelled to Haran before. He spent a season with Laban and his experience will be useful."

"Of course. I had forgotten. Take him and let him choose his helpers. You will leave soon and travel with the caravan of traders going to Haran. There is safety in a group. Just keep your errand a secret and tell no one of the treasure you take with you."

Many days were spent getting ready. Lavish gifts of gold, silver, pottery, and fine cloth were carefully packed. And the bride price, Abraham had to decide the amount by himself. Usually, the fathers discussed and bickered for hours over the value of the bride. But that was not possible. *I can't ask Eliezar to do that. I will be generous, so generous her father can't refuse.* Ten camels were made ready to carry the gifts and supplies. With much care, Abraham chose warriors who were to accompany Eliezar for added safety for the valuable goods they were going to carry. When he was sure Abraham was not listening, Eliezar grumbled to himself.

"If we don't all die before we get there, how will I know the right one? Where do I look? How do I choose? Abraham says his god will provide. I wish I could be that confident. How will I convince any woman to take this journey to marry a stranger in a far-away land?" Eliezar scratched his head as he worried. "What if they have all forgotten their wandering relative? If I fail, what then? Dare I return to Abraham with nothing and no bride? Maybe I could refuse and take my punishment here and save all the trouble. But of course, I will go as Abraham asks, and deal with whatever happens."

When all was ready, Eliezar stood before his master and friend.

"I go at your bidding. If I do not return, you will know I have failed and am unable to bear the shame and have gone far away."

Abraham clapped his friend on the back. "You will return. I have no doubt. And you will bring the woman Isaac needs for a wife. Go with my blessing."

He stood and shaded his eyes from the sun as he watched the caravan move to the far-off horizon, straining his eyes until the last camel disappeared.

Chapter Three

Abraham arranged for Eliezar to travel with a caravan of traders. All went well, and the long journey unfolded without any unforeseen troubles His own soldiers, whom Abraham insisted travel with the caravan, caused curious looks from the traders, but Eliezar's group stayed together and there were no problems. Extra protection was always a good thing to have. Robbers would attack trade caravans that appeared to be weak. On the outskirts of Haran, the two groups said farewell. The traders went to the market and Abraham's group went to the village well.

Eliezar stood by the well and spoke to Benjamin.

"It's been a very long journey, but we have arrived safely. I wonder what will come of it all. Will it be worth it?"

"I know you are here because Abraham has sent you, and you asked for me. I also know it is none of my business, but can you tell me why we have come all this way? Why are we here and how long will we stay?"

"I am here on an errand for Abraham. I don't know how long it will take, but we will stay until I succeed or fail. I am here to find a bride for Isaac. He insisted that the wife of Isaac must not be a Canaanite, she must be of the clan of his father, Terah. And so, we are here at the well in Haran.

"Didn't Abraham come from here?"

"Yes. Many years ago, and I travelled with him. Over the years while I have served him, I have been asked to do many things, but this is the most difficult."

He gazed at the peak of the holy mountain, circled in a halo of cloud. "Abraham said to pray. His god would give me the wisdom I needed. I hope he spoke the truth."

He looked at the far mountain.

"What if I make a poor choice? Who am I to pick a wife for the son of my master? I have been worried about it all the way here. Almost twenty days we have been travelling and I am still concerned about my obligation."

"I am glad I do not walk in your sandals. I wouldn't know how to begin to look for a bride for another man."

"Neither do I. I have done as Abraham instructed me. I have prayed for wisdom to the god of the great mountain."

"Abraham put great faith in this invisible god of the fire mountain."

"I am not as interested in the complicated religion Abraham follows, but he puts great faith in it. And so, I have asked his god, El Shaddai, the mighty god of the mountain, to show me the right woman. All women come to the well at some time. I will ask for water from one who interests me, and if she gives me, my men, and my camels water, she is the one."

Benjamin gave Eliezer an intense look, filled with wonder but also fear. "I wish you well. But this is most unusual. I shall wait to see what happens with great interest."

"If I fail, it will be what happens to us. Would we dare go back if we have no suitable bride?

Benjamin looked even more worried, and he did what he always did when troubled. He turned his attention to the camels.

Chapter Four

Talking to herself, Rebekah complained. "Another day. Hot, dry, and dreary. The sky may be blue, but my world is brown. Brown sand, brown tents, brown mood. I sit at my loom and even this cloth I weave is brown." She banged the shuttle on the loom and hit her thumb. "Each day is a repeat of every day in the preceding months. Friends seldom visit. We have little in common. Most are married and caring for husband and children. If it wasn't for Debba, I would have no one to talk to." As Rebekah pressed the fabric snug, she let go of the tension in her shoulders. The shuttle flew across the threads.

"My parents have tried. They have paraded a throng of men past me for my inspection. Old, young, skinny, fat, hairy, bald, and even toothless. None looked me in the eye. They spoke only to my father about me." She made a face and stared at the loom. "I might be a sheep or a goat for barter." She struggled to free the shuttle that was trapped in the threads. "Apparently, I have a reputation for being difficult. I am too opinionated, not subservient, as a good wife should be." She paused. "Well, it is probably true. But I will not marry, simply to be married. I'm not expecting a prince or a rabbi, but I do need someone I can respect." Her brow relaxed its frown and she grinned.

"At least my father considers me and my feelings. He won't sign a contract unless I agree. That is rare. What a wonderful man he is, and I am grateful. Grateful for the respect he shows mother and me, and not just us but all women, even the servants and slaves."

Deborah entered the tent and stood in silence.

Rebekah looked up. "Good afternoon. I have been thinking about my life and I am not in a particularly good mood. Your presence is welcome."

"What troubles you today?"

"It is time for me to go into seclusion. You know how I dread that time. Alone in my rooms. Feeling miserable, nothing to do but mend and sew."

Deborah sighed. *I am with you, but perhaps I am invisible.*

"Enough! I will go to the well. The walk will do me good and will help to banish this dull mood." She stood and walked to the empty water jars. "Get a water jar and come with me since I cannot go alone. So many rules for women, especially unmarried women. Sometimes I think it might be easier to just get married. Happily, I come to my senses before I do what I would regret."

Rebekah picked up a green scarf and the two women walked to the well, carrying the heavy jars and talking together.

"Look, Rebekah, there is a man at the well. What is he doing there?"

"I don't know, but he has a group of servants with him. He is just a traveller, passing through."

Deborah stopped. "We should go back. It is not proper for us to be in the company of a stranger."

"It is the well of our ancestor, Terah. The strangers are the ones to leave. Go home if you wish. I came for water, and I will get what I came for. I will be alright. Don't worry."

Rebekah took her scarf and covered her face as Deborah turned and hurried back to the house. Keeping her face shielded from the men with her veil, Rebekah moved to the well and lowered the bucket. The stranger's servants stood nearby with a long line of camels. As she lowered the bucket, she furtively watched a short, heavy-set man. He stood close to the well while his servants stood a little way off. He was better dressed, but just as dusty and dirty. He coughed and she turned to look at him. He bowed.

"Peace to you and to your house. I have travelled a long way, and I am tired and thirsty. I do not have a bucket and am asking if you would draw a drink of water for a weary traveler. I would be most grateful."

Rebekah looked at him. He spoke Hebrew in a lilting voice and his clothing was a simple colourful cloak of fine quality linen, as was his head covering. His sandals were well worn and dirty, but of excellent quality leather. The men with him were dressed much the same only not such fine cloth. They stood silently with their eyes down cast. It was a sign of respect and regard for her as a woman. Rebekah was surprised and felt a little more at ease. She poured water into a bowl and offered it to the weary traveler.

He bowed as he took it. "Shalom and thank you." He drank deeply and smiled guardedly. His servants looked on with open mouths, licking their lips.

"I will draw water for your servants, and if they will help me, your animals too."

"May the god of the high mountain bless you, my daughter," and he bowed deeply. "I am Eliezer servant to Abraham, son of Terah and brother of Haran and Nahor. Long ago we lived in this valley and buried Terah in the hills not far from here."

"I am Rebekah, daughter of Bethuel, son of Nahor. The renown of Abraham our father is told and retold by our fires. I will go and tell my father of your arrival."

"Before you go, I have something for you. I am here on an errand from Abraham, and he has sent this gift." Her eyes opened wide in astonishment.

He handed her a dainty ivory box carved with flowers, vines, and leaves. With a bow, she took it and tucked it into her sleeve. *A gift for me. That is strange. Why did he bring a gift and then give it to me, not my father or mother?* Rebekah picked up her jar, lifted it to her shoulder, and hurried toward the village. On the way, she saw her brother, Laban, striding down the hill, scowling severely, even more than usual.

Deborah must have told him of the stranger. No doubt he is on his way to avenge my honour.

As he came alongside her, Laban stopped as if to speak, but Rebekah kept right on walking, ignoring him completely. He stood with his mouth open, glowered as she passed him by, then walked on.

I don't have time for Laban, I need to speak to father and prepare him for our guests.

She hurried to the door of the compound, put down her water jar and called, "Father, I have news of Abraham. His servant is at the well."

He came running, his arms outstretched. "News of Abraham! Tell me."

"Well, I don't have any real news yet. I didn't stay and talk to the man but came at once to tell you so that you could prepare a welcome for the servant of our ancestor Abraham."

"So, my uncle is still alive. It is many, many years since he left Haran. But the traders have told us news about him. I heard he has two sons and is a wealthy man in Canaan." He stood and turned toward the courtyard of his home.

"I will get the house ready while you get your mother and start preparing a welcome meal for our guest. A servant of Abraham. I wonder what he wants."

Rebekah found her mother tending her flowers in the garden and explained the news.

"You talked to a stranger at the well. Do you ever listen to me when I try to teach you how you must behave?"

"Let's not talk about this now, mother. We have much to do to welcome the servant of Abraham. I'll look after drinks. You get food ready. And I'm sure you'd like to put on a clean tunic and fix your hair."

Rebekah walked to the back of the house to find servants who would start getting food and drink prepared. She knew that the mention of a change of clothes would put Ruth in a frenzy and she would neglect her duty to her husband and to their guest. With her out of the way, Rebekah could get the tasks done. *I wonder how this house would manage without me. Maybe that is why the men father brings home are so unsuitable. He doesn't want me to leave him.* With a smile, she worked to prepare the food for this stranger from the house of Abraham.

Chapter Five

Benjamin examined his camels, checking their feet with exaggerated care. His eyes watched Eliezar, who stood near the well, waiting. How long is he going to stand there? I can't look at these feet for much longer. One of the soldiers spoke. "There is a man coming to the well. That is very strange and look how he hurries!"

Eliezar looked up. "I will deal with him. Just stay back and don't interfere."

Laban strode up to the well and stared at the stranger. He looked at the camels, laden with boxes and bundles.

"You do not look like traders, and traders go to the market square. Who are you? Where do you come from? Why are you here?"

"You are right. We are not traders. We are honest men who are here on an important errand."

"If you are honest men, why did you insult my sister? And that insult extends to me and to my family."

"I meant no insult to your family nor to your sister. I am here on an errand from the great sheik Abraham, son of Terah, brother of Nahor. I have gifts for the family and have given one to the woman who said she was of the tribe of Abraham. I will answer your impudent questions when I speak to your father. Take me to him, please."

"You dare to ignore my questions. You have no authority over me and no right to give me orders. I could call for the officials to arrest you."

"Yes, you could. But you would have to answer to Abraham for your disrespect towards the head of your family. It would be wise of you to take me to your father."

Laban stared at the stranger and shuffled his feet while trying to decide what to do. The man unpleasantly stared right back at Laban, and he did not flinch, nor did he blink. Laban turned and started to walk away. “I shall ignore your ill-bred manners and let my father deal with you. Follow me. Bring your camels and slaves.”

The two men climbed the hill leading to the village, and the entourage followed. Eliezar noted the well kept fields, the sturdy homes, and the curious people who stopped and stared. At a large, walled compound on the far side of the village, Laban stopped.

“Wait here. I will summon my father. All you see beyond the dwellings, the sheep, goats, vineyards, and fields belong to my father. His name is honoured and respected throughout the land. We will see if you deserve to be heard or to be flogged.”

Eliezar did not acknowledge Laban, but his knowing eyes looked with interest at all he saw. And it pleased him. From the house, he heard Laban’s voice, loud and shrill as he spoke to his father.

“This stranger stood at the well and insulted your daughter. He spoke to her, and he gave her a package, which she unwisely accepted. I have brought him here for you to judge.”

Eliezar heard a different voice reply. *That must be Bethuel.*

“As you have heard, he is a servant of Abraham, your esteemed uncle. To refuse the gift would insult Abraham, who sent his trusted servant on an errand to us, his family. There is no affront and no need for your haughty anger. I must go and welcome this important messenger from Uncle Abraham."

Chapter Six

A servant came to the guest house where Eliezar was staying and announced that the meal was served in the main courtyard. Eliezar nodded. He brushed his fresh tunic once more and hoped he looked presentable. It was important to represent Abraham in the best possible light. He followed the servant into the large house at the edge of the village. Bethuel greeted him with a quick bow, which Eliezar returned deeply. The host led the way to a central garden where servants were waiting.

"Welcome to my home. Please be seated here at my right hand. You are the guest of honour tonight and I hope my simple meal will please the representative of Father Abraham."

Again, Eliezar bowed to his host. He acknowledged Rebekah with a smile and a nod.

The meal that followed was a feast worthy of an important official. They dined on venison in an onion sauce, lamb with mint and roasted fish with slices of lemon. Barley, wheat, and a grain unfamiliar to Eliezar, were served with platters of roasted vegetables.

"I am not familiar with this delicious grain. May I ask what it is?"

"I am glad you like it. It is emmer, cooked with onions and garlic. It comes from Egypt, and we buy it from the traders. It is a favourite at my table."

The wine glasses were refilled with every course. Small cakes made with dates, honey and pomegranate juice were offered. The meal ended with cheese, fruit, and strong tea.

Conversation was easy and comfortable as Bethuel wanted to learn about Abraham and his family.

"You said earlier that Abraham carried his years well."

"Yes, he is still strong, observant, and alert. Nothing escapes his watchful, knowing eye. His grazing flocks cover the hills, and his vineyards produce bountiful crops. The wine in his casks is sought after by all who come to our village. Oil flows from his presses and the wool from the sheep makes warm clothing for our cool weather."

Bethuel nodded. "And his wife and sons. I think he has two. How are they?"

"Many years ago, Ishmael, the firstborn of Hagar, left with his mother to return to Egypt where she came from. Trader's gossip tells us he does well and is a man of importance. Sarah has lain at her final rest with the ancestors in a cave at Machpelah for many years. The son of Sarah and Abraham, is the purpose of my journey."

"Tell me of Isaac. What sort of man is he?"

Eliezar thought for a long moment. He closed his eyes and asked for wisdom to help him answer this question. Bethuel coughed, and Eliezar opened his eyes and cleared his throat. "My master Isaac is capable and strong. He can run like the wind and is a man of many talents. His flocks and herds are the envy of the village. He kills the lion, the jackal, and the poisonous snake with a flick of his wrist and the thrust of his spear. His arrows fly true to the mark. His courage and bravery are spoken of with great admiration."

"But what kind of man is he? A man of reason or reckless? Wise or foolish? Kind or cruel?"

"He is the son of his father in many ways. Not given to anger. Slow to judge. Prudent in his rulings and fair in his dealings."

Bethuel listened without comment. His piercing eyes watched Eliezar with a wariness borne of the years. "You said you came on an errand, and you have a task to complete for Abraham. What has it to do with me and my people?"

"We of the tribe of the great sheik Abraham live among those who worship idols and follow many gods. Abraham and his followers worship only the almighty one who dwells on the far mountain."

"I too worship the god of the mountain. The god of Terah and Abraham."

"Of this Abraham was aware and greatly pleased. Because you and Abraham are both descendants of Terah, he sent me here to find you. It is time for Isaac to take a wife and she must be a follower of El Shaddai, the god of the mountain that breathes fire. I am here at

Abraham's request to seek a bride for Isaac from his kinfolk, from the descendants of Terah."

"There are many families here where you could seek a bride for Isaac."

"Abraham has heard of the beauty and wisdom of the daughter of Bethuel. And he sent me to the house of his nephew on my search."

"Do you have authority to conduct this business?"

"I do." He reached for the sleeve of his cloak and handed Bethuel a skin with writing on it.

"Thank you. I will read this later."

"The beauty of your daughter is known by Abraham, and he has heard that she is as wise and reverent as she is beautiful."

"My daughter Rebekah, whom you met at the well, is as you describe."

Rebekah blushed and smiled as she hid behind her veil.

"When I came to your well, I asked for wisdom from El Shaddai. I prayed for a sign. I asked that the woman who gave me water and watered my servants and flocks would be the chosen one. Rebekah fulfilled the sign, and I gave her a gift as a token of my gratitude and respect."

"Abraham wishes to negotiate a betrothal between my daughter and his son Isaac?"

"That is the reason for my journey. I am entrusted with all the details, including offering the bride price Abraham has sent. The gifts of camels, gold, and silver are not the bride price. They are tokens of affection and esteem from your uncle."

"Is Isaac coming here for the wedding betrothal?"

"No. He has many responsibilities at the house of his father. It is not unusual for the couple to meet at the wedding. Abraham wishes, if it is agreed, that the bride accompany me when I return to Hebron."

"This is all most unusual, and a serious matter. My wife, Ruth and I must give it much thought."

Rebekah rose from the table and stood before her father. She bowed to him and then to Eliezar. "Am I to have no say in this matter? It concerns me more than any other and I wish to be heard."

Ruth slapped her forehead with her palm. "This happens because you gave our daughter so many freedoms. You have led her to believe she has the right to an opinion on matters that do not concern her. See what you have done?"

"Hush, wife, but you are right on one point. I have taught Rebekah that she is able to think for herself, and I do not regret what I have taught her. Well Rebekah, what do you wish to say?"

"I wish to be a part of all the discussions. Between you and mother and between you and Eliezar. She turned to Eliezar, gave a slight nod of her head.

Ruth wrung her hands and scowled at Rebekah. "Always you have been headstrong and bold. You do not seem to understand your place as a mere woman. Obedient daughters do not speak to strange men at the well."

Bethuel smiled. "What else Becca?"

"I know the rules, mother. Father has taught me well." She looked at her father and they shared a smile. "But surely a thirsty traveller is more important that rules and customs. He meant no insult, and he was humble in his manner. And my future is mine to choose. I am no longer a child, and I would decide for myself.

"My daughter, I know that you are not a child but a woman who is learned and shrewd. You have courage Becca. You are strong as well as beautiful. Wise as well as charming. I will give this matter some thought and will listen to your words. You must listen to your heart but hear the words in your head as well."

He stood and nodded to Eliezar. "We will speak of this in the morning."

Eliezar bowed and left to return to his rooms. Bethuel left the room, and Ruth followed him. Rebekah and Deborah stayed. They sat on the cushions and watched the stars peek out from behind the clouds through the windows in the room.

In a short time, Bethuel and Ruth returned. "I have asked Laban to be present, but he has been told he is to listen and not to interrupt. I hope that is acceptable to you.

"That is your right, father. It is fine. May Deborah stay?"

Deborah stood. “I have things to do, and this is a family matter. Good night to you all.” And she bowed to Bethuel and left the room.

“I had no objections to her presence. However, as she leaves us, she shows that she is wise and courteous. When he arrives Laban would have made a scene if she were present. Ah, here he is now. Sit across from me, Laban. Remember, you will speak only when I ask you to.”

Laban sat down and slouched on his elbow. He tried to look bored, but anger flashed in his eyes, and he sneered at his sister.

“We will begin at the beginning. Rebekah, please explain exactly what happened at the well.”

Rebekah told how she and Deborah went for water and saw the group of men at the well, and Deborah left. “I continued to go and get the water I needed. I had my face covered and kept my eyes on my task. I heard the man cough and looked at him. He spoke and asked for a drink, and I offered him my bowl.”

Laban snorted. Bethuel glared at him. “Go on. Rebekah.”

“He said he had travelled a long way and was thirsty. He was polite and soft spoken and asked for water. and gave it to him to drink.” She looked at her brother, swallowed her fear and took a deep breath. “I saw his animals and knew they were thirsty too, so I offered to draw water for them and for his men, if the men would help me. They were grateful and drew many buckets of water and everyone and all the animals had a drink.”

She paused and looked at her mother, who did not look pleased with the story Rebekah was telling. Laban was near bursting with rage.

“Continue, my daughter.”

She told her father who he was and why he was in Haran. She rubbed her forehead and took another deep breath. “Then he spoke of a prayer he made, asking for direction. The sign was to be a woman who gave him and his camels water. And when I did that, he said that I was the answer to his prayer. That was when he said he was here to see you father.” She held the ornate box out to show her father and placed it on the table near him. “And he gave me this gift in appreciation. I left him and came home to tell you all that had happened.”

"You are sure that is exactly what occurred."

"Yes father, exactly as I remember it."

"Laban told me he met you on his way to the well. Your story now, Laban."

Laban sat up tall and raised his head. He straightened his tunic and folded his arms across his chest. His eyes flashed with white hot anger, belying the smile on his lips. "Deborah came into the courtyard, out of breath and all upset. She said there were strangers at the well and that Rebekah would not come home but went to the well to meet them."

"Hm," Bethuel muttered. "Go on."

"I hurried to the well, I passed my sister on the road. She walked right past me and refused to stop when I spoke to her. I could do nothing but walk on down the hill. I arrived at the well and the stranger was standing there as if it was his well. I challenged him as to his treatment of Rebekah. He refused to answer my questions. He said he wanted to speak to you and that he would answer your questions. I told him I would get the authorities over his rudeness."

Bethuel took a drink. "Look at me when you talk to me."

Laban lifted his eyes to meet his father's gaze. "He dared me to do that and said I would look bad because I treated him in this way. I turned to go home and ordered him and his men to follow me. You know the rest."

"You stormed into my house, angry and not making much sense. I think we all have the picture. Does anyone else wish to say anything?"

There was silence around the table.

"Your stories are similar to what Eliezar told me. Now the question. He is here to settle the terms of a marriage between our Rebekah and the man, Isaac. That is our business at this time. Do you have nothing to say, Ruth?"

"This man is a stranger to us and to Rebekah. No woman wants to marry a stranger. It is just not done."

Bethuel smiled at his wife and patted her hand. "We met for the first time when I entered the bridal chamber and the marriage bed to take you as my wife. That is what is done in most marriages. It has worked for us, I think."

Ruth snorted. "That was different."

"We will leave that discussion for another time. Rebekah, what do you say?"

"I am your only daughter and you have raised me to be confident and self-reliant. I am past the age most girls marry, and I know that is my own choice, for I have refused the suitors that you presented. But I do wish to marry and to give you grandsons to continue your great legacy."

Laban sat up and opened his mouth to speak. Bethuel held up his hand. Laban snapped his jaw shut.

Rebekah continued. "At the well, when the stranger asked for water, I was astonished, and was about to turn and run. But inside I felt a tender, comfortable warmth. It was as if something told me to draw the water and so I did."

Laban waved his hand in disbelief. "What do feelings have to do with this? This is business." Laban was almost shouting.

His father glared at him, and Laban shrank back into the cushions.

"What was the gift, Rebekah?"

"This gold bracelet." She held out her arm and showed a dainty chain, plain and elegant.

"All right. Ruth and I will discuss this and the rest of you can go. We will meet with Eliezar at the morning meal. Good night and sleep well. Tomorrow is an important day."

When the others had gone, he walked to the house he had given to Eliezar. A servant opened the door and showed him to the room where Eliezar sat. They greeted each other and Bethuel accepted a goblet of wine. Soon they were sharing stories of Abraham and his journeys. Many hours later, Bethuel took his leave.

"I say goodnight and wish you a pleasant rest. We will meet in my courtyard for the morning meal."

Eliezar stood at the door and watched his host walk away. *It bodes well. I have been welcomed to stay the night. We meet in the morning. That will tell my fate and the probable future of two people. Their lives will be changed by this event, whatever the outcome.* He shut the door and went to his mat to try to sleep.

Chapter Seven

Deborah spent a restless night. That her beloved Becca would marry the stranger she had no doubt, but what would follow concerned her.

When they leave, will Becca take me with her? She must, for she needs me. I need her too, but my needs are not what is important.

All night, strange images floated in Deborah's dreams. She saw people with ugly, cruel faces. Grasping hands reaching out to steal anything they could touch. Children crippled and broken, begging for a crust of bread. She woke shaking and crying. She got up and, taking a broom, attacked the sand and dust. *Nothing but foolish dreams. You don't know where you are going, but surely it will not be what was in that terrible dream.* Giving herself a good scolding, she put the broom down and set to work sorting her simple belongings, all the while talking to herself.

"How can I decide what to take? I don't know where I am going. Or even if I am going. I must have hope and prepare myself to leave with Becca. It will be some time before we go but getting ready will keep me from worrying. There is a wedding to plan, new clothes for a bride and all her things to pack. But mine first."

She picked up tunics, cloaks, and scarves. Barely noticing them, she shoved them into a canvas bag that lay at her feet. Wringing her hands, she stared at the pack, then dumped the clothes out of the bag and started the task again, all the while her mind was whirling.

When the sun shone on the camp and chased the dark shadows away, she picked up all the clothes and threw them on the bed. Determined to hide her anxiety, she slowed her pace as she walked toward Rebekah's tent to prepare the first meal of the day.

The quarters where the slaves and servants lived were alive with a vibrant hum. Word travelled like a desert fire through the quarters, and the tales of the stranger at the well were growing more bizarre each minute. Deborah didn't answer when she heard her name.

"I don't need their fears to add to my own," she muttered.

At the tent she saw the fire was already glowing and Rebekah was stirring what was simmering in a pot on the stones.

"I guess you haven't slept well either."

"Good morning, Deborah. No, I didn't sleep much. I am so happy and excited?"

"Happy? Excited?"

Rebekah smiled at her with joy. "Of course, I am happy and excited. Yesterday I met the man who will take me to my husband. There is so much to do. We are having a meeting shortly and then it will be final. While I am doing that, you can start sorting my things to decide what I should take with me. Pack only the things we cannot be without."

Deborah held her breath. *Does she mean that I am going with her? Please, let that be what she is saying.*

"I am confident we will have all that we need when we arrive. We won't have much time, so you need to decide about your things too."

Deborah's tense body relaxed. The tightness in her chest floated away and her headache vanished. "I am going with you?"

"Of course, you are. How could I ever leave you behind? You weren't worried about that, I hope. We need to start thinking about our journey for we haven't much time."

"Why do you say we haven't much time? It will be days, if not weeks, before we leave. There is much to get ready for your wedding."

"That is not my plan. I hope to leave today if possible."

Deborah gasped and opened her mouth to speak, but Rebekah had turned away. In the centre of the courtyard, Bethuel was busy arranging chairs and cushions and a table with cheese and grapes and wine.

Rebekah started to walk to the house but stopped when Deborah spoke.

"Becca, what about some food?"

"I am not hungry. You look after your own needs."

"Where are you going? We have many things to do."

"I will have something to eat at father's table. He and Eliezar are going to make the arrangements."

"Are you daring to listen to the negotiations about your marriage?"

"I am going to be part of the negotiations. I am not going to be traded or sold like a sheep or a goat. I will have to agree, or I stay here. Now, please get busy packing my clothes, as I asked you to."

Deborah stood, eyes wide in shock, mouth agape, but no sound came. She watched as her mistress strode to join the gathering of men around the table. Shaking her head, she cleaned up the tent and began to rummage through the tunics and cloaks.

Chapter Eight

Rebekah went to her father's house and into the courtyard.

He saw her and smiled. "Come and see the table. Your mother insisted on flowers. What do you think?"

"They are lovely, father. We can leave them there till the meal has ended and then remove them for the business. Are mother and Laban coming?"

"Your mother is still not sure she agrees to this marriage, and she is not coming."

"Poor mother. She wants me married but is not sure about this one. Perhaps she is upset because it is happening too quickly, and she has little to say.

"This is our decision, mine, and yours. Last night I was ready for bed when your brother stormed into my room shouting at me. I told him that was not acceptable, and he had just answered my question concerning his presence at the table. I told him no. He stormed from the room, and I expect he went out and got drunk. He won't be up and alert till much later today.

Rebekah walked to the table and smiled at her father.

"I need to be sure, daughter. Are you agreed to this marriage?"

"If the conditions are acceptable, yes, father. I will marry Isaac."

She walked around the table fluffing the cushions and sat on a bright yellow one. Bethuel looked at his daughter. She wore a yellow tunic and beside her, she placed her deeper yellow cloak. As she moved her arm, he saw the glitter of a dainty golden bracelet.

Bethuel smiled at his beautiful daughter, and she sensed his pride. "I hope you slept well and are ready for this auspicious day."

"I was too busy thinking to sleep, and I am too excited to eat."

Eliezar entered the room and bowed to Bethuel, then smiled and nodded at Rebekah. To the surprise of father and daughter, Laban walked into the room and bowed to his father. He sat beside Rebekah.

Servants appeared at once with bowls of food that they placed in the centre of the table. Eliezar and Bethuel both ate with smiles and nods. Rebekah and Laban drank the juice and nibbled at the bread. When they finished the meal and the servants removed the dishes, Rebekah stood and placed the flowers in a corner.

She gave a respectful nod to Laban and said, "Shall we begin?"

Laban jumped to his feet. "Father, this is outrageous. Women cannot even listen to business dealings. Rebekah, apologize and go to your tent."

Rebekah smiled.

"Laban." His body jolted at the booming voice of his father.

"I told you that you were to listen to this discussion. If I want your advice, I will ask for it. Now, will you sit respectfully, or will you go to your tent?"

Laban glared at Rebekah and stammered, "This is an insult and I —"

Bethuel pointed to the door. "Sit or leave."

Laban hesitated, then sat, arms folded and his face red with anger and embarrassment.

Bethuel turned to Eliezar. "Please forgive this unfortunate intrusion. It is a family matter and not an insult to you as the emissary of our esteemed ancestor, Abraham. Please tell us about your journey to Haran."

Eliezar took a drink of wine and paused. "I thank the house of Nahor for its generous welcome and hospitality. The journey from the tents of Abraham was long and tiresome. But we were never in danger, and so give thanks to the god of the mountain."

"God is good, and we must make a sacrifice to pay homage to the god of the mountain. He sleeps now, and grain and wine offered to him at the high altar will help our future plans and your return journey to the house of Abraham."

"So be it. You have heard of the events at the well, and I am in debt to the daughter of Bethuel."

The voice of Rebekah interrupted, "Please, tell us about Isaac."

Laban snorted and Bethuel glared at him. Eliezar's expression never changed.

"Isaac is much involved with the flock and herds, seeing that they are well fed and watered. He takes great care of the ewes and the lambs. Because he is diligent in caring for not only the herds, but all the needs of our great tent city, he has given little thought to his needs or to the need for an heir to the holdings of Abraham. It is past the time for him to be married."

He paused and looked around the table.

Rebekah fidgeted, loosening her head covering. Laban opened his mouth and snapped it shut without speaking. Rebekah smiled sweetly at him.

Eliezar continued. "Before she died, Sarah, wife of Abraham, mother of Isaac, spoke of the need to find a suitable wife for her son. The people who live in Canaan are idol worshippers and the wife of the heir to the lands and titles of Father Abraham, must worship the god of fire who lives on the high mountain. And so, he sent me here; to Haran where Terah, son of Nahor, son of Seth, sleeps the long sleep of eternity. I come bringing gifts, and the bride price. There are the best camels in the land, fine wool and linen, gold, silver, and pottery gifts. They are not worthy of one so beautiful and upright, but riches and honour await the daughter-in-law of Abraham."

A servant silently passed little sweet cakes, figs, and goat cheese. Eliezar hoped he had done justice to Abraham's command. Rebekah could hardly contain her excitement, and Bethuel rubbed his head, as if deep in thought. Laban sat rigid, anger and resentment evident in his flashing eyes and twitching hands.

Bethuel stood. "We must consider this very carefully. I will talk with my wife, and we will meet in one hour here for further talk."

With many bows and nods, Eliezar left and went to his house muttering as he walked. "It seems to be going well and Abraham will be pleased, I hope."

"Wife." called Bethuel. "You can join us. Come from behind the fig tree and have some wine. You must be thirsty."

Laban had been sitting quietly. He raised his head. "May I speak, father?"

"If you are respectful."

"Thank you, father. We all know of the fame of Uncle Abraham, and his servant speaks well."

Rebekah muttered. "The wealth he brings speaks even better to you."

Ruth gasped, Bethuel chuckled, and Laban growled.

"I will ignore my ill-mannered sister. The bride price is tolerable, and Rebekah should be grateful they do not know her reputation. We will never make a better bargain for her. I say send her to Isaac when the time is right."

"What time? What do you mean?" Rebekah challenged.

"Your turn to speak will come, Rebekah. What do you say, Ruth?"

"Our daughter is indeed precious, and we must do well by her. The dowry is generous, the family acceptable and Isaac has a goodly inheritance and promising future. It is a long way from us, and we will not know how she is, nor will I cuddle my grandsons. But I am grateful such a match has been found. And I give my blessing."

Rebekah smiled a warm smile at her mother and blew her a kiss.

"Rebekah, what do you think?"

"I am ready to go with Eliezar. Deborah is supposed to be packing my things as we sit here and talk. But I think she is crouched behind that pomegranate bush."

The leaves of the bush rustled, and Deborah scurried away.

Ruth clutched her throat. "Why are you packing? The decision has not been made. And even then, you will stay with me for a long time. I need time to get used to you going away."

Rebekah sighed. "Mother. You have been trying to marry me off since the day I first showed the woman's blood. Don't pretend you are sorrowful at my marriage."

At the word blood, all the men covered their ears.

"Has the decision been made, father?"

"I think it has. I am at peace with your wish to marry Isaac and if you wish to go soon, I understand."

"But she must pack all the things she will need for her new home. Pots, bowls, dishes, stools, rugs, curtains—"

Rebekah interrupted her mother's long list, knowing it would go on and on. "I will need nothing but my clothing, a few personal things, and Deborah's bundle. I am sure that Isaac can provide everything else. We need to travel fast and light. I am ready and eager to start my new life."

"How soon do you want to go, daughter?"

"I had thought today but will leave at first light tomorrow."

Ruth started to cry. Bethuel nodded at Rebekah to go to her mother.

She stood and walked to her mother's side. Rebekah hugged her mother, then stroked her damp cheek. "Mother, you have been preparing me for this day since I was a young girl. You have taught me well. I am ready, and that is because of your wisdom and teachings. I know it is happening quickly, but one day, one week, one moon will not change the fact that I am going away. Let us enjoy the time we have, and we can have a celebration at dinner tonight. I will stay until the sun lights my path in the morning."

Ruth smiled through her tears. "Yes, of course. A dinner. There will be no wedding banquet here, but a feast in farewell will have to do." She bustled off to the cooking rooms, Rebekah smiled as she heard Ruth clapping her hands for her servants to come.

Bethuel took his daughter's soft hand in his gnarled one and spoke. His voice was gentle and kind, but a catch was in his throat.

"I have loved you since your first smile and first steps. I have tried to teach you to be strong, independent, and wise. You are, and you are also clever and shrewd. Remember what I have taught you. Be an attentive wife but take care of yourself as well. Life for a woman is never easy. We do not know this man you marry, but I am confident you can take care of your interest as well as his and the larger family.

Rebekah looked into her father's deep brown eyes. In them she saw wisdom, compassion, hope and pride. She squeezed the hand which held her own.

"Trust Abraham. He is a good and wise man, and from what I have heard, he treated Sarah as an equal. Do you know it is rumoured that he even taught her to make the marks on the skins that tell what is said and done? I am not the first to teach a woman. Use that skill, but don't flaunt it. But you know that. I taught you well. Go in peace, my daughter, and may the holy one guide your steps."

He reached out and took Rebekah in his arms. They clung to each other in a warm, tender embrace. When he released her, he wiped the tears from her cheeks, and she kissed the wet spots on his wrinkled face.

"Thank you, father, for treating me with respect. I promise I will never disgrace you or the family. But especially you father." Her father turned and walked to his rooms.

He is wiping his brow. My father's tears are real tears. Mother's tears are always strategic and start and stop at her command. She stood and wrapped her shawl around her shoulders. *I love and respect father, for he is genuine and honest in all things. I will try to be like him, at least I will always remember him and try to be a daughter he can be proud of.* She walked with firm but thoughtful steps to her room and a night of happy thoughts and dreams.

Chapter Nine

Isaac stood near the river. Because his father had summoned him, he had returned from tending the herds. He stood at the bottom of a small hill. The river, the lifeblood of the camp, gurgled beside him as it cascaded over the rocks. He used these stones as a crossing place from the grazing fields to the camp. Ahead of him, dotting the small rise in the land, stood the tents of his village.

Someday, all this will be mine. Do I even want it? I prefer to live in the hills, surrounded by the flocks. The wind and the bleating of sheep is all the song I need to calm my soul. Here amid the tents, there is too much noise, too many people with their quarrelsome ways. He picked up a stick and threw it into the river.

He looked at the tents, arranged in a great circle. Each had its own story. The largest was his father's and beside that, a smaller one for him. He smiled as he saw his mother's, remembering all the time spent there, as a boy and lately as a grieving son. In the centre was a large open common area, where the villagers met to sing, to dance and to share stories, to laugh with each other and at other times, to grieve together. It was where the clan chief, Abraham, spoke to his followers. There were only a few still alive of the ones who had travelled from Ur to Haran and finally to this fertile valley where they settled near Hebron.

And I am the eldest son, born to the first wife, and the heir to the promise. I must get ready for the responsibility. I hope it is years away, but my father is growing old. He kicked at the sand as he walked to his father's tent.

At his tent, Abraham was sitting on a bench, warming his hands by the coals of his fire.

"Have you eaten, my son? There is food keeping warm by the coals. It is not bad, but Jacob is not as good a cook as Eliezar.

"I am hungry. Where is Eliezar? I haven't seen him for days. Is he ill?"

"No. He is well, I assume. I have sent him on a long errand, and that is part of my need to talk with you."

Isaac took a bowl and filled it with stew. He grabbed his spoon and was about to start to eat when Abraham held up a hand.

"Once again, you have not given thanks for the food. It matters not how hungry he is, a man must offer thanks before he eats. How often do I need to remind you?"

Isaac mumbled the required prayer and shovelled the first spoonful into his mouth. Abraham watched him eat and felt shamed by his rough, uncouth son.

"There are some things I need to tell you. We will talk when you have finished your food."

When Isaac tossed aside his bowl, Gershom immediately appeared and picked it up. He squatted near the fire and cleaned the bowl with sand and leaves. He also cleaned the spoon and put them both carefully into a box in the doorway of the tent.

"Thank you, Gershom. You may leave now and finish up later."

Gershom bowed to Abraham, gave Isaac a brief stare, and walked away.

"Father, what is so important at this time that you call me from my work?"

Abraham sighed and shook his head. Taking a deep, calming breath, he spoke slowly and thoughtfully.

"I am an old man, Isaac. I do not know why I have been spared so many years. I would have been content to rest in the tomb on the hill beside Sarah many seasons ago."

He looked toward the southern horizon. Lost in memories, he sat motionless.

Isaac cleared his throat. "You have something to tell me?"

"Oh. Sorry. As I said, I am old, and my death cannot be far away. It is time you took up your responsibilities as my heir. You must start to live as the leader of this great family."

"I understand and will do as you ask. You said there were two matters?"

"The other is more difficult. You are the heir to everything I own. It is time that you left the flocks and the fields to our hired overseers. They are good and capable men, and I have trained them well. You need to assume your responsibility here, for the good of the people and our holdings."

"But father,"

"There is no but. There is only the truth. The truth is that I will die and also the truth that I fear you are not ready for the task ahead of you. I have not given you many orders over the years, and I may have been remiss in that. But I am giving you an order now. You will move into your tent, and you will spend time each day with Enoch, my scribe and bookkeeper."

Isaac appeared as if he wanted to speak, but his father held up his hand.

"There is a time to speak, and a time to listen. This is the time for you to listen. You need to learn many things. You know little of what I do, and you must learn it all before you are in charge. I have honest men who work for me, but someday you will need to hire your own workers. You must know what needs to be done, and it is important to watch carefully, or you can be cheated. All I have worked for a lifetime to build up can be stolen from you and thrown away in a season. That must not happen, and you are the only one to guard my legacy and your inheritance."

Isaac looked at the ground and made random marks with a stick.

"I hope those scratches in the dirt are a sign that you can still read the marks and make your own."

"Yes, father. I am distressed by your lack of trust in me and in my ability."

"You will have time to prove me wrong, and I hope you do. Now, to still another matter."

Isaac yawned and tossed aside the stick. "What else?

"Before her death, Sarah and I spoke of the need to find a wife for you. That is the errand I have sent Eliezar to accomplish."

Isaac jumped to his feet and sputtered. "Wife! A wife! Do you not think I can find my own wife?"

"You have had years to do just that, and you have neglected that sacred duty. It is well past time for you to marry. But I will not have you marry a woman from this land, Canaan. No idol worshipper will do. You will marry a woman who fears our god. The god of the fiery mountain. Idols will not have a home in your tent, or your life. The women you have brought to your tent in the past are not suitable for the wife of a follower of El Shaddai. I would pass the inheritance to another before I agree to an unsuitable bride for you."

Isaac growled. "The inheritance is mine. You gave it to me with your blessing."

"I cannot take back the blessing, but I can take back the inheritance. I do not know how much time I have left, but short or long, that is the length of time you have to prove yourself worthy. Now sit down and listen."

Isaac flopped to the ground and stared at the fire.

"Look at me while I talk to you."

Isaac met his father's eyes, hesitantly.

"Eliezar travels back to Haran to our people. He will complete the negotiations to acquire a wife for you. I have given him great riches to secure a suitable woman from our relatives. Your uncle, my brother Nahor, lived in Haran and his sons and daughters are still there. His son, Bethuel, has a daughter of marriageable age, and I hear she is both beautiful and wise. Perhaps she is the one that Eliezar will bring to you. But the woman he brings will be your wife or you can leave. You have had years to bring a woman of your choosing for my approval."

"I brought women to my tent. You would not acknowledge their presence."

"I do not speak of idol worshippers and harlots, but a god-fearing woman fit to be the mother of the heir after you. It is a great responsibility."

Isaac shrugged.

"I pray that you have enough respect for the memory of your mother, and perhaps for me, but mostly for yourself, that you will do your duty."

"It seems you leave me with no choice."

"You have always known what was expected of you. Your mother indulged you far too much, but that is in the past. Now it is time for you to stand tall and become a man she would be proud of. We begin our work in the morning. Sleep well."

Abraham called for Gershom to make his bed ready and, nodding to Isaac, walked into his tent. Isaac was left alone with his thoughts. He sat by the glowing coals, and Abraham's pet lamb came and sat at Isaac's feet.

"Well, little lamb. Enjoy your freedom. It can end in a moment. Mother told me this day would come, and she was right. A wife, chosen for me by a servant! She never told me that would be the plan." He rubbed his head and made a face. "I accept or I leave." He sat motionless for minutes. "Yes, father, I accept. I can always take another wife of my choosing, or a nighttime companion. Guess I knew that all this was somewhere in my future and now my future is here."

It was turning cold, and he pulled his cloak around his shoulders.

"I haven't thought much about marriage. I watched father and mother. They seemed to be happy. But I remember times of dark silence between them, but they always got over whatever caused it. I think I can handle the marriage part, but looking after all these people? He picked up the lamb and stroked its soft head. "The responsibility of all the flocks and tents and I don't know what else, petrifies me and I don't know how to talk to Father. We are almost strangers, but I see that I will have to change that. You have gone to sleep, little one, and I must too. I hope I can keep the dreams pleasant, but I doubt it."

The coals turned to ash, and he sat there uneasily until the moon was leaving the sky to make way for the sun and another day.

Chapter Ten

Early the next morning, Rebekah dressed for the journey. She put on a sturdy shift, a sand-coloured tunic, comfortable sandals, and a scarf to protect her hair and cover her face when needed. They were not her best garments. Those were carefully packed and tied securely on a camel. The great beasts were lined up, ready and eager to get moving, loaded with their packs. Eliezar greeted her as she approached. "Good morning. I trust you are rested and have broken the night fast. The servants are just finishing getting the water jars filled and securing all the boxes and bundles."

"Good morning to you. Yes, I have eaten. The sky is clear, and the breeze is comfortable. It is a good omen for our journey. Where is father?"

"Earlier he went up the hill to the high altar to offer prayers for your safe journey. He inspected every move as we prepared for the long trip. He is concerned for your safety and well-being."

"Here he comes now, and I see mother and Deborah coming as well."

"I will make one last check of everything as you say goodbye."

Rebekah was calm and confident as she hugged and kissed her parents. Her father held her in a warm, loving embrace while her mother wept noisily. Laban watched from a distance.

Rebekah went to him. "We may never see each other again, my brother. Be kind to mother and honour father in their last days. Do not be concerned about me. This is my destiny, just as you have yours. Goodbye and may the holy one watch over you and our parents."

Laban nodded and gave a slight bow. "I wish you many sons and a long life. Goodbye." He turned on his heel, and without a backward glance, disappeared into the house.

Deborah spoke to Ruth, holding her hand, perhaps for the first time in their lives and most likely the last. Deborah paused then walked over to Rebekah. "Don't you find it strange that the village is so quiet? Where is everyone?"

"I don't know, and it doesn't matter. It is time to get on our way."

Eliezar led them to the centre of the line. "Have you ridden in camel baskets before?"

They shook their heads. Deborah looked as if she was ready to run, while Rebekah covered her mouth with her hands and uttered a squeal, excited at this new adventure. The camel carried a very large woven basket on each side, held by leather straps and ropes.

Servants helped both women into the baskets, one on each side, and with a wave of his hand, Eliezar signalled their departure. As the camel unfolded his back legs, the women were pitched forward. Deborah shrieked. Rebekah laughed. Then the front legs straightened, and they were thrown backward. Eliezar watched and grinned at their reactions. The camels took their first steps and Rebekah looked back at her parents. They were waving farewell. She returned their wave and then looked ahead to the road out of the city. Tears filled her eyes, and she brushed them away with the back of her hand.

As they crested the hill, Rebekah was surprised to see the road on both sides lined with villagers. They were waving scarves in a rainbow of colours and carried lighted oil lamps. The scene blurred as she rode past.

"Is this my marriage procession?"

"Perhaps it is, so enjoy it." Deborah began to sing an ancient song about new life. But the sound was feeble and unsure. She lapsed into silence.

The trail ahead of them wound around hills, over grassy meadows, and disappeared into the clouds far ahead.

I wonder how long it will take. I didn't even ask. Too late to ask now. Too late for regrets. Too late to change my mind. But I will ask Eliezar when we stop for the night. She shifted her weight a little in the basket. *I didn't see tent poles or material for tents. I guess we will sleep under the stars. I have always enjoyed the night sky, and now I will get plenty of time to delight in those twinkling lights. Mother moon will keep watch over us, as well.*

"How are you doing, Debba?"

"All I can say is, I am glad we don't have to walk the whole long way."

"I think it is so exciting. From high up here, I can see a long way in the distance, and the changing scenes are interesting. But this rocking is making me sleepy. I didn't rest much last night, so if you forgive me, I am going to try to have a nap."

Rebekah looked at Deborah in her basket on the other side of the camel and saw that her eyes were closed, and her head rested on the pillow behind her. "Sleep dear friend. Sleep and I will join you."

They slept until a sudden jerk pitched them forward. They both let out a scream. Benjamin was at their side in an instant. "I am so sorry. I did not think to wake you before the camel started to kneel to let you dismount. You are in no danger, but it is best to hang on as you get tipped forward and back again."

Deborah climbed out of the basket, refusing Benjamin's hand. She frowned and walked away.

Rebekah stood beside the camel and laughed. "That was a surprise. I would definitely like to be awakened before we stop again."

Benjamin smiled and promised he would remember.

Eliezar approached. "This is a short rest stop. One of the camels seems to have some trouble with a foot. Better tend to it, Benjamin. I can look after things here." And Benjamin hurried off. "I hope the morning went well. We don't often stop until mid-afternoon, but this was necessary."

Rebekah smiled and rubbed her back. "We did very well, thank you. The baskets are not as uncomfortable as I feared. As long as we can stretch our legs once in awhile, it will be fine. How long will this journey take us?"

Eliezar shrugged. "I can't say. It is many long days of traveling. I assure you; I am as anxious as you to arrive safely at Abraham's tent. We will travel as quickly as safely possible but there are things that can slow us down. Your strength and endurance are always on my mind and your safety is my first concern."

Benjamin returned. "It was just a small pebble, and it is taken care of. We can be on our way again. I have told Deborah—ah, here she is. I'll help you back into your seats."

Rebekah wiped her face on her sleeve. "I think, in spite of the heat, we will walk for a while. All right with you Debba?"

"I will gladly walk with you.

Benjamin nodded. "I will keep an eye on you and when you are ready to ride again, just give me a wave. We won't stop often so you will need to ride after a time."

"Debba,I think you were a little upset when we stopped," Rebekah said.

"That was not a pleasant surprise. Jolted awake. I thought I would fall out."

"He has promised to awaken us before we stop from now on."

Deborah took Rebekah's hand. "I have always feared camels. So big and nasty. They spit and snort and I don't trust them. I would rather ride a donkey."

"If we were riding donkeys, it would take far too long to reach my new home. I want to get my new life started."

As they walked toward the sunset, they made a game out of imagining their new life.

Chapter Eleven

Benjamin rode his camel with authority. It was the largest, swiftest camel in the long train. At present, he rode with Eliezar at the head. At times, he would be following to make sure everyone was keeping up. He also rode along-side in the centre. He took his responsibility seriously and was always watchful. He turned to Eliezar. "I have wondered why you chose me to be the drover for this long trip. I have never worked this closely with you before."

"I know how skilled you are tending camels. They are so important on this trip I needed you, and so I asked Abraham if you could be my drover. And here you are." He pursed his lips. "But there is a more important reason. I know you went to Haran years ago with a trade caravan. You stayed there for the whole rainy season. Perhaps you learned about life in that city while you were there. I hoped that you might have met Rebekah or Deborah and could help prepare them for their new home."

"I saw them both, but only at a distance."

"But you lived there and must know something of their customs, their god and worship practices.

"I have some knowledge and if you think I can help, just tell me what to do." Benjamin's brow drew into worry lines. "Why is the old toothless one along on this important errand?"

"Asher was with Abraham on the original journey from Ur, so many years ago. He has also been back to Haran at times. He knows the way. I didn't pay much attention when I came. I spent my time tending to Abraham, but Asher is a tracker. He will remember every grain of sand."

Benjamin laughed wholeheartedly at the jest.

They rode together, companions, sharing a journey and the great responsibility.

The miles dragged on, camels grumbling, slaves and servants singing to pass the time.

Eliezar called a brief rest at a watering spot. The orange sun blazed down from high above and the shade of the few palm trees was welcome. He walked to where his two charges were sitting under the leafy branches of a large tree.

"I know it feels good to just sit in the shade, but you must move around whenever we stop. The days will be long, and you need to walk. The camels need to rest, but you need to move about. It will help you sleep when we stop for the night."

Rebekah and Deborah walked around the area and chatted as Eliezar had suggested.

"You know, Debba, this makes me think of Sarah. She made this same trip, but she walked most of the way. I can't imagine that, can you?"

"Not really. I am grateful that we can ride for part of this journey. Sarah must have been as incredible as all the stories I have heard suggest. And there were also old ones and babies, toddlers, and young folk. It must have been a remarkable sight."

Rebekah adjusted her head scarf. "And an unbelievable experience. I am looking forward to meeting Abraham. He must be getting old and what stories he will be able to tell us of his long life."

"Aren't you looking forward to meeting your husband as well?"

Rebekah gave Deborah a playful push but did not answer.

Too soon, Benjamin was ordering everyone to get back on the camels. Rebekah and Deborah settled into the large baskets, hung across their camel's back—one woman on each side of the beast. As the animal stood, again they were tipped forward and back, but they were getting used to it. And this motion went on with every lurching step, but much more gently.

"If I think about this rocking, I get sick," muttered Rebekah.

"Then don't think about it. Just sway with the motion, and let it rock you to sleep."

"How can I sleep? I am full of so many thoughts and feelings. They spin around and around in my head. And my stomach spins too."

Eliezar and Benjamin came alongside the women. "Eat a few bites of the bread I gave you. It will help with the sick feeling. Then I recommend you cover up with your scarves and try to get some rest. In a few miles, we must climb some rocky crags, and you will need to walk for your safety. Rest until then."

"Why would we need to walk?" Rebekah complained. "I don't much like this rolling gait, but I don't feel like climbing in this heat either."

As Eliezar rode off, Benjamin spoke. "You will be sorry if you try to ride up the hill in the basket. The rough, steep climb could throw you out onto the stones. If you are all cuts and bruises when we arrive, Eliezar will have whip marks to match." He wheeled away.

Deborah snorted. "Surely, he is not serious. Whips are not for trusted servants, like me, only for rebellious slaves."

"That was the custom of my father, but we do not know what life will be like in our new land. I think we must be prepared for anything."

"Is it too late for me to go back to Haran?"

"I know you don't mean that. You would never leave me to whatever fate waits for me. We are in this together. And for forever as well."

As they became quiet, they were both soon sound asleep.

The caravan plodded its way east and south, following the routes of the trader caravans.

The two leaders rode side by side, sharing memories of their work and lives with the great chief Abraham. The miles passed and soon they came to the bottom of a long, steep hill.

"Good, it is time we stopped. I will wake the women," offered Benjamin.

He approached the camel of Rebekah and Deborah and called their names. They both woke with a start and rubbed sleepy eyes.

"Where are we?"

"At the base of the climb I told you about. A walk will do you good."

He made the camel kneel, and the women held on tightly as they pitched forward and back. Benjamin held out his hand to Deborah. “I will help you down and you can then help your mistress.”

Rebekah appreciated that he knew he should not touch her in such an intimate way. The women stood and stretched. Muscles were stiff and sore from sitting so long. The cushions in their baskets were comfortable enough, but there was little room to stretch their limbs. Ahead was a rocky path that wound around great boulders and bushes. The men and the camels were moving ahead slowly, and Deborah suggested they needed to get walking, too.

The path was treacherous, and they held each other’s hands as they walked. They had only gone a short way when Rebekah stumbled, Deborah grabbed her arm to keep her from falling.

“This is going to be a long, tough climb.”

Eliezar was beside them in an instant. In his hand he carried two sturdy walking sticks. “I am sorry. I should have given these to you at the start. They will help you keep your balance.” And he returned to the rear of the string of men and camels.

The sun beat down on the stones, and heat radiated from the rocky trail. Rebekah held on to Deborah’s shawl as she walked behind her, watching her feet at every step and would have fallen except for her stick.

“You should look where you are going as well as watching your feet. Glance ahead to see what the footing is like. This is not like the smooth path to the well.”

“I am getting the idea. How come you aren’t having any trouble?”

“The path a servant walks is not always a smooth one. All my life, I have tried to make your path easier for you. Perhaps I have not done you a favour by shielding you from the rough patches along the road called life.”

“I guess I will be learning a lot of new things. I’m glad you are with me to guide and advise me.” Rebekah struggled up the steep incline leaning heavily on her walking stick.

“And while I think of it. Becca, how you feel each day is up to you. Look for the worst and be miserable or look for the surrounding good in people and in the journey and find hope for your future. We will do this together, whatever our new life brings."

Deborah began to hum a cheerful tune as they continued up the hill.

Eliezar joined them. "Almost there. Well done. We will stop at the top and enjoy the view, have a drink and some grapes to refresh us."

At the crest, Benjamin took them to a grassy spot in the shade and brought them food and drink. Rebekah looked ahead. The thin thread of the road wound its way down the hillside and spun out as a twisting path through a beautiful valley.

"Where are we?"

"Below in the valley and heading south is the trade route from the East to Canaan. It meanders through the Jezreel Valley which is between the desert and the sea. We will follow it all the way, and there are no more hills like this one. There will be water, safe places to stop, cool breezes, and food for the beasts. We will pass near two or three settled towns, where we can get provisions.

"Where will we find food for all these camels? They must eat a great deal, don't they?" Rebekah asked.

"They can go for lengthy periods without eating, but they will find food along the way. When we stop, they eat the leaves from many kinds of leafy bushes, and they do quite nicely eating thorn bushes as well. As long as they have those, they are fine. When they rest, they chew their cud, and they are little trouble." He gave a slight grin. "But I would like them better if they weren't so grumpy."

Deborah made a face. "I'd be grumpy too if I had to eat thorns."

Benjamin laughed. "Come, we need to press on to reach a good place to spend our first night."

Eliezar rode up beside the women. "We are getting ready to stop for the night. Darkness is still a few hours away, but we need to set up our camp. You two are the only women, and I must take care of you. Abraham made it very plain what I would face if anything happened to Isaac's bride."

As he rode, he explained the plan.

"The camp will be the same each time we stop. We will construct a small room, blankets held up on poles, to ensure you have privacy. You will stay inside that room unless Benjamin or I take you someplace for a walk or to meet your needs. The others will sleep in a circle around you, but not too close to your room. Benjamin, and I, as well as two trusted guards will take turns on watch around you."

"Is that necessary? I feel as if we are prisoners, and I don't like it."

"Rebekah, you must understand. My future depends on your safety. You are travelling with servants and soldiers of Abraham. But he is not here, and his influence is far away. We can only trust these men so far. And we may encounter anything on this road. I have ordered what is needed for your protection. Do not test my words or actions. I obey Abraham, not you."

"But we have seen no one, and I feel quite safe and quite able to protect myself. I am not a child."

"You are a very beautiful woman. If you were a child, you would not need to be protected so much. This is the way things are, whether you like it or not. And you will obey. Now when we stop, I will help you down and stay with you while the shelter is erected.

He gave a brief nod and rode away. *That bride has an obstinate streak. I like it, but how will Abraham deal with her? And Isaac? It will be an interesting meeting. I hope I get the chance to see it.*

He bustled about giving orders, all the while keeping a keen eye on the women. It wasn't long before a simple structure of blankets and poles created a small private space for them. In it, they could take care of their personal needs and roll out their bedding for sleeping. He led them to the simple opening that served as a doorway to their room.

When Benjamin and Eliezar were satisfied with the arrangements, they were ready for sleep. Benjamin looked to the sky and saw the dots of twinkling light, against the midnight blue sky. He stretched out on his blanket as Eliezar yawned. "I hope we have a quiet night." He lay on the grass close to the crude shelter erected for the women. In a moment, he was asleep, snoring gently into the quiet night.

Chapter Twelve

Deborah awoke to sounds from the camp. Birds singing, camels snorting, sheep and goats bleating, and the familiar sound of Eliezar's voice, at the door to their private space.

"Good morning. I hope you slept well. Your breakfast is ready. Will you eat it here or by the fire?"

"By the fire, thank you."

She looked at Rebekah, her blanket rolled around her, and her bed was a tumbled mess. *I guess she didn't sleep well. Not a good start to the day. I will get a warm cloth to bathe her face. That might help her wake up and soften her mood if she is irritable.*

A bowl of water stood outside the door and Deborah took a soft piece of cotton and dampened it in the warm water. She knelt by her mistress and gently rubbed her back.

"It is morning, Becca. We need to go to our morning meal." She handed her the warm cloth.

Rebekah sat up and blinked as she looked around the messy circle of blankets. She took the cloth and held it to her face. Without a word, she handed it back.

Deborah took the wet cloth. "I spent a comfortable night and I hope you did, too. I was very tired, and I fell asleep at once."

"That is nice. I hardly slept at all. But thanks for the warm cloth, it feels good. Where are my clean clothes for today?"

"Travelling, we must give up luxuries we are used to. We will travel for days in the clothes we are wearing, and we sleep in them too. It saves time, don't you agree?"

Rebekah made a face. "Where is our meal?"

"Slip on your tunic. We eat with the others by the fire. Hurry! We don't want to start the day by being late and causing a fuss."

Rebekah mumbled the words of Deborah from the evening before. "I am in charge of how I feel. Miserable or happy. Ugh. Today I will try for something in between. It's a start, anyway." She nodded to Deborah.

"I think I am ready. Let's go," and she walked out of the room and went to the fire.

The meal was a hearty one. Wheat porridge, cheese, fruit, and goat's milk. Rebekah had to admit she enjoyed it and felt a little better.

Deborah took the dishes and put them away. "Listen to the birds, Becca. They sound so lovely. I wish I could sing like the birds or like you do. Your voice always cheers me up."

"Maybe later I will feel like singing." As Rebekah looked around, she saw that their small room was already packed up, and the bundles had been tied to a large camel. Everything else appeared to be ready as well. She realized that most had eaten before she arrived and were nearly ready to start the day's journey.

"I'll bring your camel." Benjamin's voice caught her attention.

She stretched her arms wide and looked at the trail. "Thank you. I think I will walk for a while this morning. I am rested and it will be good to move about. Yesterday, I sat for too long in my basket. Does that mean that Deborah must walk, too?"

"No. I can put something in your basket to balance it. It is kind of you to think of that. I am surprised and pleased." The smile on his face was broad and friendly. "Ready to climb on board, Deborah?"

"I will walk too. We can talk more easily as we walk together, and it passes the time."

The caravan set out, following the ancient trade route. As they walked, the green expanse in front of them was beautiful.

Deborah pointed at the distant hills. "I have never seen so many shades of green. From the pale yellow of the young saplings to the nearly black of the far away forest."

"So many trees. In Haran I couldn't see the forest for all the houses. This is certainly beautiful. Oh, I loved the city, but it was brown, just plain brown."

"That is true, Becca, but the market had colour from the flags of the traders that marked their stalls, and bolts of cloth in vibrant hues."

"Yes, it did. And it had noise. Voices, animals, birds, people bargaining, trying to out shout each other. I thought the noise of travelling would be irritating, but it is most pleasant and almost soothing."

Deborah smiled. "Sing to me as we walk. Becca." *She must have listened to me last night, and I can tell she is trying awfully hard.*

Rebekah began to hum a meandering tune to match the winding road. She turned as someone tapped her shoulder. Benjamin handed her a lyre. She smiled and began to pluck the strings.

Each day began the same, unfolded the same, and ended the same. Rebekah knew it was a long way to her new home, but as the time crawled by, her feet hurt, and her head ached. She and Deborah walked in the cool morning, rode, and dozed in the heat of the day, and walked again in the cooler evenings. Deborah never complained. At times, Rebekah found her constant cheerfulness irritating.

"How do you do it?" She asked on an afternoon when it was too hot to even take a nap.

"Do what?"

In a cranky voice, Rebekah snapped, "Always smile, keep so cheerful and happy."

"Becca. We have chosen a path. It is unwinding as it should. We are well fed, kept safe by Abraham's men and we walk toward a new future. And best of all, we have each other." She took her friend's hand. "At the end of this journey, your husband awaits, and your new life will open before you. I am thankful for all these things and have good feelings about our future. There is nothing we can do to change the days before us. I choose to be content with life, especially when I can't change it."

"Oh, I wish I could be as innocent as you are."

"I am not an innocent. I have seen and lived some of the worst that life has to throw at us. Don't forget, I was born a slave. Your parents saved me from a terrible life when they bought me and gave me my freedom. Compared to my early years, I live like a queen now."

"Well, I don't have your ability to accept things that are unknown, and I do worry about the future."

Deborah smiled at Rebekah and squeezed her hand. "What can you change by worrying? You are just borrowing trouble. Live today and let tomorrow come when it comes."

"But I knew what life would bring back home. I had no worries or fears."

"Are you sure? What if your father died? Laban would have forced you to marry the man who offered the biggest purse for you. You would have had no choice. You could have been the fifth wife and a servant to the other four."

Rebekah kicked at the dirt at her feet. "I hate it when you are right, as you nearly always are. But I was born to parents who love me and —"

"And gave you everything. Also, they protected you from the harsh realities born by many women in our world. You have lived a privileged, sheltered life. Nothing you can do about that. But think about some of the women in that village. Do you think they all had an easy life?"

Rebekah frowned and heaved a deep sigh. "I tried not to think about the cuts and bruises I saw at the well. I convinced myself the women were clumsy and fell or bumped into things?"

"I don't mean to make you unhappy, or feel guilty, Becca. I am just suggesting you need to feel gratitude for what your life has been."

They walked in an uncomfortable silence for miles.

"Deborah, I have decided that each night with my evening prayers, I will name three things for which I am grateful. Tonight, I shall name Mother, Father and my wise and kind companion, teacher, and friend."

Deborah raised her eyes to the deep blue sky in thankfulness.

The two women smiled at each other as if they shared a special secret. The camels slowed their pace and turned into a grassy meadow. The day's travel was at an end. It was time for a meal and sleep.

Chapter Thirteen

Eliezar woke before the sun. He rolled up his mat and took a walk around the camp. All was peaceful. Guttural snoring ruptured the silence of the dawn. *I can't tell if it is camels or men making all the noise.* The weight of his responsibilities meant that others seldom saw his humorous side. He roused two camel drovers, and they sat up and yawned.

"Time to get the day started. We have a long journey today. Tonight, I'd like to stop near Laish. Things are going well, and we'll pause there for a rest."

"Will we be in the city?"

"No. We will stop at the narrows in the river. I don't want the women to go into Laish. They need time to rest and refresh. But the men can go if they wish."

"We wish, and the others will too."

"Fine. But you are responsible for seeing that we have an able group when it is time to leave. I will not have drunken dolts on this important journey. Now better get moving and get us underway. I don't like to travel after the sun sets."

Eliezar walked away and went to see that the fires were started for the morning meal.

The noise of the waking camp woke Rebekah and Deborah. They washed in the water near their tent and tried to brush the creases and sand from their clothing.

"How much farther, Deborah? I am getting so tired of these monotonous days. Everyone just like the last. Sleep, eat, walk, ride. Sleep, eat, walk, ride. That is all we do. Day after dreary day."

"I have heard tales of travel in the olden days. Wild beasts attacking the animals we need for our food and milk. Robbers and bandits hiding in the rocks and bushes. That is what Sarah had to endure when she walked this trail so many years ago."

"I've heard the stories, too. And I think they followed the rocky sea route, not this lovely valley."

Deborah couldn't help but smile. *She is trying so hard to be more accepting of our hardships. I am proud of her.* "This trade route is a safe way to go. There are shady trees, beautiful scenes, and plenty of water."

"It would be interesting to talk with others, traders, and travellers, who stop at the same places we do. I wish that Benjamin would let us buy a few things, but he says, 'No room, no room." Rebekah threw up her hands in imitation of Benjamin. They both laughed.

Eliezar walked among the men who were saddling camels and loading all the bundles they carried.

"Keep moving. We need to cover a lot of distance today. More than two Sabbath journeys and in record time. Less talking and more working, or I will have to get my whip."

As he walked away, the men chuckled. They knew that Abraham never whipped his labourers, and neither did his overseers. The slaves and servants worked hard in gratitude for the kindness shown to them. On the trail, Eliezar always sat with the hands and ate the same food.

The morning meal to break their fast was even more hearty than usual. Along with the porridge, fruit and bread, there were lentils and even cheese. Eliezar approached his charges. "Eat well, ladies. We have a long way to go today. I want to reach the village of Laish before dark." Eliazar frowned as Rebekah squealed in delight.

"A town. A real town. We are going to stay in a village, with shops and—"

"Whoa. Just hold on. We will camp near the river just before we reach the village. The men will go to the market and replenish our supplies, but you women will stay near the tents."

Rebekah put her hands on her hips with a deep scowl on her face, and blurted out. "Stay at the river? Not go into the town! You are not my father nor my brother nor my master. I will go where I want."

Speaking softly and patiently, as if to a naughty child, Eliezar replied. "True. I am none of those. But I am Abraham's servant, and he has ordered me to bring you safely to his tents and to your husband Isaac. I will do as I have been ordered, and you will do as you have been ordered. It is the way of the world, Rebekah, and you cannot change it."

Her eyes, black with anger, flashed like sparks from a fire. "I will go where I will go."

Deborah stood quietly. She knew Rebekah's temper and held her breath.

"Rebekah, this is not done out of cruelty, but out of the respect I have for the future bride of Isaac." He held up his hand as Rebekah started to speak. "Hear what I have to say. You are young and full of life, and I understand how tedious this journey is. But I am just a servant. I must do what Abraham expects me to do. I will protect the property that has been entrusted to me."

Rebekah screeched, "Property." She stamped her foot and stomped away.

"Try to reason with her, Deborah. I am sure you understand my position. I do not do this with any malice, but she will stay at the river, under guard, and tied to a tree if I must."

"I do understand, Eliezar. We are in for an unpleasant day. I will leave her alone for a while and let her think about the situation. She will see reason, I am sure."

Benjamin came and announced the camels were ready.

"I will fetch Rebekah. If I don't return..." Her voice faded as she walked away to seek Rebekah.

She found Rebekah sitting on a large bundle, which was ready to be loaded on a camel. She was sobbing. Deborah sat beside her, their body's touching, but she did not speak. A servant came to get the pack, but Deborah waved him away.

I hope she calms down before long. Deborah put her hand on Rebekah's tightly clenched fist. Rebekah did not pull it away. *Hopeful sign.* The sobbing diminished, and Rebekah rubbed her eyes.

"I know women are just possessions, but I never expected to be called one. And by a mere servant."

"Eliezar is a servant. But the respected servant of the powerful patriarch of our family. Eliezar is no ordinary fetch and carry. He has status and when acting on Abraham's behalf, he has power. Power over other men, and certainly power over lowly women. We may not like it, but that is the world in which we live."

Rebekah howled. "I left my home, my parents, my friends. I miss them all, and I even miss my miserable brother. What have I done?"

"You have contracted to marry the son and heir of the most powerful man in your entire extended family. At the time you agreed, you were happy and confident. All that has changed is that you are weary of this long and dreary journey. We still do not know what life will be like in Hebron. But you need to remember, you are Rebekah, daughter of Bethuel."

Rebekah sniffed and wiped her face with her dusty sleeve.

"You have been raised to stand tall and proud. This journey will end and then, as the wife of the heir to Abraham's land and titles, you will stand an important person at the door of Isaac's tent."

Rebekah looked with admiration at Deborah. "How did you get so wise?"

"Just age and experience, my friend. Age and experience. Plus the fact that as a slave, I learned that I could control nothing but my thoughts and attitude. Not much changed when I was given my freedom by your father and became your servant. And always remember we are only women."

"Mother once said 'listen silently, watch quietly, wait patiently and act shrewdly.' I think I finally understand what she was trying to tell me."

"Your mother was wise, and you are her daughter. Now let's get your face washed and get on that stinking camel for another day's journey."

Eliezar stood a short distance away. He said nothing and gave no indication of his impatience. As they walked past him toward the camels, Deborah shrugged her shoulders and smiled. Eliezar nodded his understanding and appreciation.

All day long, the fiery, red ball of the sun poured its heat on the travellers. The camels plodded along, grumbling, and irritable. The sheep and goats bleated and fussed. Leather straps creaked and groaned. Dusty, dirty men shuffled along in silence. The two women slept fitfully in their baskets. Rising over the muffled sounds, Benjamin's voice echoed down the exhausted line.

"We are at the rest spot. I can see the bend in the river."

The women woke up and stood up in their baskets. Eliazer held his breath but realized they needed to see what was ahead. In front of them lay a flat grassy field, circled by trees, and dotted with a colourful display of dainty wildflowers. The river babbled over its rocky bottom and the sun danced on the ripples. A cheer went up from the group. In the west, the sun was slipping behind the hills and turning the sky pink and gold.

Eliezar raised his hands. "God of Abraham, you have led us to this destination in safety and in peace. May you hear my thanksgiving prayer. Blessed are you who inclines his ear to my humble prayer."

Chapter Fourteen

Excited chatter broke out all along the line of camels. Men were calling back and forth and laughter filled the air. Someone started to sing a work song, and many joined in. It was the first song heard for days. The rich voice of Benjamin could be heard above all the others.

The camels were soon relieved of their burdens and taken to the river to drink. The noise of splashing water sounded as it cheerfully rang out along the clearing. Men were unrolling provisions, collecting dung for a fire, and humming or singing while they worked.

Rebekah and Deborah climbed out of their baskets and rubbed stiff aching joints. They walked to the river. Benjamin called out to them. "Be careful. The water hides many dangers. Do not be long. We need to get the camp settled for the night." He turned back to his duties, and Rebekah stuck out her tongue at him.

Deborah flinched but said nothing.

Rebekah stood on the bank watching the sparkling water flash past. "I would love to just jump into that clear, cold water. Maybe I will."

"No, you will not. Not while I have to look after you. Can you imagine what Eliezer would do to me if I let the precious bride of Isaac play with the crocodiles? He would break his rule about a whipping."

Rebekah managed a smile. "I know I cannot, but still, I would like to. Wouldn't you?"

"Time enough for that later. We are staying here for a few days, so we will be able to bathe and wash our hair. Even wash our soiled clothes, I think."

"Wonderful. Do you think he will change his mind and let us go to the village?"

"He will not. So, get it out of your head and do not bring it up. You might find yourself tied to a tree, or worse, a camel. Let us see how our room is coming along and get our beds ready for the night."

Benjamin was beside their space and smiled as they approached. It was ready for them, and Deborah noticed a large roll of tent material and a bundle of long sturdy poles.

"What are these for?"

"I have arranged for a section of the river in the quiet little bay to be set apart for you to bathe and do your washing. These poles and the fabric will make a small private space for you. I will guard it personally when you are using it.

Deborah looked at Rebekah, but she did not appear to be going to respond.

"Thank you, Benjamin. This is very thoughtful of you. We are most grateful for your kindness.

She poked Rebekah in the back. Startled, Rebekah cried out, "What was that for?"

"I will talk to you later. Let us get ready for our meal and then for bed. Despite napping today, I am ready for some real sleep."

When Benjamin had moved away, Deborah spoke in her soft voice. "Rebekah, why do you treat me with consideration? After all, I am just your servant."

"You are more than a servant to me, and you deserve my kindness, for I depend on you for so many things."

"You do not seem to recognize it, but you depend on Benjamin and the other servants as much, or even more. For all they do for your comfort and safety, they deserve your respect even more than I do. Think about it and see them as people. People with loved ones, dreams and hopes, fears and concerns."

"But they are just servants."

"There are no buts. Consider what I have said and change your haughty ways."

"Why are you so bossy? You were not like this at home."

"In Haran, it was the task of your parents to teach you. They gave you wonderful examples, but you seem to have paid little attention.

You will be one of the leading women in our new home. You cannot act like a spoiled child anymore."

Rebekah changed her pout to a half smile.

"You must act like the wife of a leader in the clan. I know I sound harsh and critical, but I am afraid for you if you do not take your responsibilities more seriously. Think of how your mother acted as the wife of the leader and try to be more like her."

"There is too much change. Too much to learn. I cannot do it and you can't make me." She started to stamp her foot but shuffled it instead.

"You are right. I cannot make you. But you have the power to control your attitude and your behaviour. How you act can make or break your position in Abraham's house."

"Enough. I am hungry and tired. I am going to the fire to eat and then to bed. I can get myself settled. You need not bother."

Deborah watched her walk away. She turned and entered their private space. *I have half a mind to leave her bed all tied up and let her fix it herself. But I cannot. I have been hard on her today, so this will help to ease her into thinking about my words. I hope.*

When the room was fixed to her satisfaction, Deborah went to the fire and got her bowl of stew. She sat on the opposite side of the fire from Rebekah and started to talk to the camel driver beside her. When Rebekah got up to leave, she almost jumped up to go to help her.

I will stay here until she is asleep. Enough words. Time for me to pull back a little and let her learn to stand on her own.

Benjamin took her bowl to the cleaning stand and when he had wiped it, added it to the pile of clean dishes. He returned to Deborah and asked permission to sit beside her.

"Of course, Benjamin. And thank you for tidying up my dish. I can do that myself."

"I know you can, but I wanted an excuse to talk with you for a while. I have thought the job of a camel drover was a hard one. But to be honest, you have a much more difficult task. Has she always been so impossible?"

"Be careful how you speak of my Becca. I am devoted to her; I understand her and will defend her to the end."

Benjamin chuckled. "You are certainly loyal, patient and wise. I also am sure I do not want to get on your bad side if you have one. Tell me about her."

"Not much to tell. Her father spoiled her. Her mother mostly ignored her. That is about it."

"And you loved her. She is lucky to have you to teach her. I think she will do fine. Isaac will be a handful, as he, too, was spoiled. But it was his mother who indulged his every whim. She kept him so close Abraham spent scant time with him and so had little influence."

Deborah looked at him and her eyes smiled. "They should at least understand each other if they share their stories."

"They will either spend their lives in petty squabbles or they will make a formidable team. Let us hope it is the latter, for all our sakes. It is late; time we both went to our rest. Sleep well and have pleasant dreams. Goodnight Deborah."

She nodded to him and went to the makeshift room that was their home. She entered quietly and saw that Rebekah was sleeping soundly.

"Good night, my child. Sleep well. Tomorrow, we begin a new day and a new life."

Benjamin had watched Deborah as she went to her tent. *I am glad Deborah is taking our temperamental princess in hand. I was hopeful that she would. I was very afraid that I might have to step in. That thought is scarier than a runaway camel.* He yawned and let out his breath in a great sigh and went to his tent for a well-earned rest.

Chapter Fifteen

The lazy days spent by the river floated by in happy moments, just like the fluffy white clouds in the azure blue sky. Rebekah splashed in the cool water, washing away weeks of sand and grime. The fragrance of the water lily clung to her hair and skin.

As Deborah dried her hair, she teased Rebekah. "Your hair is different today."

"What is the matter with my hair?"

"Nothing. It just smells different. I like it better than camel as your favourite perfume."

The women's laughter echoed across the water.

Benjamin listened with a sense of relief. He stood with Eliezar on the riverbank. "This has been a good place to stop. Rebekah is much happier and calmer during this stop. I will try to find the time to talk with her at the first opportunity. I do not have much experience with women, I hope she will listen."

Eliezar clapped him on the back. "You are young, handsome, and smart. You will not have any trouble as both she and Deborah look up to you. You are taking good care of them, and they know it. She will listen."

Each morning, Eliezar chose four men to go to the city to buy supplies for the next part of the journey. They returned with boxes and bundles before the evening meal. Around the fire, they spoke of the things they saw and heard. Each night, men went to the town for time away from the work they did each day.

Later in the day, Rebekah watched with envy as the men went to Laish. She sighed with disappointment as she watched them leave. "Don't you wish we could go to see the city? How I would love to look at the goods for sale. Just to walk in a market, see the colours, smell the spices and perfumes, to hear the noise of barter and trade would be wonderful. I have no coins to buy anything, but just to see it all would be a wonderful day."

"Of course, I would like to go, but you know it isn't possible, and for good reason."

"All right, wise old woman. I will just enjoy the fresh fruit and the meal of fish they bring."

Deborah shook a finger at her friend. "Be careful. Watch your tongue. Wise of course, but old?"

Around the fire after the late day meal, the mood was relaxed and carefree.

The two friends laughed and joined in the singing that was drifting upward from the fire to the stars. When they finally went to their beds, they were happy and very tired.

Much later, they were jolted awake by more singing. Deep, slurred voices. Howls of pain and curses as someone fell.

Rebekah sat up and shrieked.

"It is nothing Becca. Just the men who went into town, returning and the wine and beer are talking. I would not want to be in their sandals in the morning."

"I hope they quiet down. I need to sleep."

"It should not be long. They will soon be away from our tent and in their own spot."

After four restful days, at the evening meal, Eliezar stood on a stool so he could be seen and heard by the workers. "We have had a pleasant pause in our journey. The camels are ready to travel again, rested, watered and fed. Our supplies are replenished, and so we can move on. We have enjoyed the river, the quiet afternoons, and peaceful evenings." He paused and stared at two of the men. "Most of the time. Tomorrow, we leave at sunrise, ready for the last days of our journey."

Murmurs travelled around the circle and quick looks were exchanged. But no one spoke.

"Good. There are no questions, so get some rest. No one goes to town tonight. If anyone decides to test me, he had better just stay in Laish. He will not be going on with us. Good night."

The circle quickly broke up as everyone walked to their sleeping place. Rebekah and Deborah took one more walk along the gurgling river, then went to their beds. Rebekah stretched out on her mat.

"How will I ever get to sleep tonight?"

"The same way you have every other night on this journey, Becca. It is no different. Tomorrow, we start walking again."

"You are so sensible. Sometimes I wish you could be foolish like me. Just for a little while, be young and girlish again."

"Go to sleep and let me do the same."

But Deborah did not fall asleep. She lay for a long time until she heard the regular quiet breathing of Rebekah. Then she got up and, in her bare feet, went out to sit under the stars. She loved to watch their reflection in the water. They winked as if they had a wonderful secret that only they knew. She jumped in alarm when a twig snapped behind her.

"It is just me, Benjamin. I saw you here and came to make sure you were all right. If you are, I think you should go to your bed."

"I am just too excited to sleep. Soon I will be in the place where I will spend the rest of my life. Then I can sleep when I know my new life."

"The nights get very cold here in this valley. I suggest, even if you can't sleep, you lie on your pallet and rest. Get warm for the rest of the night. To be honest, I would like to sleep, and I can't until you are safely in your tent."

Deborah apologized, got up, and walked away. *Is he our friend and guardian or our jailor? I hope Rebekah and I can walk about on our own when we are at home in Abraham's village. Freedom cannot come soon enough.* She lay down on her mat, and despite her annoyance and excitement at what the next few days would bring, she was soon asleep.

Chapter Sixteen

Benjamin was up before the sun. He inspected the camels, checking their feet for sores or bruising. They all seemed healthy. On such a journey, the safe arrival of everyone depended on these magnificent animals. *How can a creature that is so bad tempered and so awkward looking be the means for us to survive? But they are, and they are my responsibility.*

Benjamin had been completely surprised when told he was to be in charge of the camels on this important journey. But he relished his new responsibilities. Each day, Eliezar spent time talking to him about all kinds of things, and he asked Eliezar if this was some kind of test. The response was unexpected.

"In a way, it is. I asked Abraham if I could have you for my camel drover on this journey. He agreed and then asked me to watch out for you and to teach you anything I thought would be good for you to learn. That is what I have been trying to do. Have you learned anything?"

"A great deal, and thank you, not just about how to survive on such a journey, but the stories of the family too. I never knew much about Abraham's early life or why he came here. It is good to know. It helps me to understand why his worship of El Shaddai is so important to him."

"The safe arrival of Rebekah is important to him and, therefore, to us. She knows little of our way of life. Make it your task to talk to her and tell her about Abraham's family and our worship. I saw signs that she has grown up in a family that paid little attention to the god of Terah and of Abraham. There were idols in their house, and you know how that will not be accepted. Teach her of the tribe's religion."

"You mentioned this before. Why me? Why not you?"

"Two reasons. I am an old man in her eyes and besides that, I am not very religious. And so, it is not fitting for me to teach the wife of Isaac, and certainly not about the god we worship. You are young, better you tell her the stories of the god of the mountain. Now I must move on."

Benjamin walked around the camel pen, checking the harnesses. *What do I say to a stranger and a woman who lived in a distant land? I hardly have this god stuff figured out for myself. I better do some thinking about the powerful god of the mountain.*

The long journey was nearing its end. Benjamin had little time left to have this challenging conversation with the spirited woman in the caravan. *I'll think about what I can say as we travel today. Then tonight I will find a way to talk to her. Eliezar has managed to give me the hard tasks. Camels I know. Women are a mystery.*

Early the next morning, camp was stirring, fires were glowing, and the camels were fed and watered. Benjamin listened to the chatter that was filling the damp morning air. He looked to the east, and the sun was climbing up over the hills.

"Good day Benjamin. All the signs point to pleasant weather. Have you checked the camels?"

"Yes Eliezar. I didn't sleep well and so I am up early to look after things."

"Any reason you couldn't sleep?

"I was worrying about the task you have laid upon my shoulders. I don't know how to begin or what to say."

"Don't think too much about it. Just talk to her. Ask if she has any questions. That is always a good start."

Benjamin watched Eliezar walk away to get the meal started. *If it is so easy, why don't you do it?*

The women were seated near the fire. He filled two bowls of porridge and took it to them. He got a bowl for himself; he sat down with them. He took a deep breath. "Blessed are you, god of the mountain, who brings forth grain from the earth."

Rebekah looked at him, eyes wide with wonder. "Do you say that every morning?"

"That is the prayer before we eat. Well, that is the short version. There is a much longer one as well. People who worship El Shaddai repeat this blessing before every meal. Don't you have a prayer of thanks before eating?"

"Sometimes Father says something. But he mumbles, and I never paid much attention."

"If I remember, Rebekah, he only did that on special days. The Sabbath was one time," murmured Deborah.

"You are right. There was always a candle on the table too now that you remind me."

"Is that important to you, Benjamin?"

"There are many important things to do and to say to please the almighty one who lives on the holy mountain."

The commanding voice of Eliezar interrupted them with his call to get the meal things cleaned up and packed. "We need to get on the trail. Get moving everybody."

The long line formed up as before and a shout to move rang out over the water to the distant hills. The faint echo whispered back. With noisy grunts, the camels were plodding along once again.

The caravan continued travelling south through the great river valley. The route was well used by traders and the road was broad and a good distance was covered each day. Everyone knew the daily pattern and since all were eager to arrive in Hebron, the work was shared by all with little dissension.

Rebekah and Deborah took pleasure walking in the cooler times of the day and riding when it was hot, or they were tired. Eliezar and Benjamin kept a close eye on them and spent time each day entertaining them.

Rebekah asked about her husband, but Eliezar gave no new information beyond what he had shared at Haran. She needed to know more, and asked Deborah to help. That night Deborah engaged the servants in conversation around the fire. She had the opportunity as Rebekah retired early most nights, and that gave Deborah some freedom to help her mistress.

She asked questions. What did he look like? Was he a good manager of his flocks and herds? Was he kind to his slaves and servants?

The answers came easily as the men talked about their master and shared memories of the family. Deborah learned that he was born to Sarah after long years of barrenness. Sarah considered him a miracle and a gift from El Shaddai and was very protective of him. This gave truth to Deborah's opinion that he was pampered and even spoiled by his mother. He got whatever he wanted. Abraham had little time with his son, and his influence was often negated by Sarah. Isaac was a good man with animals, and since his mother's death, spent most of his time living in the fields with the flocks. He seldom went into the city, but when he did, those servants who went with him told tales of drunken nights and loose women.

Deborah asked about his god and the devotion of Isaac to the faith of his father. The men looked at each other with blank stares. Their responses were short and guarded.

"It isn't our business how or what god he worships,"

"Sometimes he went with Abraham to the high altar, but not often."

"I never knew him to follow the ritual prayers or blessings."

"He spent more time cursing than blessing the mountain god."

All this was pondered by Deborah. Benjamin was a much more religious man from what she had seen of his habits. *I will have to think carefully about this. I think, perhaps, Abraham is more devout than Isaac. I wonder what I should tell Becca.*

Days unwound in the same fashion as they had for the past week, but Deborah sensed excitement in the servants. She gathered that they were nearing the end of the journey. Near the town of Shechem, they stopped, and Eliezar ordered a rest for the caravan. The rules were the same as at Laish. No visit to the market for the women.

After the meal on the last night in camp, Benjamin asked the women to take a walk with him to the river. He carried blankets and had a flash of wine and honey cakes. Deborah eyed him with a questioning look.

He spread the blankets on the ground, took a bowl, and got water from the river. "Just in case we get thirsty as we talk. I have a purpose in this walk. We are nearing the land of Abraham. Eliezar has sent a fast runner to let Abraham know we are almost home. By the time the sun is high in the sky tomorrow, we will be on his property, and in a day or two at his tent. Do you have any questions that I might answer for you?"

Rebekah looked puzzled and twirled a curl around her finger.

"Well then, let's start at a different place. Will you answer some questions for me?"

Rebekah looked at Deborah, who smiled and nodded.

"If I can. But I don't understand what you want to know."

"Just getting to know you. I thought since we are about the same age, maybe I could help you understand the family and make it easier for you to fit in."

"I have heard that Abraham had a son before Isaac. Is this true?"

Benjamin repeated the story of Isaac's birth, the birth of Ishmael and the fact that Isaac was the heir to the inheritance when his father died.

"If Ishmael is older, why is he not the heir?"

"He is the son of a former slave. Hagar was neither wife nor concubine to Abraham and the first-born son of his wife is the heir to the birthright and the land."

"That might explain a lot of things. I have heard that Abraham worships a god who lives on the fiery mountain and only this one god. That is strange to me. Tell me about this one they call the almighty one."

"I will start a little earlier. Terah and Abraham left Ur because of the evil they saw in that great city. They stopped at Haran to rest, and Terah died and was buried there, as you know. Abraham always said that his god told him to leave Ur."

"This mountain god speaks?" Rebekah interrupted.

"Not to me or to many people. But Abraham hears an answer to his prayers. A voice, or a thought, a vision, a dream. I don't know. But he was sure god told him to go to a new land. And that land was Canaan, where we now live."

Rebekah took a long time to drink some water. Benjamin waited.

"This is very strange to me. Tell me more."

"El Shaddai, dwells on the sacred mountain. When it is quiet, he is pleased and is resting. When it smokes and thunders and covers the land with the river of hot red fire and ash, he is angry."

Rebekah shuddered. "What makes him so angry?"

"El Shaddai demands our allegiance, and we must not worship any other gods. We need to offer sacrifices to him on the altars. Grain and oil and sheep or goats are burnt or slaughtered to show our devotion and obedience."

"I don't know if I want to see that."

"You won't have to. Only the men go up the mountain to offer the sacrifices. Women have their own rituals."

"What are they? What do the women do? What gods do they worship?" The questions tumbled from Rebekah's lips.

"I can't answer that. The women go to their house and men can't enter. You will have to ask the women, about their rituals and their worship."

Deborah and Rebekah shared a puzzled look.

"We have much to learn about our new life, Rebekah. There are many things that are new to us." Deborah patted Rebekah's hand and then clasped it gently, trying to keep her calm. "This is a great deal for us to grasp. We need to think about it for a while and then talk some more later."

Benjamin gave a sigh of relief. "Yes. It is time I found Eliezar. He may have work for me to do." And he hurried away.

"You know, Rebekah, I have vague memories of these customs from my family. It seemed to me, Father said prayers over everything. Mother lit candles at our meals and we children sat quietly and respectfully."

"Your family worshipped this invisible mountain god?"

"I think so. It is so long ago, and so much has happened to me, it is hard to remember. It was before I was taken from them and sold at the slave market. I was glad your family bought me, as they were always kind and just in their treatment of slaves and servants."

"I thought marriage was a simple thing. But this is getting very complicated. But we will figure it out. I am strong and smart, and I can work this out. Maybe even to our advantage."

Together, they walked away from the water and back to their circle of safety inside the room Eliezar had arranged for them.

Rebekah was deep in thought as Debba braided her hair for the night. *I must find a woman I can trust and talk to her about this god of the mountain. Perhaps she can help me understand my duties and my place in the village. I always said that our life in Haran was dull. I think the next phase of my life will not be dull. It may be challenging, but it will be interesting, and I hope satisfying.*

Her hair was done, and Deborah said goodnight. Rebekah lay on her mat and tried to think about her life in the coming years. Still pondering the mystery of the future, but before long, she was breathing softly as sleep stilled her questions.

Chapter Seventeen

Abraham sat looking at the bowl of porridge. He stirred it listlessly. *Gershom is not a cook. If Eliezar doesn't return soon, I will be very hungry.* Each day, he tried to keep busy. Working at something, anything, helped to keep the worries about Eliezar and his errand at the back of his mind. There was no way to get a message to him, and Abraham knew Eliezar would not be trying to contact him. If all was going well, there was no need, and if he had failed, he had threatened to run away. Sometimes, because of his age and stiff joints, Abraham was not able to sleep or to do much physical work. And when idle, he worried.

He turned to Gershom. "How long has he been gone? It seems like a long time."

"It is a long way to Haran and back. And travelling with a woman will make him move more slowly."

"I don't see why. Sarah never slowed me down. Never complained, just walked, and still looked after me every day."

Abraham had been thinking about Sarah. Ever since he set in motion the plan for the marriage of Isaac, he often spoke of her in loving terms.

Someone was running hard toward the tent. Gershom pointed at the runner. "Look Abraham. A runner is coming up the hill."

The man stopped in front of Abraham, dripping wet from his exertion, and gasping for breath.

Abraham poked Gershom with his cane. "Get him some water and a seat." Gershom jumped to obey.

In a few minutes, when he caught his breath, the messenger spoke. "Abraham, chief among all chiefs, I bring you a message."

"Fool. Why else would you be here? Get on with it."

"I bring news of the caravan. They are soon going to be on the vast lands of Abraham, and will be here at your tent, at sundown in two or three days."

Abraham raised his hands and offered a blessing. "Holy One. You have granted your servant Abraham good news this day. Blessed be the holy name. Gershom, where are you?"

"Here, master. What is your desire?"

"Take this messenger to a tent where he can rest. But first, get water for him to bathe and food. Then find Esther, the healer, and send her to me."

In a short time, Esther was walking up the path to the tent.

"Esther, Esther, they are coming," shouted Abraham.

"Who is coming? Raiders to rob the camp of Abraham?"

"Why would I send for you if raiders were coming? And who would dare to attack me?"

Esther's giggle made Abraham laugh with her.

"Why do you like to tease me?"

"It is good for you. You get all excited and that gets your blood moving. Now who is coming?"

"Eliezar and the bride for Isaac."

"Maybe he couldn't find a woman willing to come so far to marry a stranger?"

"If he failed, he threatened to run away. He has not, so let's get busy. They will be here by sunset tomorrow or the day after. We have a great feast to prepare, fine wine to get ready, and meat to roast. We'll need a bridal chamber, and I will need a lamb to sacrifice at the high altar. Why are you standing there? Get busy."

"It is good news, Abraham. I will get everyone to work at once. Have some wine and then rest a bit. Should I find Isaac and have him come to you?"

"I will send Gershom to get him. You have plenty to do." He watched her walk down the hill. *What would I do without her?*

In a short time, the whole camp knew and anyone who could leave their own work was busy with the preparations.

Isaac ambled up the hill to his father's tent. "You wanted to see me?"

Abraham jumped.

"Sorry to wake you, father, but Gershom said it was important."

"Eliezar will be here by sunset tomorrow, and he brings your bride."

Isaac dropped to a stool with a thump. "It is really going to happen. I am getting a bride."

"Yes. And you have much to do. You will need a fine tunic and robe. No dirty, smelly skins for a bridegroom." Abraham looked at Isaac's tunic with disgust. "The bridal chamber needs to be prepared. Sarah's tent will be the proper place. You will need flowers and lamps, well swept carpets, and fresh clean blankets for the marriage bed. Why are you looking at me like that? You knew this was going to happen."

"But it will be many moons till the wedding. There is the contract and the bride price to settle."

"I paid the bridal price to her father before Eliezar and the woman left Haran, and Eliezar signed the contracts in my name. It is all done. All that's left is the marriage bed."

"Do I have no say in my own wedding?"

"Not at this late date. If you had acted years ago when you should have been married, it could have been different. But you have left me no choice. And besides, fathers arrange marriages. Always have, always will."

"But I have never seen her. What if she is fat, old, or ugly?"

"Unimportant. Women have been married to men for ages and they have had no say in the matter. And most men don't see their bride till the bedding. You will dine with her at the feast I am planning for tomorrow. Be glad about that. Now, off with you to the market to buy some decent clothes. If you need advice, take Gershom with you.

Isaac sat numb and still as a stump.

"Why are you still here? Do you have a question?"

"No father. I am just totally surprised. "

"Well, be surprised on your way to find Gershom. And when you return, we will go to the high altar to make a thanksgiving offering to the all mighty one." Abraham watched his son walk down the hill. "At times, I find it hard to believe he is the son of my loins."

Chapter Eighteen

Eliezar sat alone by the fire. He reviewed the journey to this place. It had gone well, and he was glad there had been no major incidents that required his intervention. After a few more hours, he could relax. This heavy responsibility would be over. If she was the wrong woman, he could blame the god of the mountain, or at least his misunderstanding of the sign.

His mind turned to Deborah. Now there was a woman! She was wise, intelligent, strong, and yet kind and considerate. *I think she has seen life at its worst and at its best. She takes changes with quiet composure. Her devotion to Rebekah is admirable. What a wife she would make. Some lucky man will surely claim her for his own.* His thoughts were interrupted by the cheery voice of Benjamin.

"Good morning to you. Up early again." Benjamin grinned.

"Our journey is nearing its end and I just need to make sure I have not forgotten anything. I am rather surprised that we received no word from Abraham."

"He is no doubt busy getting ready to receive the bride. And remember, there is no one there to send out a reply. You are here. No one would think of the courtesy of a reply except you, Eliezar."

He chuckled. "I suspect you are right. Can you imagine the confusion as they try to get this marriage arranged? I wonder how Isaac is feeling."

"Honestly, I can't imagine, and it is of no concern to me. I have to get my camels ready for this last day of our journey." He waved and went to the holding area where the camels were pastured for the night.

Eliezar looked with satisfaction at the camp. Cooking fires were glowing to prepare the last meal on the trail. Food supplies had lasted, and fuel had not been a problem. Shadows were moving in the women's tent, and that was a good sign.

As everyone ate their meal, there was little talk. That this was the last day was known by all, and they were both happy and sad that their journey was ending. There was always excitement and mystery when travelling so far from home, and there was gratitude that all had gone well along the road. But there was also eagerness to return home, to wives and families, and to the comfort of the daily routine of life in the village.

Just as the sun appeared in all its glowing morning colours over the eastern hills, Benjamin lined the camels up. He walked over to Deborah and greeted her.

"How are you feeling today? There must be a lot of different feelings for you and Rebekah."

"Yes. She has been quiet this morning. I am sure she is feeling nervous and even afraid. But she will be fine. Thank you for helping us understand a bit about the life we can expect. I hope the women welcome us and are willing to help us fit in to life here.

"The head leader of the women for the time being, until Rebekah learns her role, is Esther. She has been trained by Rivkah, who was the healer Sarah trained. Rivkah was very close to Sarah and replaced her as the healer when Sarah grew too old and tired for the work. They will both be there to answer questions."

Deborah was nodding her head as she listened.

"Esther is on good terms with Abraham. She is the only one who can tease him and make fun of him. She is loved and respected by all. You would do well to make her your friend. Tell Rebekah about her. She will need her too as a friend and a mentor."

"Thank you, Benjamin. You have been a good friend. I hope we can continue to rely on your advice and friendship."

"I will return to my regular duties in the camel yards, but I will always be around if you need me." He reached out to take her hand, but at the sound of steps, retreated into himself once more.

"Good morning, Rebekah. Will you ride or walk this morning?" Rebekah looked thoughtful as she stopped beside him.

"I will walk. I am too excited and too nervous to sit still. You say we will be there for the meal at sunset."

"All being well, yes."

Benjamin gave Deborah a warm smile and turned back to his duties. He called the order to start moving, and the camels grunted and heaved to their feet, lifting their burdens high into the morning mist. The pace they set was faster than they had walked before. It seemed that even the camels knew they were nearing home.

Rebekah had been asleep in her basket for most of the afternoon. She heard her name and roused and stretched. Benjamin was speaking to her, and Deborah was at his side. Her camel was down, and she climbed out and stood on the grassy hill.

"I have called a brief rest stop. In the valley, you can see large flocks of sheep. They belong to Abraham, and it is possible that Isaac is there watching them. You might want to tidy yourself a bit, brush the sand from your cloak, for you will soon be at Abraham's tent."

He pointed to the distant hill. Rebekah could see white dots on the lush green, grassy slopes. More sheep than she could ever count. Deborah had a brush and was sending clouds of dust into the air as she cleaned Rebekah's cloak.

"Such a lovely blue colour, but it is grey with dust and sand. I'll get it clean and then we will tidy your hair and get your head covering and veil in place."

"What will I say them, to Abraham and to Isaac?"

"I think a simple smile and a graceful bow will be all you need for now."

"You make it sound so simple. But the first impression can set the tone for the rest of my life. I know we are caught up in this contract, but I would like it to be pleasant for us both, Isaac, and me."

"I wonder how he is feeling. What has he been told about you? Is he scared, angry, resigned, excited? Surely you must wonder how he feels?"

"I can barely manage my own mixed feelings. I can't think about his. And remember, if he is not happy, I am gone, divorced, thrown out."

"I know, but I am sure that he is a man of honour, and you will be treated with kindness and justice."

"Maybe. Maybe not. That is why I have the money and the gold that father gave me. Security. Father said that we would be always welcome in his house if I found myself in trouble."

Deborah smiled broadly to make light of Rebekah's worries, but she was relieved to hear that no matter what happened, they could survive.

Too soon, the camel train began to move, and Rebekah and Deborah walked the last miles to meet the two strangers, the men who would be husband and father, to Rebekah.

The two women walked in silence along the smooth road that led to the village that was to be their home. Many tents dotted the hills that rose in countless shades of green behind the tents. Most of the tents were black, but two were adorned with panels of colour along the sides and bright flags waved from the posts. A wide river ran through the valley between the verdant hills. The sun was still above the trees when they reached the bottom of the hill. A man stood by the side of the road. He was wearing the sturdy cloak and rough sandals of a shepherd.

Deborah whispered in Rebekah's ear. "Your husband. That is Isaac."

Rebekah quickly covered her face with her veil as he approached. She barely glanced at him, then bowed. He nodded and spoke to Eliezar who had quietly joined them. "Welcome back Eliezar, father is waiting for you at his tent. Please take this woman to Sarah's tent, and I will meet her there later." And he strode away, back to the sheep.

Deborah took Rebekah's hand and started walking. Rebekah fell into step, and they moved toward the tents. Neither spoke. Surprised and shocked at the lack of courtesy or welcome, they were filled with apprehension. In silence, they continued into the settlement.

As they walked past tents, where women and children stared. A few smiled, and one or two waved a small greeting. They climbed a hill toward two large tents. Eliezar led them to the smaller one that had flags fluttering in welcome on the posts. "This is the tent of Sarah," he said and scurried away.

The entry flap opened and a woman with a wide and welcoming smile came out.

"I am Esther. Welcome to the tent of Sarah. I have scented water for you to wash in and cool pomegranate juice for you to drink. Please come in and be at home."

The two weary, nervous travellers relaxed their shoulders and the tension floated away on the gentle words of Esther. Rebekah warily entered the tent of the matriarch. *I hope the smile of Esther is a sign of welcome to this place. Perhaps being led to the tent of Sarah is a good omen.* They removed their dusty cloaks and eagerly drank the cool juice.

At his tent, Abraham greeted Eliezar with a warm handshake. "Tell me about your choice."

"She came as an answer to my prayer. Her name is Rebekah, and she is the daughter of your nephew, Bethuel. Her father is wise, kind, and generous. Her mother is not happy to see her go away so quickly. And her brother has the air and manners of a tyrant."

"But the bride? What about the bride?"

"She is beautiful as was rumoured. She is wise and learned. There is a strong independence about her. Bethuel gave her the right to choose her husband, and she has refused many. She has much to learn about our ways but seems eager to listen. Her servant Deborah is a woman to be respected. Experienced in the ways of the world and smart and canny. I am impressed with her. They will keep Isaac on his toes, and he will need to measure up."

"Good. Well done. Go to your tent, I will send food and drink to you. I am glad you came back. I cannot survive much longer on the meals Gershom prepares."

Eliezar laughed. "It is good to be home, very good."

Chapter Nineteen

Rebekah followed Esther into the tent. She stopped, enthralled. Deborah bumped into her and gasped. Never had they seen a place like it. The air was fresh and sweet, and some panels of the tent fabric held up by cords allowed fresh air and sunlight to enter through these unique windows.

Deborah spoke in awe. "The tent walls are decorated with circles of dried leaves and flowers. How lovely."

Rebekah found her voice. "This is where Sarah lived? It is so inviting."

Esther nodded. "Yes. This was Sarah's home. And now it is to be yours. Isaac will join you here soon. He is getting cleaned up to welcome you. Would you like to put on fresh garments to greet him? I know your baskets have not been unpacked, so I have chosen a few things from my trunks. We are about the same size. They are on those pegs to your right." She pointed to the colourful garments hanging beside them. "I will leave you and Deborah to get ready. There is no rush. Take your time. Isaac will need more than a few minutes to get the smell of goat out of his hair."

Deborah thanked Esther and went to the clothing hanging in the tent.

"Rebekah, these are beautiful. Which one do you want?"

"None, thank you. I refuse to wear borrowed clothes for my wedding night. I want my own and I will wait till my trunks arrive."

"But Isaac?"

"He can wait until I am ready. Now go and see about my clothes. You know which basket has my wedding garments in it. Don't stand there with your mouth open. Go!"

Deborah left the tent. Esther was standing just outside, and she must have heard.

"I am sorry. Rebekah is proud and used to having her own things. Please forgive her lack of appreciation for your kindness."

"No need to apologize. This must be difficult for her. I will help you find what you need and get it here quickly. I will also get scented water for her to bathe. Come."

In his tent, Abraham was urging Isaac to make himself presentable. "You were not supposed to be in the fields. I expected you to be here, as I asked, learning how to oversee all my holdings. Do I have to teach you how to be a man? And I dread to think of you as a husband."

Isaac started to speak, but Abraham shushed him. "Eliezar tells me Rebekah is a lady. Well spoken, gentle and refined. She is expecting a man who is her equal. You will be sorry if she turns around and goes back to your uncle. He will be enraged if his only daughter is mistreated. Gershom is waiting to help you. Now get to work."

Isaac dragged his feet as he went to his tent. *Why is everyone in such a hurry? Marriage is for a very long time. It can wait while I get used to the idea.*

Gershom called. "Hurry up Isaac. Your father has told me most forcefully to get you cleaned up and over to your mother's tent. Your bath is ready. Enjoy it while it is still hot."

When in the bath, Isaac had to admit it felt good, until Gershom started to scrub.

"You will take my skin off. Take it easy."

"When was the last time you had more than just a quick dip in the river to bathe? It will take a strong scent to get the stink of goat out of your hair. Your wife is lovely, in case you didn't notice. You need to impress this lady from the land so far away."

"Why do you say I need to impress her? She needs to impress me."

"I am sure you will be excited by the first glimpse of her. It will be a diplomatic disaster if she takes one look at you and gets back on the camel to return to her family."

Isaac shook the water from his hair and took a towel to dry himself.

"And I assure you, you have not felt your father's full wrath yet. But you will if this meeting fails. Take care, Isaac; there are more important matters at stake here than what you want."

Gershom held up the tunic and cloak that had been purchased for this meeting. Isaac felt the fine fabric of his new clothes. *I must admit this red tunic is very handsome and so will I be when I wear it.* Gershom handed him a cedar branch to brush his hair and beard. The new sandals had been polished till they gleamed. The light brown cloak with the red pattern stitched on it impressed him as he draped it around his shoulders.

"I am ready. Walk with me to the tent."

Rebekah was ready and waiting, trying not to fidget. She had chosen a tunic of fine, pale blue linen. It was embroidered around the neck and the cuffs with her spirit emblem. She touched the delicate embroidery and thought of Zera. *I wish you could have lived to see me married, and to watch over me in this new life and keep me strong.* Her cloak was a deep, sapphire blue with the same embellishments. Her sandals were soft leather and had dainty blue beading on the straps. Deborah had brushed her hair until it shone and scented it with cedar. It was held in place with white ribbons and blue combs. Deborah paced in the tent and Rebekah sat on a silk cushioned stool. The sun shone on her from the opening in the roof, making her glow in the dim light from the windows. They waited.

"I hope this delay means he is taking proper care to dress to meet you. He needs to show you proper respect."

"Deborah, I need you to be calm. I am not concerned about this delay. I will be married for an awfully long time and a few minutes to settle my nerves is a good thing. And we must impress him. He can not go back on his promise to wed, but it will be very awkward if he is displeased." Rebekah smiled at her faithful companion. *I know you are worried, dear friend, but it will be what we make it.*

The sun was just kissing the top of the hills in the west as Isaac walked down to Sarah's tent. *I will have to start thinking of it as Rebekah's tent. I hope she will be worthy of living in mother's tent.* As he neared the dwelling, he realized his heart was pounding. *What do I have to worry about? She has to please me, and I must remember she is just a woman who will be my wife. Better get started right away by letting her know her place.*

He stopped at the opening flap and clapped three times. He waited for permission to enter. *I won't be begging entrance at her door when she belongs to me.*

The men who had accompanied Isaac walked away. Benjamin turned to Gershom, "I hope they don't kill each other."

A gentle voice from the tent answered. "Enter." Esther, standing outside near the doorway, smiled, and whispered. "Be kind Isaac." He never acknowledged her presence.

Isaac opened the flap and strode inside. He paused while his eyes adjusted to the dim, shadowy surroundings.

His bride sat on a stool in the centre. Isaac stared. Something was wrong. Something was very wrong. The tent looked different. It took a moment and then he realized what it was. Where was the cedar stump that cradled the green stone of his mother's life? It was gone.

He shrieked. "Where is the stone? What have you done with the stone? It stands in the centre. Always."

Esther rushed in. "Isaac. You told me to fix the tent for the wedding night. You said to me that it was now Rebekah's tent and to fix it up for her. I moved the stone. I put it on the south side that looks toward Sarah's sacred grove. The pedestal leans toward the cave where she is buried. That is proper now that this is Rebekah's home. This is no longer a shrine to your mother."

She paused as the tent flap flew back and Abraham burst into the room. He had heard Isaac's outburst from where he stood a little way off. Deborah led him to a stool. He did not sit, but stood rigidly, dishevelled, and breathless.

Esther continued. "Sarah would have wished for a better welcome for her new daughter. You have been rude, and your behaviour is an insult to Rebekah and to your uncle and your father."

Abraham spoke in a cold, steely voice. "I heard the shouting, and I came at once." He bowed to each of the women, then jabbed Isaac with his walking stick. "You. Come with me."

As they left, a woman pushed past them and into the tent. Abraham nodded and said, "Rivkah. It is proper that you are here."

Taking a deep and calming breath; she entered the tent. Rebekah sat rigid on the seat and Deborah was cowering on the floor at her feet. Esther stood white with anger or fear but managed to say, "Welcome, Rivkah, teacher, companion and friend to Sarah."

Deborah stood and went to the rear of the tent, where a small fire was burning. She took hot water and made a pot of mint tea. With steaming cups, she walked to the women and sat on the floor beside her mistress. They took the cups and looked at Esther, their eyes full of questions.

"Where do I begin?" Esther wondered aloud.

Deborah looked up. "If I may speak, perhaps I can help." Esther and Rivkah nodded. "We have heard talk of Isaac. Talk that he is self-centered and strongly attached to his mother and her memory. The servants spoke of his lack of discipline and his practice of putting his own needs before those of others. Does this help?"

Rivkah sighed. "Yes, it does. I am glad you were somewhat prepared. That describes Isaac very well. He was born to Sarah late in her life. They had given up all hope of a son and heir. That is why Hagar was sent to Abraham and bore Ishmael. That turned out to be a tragedy, for Sarah had Isaac after Ishmael. And he, of course, became the heir, and Ishmael became the second son. Hagar was teaching him that he could supplant Isaac and that led to their being cast out and they went south to Egypt."

Rebekah sipped her tea. "There was talk of a long lived, deep estrangement between Abraham and Sarah. Is that true?"

Rivkah looked at her feet and chewed her lip. After a thoughtful pause, Esther spoke. "It is true. The details are not important, but Sarah never totally forgave Abraham for putting Isaac in danger when he was a young boy. They managed to live in outward harmony, but I believe the scar ran deep. It affected Sarah's relationship with her son. She kept him close to her, pampered and indulged him. Abraham had little contact and was never able to teach him how to be a strong, independent man. After Sarah died, Isaac spent most of his time with the animals and the herders."

Deborah went to the fire and stirred the embers. She took some dried leaves and dropped them on the embers. Soon, the tent was filled with the soothing aroma of lavender. As she sat down again, she patted Rebekah's shoulder.

Esther continued. "Whenever he was summoned here by his father, he slept in this tent, even though he had his own tent, near his father's. Gershom and Eliezar kept this space clean and tidy, and they fed Isaac. A few weeks after Sarah's death, Eliezar came to me. He told me that in the centre of the tent, resting on a cedar stump, was the green orb that is now at the back of the tent. I know nothing of its story, but this has been a shrine to his mother ever since, and I believe that for him, the orb is a powerful symbol of his mother. Eliezar says he talks to it, prays to it, and sometimes sits and sings songs here hour after hour."

"And now I have come and violated this space." Rebekah spoke in a voice filled with sorrow.

Rivkah touched Rebekah's arm. "None of this is your fault. He knew this was to be your home now. That is our custom. He ordered it swept and cleaned and told Esther that it was to be yours. He told us to do what was needed to make it a good place for you. It is so typical of him not to think of what would have to change. Isaac cannot seem to feel for another or understand how his actions will affect them."

"What will happen now?"

"We will just have to wait. Abraham will have to deal with this and sort it out."

Deborah stood. "I don't know about you two, but we have not eaten for hours. I am hungry. I will get cakes from our food pack and make fresh tea. Let us share a simple meal while we wait."

"Good idea. Can I help you?" Esther offered. "Rivkah will sit with Rebekah."

"Thank you, no. Please stay with Rebekah."

They ate the simple food in silence. As Deborah stood to clean up, Esther spoke. "I wish I could be outside Abraham's tent and hear what is going on."

Deborah clattered the clay dishes and chuckled. "I suspect Isaac will receive the wrath of Abraham and maybe even the sting of Abraham's cane."

A long sigh came from Rebekah. "This is not the way I imagined my wedding banquet."

Abraham strode to his tent and Isaac followed meekly. They were barely inside when Abraham roared. "I have raised a fool. Bethuel is a great and powerful man in Haran. You have insulted his daughter, your wife. She is not one of your street women. She is the esteemed daughter of your uncle, and you treated her abominably." Abraham continued to prod his son with his stick. "The full wrath of Bethuel's army can wipe out this miserable village if she returns to her father in shame." He paused to catch his breath and took a moment to calm himself. "You will go to the mountain to ask for mercy from the Almighty One. Then we will return to the tent of Rebekah where you will beg, yes beg, for her forgiveness. I can only hope she is as forgiving as she is beautiful."

The women were trying to act as if nothing had happened, and they talked about the warm days and pleasant evenings.

"Shh! Someone is coming." Rebekah sat once more on the stool, and Esther and Rivkah stood beside her and a little behind. They each rested a hand on her shoulder. Deborah stood in the shadows near the fire.

There was a soft clapping at the tent. "May a humiliated father enter?"

"Enter, Abraham, esteemed father of Isaac." Rebekah's voice was soft and gentle, but firm and steady.

He came in and knelt before the astonished women. "May I speak? My tongue sticks to my mouth and words are hard to say, but I will speak with honesty and with deeply felt shame."

Rebekah pointed to a cushion near her feet. "Do not kneel. Rise and sit on the cushions on the floor. If there is any shame, it is not yours."

Abraham went to the cushion and looked at the woman who spoke. "You remind me of my brother Nahor. I can see him in your face."

She sat with poise and dignity. Only the bright spots of colour on her cheeks gave a hint of her feelings.

Her beauty pleased him, and he saw his brother, in her strong cheek bones and ebony hair. "My son has shamed the house of Abraham. His shame is mine. He is now on his way to offer a sacrifice and to pray for the forgiveness of the holy one. On his return, he will cleanse himself with water and hyssop. Then he will come and beg for your forgiveness. And I hope you will make him beg. He needs to learn humility and compassion."

He paused for breath and wiped his brow.

Esther spoke as Abraham paused. "Abraham. If it pleases you, I have told these women why the orb was here and what it represents to Isaac. I think it is enough for now. If you wish to say more later, that is up to you."

"Thank you, Esther. You have the heart and the wisdom of your teacher." He managed a smile. "The orb will be moved to a small tent I will put beside mine for the present. I will deal with it later."

Rebekah stood and walked to the cedar post. She deeply inhaled its aroma, then reached out and touched the green orb. As her hand rested there, her shoulders relaxed, the tension drained from her body. She turned and there was a peaceful smile radiating from her eyes and mouth.

"The pedestal and the orb can stay. Cedar is my spirit symbol and I find comfort in its presence."

"It will be as you wish. If you change your mind, I will have it removed. The family will gather for the meal that has been prepared. It will not be a wedding feast, but a welcoming feast for my beautiful daughter and her faithful maid servant. There will be music, dancing, and entertainment. I know you must be tired, so you may retire here from the festivities to your home, whenever you wish. Isaac will sleep in his tent."

He rose, bowed, and turned to leave.

"Father Abraham. I am pleased to meet my esteemed uncle. I look forward to getting to know you and to hear your stories. Tales of your wisdom are spoken at the ceremonies in my father's house."

She walked to his side, and standing on tiptoe, placed a kiss on his whiskered cheeks.

As he left, he wiped tears from his beard. "She is just what he needs, but she is too good for him." He looked at the stars and the holy mountain. "Blessed be the god of my fathers. His goodness fills my heart, and his kindness overwhelms me with joy. Blessed be the holy name."

The women finished their tea and Rivkah invited them to bring their cushion near the fire.

She spoke and her voice rang out strong and steady. "A fire offers warmth, beauty, and strength. We surround our fires with stones. Stones that contain and control the flames." At that moment, a log broke, and sparks danced upward. "The flames cook our food and warm our tents. But fire can burn our bodies, scar our skin, and destroy our possessions. Our feelings are like the fire. They can be helpful, or they can harm us and others. The stones remind us that the fire which burns within also needs to be controlled or it can destroy the mind and spirit."

She raised her arms and held out her hands. "Please, may we join hands around this circle of stone and fire?"

They moved their cushions closer and linked their hands. Rivkah went around the circle and made eye contact with each one. Her powerful voice filled the tent with a haunting melody as she hummed a tune. The singing stopped, and she spoke.

"El Shaddai, mother of us all, from your dwelling place on the fiery mountain, you feel the pain of all your daughters. Let the flame of your presence fill our hearts, heal our wounds, and give us strength and courage. We welcome Rebekah and Deborah to our land and ask for a blessing on them as they learn our ways and customs. In love we gather, in love we separate, in love we live each day. Blessed be this night of welcome."

They stayed supported by the comfortable silence of sisterhood and friendship. The silence was broken by the sound of footsteps in the tent doorway.

"It is Abraham. May we enter?"

"Come into my home, father Abraham. You are always welcome."

The flap was lifted, and he came in, bending low in a bow as he did. Behind him came Isaac, his eyes looking at his feet. Then Eliezar and Gershom. The women around the fire stood and all but Rebekah started to leave.

"Please. You must stay. The offence was public, and the apology must be witnessed by those who heard the insult." Abraham gestured for everyone to sit.

They gathered on mats in a larger circle around the fire. Abraham reached into his sleeve and withdrew a small bag. He opened it and sprinkled leaves on the fire. Its minty scent filled the air. "May the fragrance of this hyssop purify the air in this space and the resentment in our hearts." He gestured to Isaac with a wave of his hand.

Isaac glanced at Rebekah, then lowered his eyes to the floor. "I am Isaac, son of Abraham, son of Terah, son of Nahor, son of Serug. I have embarrassed and offended my revered cousin. Instead of a welcome, you received rudeness. Instead of praise, you received insults. Instead of respect, you received dishonour. My esteemed father has shown me the wrong I have done. I am truly sorry, and I regret the shame and hurt my thoughtless words have caused. Before these witnesses, I request your mercy and compassion, which I do not deserve. I beg your forgiveness and seek reconciliation."

No one breathed. The fire spit and crackled. The hyssop burned, its woodsy scent cleansing the air. Smoke curled up to the roof and drifted off into the twilight. Isaac sat rigid; his eyes fixed on the fire.

Rebekah coughed. All eyes turned to her. Her calm presence and steady gaze took control of the situation.

"I am Rebekah, daughter of Bethuel and his wife Ruth. Bethuel is the son of Nahor and his wife Milcah. Nahor is the son of Terah and his wife, Amathlai. I have travelled from Haran to this place as the bride of Isaac. The contracts were signed in Haran, by Eliezar, agent for Abraham. Gifts were given and received; the bride price paid." Rebekah's eyes never left the tormented face of Isaac. "Isaac has offered his regret at any insult he unknowingly caused. The smoke from the fire has carried the unfortunate words up into the sky and they are blown away by the wind. It is forgotten."

Isaac looked at Rebekah and their gazes met. A smile flickered across her face and lit up her eyes.

"We will prepare ourselves and attend the welcome dinner made ready by Abraham. Isaac and I will meet there and be introduced properly. Let it be noted by these witnesses that will be our formal meeting."

One by one, the men left, each bowing low to Rebekah. Abraham was the last to leave. He kissed the hand of Rebekah and whispered. "Such a woman of honour and compassion is truly a blessing from El Shaddai. May the holy one be praised for sending you to us."

Chapter Twenty

Rivkah and Esther left the tent of Rebekah and walked together to prepare for the dinner. Deborah let out a quiet cheer. "You saved the day, Becca. I am proud of you. What courage, wisdom, and compassion you showed. I would have liked to whip him as he deserved."

"I don't know how long he has lived, but he is like a spoiled child. I think he is learning that his life has changed in many ways. I will be patient with him, for he is very frightened."

"They say he kills lions, bears, and snakes. Why would he be frightened of a woman?"

"He is afraid of marriage, and he is afraid of his father. Abraham spoke no words of forgiveness. The son has much to prove to his powerful father."

"He may not be afraid of me, but he has much to prove to me before I consider him worthy of being your husband. Aren't you worried, Becca?"

"Not in the least. Forgiveness can be powerful when offered without conditions to one who is begging for mercy. At least for now, I have some power in this new world. I only hope I use it wisely. Now, get busy and fix my hair. I must look my best when I meet my husband."

Rebekah entered the tent of Abraham and saw a table laden with food. There was goat, lamb and fish heaped on platters, surrounded with spices, herbs and lemon slices. Steaming bowls of vegetables of vibrant colours waited to be consumed. Bread, warm from the ovens, dripped with flavoured oil. Richly painted bowls of dates, figs and pomegranates added their colours and aroma. Goblets of hammered gold were filled with the finest wine from Abraham's store house.

Abraham, Isaac, Eliezer, and Benjamin were waiting to greet the guests. An old, wizened man stood beside Benjamin. Rebekah remembered seeing him in the caravan but did not recall his name.

Deborah leaned close to Rebekah. "That is Asher. He was the guide on our journey."

"Thank you, Deborah. I had forgotten."

"You are going to have to make an effort to learn the names of those who help you."

The women stood at the other side of the doorway from the men. Rebekah smiled at them, Esther and Rivkah smiled in return. Rebekah took a step toward the table, but Deborah held her sleeve and restrained her. Again, Deborah saved her from a mistake.

Abraham held up his hand, and the room became still.

"Blessed are You, Lord God, King of the Universe, who brings forth bread from the earth.

Blessed are You, Lord God, King of the Universe, who brings forth the fruit of the trees.

Blessed are You, Lord God, King of the Universe, by whose word all things came to be."

Abraham invited Rebekah and the women to the table to fill their plates. The men followed from the oldest to the youngest. Abraham motioned for Rebekah and Isaac to sit at the centre of the long table. When all were seated on cushions around the low tables, servants appeared and offered wine. The lavish meal was followed by fruit, honey and almond cakes, and wine flowed freely.

Isaac smiled gingerly at the beautiful woman sitting beside him. "May I say that you look lovely in that dress? Your beauty has not been exaggerated."

"Thank you, Isaac. This is a wonderful feast. It is most delightful, whether you call it a welcome banquet or a wedding celebration."

"I am glad that you are pleased." They continued to talk about the food, and then Isaac changed the subject and they talked about her long journey. When that conversation lagged, Rebekah asked about the village and its people.

Deborah was seated between Rebekah and Benjamin. “It is good to see them talking to each other,” she offered, to start a conversation with Benjamin.

“It seems civil and polite. It must be difficult for both of them. They are married strangers.”

“I expect all married couples have awkward moments at the beginning. I am simply happy that they are relaxed and enjoying the meal.”

All conversation stopped when a gong sounded, and the entertainers entered. Musicians and dancers took their places, and the music began. Rebekah enjoyed the singing and the music. The graceful dancers were enchanting, and she clapped in appreciation. A storyteller came and sat in front of her. He told a long story of a great battle fought and won by Abraham.

“I have heard this story in the house of my father. Abraham rescued Lot from the Five Kings. It was a great victory.” She whispered to Deborah. “I had not heard of Reuben and Eliana before.”

Deborah whispered in response. “I think we should ask Rivkah to tell us the rest of the story.”

“Yes, we must. I wonder who she was.”

Abraham got to his feet and thanked all the entertainers. He pronounced the dinner a success and offered more wine and honey cakes.

Rebekah whispered to Deborah. “You know what you have to do. Go now.”

Deborah slipped unseen into the night.

Rebekah started to rise, and Isaac stood beside her at once. “If you wish to retire, I would be honoured to walk with you to your tent.”

“I should like that very much, Isaac. But first we must say goodnight to our guests and thank our father for the wonderful banquet.”

Rebekah took her time and spoke to each one present. As she called Asher by name and thanked him for guiding her to this place, his face lit up with joy. Isaac followed her around the room. He was surprised at the way she spoke to everyone, and he marvelled at the ease she showed. Each one responded with a smile and kind words. He got her cloak and wrapped it around her shoulders. They walked out into the night.

The stars were reflected in Rebekah's eyes as she looked at Isaac. "It is a lovely evening. The stars are so close I can almost hear them singing."

Isaac laughed softly. "I have never even thought about them. But they are quite pretty tonight. Imagine hearing the stars sing. You have a wonderful imagination Rebekah ."

They walked in silence down the small hill to Rebekah's tent. Isaac remembered the roaring voice of his father and his chest tightened and he rubbed his throbbing temples. He could still hear every word Abraham shouted at him.

Isaac trembled as he remembered. He took a moment to calm himself and then spoke in reply. "I said the stars were pretty and they are. But they fade into nothing when compared to the beauty of my wife."

"Thank you, Isaac. I am glad that I please you with my pleasant face. I hope that there are many ways that I can please you tonight and for many more days and nights."

Isaac frowned, puzzled by her words and unsure of Rebekah's meaning.

At the door of her tent, she paused. "Deborah has lit the lamps to welcome us. I know father said that this was not a wedding feast. But it felt like one to me. I am ready to be your wife in every way, Isaac." She looked up at him and her eyes betrayed her thoughts.

He felt overpowered by her invitation. For he was sure that was what she had just offered.

"Are you sure, Rebekah?"

In answer, she put her arm around him and gently kissed his cheek.

He followed her into her tent. Oil lamps glowed in every corner. Flowers were on each table and a bed had been made ready. Isaac removed his cloak, took her cloak, folded it, and laid it carefully on a stool. When he turned back, Rebekah had dropped her tunic to the floor and stood an ivory goddess in the moonlight.

He fell to his knees and reverently kissed her hand. She reached out and raised him to his feet. Taking his hand, she led him to the waiting bed.

Outside, the glittering stars filled the sky with light and with the music of love.

Chapter Twenty-One

Deborah tip-toed to the small opening at the rear of Rebekah's tent. It was for her use only. She listened and heard no sounds, so she entered, prepared to leave at once if Isaac was present. Rebekah was curled up sleeping peacefully, alone. Deborah started the fire and put water over the flames to boil. When she dropped a log for the fire, Rebekah stirred and sat up.

"Good morning, sleepyhead." Deborah teased. "It is a gentle morning outside."

"Did you scare Isaac away?"

"I made sure you were alone before I entered. How does it feel to be a married woman?"

"Deborah, all you need to know is that I slept well and am happy."

"What do you think Abraham will do when he learns that Isaac disobeyed him?"

"If he is displeased, I will set him right. Marriage is what he wanted for his son. Marriage is what he has. Nothing to be upset about."

At the front of the tent there was a commotion and men's voices. Rebekah quickly pulled on a clean tunic. "Enter Abraham."

Surprised, Deborah stepped back into the shadows. Abraham burst into the room and Isaac followed, eyes cast down as usual when he was with his father.

"Father Abraham. I sense you are displeased, but I can't imagine why. I will tell you what happened last night. I asked Isaac to accompany me here. The walk was pleasant, and I felt very warm feelings toward my husband. I kissed him and invited him into my tent. He accepted the invitation to complete our marriage. I trust that is what my husband told you."

Abraham looked at Isaac, who met his gaze with new confidence. "I apologize for intruding this morning. I am apologizing a great deal lately. I will leave you to have your morning meal." And he walked out and returned to his tent.

"Good morning, Rebekah. I hope you slept as well as I did. I will leave now, and I hope I can show you the village later today."

"I would love to walk with you and see my new home."

Deborah spoke from the shadows as Isaac left. "You are a wonder. What a change from the unhappy woman I had to manage on the trail."

"I am grateful for the lessons you taught me. Father raised me to be independent and proud. I'm afraid I turned it into selfish and arrogant. Thanks to you, I see the difference. I hope you will still be my guide in this new life."

"Just try to get rid of me! Let's eat."

They were just finishing putting away the dishes when three gentle claps were heard in the doorway.

"It seems we live on the main road of the village." Rebekah called, "Enter."

Rivkah stepped into the dimly lit space. "Forgive my intrusion, but I thought you might have some questions that I could answer."

"Come and sit. I have many. First one, who are Eliana and Reuben? I had never heard of them until the storyteller named them last night."

"Abraham found Eliana alone and crying in a wheat field when they were both young, children really. Binah, Sarah's mother, took her in. She became Sarah's friend and companion until her death. Reuben was a soldier in Abraham's army. He died in battle when Lot was rescued from the Five Kings. Eliana was carrying his child when she learned of his death. She died of her grief a few hours later and delivered a still born girl child. It sounds so simple when I tell it like that. They were both dearly loved, and all the camp shared the grief of Sarah and Abraham. It was then that I became her servant and companion."

"I have so much to learn. I hope you will be my teacher and guide me."

"I will be your teacher and your friend. The women are planning a welcome ceremony for you when we gather in the moon tent tonight. Some of us gather each month to welcome the new moon. It happens tonight and we will have a ceremony to welcome you into our circle of women."

"What is the moon tent?"

"Didn't you have a special room to go to as women? Where did you go for your seclusion when you had your bleeding at your moon time of the month?

"We just stayed in seclusion in our homes. Our shame was our own, and we kept separate from all but our mothers and women servants."

"That is not our custom. We women gather, not in shame, but in a circle of sisterhood. When you are ready, I will take you to the women's place. I can help you learn our customs easier there. You come too Deborah."

"We are ready."

The three women walked together along the well-worn path to a large tent on a hill south of Rebekah's tent. Rebekah and Deborah were surprised at its size.

"Abraham gave us this tent before he raised one for his soldiers. Thanks to Sarah, he understood its importance to us."

The tent was made up of two colours of fabric. The usual dark fabric was all around the outside but at the doors the colour changed to red. A colour that said this place was different. They entered, and Rebekah could not believe what she saw.

"Look Deborah, cushions, and mats everywhere. Many women could gather here."

"The walls! They are decorated with soft flowing scarves in every colour. And there are moon carvings showing her in every phase."

"Flowers, and herbs and spices. What wonderful perfume. I smell cedar." The smile on Rebekah's face glistened in the tears of joy that dotted her cheeks.

"Come," Rivkah led them to the cushions, and they sat close together. "As I said, all women come here for their personal moon time. There is no shame here. We celebrate the wonder of our bodies, and we offer our sacrifices to El Shaddai. We offer grains, bread, and oil. The only blood we use is to pour a drop or two of our own body's shed blood back into the soil of our mother earth. It reminds us that we are one with her. There is no altar, only the sacred fire which burns in its consecrated circle."

"You said Deborah and I can come too?"

"Of course. You are women and you belong here from now until the time when your deaths will be honoured here."

"You said there would be a gathering tonight. The new moon time?"

"That is right. At each dark of the moon, any who wish can gather here to wait for and welcome the new moon. It is usually a quiet time for reflection and prayers. Of course, we sing. We always sing, and we share food and wine. But this one will be special as we welcome our newly arrived sisters."

"How will we know what to do?" Deborah wondered aloud.

"It is all quite simple, and you will catch on easily and quickly. Remember, it is to welcome you, not to embarrass or frighten you. If you have no more questions, I think we should return to our homes. Others may want to greet and welcome you."

"I am so glad you came here and brought me with you," whispered Deborah as they walked to their tent.

"It is a friendly and safe place for a woman to live. I thought I was well off in Haran, but this is almost too good to be true."

They were astonished as they saw the door of their tent. Piled around it were flowers and gifts of spices and grain. There were loaves of bread and cakes and gifts wrapped in pretty cloth. They gathered it up and took it inside. Their hearts were filled with warm and tender thoughts of gratitude.

Rebekah was resting on cushions when she heard Isaac's voice at the door of her tent. "Are you ready to go for a walk with me? I can come later if you would, rather."

"Oh, no. I am coming now. Just a moment."

She patted her hair and smoothed her tunic. Picking up a scarf, she went to the door.

Isaac looked deeply into her eyes, touched her cheek, and took her arm. "There is so much I want to show you. We will start at the river."

At the river, they sat on a log and watched the water bubble past. The sunlight sparkled in the ripples, and the river sang its song. Rebekah was enchanted. "Tell me about Father Abraham."

"You know that he is the leader of this tribal family. He brought them here from Ur. They stopped for a rest in a valley near Haran. That is where his father, Terah, is buried."

"And his mother?"

"His mother stayed in Ur. She was not well, and she died not long after they left."

"How sad that they were separated in their last years."

"I understand that Terah was not a very loving husband. Once she had given him sons, she lost her importance. She was replaced in his affections by a wine bottle. They were both happier apart from what I have heard."

Rebekah pondered this information in silence.

They left the river and walked to the market. It was not busy, and they strolled among the stalls.

"When is market day?"

"It is here all the time. The sellers come in the early morning and that is when it is most busy. We never know when a trade caravan is coming, but when one does, the news spreads on the wind and everyone hurries here.

"Do traders come often and where do they come from? Haran?"

"They come from far, far away, from cities in the east, and along the coast of the great sea, and yes, they come from Haran."

"I could write a letter to my father. He would love that."

"You can write? Or did you mean someone write for you?

"Father told me not to reveal it, but yes, he taught me to make the marks and to understand them. Most of them, anyway. Please don't tell anyone."

"I will tell father as soon as I see him."

"Why must you do that? Do you want to see me flogged or worse? Why do you wish harm to me? I will not let anyone else know, and I will use a scribe if you order me to."

"Rebekah." She heard tenderness in his voice, not reproach. "Father taught my mother the signs. She was much better at it than I ever was. The marks never stayed still for me. They seemed to jump around. Mother always made an excuse for me. She said my eyes were bad, and I needed to take care of them for the hunt. Maybe you will read the skins for me. I have had to ask father since mother died, and he is impatient with me."

"Of course, I will help you. And no one needs to know. That is what husbands and wives do. They help each other. They look after one another. Father always said that marriage was not about owner ship but partnership."

"I see that you have much to teach me."

The path took them to the central square. Once again, they sat, this time on the grass.

"This is lovely. Does it have a purpose other than beauty and peace in the middle of your busy city?"

"This is where we gather. People come here to visit, to barter, to make contracts. They come to gossip, to sing and tell stories. The young ones play, and the older ones look for marriage partners. Didn't you have a common gathering place in Haran?"

"Our houses were big; each was made in a square. In the centre was a garden. Families and friends gathered there. For important things like announcements and orders from the leaders, we met in the market square. I must confess I don't know what the poor or the slaves did. My life was spent in my home, or at the well. It was a gathering place for the women." She paused and stretched out her legs. Her tunic crept up almost to her knees. Isaac leaned over and pulled it down. As he did, he looked into her eyes and let his hand brush her leg. Rebekah blushed and smiled at him. A small cough and she continued. "But I saw little of the ordinary poorer people. Father kept me close to him, for my protection, he said. But he never said from what. I am beginning to think he kept me with him for his own selfish reasons."

"Here we all live on top of each other. I think that is why I spend so much time in the fields with the animals. They ask little of me and I don't have to explain anything to them."

He stood and took her hand to help her up. He held her in a close embrace for just a moment. As she drew away, she spoke.

"This has been a wonderful walk, Isaac. I am learning new things all the time. My poor head is spinning trying to understand it all. I knew I would find things quite different, and this time has helped me a great deal. Thank you, husband. I would like to go home now to rest before the women's gathering for the new moon tonight."

"You will be busy getting ready, and you will not be home till late. I will come to you tomorrow morning if I may."

"I look forward to it." She leaned toward him, and he held her close and kissed her, taking her breath away.

Rivkah appeared at the cooking fire, carrying a pot of barley stew. "I thought I would get your meal, as I know you have a lot on your mind. Would you both like help to choose something to wear tonight?"

"Oh, yes." Two voices sounded as one. They all laughed.

After they had eaten, she helped them choose simple tunics, and explained the women only wore jewellery for special occasions. "We live simply and the women work hard. Fancy clothes and jewellery would be ruined or get in the way".

Rebekah settled on a bright green dress, simple and practical, and Deborah a yellow one with a green rope belt. They braided their hair and wove matching ribbons into the braids.

Rivkah smiled as she spoke. "You have wonderful colours for your clothes. Perhaps you can teach us about dyes. We don't know how to make as many colours as you seem to. I think those plain, sand-coloured cloaks will make the tunics appear even lovelier."

The bright yellow sun was just stroking the tops of the hills with golden ribbons as the three women walked together to the moon house. Rivkah was calm and relaxed. Her companions were nervous, excited, and eager. As they neared the tent, they heard the sound of women's lilting voices singing together and it filled the sky and their hearts. Rebekah's heart was pulsing in rhythm to the drum that kept the beat for the song.

I never knew I could be so excited and so calm at the same time. So far, I love my new home.

Rivkah bade them enter and held the tent flap open. "I know that you will enrich our lives and open new doors for us. I trust we can do the same for you."

Chapter Twenty-Two

As they stood at the entrance to the moon house together, Rivkah gave them instructions. “The women are all gathered and seated. The room will be filled with friendly faces. I suspect I will have not seen so many come for the new moon ceremony in a very long time, if ever. You will go to the far end of the room. Esther and Ayla, the primary midwife, are waiting there for you. I will stop at this north end and take my seat.”

Deborah turned to Rivkah. “Do we sit or stand?”

“You stand between the two leaders. You will be introduced and then invited to sit. We have a beautiful hand gesture. We raise our hands, palms turned outward, and we flutter our fingers and twist our wrists. It means welcome, thanks, honour, and blessing. You will see it often tonight. Since it is for you, you smile and bow your head in response.”

“What else do we need to know?” Rebekah asked.

“There is a prayer before we eat our simple but meaningful meal. It is the role of the leading woman to say the prayer. That is, you.”

“Me! I don’t know the prayer. I thought women only prayed in their own homes.”

Rivkah heard the panic in Rebekah’s voice. “Esther will whisper the words to you, and you repeat them loudly, so that all can hear. You can do this. I know you can.”

Deborah hugged Rebekah. “Of course, you can. You were born and raised to be a leader. Your time has come. Embrace your new role.”

“Well spoken, Deborah. The women are singing a song of joy and hope. We will stand here until they finish and then enter. When we come through the door, they will sing a welcome song for you.”

Rebekah took a deep breath and was pleased that she was calm and relaxed. *Maybe I was born for this. I am at peace in my heart.*

The singing stopped, and they entered. As they walked to the far end of the room, they felt the presence of many women. A fire burned in the centre of the rainbow-coloured circle created by the clothing of the women. They carefully walked around the fire, one on each side. Esther smiled broadly and nodded. The air smelled of flowers and cedar. Standing between the two leading women, Rebekah was overcome with emotion. The song just didn't stop, it gradually faded away into total silence.

Esther held up her arm and spoke. "We are gathered to welcome the new moon and to welcome these women from afar to our circle." She turned to Rebekah. "This is Rebekah, daughter of Ruth, and Ruth is the daughter of Zera. Rebekah has travelled here, and she is the wife of Isaac, and the leader of all the women in our settlement. We welcome you, Rebekah."

Hands fluttered all around the circle. Rebekah's heart fluttered in her breast.

Esther turned to Deborah. "This is Deborah, daughter of Hada, the daughter of Tala. She comes as a companion and friend to Rebekah. We welcome you, Deborah."

Again, the welcome flowed around the circle. Deborah's eyes filled with tears.

"All rise as our new leader offers the prayer of blessing before a meal."

Rebekah took a deep breath as the words from Esther touched her ear.

"Blessed are you, El Shaddai, creator of all. You supply all our needs. You hear our cries and weep with us. You share our joys and laugh with us. The wisdom of the grandmothers comes to us in the smoke and flame of the sacred mountain. Blessed be the mothering god of our people. Amen."

"Please be seated." Led by Rivkah, a small group of women left the circle. They uncovered a long table at the back of the room and stood behind it.

Esther spoke in her firm but gentle way. "A symbolic meal has been prepared. There is bread for our journey, honey for the sweetness of life, bitter herbs for our sorrow, eggs for the nourishment of our bodies and pomegranate wine for the life blood that flows in our bodies. We will lead the way to the table. Please follow around the circle from both sides."

A flutter of hands blessed the women as they made their way to the table. As they received their meal, the sound of happy voices filled the room.

As the meal was ending Rebekah asked if she could speak. Rivkah nodded and held up her hand. Gradually the room came silent, and all eyes turned to the four women seated by the fire.

Rebekah spoke, her voice shaky with emotion. "I have never felt so moved by a shared meal. I think I speak for both of us when I say thank you." And she fluttered her hands in salute.

The meal ended with the singing of a blessing song. The words echoed the prayer Rebekah had repeated, and the melody floated all around the room.

The mid-wives, Rivkah's helpers, carried small lamps in a smaller circle within the large circle of the women. Ayla took a long straight piece of wood. With quiet, dainty steps, she went to the sacred fire and added fresh cedar branches to it. A fountain of sparks flew upward, and Ayla lit her taper. She went to the mid-wives and passed the flame to the little lamp each one held. They walked around the circle and lit the lamps on the floor. These smaller lamps repeated the flame from larger lamps placed on pedestals around the outer edge of the room. As the flames flickered, the shadows of the women danced on the walls of the room.

Shira, the best singer's strong voice, filled the room with a haunting melody.

Esther whispered. "She is calling the new moon to come from its hiding place to light our path. She speaks the ancient tongue of our people," Softly, other voices joined the song until the whole room was vibrant with the call to the moon.

The song gradually died away until only Shira was humming its melody. Her voice floated in the air and called the new moon to life.

Rebekah and Deborah were enchanted by the simple beauty of the ceremony. Ayla left the circle and stood near the doorway. She was holding a basin of scented water. "When you are ready, come to the basin and wash your hands. This cleansing ritual prepares you to greet the silver arc of the new moon. I wish you all a good night and may you dream only happy dreams."

Slowly, reverently, the women began to leave, some alone, some in small groups. As they stood, many offered a smile, a hand flutter, or a brief bow to the women still seated at the head of the circle. The two honoured guests were overcome. Esther put an arm around each one and said, "Welcome, sisters. May El Shaddai bless you and give you peace."

As they prepared for bed, Rebekah and Deborah hardly spoke.

"Tomorrow we will speak of all we have seen and heard. Tonight, I am overcome with many emotions."

"Yes, and I have questions, too. But tomorrow we will talk." As she finished speaking, Deborah extinguished the lamp in their tent. "Tomorrow."

Rebekah was awake before the sun. She walked outside and sat near the cold fire pit facing the east. The sky was tinted with a warm rosy glow. As she watched, the whole sky bloomed with colour, pink, red, gold, and lavender. Deborah came and sat beside her. "Lovely morning and don't the colours remind you of the beauty of the room last night."

"They do, indeed, Deborah. Wasn't that something? I have never felt so comfortable and at peace in a roomful of strangers. Never before in my life."

"And I have never been with that many women in one place before, either."

Deborah laughed a deep warm chuckle. "I wouldn't have believed it if I wasn't there. I wonder what other surprises this place has for us?"

"If they are all as wonderful as that was, I can hardly wait. The rituals were so simple and yet so deeply meaningful. I can still feel the warmth from their greeting song and the smiles."

"And the ordinary foods felt like a grand banquet in that setting."

Rebekah hugged her knees and agreed. "It was all amazing, and to think it happens every new moon. What a wonderful way to mark the passage of the days."

They sat in comfortable silence until Deborah spoke.

"I expect you will be spending some time with Isaac today."

"Yes, we are going to visit more of the village so that I can begin to feel at home here. What will you do? I am sorry that I am leaving you alone so much."

"Don't worry. Other servants and maids stop by to talk, and I am learning from them. This is a good place that we have come to. You made a good choice, and I will be happy here if you are content, too."

"I am very content, Debba. I am sure there will be struggles, but that is true of life anywhere. Let's get our meal ready and enjoy that time together on this wonderful morning."

Chapter Twenty-Three

Deborah had just finished cleaning the dishes and after putting them away went outside to join Rebekah. Esther was coming toward them, and Deborah got another stool.

"Good morning."

Rebekah turned and smiled at Esther. "I am so glad you have come. Sit here with us. We were just enjoying the golden sunrise. Have you eaten?"

"Yes, I have. I came because I thought you might have some questions this morning."

"Yes, I do. But first we both want to tell you how moved and touched we are by the beautiful welcome we received last night."

Deborah could hardly contain her happiness. "I, we, have never experienced anything like it. To be a part of so many women, celebrating the new moon was…" She hesitated.

Rebekah picked up the thread of conversation. "I think she is trying to express the wonder and joy we both felt. Back home, there is no place for women to gather and celebrate our lives."

"I find it sad that you say that, and yet I know it is true for many women. Abraham learned from his mother that women were not possessions. Sarah's mother, Binah, was a wise woman, and she taught Abraham's son well. We were meant by the holy one to be partners with men. We don't always do it perfectly here, but we do strive for that feeling of partnership. Dare I say equality? Often, we miss that mark, but it is good to strive toward an ideal."

Rebekah sighed. "I have so many questions I don't know where to begin."

"We will have many times to share our stories. The rainy season is almost here, and we spend much time in our tents. Mine will always be open to you and to your questions. But is there a special one?"

"Did someone teach you the ceremonies? Are they new or ancient?"

"The ceremonies began long ago with the ancient grandmothers. They were passed down, through the midwives and from healer to healer, from mother to daughter. Since the women had no marks to write it down, it was told and re-told from generation to generation.

"How wonderful that we can hear the words that our grandmothers heard. Perhaps in Ur, Hada and Talia heard these same words." Deborah felt deep joy as she thought of her mother and grandmother.

"They may have heard words at their ceremonies, but they could have changed over these many, many years. If I tell you a story, then you tell Deborah a few of the words would change. Not on purpose, or not to change the story, but that is the way it is when people share what they remember."

Deborah looked thoughtful. "Are you saying that the words may have changed over the years, but the meaning and the purpose are the same?"

"That is exactly what I am saying. It is the same with the actions that we do. Years ago, when I first went to the moon house, I don't remember the hand waving way to express agreement. It just started at some time, maybe with just one woman."

"But because it is respectful, quiet and beautiful, everybody now does it."

Rebekah paused in a thoughtful moment. "I like that. Change. Our world is always changing, and I think it is a good thing that the words and actions can change in time. It means that each generation makes them their own."

Deborah smiled. "Do you think it also means that we all are learning every day?"

"I am so glad you are here. You are both smart and wise. I look forward to seeing you take your place in our village. You did a very good job of the prayer. It seemed like you had been doing it all your life."

"Thank you, Esther, but I was very nervous. I can hardly remember what I said.

"That is exactly what I mean. Next time you do it, you will change a word or two and that will be just fine. It will come from your heart and that will make it special."

"Oh Esther. I hope the next time, you will still help me with the words. I have so much to learn. When I agreed to marry Isaac, I had no idea I was expected to be a leader. Isaac is not the leader yet, so why am I?"

"When Sarah died, there was no one to take her place. Abraham did not have a second wife, although I am not sure that would have been the proper thing to do, anyway. Rivkah, Ayla, and I have shared the task, but we are glad that you are here. We will answer your questions and help you if you need it, but it is now your place to lead us."

"I will need help because your traditions must be honoured. I can't just do whatever I want. I must respect the old ones, and I will need lots of direction, especially since it is all new to me."

Deborah looked lovingly at her companion. "You will be wonderful Becca; I know you will."

"Becca?"

"That is a pet name Deborah has called me since we were young girls. She only uses it now, I think, when she wants to get my full attention or to tease me."

Deborah stood up and went into the tent. She returned in a short time with cool water and barley cakes for everyone. "I thought we could use a drink and I hope you will tell us more about Sarah."

"Please, do Esther. It would help me understand Isaac better if I knew more about his mother."

"Where do I begin? Terah was the father of both Sarah and Abraham, but they had different mothers. When Terah married Binah, he had three sons with his first wife, Amathila. She died when the youngest was born. Sarah was the only daughter Binah had, but she bore more boys. In spite of being surrounded by brothers, Sarah learned to be a woman at her mother's side. Binah was a strong woman, and Abraham respected her as well as her daughter. Sarah grew up thinking all women were treated with love and respect. In fact, she demanded it. Abraham disappointed her a couple of times, and she made him pay for his disrespect. I wasn't there, but Rivkah has told me the stories."

"Will she tell us?

"I don't know, Deborah. It all happened long ago and maybe it should rest with Sarah in her tomb."

"Where is she buried?"

"In a cave in a field that Abraham bought for that purpose. He bought it from Ephron for many shekels of silver. He will be buried there with her when that time comes. On the day of her burial, the whole village walked to the grave. Some were weeping, but most walked in a mournful, respectful silence. Isaac used to go there often, but not so much since the green orb appeared in Sarah's tent."

"Yes, the orb. Tell us about that."

"I know nothing about it except that it appeared a few moons after her death. I don't think Abraham knew it was there until the day you entered the tent. You will have to ask Isaac about that. Now may I ask you a question?"

"Of course. You know little about us, and I am sure you have questions." Deborah picked up a piece of cloth and began to mend it.

"I know the story of how Sarah and Abraham were married, and it is a lovely story, for another time, I think. And I wonder if your marriage customs in Haran are the same as ours, here in Canaan?"

Rebekah settled herself on her cushion. "I think they would be similar. Marriages are arranged by the two fathers, often when the bride is very young. Most girls are betrothed before they come to their woman's time. The betrothal is really a marriage except for the intimacy of the marriage bed, which seals the contract made by the father."

"That is the same here. Sarah was only nine when the contracts were signed, and they were married about four years later. The time is to allow the groom to acquire the bride price, and for the girl to reach her woman's time."

Deborah asked her question. "How old was Abraham at the marriage?"

"He was ten years older than Sarah, so he would have been twenty-three. Were you betrothed at a young age, Rebekah?"

"No, I was not. My father kept me very close to him. For my protection he said, but I think he just wanted me around. He treated me more like a son than a useless daughter. I was taught many things that girls are usually forbidden to know."

Esther's interest was obvious. "What things?"

"He taught me about trading with the caravans, and how to haggle for a good bargain in the markets. What I tell you now, you must promise to keep secret, he taught me how to read the marks on the skins."

Esther smiled. "Sarah could read the marks and make them too. So, it is not unknown in this tribe. At least by the leaders. Forgive my boldness, but you are older than most brides."

"There is a good reason for that. My father considered my wishes in choosing my husband. He would not marry me to someone I did not wish to be given to."

"And she was very particular. Very, very, particular." Deborah teased, and chuckled.

"And so, like most couples, you and Isaac did not meet until you arrived here."

"True, but I asked many questions on the journey. I think I knew more about him that he did about me."

Deborah looked at Rebekah, "I have one more piece of this story to tell you, if I may." Rebekah smiled and nodded.

"Bethuel and mostly Ruth, her mother, wanted Rebekah to stay with them while arrangements were made. My Becca, spoke up and said, 'in the morning, I go with Eliezar to meet my husband'."

"You had an unusual amount of freedom. I hope you don't expect the same here. The traditions of Abraham are still very strong."

Rebekah grinned. "It will all work out, I am sure." The women shared a knowing laugh.

Esther stood. "I must be going. I hear Isaac's voice calling to someone. I will go now and let you have time with your husband. Farewell." And she was gone, down the path to her own tent.

Chapter Twenty-Four

A few days later, Rebekah awoke. She stood and stretched, ready for another day. Pausing, she felt that dull ache in her gut and knew that her time of seclusion was upon her once again. The time alone, just because she was a woman having her normal monthly blood flow, irritated her each time it came. To spend days alone, with only the most fleeting contact, was agony for her. She called Deborah.

"It is my moon time. And now I spend it in a tent. I was looking forward to walking today with Isaac. And worse, it is beginning to rain." She was holding a cup, and she threw it across the room. It broke when it hit a wooden chest and she burst into tears.

"Calm down Becca. Esther said something about moon time each month in the women's tent. Don't you remember?"

"Yes, now that you remind me, I do. Find Esther and bring her here to explain it to me."

Without a word, Deborah left on her errand. Esther was standing outside her tent watching the rain as it moved across the valley.

Deborah greeted her and told her why Rebekah was asking her to come to her tent. "Just so you know she is in a nasty mood. The isolation she had to endure at her home always makes her angry."

"Thank you for the warning. But I think she will feel better when she hears how we deal with it here."

The two women walked to Rebekah's tent and entered. Esther greeted her with a cheerful smile. "I understand it is your moon time and you are wondering what happens here. Let's sit and have tea while I explain it to you."

Deborah soon had tea ready, and the three women sat together in a close circle.

Rebekah put down her cup. "I woke with my usual signs that today will be my moon time, and I need to find out what I should do, and what will happen."

"I must be honest; I was shocked when Deborah said you spent this time alone in your room. Sarah brought the custom from Ur, that women shared this time together. They had a whole house in that great city. Abraham provided the large tent you saw a few days ago. There is no shame for us, in fact we rejoice in our role as life givers. For we are the ones who bear and raise the next generation of the tribe."

Rebekah picked up the cup and sipped the now cold tea.

"It will be new to you, but I am sure you will find it warm and comforting. The women simply gather at the tent. There are few formalities. Just enter the tent and find a space to put your sleeping mat and whatever else you bring?"

"What do women bring with them? Food? Water?"

"We all bring food. Grain, or fruit, or anything we can share. Women who are still in their tents also leave things at the door for us. The men see that our water jugs are kept full. They are left at the door of the tent. We take turns making the meals and we all keep the tent clean and tidy. It all works out."

"It sounds too good to be true. What happens if Becca decides she wants to use her position and do nothing and just be looked after?"

"Deborah. I would never to that."

"Just asking. What if that happens if someone won't help?"

Gently Esther answered. "We would think that she must have troubles and needed time and space for herself. We don't judge and we don't talk about each other in hurtful ways. This is a time to be at peace, with oneself and with each other. As I said, it just works out."

"I need some practical help. What are the rules about keeping clean? How do I manage that?"

"There is a basket of wool balls, and we all use them, then wash and set them near the fire to dry. Then they are put outside in the sun to be further cleaned by the warmth and the air. Meals are by work groups."

Deborah stood and began to clean up. Rebekah motioned for her to leave it all till later. She smiled and sat down. Esther continued. “Each sleeping area has a colour and when it is your time to work, a pennant with your colour will be in the food area. Same with any big cleaning jobs. It is a good idea not to always sleep in the same colour area. That way, you get to know more women. But you could figure this out, and as I said—”

Two laughing voices finished Esther’s thought. “It all works out.”

“Just watch and follow the rhythms of the day. In the end, when you are ready, you just leave. There is no formal goodbye. Any other concerns?”

“No. That is very helpful.”

“When ready, just go to the moon house and walk in. You will be welcomed. They know who you are. Take some work to do, mending or a small weaving. One more thing. If you wish, you can put a bit of red cloth on a rope at your tent. Isaac will know what it means.”

They sat in total comfort together, talking as if they had known each other for years. Esther picked up her shawl, smiled and left to return to her tent.

At their tent, Rebekah gathered up her clothing, including a warm shawl and the sewing she was doing. She took her sleeping mat, rolled it up, and covered it with a sheepskin to keep it clean. From their supplies, she took dried figs, bread, and a batch of cakes made late yesterday. Deborah walked with her to help her carry her bundles. They went out into the warm day.

I am surprised. I don’t feel anxious at all. Actually, I am looking forward to this time of quiet and peace. I am sorry that my bleeding came. I was hoping for happier news, but next time.

The space looked a bit different. Around the outside edges, instead of piles of cushions, there were sleeping mats of many kinds. The sacred fire was not burning, but there were three other fires warming the room and casting swaying shadows on the walls. She was greeted with smiles and words of welcome. One woman asked if she would like to put her mat near hers. ”

“Thank you. I should like that very much.”

On that friendly note, Rebekah settled in for this new and exciting experience.

Women came and introduced themselves. *I will have to learn all these names. But in time I will know them all.*

Usually, this time of withdrawing from daily life had been very frustrating and Rebekah chaffed at the restrictions. But here, working with her new friends, sharing stories, singing songs, and just being at peace made the days fly by. There was laughter and tears, as stories were shared. Sad ones, funny ones, and stories that told the legends of ancient days. Some women remembered Sarah, and Rebekah learned more about her. *I must remember she was a real woman, not a legend, as I once thought. Sarah is the women who bore my husband, raised him, and taught him. As I learn of her, and know the story of his birth, it is understandable that he worships her memory.*

The time flew by and almost too soon, she was ready to leave and return home. As she had seen others do, when it was time, almost wishing she could stay, she quietly walked out the door and went to her tent.

There was no one in the tent, but it was plain that Deborah had spent time there. In it, everything was tastefully arranged and there wasn't a grain of sand to be seen. Across the narrow end, a line had been strung for clothes to hang to dry.

I'll take that bit of red cloth down. Deborah will know I am back. Isaac too, I hope.

Deborah rushed in. "Glad to have you back. Tell me all about it."

"Hello to you too. The tent looks wonderful. Thank you for all your work."

"I thought we could arrange the cushions to look more welcoming when someone came to visit. I have hung scarves we don't wear and put out your pottery from Haran. It helped to pass the time. Anything you don't like; we can change and fix together."

"No. It is lovely. I think I can smell a hint of cedar as well. You have done an excellent job."

"So, what was it like in the tent?"

"Esther told us all we need to know. It was a wonderful, peaceful time. The women were warm and friendly, and the time passed very quickly. I will only say that I enjoyed my time there. Seclusion isn't bad at all when you spend it with other women."

Deborah raised her eyebrows and pouted.

Realizing what she had just said, she laughed. "Of course, you were always with me, and your company was all that kept me in my right mind." Deborah laughed with her. "As for the details, I think it best if you find out for yourself."

"I was afraid you would say that. I will wait since I have no choice. Now I will get the meal started. I am hungry and I hope you are too."

Chapter Twenty-Five

The next morning, as she saw him approaching, Rebekah stood to greet her husband. "Good morning. It is cool this morning, a good start to the day."

"Yes, it is. What shall we do today?"

"Don't you have animals to tend, work to do?"

"It is our custom that a newly married man is excused from routine work after his marriage. His duty is to his wife to see to her happiness."

"I did not know that. But it is a lovely custom. There are so many things I must learn."

"It will happen one day at a time. We only saw part of the village on our walk the other day. Would you like to see the market?"

"Let's go."

"You have forgotten a veil. You need to cover your head in the presence of other men. Only family can see you without a veil. It is a sign of modesty and loyalty."

She made a face but went to get a veil. She returned wearing a filmy blue strip of cloth covering her head and the long ends tossed over her shoulder floated at her back.

"I'm ready. Lead me to the market."

Now Isaac frowned as he saw the flimsy fabric. *Good enough. Her hair is covered.* He held out his hand, and they set out for the market.

"It will be quiet today. There are no traders from other cities here. It is too close to the rainy season. They are all staying home and working to re-stock their wares. Only our local artisans will be there."

"It will be fine. I can see what is available to purchase for our everyday needs."

The path led between a row of stalls. Pleasant scents drifted past. Perfume from flowers, plants, and herbs tickled her nose. Meat, raw and cured, swung from hooks, and rocked in the breeze. The odour of spices hung in the air, reminding her of home. Pottery bowls and cups, some plain and others decorated with intricate patterns, were stacked in orderly groups. Bolts of cloth caught her eye. She saw that there were expert weavers at work in their homes and shops.

Vendors called out greetings to Isaac and nodded to Rebekah. At one stall, he stopped and spoke to the woman selling almond cakes and he bought two of them.

"We can sit by the river and enjoy these, if you would like."

She smiled and took his arm.

"Are you happy with our market? Will it meet your needs?"

"It is perfect, Isaac. Are Deborah and I safe to go there without a man?"

"If you are properly dressed and respectful to the sellers, you will be safe and welcome. That is partly why we went. Now they know you are my wife and will treat you like the important woman you are."

"I don't really feel important. I feel more like an ignorant child. I am afraid of offending and thus causing you embarrassment."

"The village is not very big, and everyone knows you come from a far land. They will be understanding and forgiving of small errors. At least for a little while. But you learn quickly and so does Deborah."

"She has seen more of the world than I and will not be so likely to offend."

"Here is where I like to sit. The tree gives us shade, the log is our throne, and the river sings a song to us. You are my queen, and we reign over the creatures in this place."

Rebekah giggled and sat down to enjoy the cake. Isaac carried a flask and brought clean, clear water from the river for a refreshing drink.

"What do you find familiar here and what is different for you?" Isaac asked.

"We speak the same language, eat the same foods, wear the same clothes. It is different living in a tent and not a house. Not bad, just different. In Haran, there was no central gathering place for everyone to meet. That is very welcoming, and I look forward to going there."

"You were at the woman's tent last night."

"We had no such place in Haran. It was amazing. So many women were there to welcome the new moon and Deborah and me. I am still thrilled by everything we did."

"What did you do?"

"Rivkah told me that women's sacred time, shared in that sacred place, is our special time together and not talked about. I hope that was not a trap for me. I am just as curious about what the men do at the altars, but know it is forbidden to me."

"I did not mean it as a trap. But mother shared things with father and I thought you might with me."

"Not now. It is all too new and too wonderful. And that kind of sharing confidences must be going both ways. You are the head of our house. I will follow your lead."

Isaac looked at Rebekah with new understanding. *My wife is not only beautiful, but she is also smart and crafty. She will not be easily tricked, I think.*

Rebekah turned to him and looked deeply into his eyes, and he returned her gaze. *Strange that I thought of trickery? Trust is what I should be thinking about.* "I have heard there are many gods worshipped in Haran. Who is the chief god?

She twirled a curl in her fingers and thought for a long time. "There are more gods than I can count. I think it depends on who you are. For most, it is the idols whose statues are standing in various places in the city where people go to worship. There are families who pay homage to more than one of these gods. Others, as you do here, worship the almighty fire god of the mountain. My father worshipped him but was not as committed or devout as the way I see your father worshipping."

"Few are as committed as my father. But few have had their god tell them to move to a new land."

"Did he hear a voice? How does the fire god speak?"

"I don't really know. Visions, dreams, signs. He has not spoken to me. I suppose that is because I don't make many prayers or sacrifices."

Isaac stood. "Let's walk along the riverbank toward my tent." They were silent for a time, then Isaac spoke.

"My mother seemed to know this god in a different way."

"What do you mean? What way?"

"The way that the women know the mountain god. You must know, you went to the house of women. That is where they worship."

"I don't know very much. It was partly the new moon ceremony, and I don't know if that counts as worship. I guess I will have to ask Rivkah or Esther. It is all very puzzling."

"What else happened besides the moon ceremony?"

"The women gave Deborah and me a welcome to this village. It was the most wonderful time I have ever experienced."

"Yes. I guess your wedding was less than you expected."

"I didn't mean that, Isaac. My wedding was exactly what we needed to do on that day. The dinner was magnificent. I loved the dancers and the singing, and the story of your father's desert wanderings was breath-taking. And I might add, so was the rest of the night."

She smiled shyly at him, and he kissed her hand. He pointed up the hill. "There is Jacob, waving and beckoning us. I suspect since the sun is on the hill tops, it is time for the meal, and he has prepared it for us."

"That is kind of him. We can eat together. At your tent?"

"Of course. You can do that whenever I invite you. Remember that Jacob will have done his best, but he is not a good cook.

In front of the tent, Rebekah was surprised. A low table had been set out near the embers of a fire. It smelled of pine as logs glowed red and orange. Well swept mats had been put down and colourful cushions spread around. On the table, a candle flickered and there was a jug of wild marigold. The golden petals repeated the golden clouds in the western sky.

His face showed total surprise. "This is nice. Jacob has done a decent job. I hope the food is as good."

Rebekah pointed to the figure of a woman scurrying away down the hill at the back of the tent. "I think he has had help from Deborah. The food will be good."

As they sat, Isaac mumbled words of thanksgiving. Rebekah was a bit surprised by his effort. *I wonder, does he always do that or was it for my benefit?* They enjoyed the food and the wine, and the meal ended with fruit and cheese.

"I need to ask you something, Rebekah. Please be honest with me."

"I will always speak the truth and I trust you will too."

"Have I displeased you? Are you angry with me?"

"No. Not at all. Why would you think that?"

"You have not come to my bed when I have asked you for the last three nights?"

"When did you ask? I heard no request."

"Of course. How foolish of me. You do not understand our customs. Outside of my tent is a low stool. A little lamp sits on it. When the lamp is lit, it is a signal for you to come to my tent and we can spend the night together. Not a command, an invitation."

"A lamp? An invitation?"

"When you did not come, I felt you were displeased."

"I think we should not make assumptions. We do not know each other yet, and we may both be unaware of expectations. I am sorry this happened, but I simply did not know. I shall look for the lamp each evening.

"I don't need to light it tonight since you are here."

"Can I leave a lamp for you by my tent door?"

Isaac was too shocked to answer. *She can't be serious. What if she is? We truly are strangers, and I don't know this woman. But I know she is my wife, she is not displeased, and is coming to my bed. For now, it is enough.*

He took her hand, and they entered his tent. She looked around. It was much as she had expected. Messy, not clean and with a stale, heavy odour.

Isaac sensed her discomfort. "I never thought. This is not a room that would please a woman. Perhaps we should go to your tent."

"No, husband. This is the space where a man dwells. It speaks of manly things, of things that are important to you. You brought me here as your wife, and it is fine." She smiled at him, but her eyes did not smile, just her mouth.

She is being kind, but she is not comfortable. I will ask father what I should do about this.

He went to the bed and took away the rumpled, stained blanket. From a large wicker chest, he grabbed two different blankets. For just a moment, Rebekah caught the scent of summer breezes.

"Come, help me spread these clean blankets on our bed." He was rewarded with a genuine smile from his wife.

Chapter Twenty-Six

In the months that followed, Isaac and Rebekah settled into their life together. They spent many hours walking about the settlement while Isaac answered the questions Rebekah raised.

"Here in Abraham's valley, there are no worship places on the lanes and paths. In Haran, there were many images of the gods. People stopped and left tokens of their devotion fitting to the god or goddess in that place."

"We worship only the god of the mountain. It is forbidden to worship any other gods. In the faith of Father Abraham, there is only one God, the Almighty One."

"Father believed in this God too, but he let his slaves and servants worship as they want to. Why is that forbidden?"

"Our family lived among idol worshippers in other places. Long ago in Ur, then in Haran, and now in nearby Hebron. It is important to keep our people away from other gods. Mother was very distressed by the sacrifice of children on the altars of some of these gods. Mother taught that children were to be loved, cared for and taught all the things they needed to know."

"Your mother was an amazing woman. I wish I could have known her."

"She would have loved you Rebekah, not just because you make me a better man, but because you, too, are an amazing woman. You share many things with her."

"I struggle to learn these new ways and customs. It is hard to lay aside the things I learned as a child and young woman. At times, I feel disloyal to my father."

"You have said that Deborah is more aware of the world and some of its customs. Perhaps you could talk to her. She seems wise and well informed."

"I tried to talk to her, but she just claimed she was a slave for most of her life, and to not question. Just keep quiet and stay invisible."

"But you are happy here, are you not, dear one?"

"Yes. I must admit, life here is calmer, more peaceful and the people seem more content and happier than people in Haran. If that is what El Shaddai brings then I must let the past stay in the past. I do love my life here, and I want to please and help my handsome husband."

He laughed and squeezed her hand.

The days passed and Rebekah grew more at ease in her place as the leader of women. Their rituals, ceremonies, and understanding of El Shaddai intrigued her and comforted her. The summer season had passed pleasantly with picnics under the trees. Rebekah learned to enjoy wading in the river and letting the cool sand cover her feet as she stood at the river's edge.

One morning as the rainy season began, Rebekah woke feeling cranky. Vague pains in her gut made her feel sick. She remembered. Again, her moon time was here. These were the signs that she would have her usual blood flow before night came.

Deborah entered the tent. "Well. How are you this morning? You seem a little pale."

"I will have my moon time before the day is over. I have my things ready and the food I will offer."

"I can carry something for you. I'll grab a warm shawl and be right with you."

"Take this one of mine. It is warm and helps keep the rain away." Rebekah handed her a heavy woolen shawl.

Deborah stepped outside. "It is raining a bit. Good time to have to stay shut up in the tent."

The two friends covered their hair and wrapped the long shawls around their bodies. Walking with quick steps they followed the path to the women's place.

Deborah carried the things inside then said goodbye and left.

With a friendly welcome, of smiles and greetings, Rebekah settled in for the next few days. One evening, when the singing and storytelling ended, she lay on her mat whispering to the night.

"This is so peaceful and so comforting. Perhaps mother would have felt better about this time if she had such a place. All she told me was the negative resentment she felt because she was a woman. It is not just pleasant here but affirming and uplifting. This is truly a gift from the grandmothers of earlier times. I am to so thankful for their wisdom."

When it was time to leave, Rebekah picked up her things and with a sigh of complete contentment, left the house and returned to her tent.

"So, anything new in the tent?"

"No, I settled into the routine easily. It was a very peaceful time. The women were warm and friendly, and the time passed quickly." She laughed.

Deborah smiled and picked up a bowl. "I will get our meal started, I expect you are hungry, I know I am."

After the meal, Rebekah went for a walk to the bench by the river. As she hoped, Isaac soon joined her.

"Welcome home, dear one. I missed you every day. When father told me I was going to be married, I was really scared. I talked to old Asher. He had a couple of wives, or more. I asked him about love. He told me that he never knew his wives before the marriage bed, and it all worked out. Kindness, patience, and forgiveness are what is needed he said. He also said that to get beyond my own self-importance was what counted. Do that, he said, and love just walks in through your open heart."

"Those are beautiful words, Isaac."

"I realized when you were gone that I didn't want to be away from you. All I could think about was your smile, your voice, and your laughter. I guess that is love, Rebekah. I love you."

"I missed you too, Isaac. And you stole my heart that very first night. I knew then that you were to be my first love, and I think, my only love."

"This is a cold and wet place to be. May I take you to my tent? That is the place to speak of love, not here where we are drowning."

"I should be most happy to dry out in your tent by your glowing fire."

In the morning Rebekah woke to the sound of dishes clattering in the centre of the tent. She looked and Isaac had breakfast ready and was coming to her with a cup of steaming tea.

"What a wonderful surprise. Thank you, Isaac."

"I can get bread and cheese and fruit ready, but that is all. I am a worse cook than Jacob."

"But it is so kind and thoughtful of you. I will be just a moment and then I will come to the table and eat with you."

"I'll be waiting."

They enjoyed their simple meal, and Rebekah cleaned up while Isaac tended to the fire.

"I will need to go out and get more wood and more water. I won't be long." Around his shoulders he put a long sheep skin. It covered him from head to toe.

She looked around his tent. It was the first time she had been there alone to look at her husband's room. It was much smaller than hers and she wondered why that should be. The furnishings were simple and practical. There were no decorations or soft cushions. But there were signs of Isaac's life. Animal horns and hooves, weapons for the hunt, and perhaps for war. There seemed to be no order, just a jumble of things strewn about. It was a place to sleep and eat. Practical. Useful. Manly. Smelly. But foreign to her and not welcoming at all.

Isaac returned with water and said wood was piled under a skin just outside the door. "I hope you will stay with me this morning. It is raining very hard, and you will be warm and dry here. I saw Deborah while I was out and waved to her and pointed to the tent. She waved back and then hurried to her own tent.

"I am glad she knows I am safe and dry. I would like to talk to you, Isaac."

"You sound serious. Is something worrying you?"

"Yes. I am troubled."

"Alright, my dear wife, what is it?"

"Not easy for me to speak the words. Please let me say it all, and then we can talk."

"I will do my best to listen and hold my words till you are finished."

She sat and hugged herself, not looking at Isaac at all. "But I don't know where to begin."

Isaac took her hand. *It looks as if she is trying to protect herself, or maybe even hide. She seems so helpless.* "If I may, perhaps I can help. When I heard that I was to be married, I didn't know what to think. I knew that it was a duty I had to do and that is how I looked at it. A duty to my father, and to the tribe. Nothing more, nothing less. But that has changed. The way you dealt with my terrible outburst at our first meeting showed me you were no ordinary woman to be seen as a duty. In the time we have spent together, I have learned to respect and to appreciate you. You become dearer to me each time I speak with you. It must have been even harder for you to consider a forced marriage to a stranger from far away."

"I was not forced, Isaac. My father gave me the right to refuse. But deep inside of me, something said that this was what my heart needed. When I came, I was worried, of course I was. But I also felt that it would be a good marriage. And I too have come to admire you and to like you very much. My affection, like yours, grows with each meeting."

He leaned toward her and gave her a tender kiss.

"As you know, once again, I have come from the woman's house. I was there with my regular woman's time. We have been married for many moons and I hoped that by now I could tell you we were having a baby. But it is not happening. I want so badly to give you the son you want and need and deserve. I have done everything I know about, trying to make it happen, prayers to your god and mine. I have drunk the terrible teas the midwives make. I have eaten pomegranates when I could get them. I hate to confess this, but I found a small carving of Inana in Sarah's things and I have been sleeping with her at night. I hope this doesn't upset you. But she was desperate for a child, and I am feeling that I understand her pain. I don't know what I have done to offend our god, and I don't know what else to do. Help me, Isaac."

Tears streamed down her cheeks, and she was trembling with emotion. He took her in his arms and crooned a gentle melody in her ear. When the tears stopped and her heavy sobs slowed, he spoke.

"Dear one. No one knows why things happen as they do. I don't believe you have done anything wrong or left anything undone. Sometimes it just takes time. Think about my mother and father. But they had me at last, and all the pain and emptiness went away. I will never blame you or put you aside. I love you too much for that. Father remained loyal to mother and as I will to you. Don't suggest we do what they did. I won't. If we never have a child, that is the will of the Almighty One. It changes nothing. You are my wife and always will be my one and only. I hope that isn't what is causing those tears."

"It is a part of my sorrow and fear. But mostly I don't want to disappoint you, and my arms just ache to hold our child. I am reassured by your devotion and loyalty. It helps so much to ease my pain."

"And while we are waiting, just think of all the pleasure and fun we will have."

He raised her chin with his hand, and she saw the laughter in his eyes. She smiled at him through her tears and playfully tossed a cushion at him.

Abraham was nearing the tent and ready to ask for admittance. He heard laughter, the deep chuckle of Isaac, and a rippling giggle from Rebekah. He walked away, smiling in deep joy.

Chapter Twenty-Seven

The family sat around the fire at Abraham's tent. The stars poked holes in the black sky as sparks flew up to join the glittering points of light. Quiet chatter circled the fire pit as the younger members shared gossip and news. Abraham stared into the distance. Rebekah watched him and wondered how he was feeling. She startled as he spoke.

"I am sitting here wondering what has happened to my son Ishmael. It seems to be a lifetime ago that he was banished from our village. Have you heard any news, Isaac?"

"The traders speak of him. He is well and is the head overseer of Pharaoh's holdings in the land of Goshen. Your son is an important man in Egypt. He is married and has many children."

"And his mother, Hagar. Is she alive?"

"Yes. She lives in his grand house in Goshen."

"I would like to see him once more before I die."

"If you wish, I can send a message with the next trade caravan"

Abraham nodded and returned to his silent reverie.

As they walked home, Rebekah questioned Isaac.

"I asked Rivkah about the troubles between Abraham and Sarah, but she said it wasn't her story to tell. Can you help me to understand what happened?"

"Mother was barren and gave Hagar, her maid, to father to produce the needed heir, and she gave birth to Ishmael. After I was born, Hagar planned a way for Ishmael to receive the blessing and the inheritance of the first-born son. But it had to be given to me as the son of father's wife not a concubine. For her treachery, she was banished."

"I trust you will send for Ishmael and that he will come to see Abraham. It will bring peace to an old man."

"I hope so. I truly hope so."

Chapter Twenty-Eight

Hagar wrung her hands. "My son, I don't know what to think about returning to visit Abraham. We left Canaan so many years ago. And it was not a pleasant leave-taking. Sarah forced us to leave."

"I know the story well, mother, but it was a long time ago. After we settled here, you worked as a cook at the palace. It was simple for you to get work as you had lived there before."

He continued in a condescending tone. "It was wise of Sarah to give you the piece of gold with Pharaoh's mark on it. That is the one small reason I am grateful to her. You and I know how I worked as a helper in the farms of Pharaoh. We worked extremely hard and now I am overseer of all Pharaoh's lands, farms, fields, and stables."

Hagar looked at Ishmael. "We are rich beyond my dreams. Maybe even richer than Abraham or Isaac."

"That is of no importance to me. I think little about them. I don't know why I was summoned, for that is what it felt like. Not an invitation, but a summons."

"I think it is time to ask his forgiveness for my ambition and greed"

"Mother, you only did what you thought best for us. You had a hard life, and I do not blame you for trying to protect me. But all that is in the far-away past, another life. Isaac is my only brother, and we had good times together."

Hagar put down the cloth she was mending and looked intently at her son.

"But they are strangers to me. Since we moved here, we have lived among my people who were here in this land. It was from them I learned of my roots and the religion of my father." He paused and twisted the gold bracelets on his arms. "It is the faith I have chosen to follow, Now, I would like to see my father, and ask him some questions about my rights."

"We had no rights. Sarah needed a son; I was the means to fulfill that need."

"Exactly. By custom and the law, I was Sarah's son. What is the saying? Born upon her knees That's it, and therefore I am the eldest son and the rightful heir."

"I was wrong to fill your head with false dreams. You were a child and believed what I told you. That was our ruin. We could have had a good life there except to my ambition."

"You did what you thought best for me. You had a hard life, and I do not blame you for trying to look after my interests. But Isaac is my only brother, and I need to see him and look him in the eye.

Hagar sighed. "You want me to go with you. But I don't understand why.

"I think you need to go to put behind you all the pain and sorrow from that time in your life. You are still holding on to those bad days. If you can see Abraham and talk to him, perhaps you can find true happiness. And I would miss you if you stayed here."

"It is such a long journey. I can't face the travel, the thirst, the hunger, and the fear. I am not so young anymore, Ishmael, and it would be challenging for my old bones."

"Mother, you are not old. Your beauty has not faded, and you stand proud and tall in this magnificent land. I would not ask you to make that long, arduous journey. I will borrow one of Pharaoh's ships and we will travel by water."

Hagar shook her head. "I am afraid of the desert because I know it. I am afraid of the sea because I do not know it."

"The boat is large, mother. You will have your own private space, a comfortable bed, and a view of the coast all the way. We will feast each day on fish, fruit, and bread. The breezes will cool your brow and the waves will rock you to sleep. I would not put our lives in danger. Please come with me."

I will think about it."

In just a few days they stood together on the deck. Provisions were stored in wooden boxes lashed to the railing on the deck. Fine cotton curtains made a room for Hagar near the centre front of the boat. There, the rocking motion would be less than at the edges or the rear. Hagar sat on a stool, fastened to the wood of the boat.

"Ishmael, the sails are beautiful. Look how they ripple in the breeze. But why are there oars along each side? Doesn't the wind make the boat move?"

"When it blows, we will move quickly. But sometimes the wind is still and then we use the oars. We will travel day and night, so the journey will be over before you have time to think about the unknown future."

Hagar watched as the slaves pulled the anchor aboard and the oars flashed in the sunlight. In the blink of an eye, the wind caught the sail, and the boat leaped ahead. Hagar laughed in delight. Her maid Talia laughed with her and twirled in a circle around her.

"This will be such an adventure. Tell me about the land we are going to."

"I have not been there for many, many years. I remember a rugged land, with rocks and trees, meadows, and flowers. No vast deserts of sand, only green grassy hills. Sparkling rivers and streams with fresh water. The people lived in tents. Maybe they still do."

"No houses! How strange. What are the people like?"

"People are people. They can be kind or cruel. Generous or selfish. Honest or thieving. It doesn't matter the race or language; people are the same everywhere."

"I envy you. You have travelled and seen so much. What adventures you have had."

Hagar patted Talia's hand. "Don't envy me. My life has not always been a happy one. I have things I wish to forget."

"You were not always Keturah. You had another name?"

My parents named me Hagar. It was a good name for me, for it means forsaken or to flee. I felt forsaken by the gods, when I fled from the anger of Sarah, my mistress. In Egypt, where I went with my son, life was better. My life changed and so I changed my name. Keturah was a wise old woman who befriended me in my new life. When she died, I decided to take her name and keep the memory of her kindness to me alive."

"You have many stories to tell your grandchildren."

They sat and watched the shore drift past. Keturah was deep in thought, wondering what lay ahead. Part of her mind was trying to remember Abraham. He was a big man, tall and strong, that she knew. He had kind brown eyes and a ready smile. His relationship with Sarah was strange. They were close in many ways, but there was also a deep separation between them.

It was there on our trip from Egypt to his homeland, and it never went away. He seemed unaware of me until I went to his bed at Sarah's command. He loved his son, my Ishmael, but when Isaac was born, we were cast aside, forsaken. She stood and paced back and forth on the rocking deck beneath her feet.

She was deep in thought when Ishmael touched her arm. "Are you well, mother? You didn't hear me speak to you."

"I am fine, my son. I think I will lie down for a rest. The sea air makes me sleepy."

He watched as she went into her little room. "Maybe I did the wrong thing in bringing her. She was not eager to come on this journey. Too late now for regrets. But she is strong and resilient. She will be fine, and I think the visit can heal the scars that she hides in her heart."

The days passed quickly. Blue skies and fair winds sped the little ship quickly along the coast. They landed at a hidden cove known to Egyptian sailors. A second boat had followed them and carried food and provisions for the overland trip to Hebron. It carried gifts and treasures for Abraham and for Isaac. The trip would take several days, but they would travel quickly. They had brought a litter for Keturah and slaves would carry her all the way to their destination. The slaves were also soldiers and were ready to protect Ishmael and Keturah if any trouble arose. Keturah enjoyed the journey. She rode in her litter and watched the scenery pass by, chatting with Talia and Ishmael as they walked beside her.

As they travelled, Keturah remembered the earthy smell of the cedar trees. The fresh breezes that caressed her cheeks were so much more pleasant than the hot dry winds of Egypt. She turned to Talia one evening. "Look at the stars. I had forgotten how they danced in the dark sky and the great round moon sails the heavenly seas. Even the air seems softer and kinder in this land."

Talia looked at her. "What do you mean, softer and kinder? Stars are stars and air is air."

"In Egypt, the wind blows the sand, and it stings again my cheeks. The stars are just points of light. Here there is something in the air that makes them dance, and I can almost hear them singing."

"Sometimes your words are so beautiful I wish I could remember them for ever."

Keturah had worried that she would be anxious and afraid. But as she travelled, she remembered the lush green valleys, the forest of cedar and pine, and the streams and rivers that gave life and beauty to this land. *There is much that is good in my memory of this former life. I will only think of the good days and hope that others can also forget past troubles.*

On a cool morning, Ishmael walked beside her litter. "I remember my father as a kind man who played games with me and taught me about the animals, birds, and the land."

"Your memories are accurate. Are you worried about our welcome?"

"A little, but Isaac invited us to come, so I hope that is a sign that all has been forgiven."

"We heard Sarah has been laid to rest and perhaps the painful parting has been buried with her."

"My advisors tell me that the name Canaan, the land to which we travel, means hope. That is what I think about. A land called hope. And I hope that Isaac and I can start over as brothers. He must know that I am the firstborn of Abraham and that means something."

He smiled at his mother and walked on ahead to check the trail.

Oh, my son. The past is gone. Leave it alone. Forget what I taught you and find a new way to be a son to Abraham and a brother to Isaac. Hope. That is all I can do. Hope for a new future for you and your kindred.

She tried to lay her fears aside and watch the road ahead that led to the valley called hope.

Chapter Twenty-Nine

Rebekah frowned as she look outside. For weeks, the sky had been overcast. The sun peeked out between the clouds many times each day, and mornings were often sunny and warm. It was strange that the rains had not come as often as they usually did. It was new to Rebekah, and she wondered at the constant concern over the water supply. On a cloudy afternoon, they had walked up the hill beyond the village.

As they sat on a blanket Isaac had carried, she asked him about this worry about the lack of rain. "Isaac, we had wells in Haran, and we were never short of water. You have wells here too. Why is everyone so worried about the rain?"

"Our wells are not deep. They rely on groundwater. The wells in Haran reach way down to large pools or rivers that are underground. Here, if the rains fail, the ground dries out, the grass turns yellow and dies, and so do the crops. With no water, the herds are in trouble quickly and so are we. No water means death in a brief time. Our water comes from the rain and during the rainy season the river and the wells fill up, but they go dry if we do not get enough rain during our winter."

"Even the water in the river goes away?"

"Father tells of a time when the river was just a trickle. That is why they went to Egypt, to buy food to keep the people alive."

"That helps to explain why everyone is so worried."

"It does, and why no one really minds the wet season. We may grumble a little, but we all know our lives depend on those rainy days."

They sat in comfortable silence till Isaac pointed to the tamarisk trees. "Look at those bushes Rebekah. Behind them is a clearing that we call Sarah's grove. She came here often to pray and to ponder her life. To her, it was a sacred place."

"Rivkah has mentioned it. Is there a connection to this place and the stone in her tent?"

"Yes. It was one of the many stones that she had collected and carried with her from place to place when they moved. She collected them all her life?"

"Do you know why?"

"I think she needed to mark her experiences in some way. A stone was her spirit symbol, so it was a clever way to remember the important events of her life."

"You said there are quite a few. What kind of events?"

"Father told me as we sat by the circle after her burial, but it is hard to remember. There was one for her marriage, one for my birth, a stone from her mother's cooking fire, and many more. I know there was one from Egypt, but you will need to ask father if you want to know more about that one and the others. No one has ever talked about that time in Egypt. I think Sarah forbade it."

"It must have been an unhappy time. Didn't Hagar come from Egypt?"

"I understand when they returned to this land, she came with them as Sarah's slave. Rivkah might know something if she is willing to talk."

"But she left when you were very young, didn't she?"

"Yes. And of course, Ishmael went with her."

"Do you remember your brother?"

"A little. But as you said, I was young, and no one talked about them."

Isaac stood and helped her up. "I will take you into the grove and show you where the stones are buried."

They walked to the hidden opening, and Isaac held the branches back as Rebekah bent low and entered. In the center was a hollow that was filled with blue cornflowers.

"That was mother's favourite flower, so I planted them there."

"What a beautiful spot, and a fitting tribute to your mother. What is that place where there is a small hollow."

"That is where we buried the green jade on the day of her burial. Father did not want anyone to find them. The alabaster and jade were valuable and worth stealing. Later, I got it. I was grieving for my mother and needed something tangible to focus my memories around."

"So, you came and dug it up and took it to your tent."

"And I made the cedar pedestal it sits on."

"It is lovely. The stone is wonderful, and I like the way the base of it is not finished. That speaks to me of our lives."

"I think that is what mother was trying to say. In mother's stone circle, she has put a stone for birth and one for death. That is the circle of life for all living things."

"Rivkah has said she came here to rage, to grieve, to pray and to heal. It is the perfect spot for all those strong emotions. Rivkah called it a sacred place, and I can feel that."

"If you want to come here for any reason, please feel free to do that. I think mother would like it if this place became special to you." Isaac put his arm around her and they stood, each with their own thoughts.

Isaac broke the silence. "We had better get back to our tent."

"Before we go, I would like to say a blessing. May I?

"Of course."

"For this holy space, we are grateful. For its quiet. For its beauty. For the life that is honoured in this space. For the woman Sarah, daughter, wife, mother, friend, and healer, we offer our prayer to El Shaddai, gentle mother of us all."

Isaac picked a flower and tucked it into Rebekah's hair. Her eyes were damp with tears.

As they were walking down the hill, Rebekah pointed to the road coming from the south and leading to the village. She had spotted a group of people riding camels nearing the simple boundary wall and gate. Isaac stopped. He stared at the travellers. Then he shouted.

"Maybe it is Ismael. Has my brother come?" He grabbed Rebekah's hand and almost pulled her off her feet as he ran toward the road. At the bottom of the hill, Rebekah stopped. "You go to Ismael. I will go and tell Father Abraham."

He barely nodded and kept running. Rebekah turned and hurried toward the tent of Abraham. He was sitting outside, his head tilted back to let the sun warm his face. She approached and spoke. “Father. I bring news.”

He sat up, startled. “News. News. What news?”

“Isaac and I saw a small caravan of camels and riders on the road into our village. Isaac thinks it is Ishmael and has gone to meet him. I came here to tell you.”

“He is here? I knew he was invited but heard no more. Ishmael here? My son has come home. But there is nothing ready. What will I do? What will I do?”

“You will calm yourself, comb your beard, put on a clean tunic, and prepare to greet your son. I will find Eliezer and Deborah and they will get help and get busy with a feast for your guests.”

“Yes. Yes. Tidy my appearance. A feast. We must have a feast.” He looked for Rebekah, but she was already down the hill and talking to Deborah.

Chapter Thirty

Abraham held tightly to Rebekah's hand as the travellers approached.

"Look, Ishmael rides a camel. How wonderful."

"Actually, father, your sons look very much alike. Ishmael is leading the camel and Isaac is riding."

"That is good. I like the message I see in that. Who else is there?"

"I really can't tell, but I think a woman is on the litter just behind Isaac."

"His wife?"

"Perhaps, but it could be his mother, couldn't it?"

"Hagar. Do you mean Hagar?"

"I don't know, I am just guessing, but she looks like an older woman."

At that moment, Ishmael called, "Father" and ran. He was at Abraham's tent in an instant. They looked at each other for a long moment. Then Abraham opened his arms and engulfed Ishmael in a strong, steady embrace.

All the others stood at a respectful distance as the father and son greeted each other after so many years.

Ishmael looked around and his eyes fell on Rebekah. "Who is the lovely woman standing behind you, father?"

Abraham turned. "Oh. That is Rebekah, daughter of Bethuel, the son of Nahor."

Isaac smiled at Ishmael and stood beside Rebekah. "And my wife."

"You have chosen well little brother. I am glad to meet you, Rebekah."

She gave a slight bow. "Welcome to the tent of your father. I hope your journey was without any trouble."

Abraham grinned. "Yes, yes, it is a long and dusty journey from Egypt. I remember it even though it was years ago. My spit dries up at the thought."

Ishmael grinned. "We came in an Egyptian boat. We landed near Ashkelon and then followed the trade route to Hebron. The sea voyage was swift and pleasant. The land travel was without incident. Camels travel quickly and need little to eat or drink on a four-day journey. It was the best thing to do for the comfort and safety of mother."

Abraham's eyebrows shot up. "Your mother is here? Hagar has come to my tent?"

She stepped forward, knelt at his feet, and pressed her forehead against his hands.

"Father, this is my mother. But her name is not Hagar now. She is Keturah and her name means incense. She was unsure of her welcome here but has come to honour the father of her first-born son."

"Rise, Keturah. You are welcome. We have stories to share and to unravel."

Keturah rose, smiled at Abraham, and bowed to Isaac and to Rebekah.

"I am very happy to be with my son as he is reunited with his family."

Rebekah stepped forward and gestured to the tent. "Inside there is food and drink prepared. Please let us sit together."

Abraham offered Keturah his arm, and they led the way into his tent.

The sun was painting the blue sky as it dipped behind the hills. Isaac and Ishmael stood outside and watched the clouds as they changed shapes and colours. Pink turned to red, blue turned to purple, and yellow became dusky gold.

Ishmael gave a sweeping gesture to the sky. "We don't often have sunsets like this. The sun touches the earth, glows crimson for a moment, and is gone. I had forgotten the colours and the twilight hour. It is amazing."

"I think you arrived just in time. To me, this looks like a promise of the rain we need. It will be good for the land, but we will be staying in these tents mostly. I expect you will need to borrow a heavy cloak to try to stay dry."

Deborah spoke from inside the tent. "All is ready. Come in and dine."

Ishmael sat between Isaac and Abraham in the place of honour. As each course was presented, Ishmael entertained with stories of his homeland. Ishmael spoke of the land where the Hebrew people lived.

"You live in the north?" Isaac asked.

"Yes, our people live in a good fertile land. We work hard and raise crops and animals to fill the granaries and barns of the Pharaoh. We are free to live our lives, as is our custom. You would find our villages similar to yours."

Abraham reached for some bread. "I remember Goshen. It was a pleasant land, sweet water, and a gentle climate. This land can be harsh and unforgiving. It is good to know my son and his mother live well in Egypt. Do you have sons, Ishmael?"

"I have eight sons. My wife, Ayesha, has recently given me a new son, Hadar. She could not come on this journey. But she sends greetings to you my esteemed father."

The talk flowed as the lamps burned low. Rebekah broke into the stories and memories. "The moon is high in the sky. I think, Isaac, that our guests need to rest from their travels."

"You are always taking care of us. Thank you, Rebekah. Where will our guests stay?"

Rebekah, as usual, had it all thought out. "I think Ishmael should share your tent, Isaac. I know you will talk and not sleep, but that is as it should be. I saw to it that Gershom has taken care of your servants and animals. They are settled for the night."

"Thank you, Rebekah. You are as kind as you are beautiful,"

Ishmael's smile was unsettling, and she was not sure how to respond. She turned away and spoke to Keturah. "If it is agreeable with you, Keturah, I would welcome you to my tent. Before you decide, understand that it is the tent that belonged to Sarah."

"I hold no bitterness over the past. It would be my honour to come to the tent of my former mistress and share that revered space with you."

Abraham raised his hands in blessing. "Shalom to this house and all who dwell here. May your nights be peaceful."

Each one bowed to the old man and backed out of the tent to go to their well-earned rest.

Abraham watched the stars as they floated across the deep blue sky. *Hagar, no, I must remember her new name. Keturah, it is a lovely name. I had forgotten what a pleasant face she had. The lines of anger have softened, and her smile once more lights up her eyes. Tomorrow will come soon, and I need to rest.*

He entered his tent, and without even taking off his tunic, dropped onto his mat and was asleep at once. The pale silver moon smiled down on the sleeping village.

Isaac opened the flap; Ishmael entered the tent. He took a quick look around. "This is not a place fitting for the next great leader to live."

"It is small, but I spend so little time here it isn't a problem. Most of my time is at the work of the settlement, and father, our father does little these days. All my free time is spent with Rebekah, and I sleep in her tent most nights."

"That may be so, but this is still not the image of a great leader. Rebekah should be here and you in your mother's tent."

"It is of little importance. Everyone knows I am the heir and so it doesn't matter."

Ishmael frowned. "I think it does. You need to show your importance and demand the respect you deserve." The underlying rage in the voice of his brother shocked Isaac.

"We need to get settled for the night. You take my pallet, and I will get comfortable in the far corner."

Ishmael called for his servant and the man entered and together they moved aside Isaac's bedding and laid out a soft padded base and then covered it with a woven linen blanket and over that a silk one, intricately decorated with symbols of the sun, grain, and water.

Silently, Isaac picked up his bedding and laid it out on the tent floor. "I hope you sleep well, my brother. The days start early here, as we go to bed and rise with the sun." He turned his face to the wall and feigned sleep.

Keturah followed Rebekah into the tent and stopped. "This is even more lovely than I remember it. You have made it yours I can see but have honoured, Sarah, the one who lived here before."

"You must be used to sleeping in a large house. I hope you can be comfortable here."

"My beginnings were as a slave. This is a lovely dwelling. I am honoured to be a guest in your home."

Rebekah turned to her companion. "This is Deborah. She will look after us along with your maid. Her name is?"

"Talia. She is Egyptian but has taken our faith to be her own and, as you know, speaks our words perfectly."

"Welcome, Talia. I hope you can be comfortable sharing the tent with Deborah. If you would prefer, we can get a tent for you nearby."

"I think Deborah and I will do very well in her tent. She has been most welcoming and gracious."

"You must be tired after your travels, so let's get some rest and we can get to know each other tomorrow. Good night, and rest in peace. Shalom."

Chapter Thirty-One

The next morning, the men gathered at Abraham's tent for the early meal. Deborah had come to help, while Talia looked after Rebekah and Keturah. Deborah knew Abraham would appreciate a special breakfast for his guest and Eliezar would not be offended at her help. She prepared a generous breakfast, adding fresh yogurt and raisin cake to the usual foods. Isaac offered the blessing and thanked Deborah for the meal she had prepared. Abraham added his thanks as well. Ishmael looked surprised as she bowed with a cheerful smile at the praise she had heard spoken. He ate little, merely sniffed at the porridge, but seemed to enjoy the yogurt and bread.

Isaac stood and invited the others to join him outside. "It is good the rains are holding off. We can take a tour of the fields, the water systems, and the village. I am sure you will see many changes since you left, Ishmael."

"From the hill where we camped, there seemed to be more tents, but it looked much the same. It surprised me you haven't built any houses."

Abraham's eyebrows went way up. "We are wanderers. We move from place to place; how could we move a house?"

"But you don't move anymore. You have been here for my whole life."

Isaac heard the same condescension this morning that he had heard last night. He gave a small cough, glad that Abraham had not noticed the insult. "Let's get going. That mist could turn to rain at any time." He offered an arm to his father, and they set out to show Ishmael their village.

They walked about, and Abraham kept up a steady stream of cheerful conversation. He pointed out the fields, ready for planting when the rains ended. As they stopped to look at the irrigation system, he spoke with pride. "Your uncle, Lot, was a clever man, and he drew up the plans for these troughs to carry water to our vineyards and gardens."

"That's a lot of work. At home in Egypt, we have the Nile that floods our lands and we do not have to do anything. It is much better than wooden things that must need repairing all the time."

Abraham scowled. "Our river gives us sweet water and tasty fish. That is enough. We are strong and clever and can water our fields in this manner. We depend on our own skill and on the generous hand of El Shaddai for our water."

Ishmael started to answer, but Isaac broke in. "We should keep moving. There is much to see."

They toured the yards, the gardens, and the olive grove. Isaac carried the conversation. Abraham had become quiet, and Ishmael nodded and grunted. At the pens for the sheep and goats, he broke his silence.

"I had forgotten how they stink."

He held a cloth up to his nose and Isaac caught a whiff of a sweet-smelling perfume.

Abraham eyed his first born. "Those stinking animals are the life of our people. Wool, meat, milk, cheese, and tallow. At least they don't growl or spit." He turned back toward his tent. "I am tired of this. You continue. I need to rest."

Abraham slowly made his way up the hill to his tent. There was an awkward pause as they watched him. He climbed slowly and leaned heavily on his stick. Isaac regarded his brother. *Does he not see how he hurts father? This is not going well. Not at all.* He touched Ishmael's sleeve. "Perhaps you would like to visit Hebron. The city might be more to your liking."

"Oh yes. That is what I would like to do. Shall we go?"

"I will get Gershom to show you the town. I have work to do."

Meanwhile, the women had finished their meal and cleaned up the tents. In a comfortable circle, they sat on stools outside and happily shared experiences. They talked about the weather, so different in their two countries. Keturah pointed out a fluffy, white cloud that looked like a sheep. "I remember when we lived here and Ishmael was young, we would look for shapes in the clouds. You can't do that in Egypt. If there are a few clouds early in the day, the sun burns them away before they can take any shape at all."

Deborah wondered aloud. "No rain. How do things grow?"

"We have some rain, but not for long periods. It comes from the great sea to the north. The river floods and waters our crops and it is very faithful. What we have is the khamsin."

Two voices asked. "What is khamsin?"

"It is the hot dry wind that blows for days and days. It comes in the summer and whirls the sand into great clouds that blot out the sun. Then that sand covers everything and creeps into the houses and fills every crack and cranny. It is not too bad where we live, but just a little south of us, it can be deadly."

Rebekah stood. "I think every land has good things about it and things that can cause suffering. No land is perfect, and we must learn to be content where we are. Let's walk to the river. It is getting hot, and it is much cooler there."

They gathered under the huge cedar tree. Keturah sat on the bench and the others on the grassy slope. They continued to compare their lives and experiences.

Rebekah noticed Abraham returning to his tent. She stood. "If you don't mind, I will go to Abraham and see if he needs anything. Please continue."

Deborah jumped up. "I will go. I can get him water or fruit." And she was off up the hill.

Keturah smiled. "The chief has many who look after him. Is he well, Rebekah?"

"Yes, in general. He moves more slowly now, of course, and he has aches and pains. But he doesn't complain very often. When he gets grumpy, usually when suffering, we send Esther to him." Rebekah gave a rippling laugh. "Esther is our healer and along with herbs and salves, she brings laughter to his tent. She is the only one who can tease him, make him laugh, and improve his state of mind. You must meet her."

"I would like to meet the women who are here. This seems to be a very pleasant place to live and there seems to be little unhappiness."

"We will soon have the new moon ceremony. You will join us, I hope."

"I remember that time. Yes, I would love to join you in the moon house. Thank you. Could we take a walk around the village? I would enjoy that."

Rebekah stood and held out her hand. "Let's do that. It is good that the rains have not come yet. We must be outside while we can before we huddle in our tents and try to keep dry."

"I remember those wet days very well. And yet, the memory is a good one as we women spent long hours together, warm, and dry." They linked arms, and smiling, walked to the village.

Chapter Thirty-Two

Sunlight woke Rebekah early. The discomfort that spoiled her sleep told her it was her moon time once again. She stood as Deborah entered the tent.

"Good morning, Becca. You are up early. I'll get the fire going."

"Don't bother. I must get ready to go the moon tent." She cradled her belly as a cramp spread in her gut.

"I'll help you get ready and walk with you. But first I'll get my shawl. The rain is starting."

"Please get Keturah and bring her here."

Rebekah watched her go and poked at the fire. She shook her fist at the roof. "Once again, I go to the tent. At least now the faces of the others, are friendly. I enjoy their growing friendship but what I really need is a child in my womb. A son for Isaac, an heir to the inheritance. Why am I being punished by El Shaddai?" She began to pace back and forth in the space around the fire.

Keturah and Deborah entered.

"Good morning, Keturah. I have asked you here this morning as I woke with my usual signs that today will be my moon time, so I must go into seclusion. Again." She scowled. "I will leave you in Deborah's care until I return. My regrets that I cannot be here to welcome you."

"I thank you. I look forward to getting to know Deborah and to learn my way around the settlement. Abraham has asked me to join him for the early meal. Perhaps we can meet later, Deborah." She bowed slightly and with a wave left to walk up the hill to Abraham's tent.

Rebekah gathered up the clothing, including a dry shawl and some sewing she was doing. She took her sleeping mat, rolled it and covered it with a sheepskin to keep it dry. From their supplies, she took dried figs, bread, and a large bowl of lentil stew. Deborah walked with her to help carry the bundles. They walked out into the driving rain.

 help her carry her bundles. They went out into the storm and struggled against the driving rain.

Shaking off the raindrops, they entered the tent. As usual, the space was welcoming. Around the edges, instead of piles of cushions, there were sleeping mats of many kinds. The sacred fire was not burning, but there were three other fires warming the room and casting swaying shadows on the walls. She was greeted with smiles and words of welcome.

Rebekah settled in once more for the regular time of seclusion.

The days flew by and almost too soon, she was ready to leave and return home. When it was time, she quietly walked out the door and went to her tent.

There was no one there, but it was plain that Deborah had spent time cleaning, there wasn't a grain of sand to be seen.

Deborah rushed in. "So, what was it like? You looked rested and relaxed. I think it was more healing for you this moon time." *I hope this means better days ahead for her.*

After their meal, Rebekah went for a walk along the river. As she hoped, Isaac was sitting on their favourite bench. He joined her in her walk. As the sun slipped out of sight, Isaac hugged her shoulder a little more firmly. "Can I persuade my lovely companion to come to my tent and warm up by my fire?"

"Your companion would be delighted." She smiled up at him and he bent and kissed her. They walked arms around each other, to his tent.

Chapter Thirty-Three

The excitement settled into a new routine. Keturah felt safe and secure in Abraham's settlement. Few people seemed to know that she had once lived there as Hagar. Or if they knew they no longer cared about her past. She was glad to see that Isaac and Ishmael spent time looking at the flocks and herds. Each evening, the lamp in Isaac's tent burned late as they talked long into the night. The rains had been falling for many days, and Abraham stayed close to his tent and Keturah was at his tent most days. She returned to Rebekah's for the evening meal. The two women were becoming good friends and spent comfortable evenings sharing life experiences.

On a morning when the rain was very light, a mist really, Rebekah stood at the door of her tent. As she looked toward the river, she saw Abraham sitting on the bench. It was a thoughtful gift from Isaac, who made the bench with a well-shaped back on it. Anyone could sit for hours in comfort. Abraham came often to sit in the shade of the oak tree and watch the water.

I would like to sit with him, but perhaps he needs to be alone. But I feel drawn to sit with him.

She grabbed her shawl and walked to the bench. "Father, I hope I am not disturbing you."

"No, my child. I am just enjoying the river. There is something so quieting about watching water flow by."

"This is a favourite place of mine to sit, and I am glad you enjoy it, too. The bench Isaac made adds to the pleasure."

"I am pleased you have come. Do you have time to listen to the cares of an old man?"

"I have all the rest of the day. What is troubling you?"

"Many things. Ishmael mostly." He paused, and a frown twisted his brow.

Rebekah adjusted her shawl. “We just met, and I do not know him well, but he does not seem to be happy. On the surface, he seems fine, but he is a troubled man, I think.”

“I am sure you have heard at least some gossip about the time he and Hagar left. It is long in the past, but I suspect he is bitter and angry about it still.”

“You are right. Long-ago events shouldn’t matter now. All that matters is the damage they have done. He was young when they left, was he not?”

“He was. His mother seems to have let the past stay in the past. She may still have some guilt about it all, but no anger or need for revenge. I cannot say the same about my son.”

“Let us hope that being with you and getting to know his brother can heal the scars he carries. I hope he talks to his mother; her wisdom would be good for him to know.”

“For young men, it's hard to listen to your parents, especially as they are getting old. But I too hope he can find peace amongst us.”

She sat beside him, and they listened to the river bubble past.

“That wasn’t what I really wanted to talk to you about. I have been very lonely since Sarah died. The days are long, and the nights are impossible. Work tires me out and that is good, but I do not rest easy. It has been a delight to be reunited with Hagar, Keturah. Sometimes I forget her new name. But it suits her. I am sure you have noticed that Keturah and I spend time together. I enjoy her company. She is a gentle, calm soul, wise and amusing. She says that she enjoys my company as well.”

“Yes, I have seen you together and you both look happy and at peace.”

“I am afraid they will return to Egypt and when I think about it, I am heartsore.”

“Has she said that she is going back?”

“No. She speaks fondly of this place and of our time together, but there is always a note of sadness.”

He pulled at his beard in the curious way he had when he was thinking.

“I am wondering if I should ask her to stay.”

"Stay here? How? As a friend, a companion, or a concubine."

"No. No. Never that. As my wife. Is it too soon, do you think?"

"It seems to me that Ishmael will go home in the summer season. If you don't ask soon, I think it will be too late."

"But do you agree?"

"You are two people forever connected by the past and by your son. You are making a new friendship now. What better foundation for a future together?"

"If that is your blessing, it is wonderful and thank you. But what will Isaac think? He feels so strongly about loyalty and being faithful. I don't want to upset him."

"You have not betrayed Sarah in all these years, and no one would see this as a betrayal. Isaac only wants you to be happy. I know he has profound respect for Keturah. He holds no ill will toward her. You will have his approval; I am sure of it."

"I will ask her on our walk tonight when the moon is full and shining down in blessing. Thank you, Rebekah." He put his arm around her shoulder and hugged her tenderly. They sat quietly for a time, watching fish jump in the shining blue waters of the river. Warmed by the pale winter sun and by their affection, they were content.

Abraham returned to his tent, changed his cloak, and combed his beard. He found his sons together and spoke to them.

"You have seen, I am sure, that Keturah and I are more than just friends. She is very dear to me, and I want to ask her to be my wife."

Isaac clapped his father on the back. "That is good news. I am happy for you both."

"I haven't asked her yet; I was hoping for your blessings. Ishmael?"

"If that is what you and my mother want, so be it." His voice held no hint of his feelings.

"I would like you both to walk with me to the wedding, will you?"

Isaac grinned from ear to ear. "It will be an honour and my pleasure."

Abraham turned to Ishmael. “Will you walk with Isaac and me to the wedding?”

“If you wish. Are you coming to Egypt with us or is mother staying here?”

Isaac gulped and swallowed his words. Abraham uttered a long, deep groan.

“I trust my wife will stay with me. I am surprised you even asked.”

“That’s settled them. I will see you later.” He walked away without looking back.

Abraham was deeply troubled by Ishmael’s response. Isaac put a reassuring hand on his father’s arm. Abraham forced a smile and, shaking any negative thoughts from his mind, went to meet Keturah for their walk.

She was waiting at the tent and greeted him warmly. He leaned close and kissed her cheek. “I am going to show you a favourite place of mine. Ready for a walk?”

“Lead the way.”

He took her hand and led her toward the high hills. They climbed upward until a small path led away from the main trail, and they turned and followed it. After a short walk, they came to a wide opening. From this spot, they could see from the east to the west the length of the valley.

“It is so lovely. The river is a silver road winding through the trees. And your tents, they seem so peaceful, and the people are too.” She laughed. “Little insects running about. The sky goes on forever. This would be magical with the moon and the stars.”

“We can come back as many times as you want. Have a meal up here, even sleep under the stars.”

The smile left her face, and she looked at him with tears spilling down her cheeks.

“Dear one. Have I upset you? What is wrong?”

“Oh Abraham. Ishmael is impossible. He is not doing well here. He is angry and vengeful. All the poison he has kept hidden all these years is bubbling in his mind. He is returning to Egypt, and it breaks my heart.”

“Him returning to Egypt or his anger?”

"Well, both. But mostly the thought of leaving all this pains me."

"You don't have to go. You can stay here."

She looked at him and a smile broke through the tears.

"Keturah, will you be my wife? Will you marry me and stay her for whatever time we have left?"

"Yes. Abraham. Yes, yes, yes."

He took her in his arms and held her closely. He could feel her heart beating and her warm breath caressed his neck.

She leaned away. "But what of Ishmael, Isaac, and Rebekah?"

"I have spoken to them. Rebekah and Isaac are pleased and happy. Ishmael was quite noncommittal, saying it was up to me. I don't think he will make a scene, but I don't expect he is pleased."

"I have given him my life and taught him all he was willing to learn. It is our time now, my love. But a wedding, so much to think about."

"It can be as simple as you want. Rivkah and Deborah will help with the plans if you wish. We are not children, years away from that. I think we can make our own plans. The boys agreed to walk with me from the dinner tent to the bridal tent. I am happy with just that simple ceremony. But whatever you decide."

They sat on the mossy grass, talking and dreaming. The stars lit the sky with a thousand twinkling lights and the moon was their lantern as they made their way down the path to their homes. Abraham to his tent and Keturah to the tent that held so many memories for her. Good and bad. *Those memories are of the past. Today is the present, and the future looks hopeful. The name of this land, hope. If only Ishmael*—she shook herself and looked at the moon. Speaking to the wind, she prayed that the future would be as kind and benevolent as the gentle moon.

Chapter Thirty-Four

Keturah awoke with the first rays of the sun and stretched energetically. *Did I sleep all night? I can't believe today is my wedding day. It looks like it will be a wonderful day, but it would be even if it poured rain.* She could hear Deborah and Rebekah whispering beyond her curtain.to "Stop whispering I am awake."

Rebekah pulled the curtain aside and Deborah came in carrying a tray. It was heaped with a wonderful array of fruit, nuts, cheese, and bread. Rebekah carried three glasses of orange juice. "Breakfast is served."

They sat on cushions in a circle and Keturah offered a blessing for the day. "Holy One of the high mountain. Today you slumber. It is a good omen for a wedding. Look on this day with favour. May joy fill every heart and let this be the happiest of days for Abraham and for me. We welcome this day with open hearts, filled with love. Blessed be your name, El Shaddai, god of peace. Shalom.

"Your dress has been hanging in the air since early dawn. It will be perfect, no creases and the scent of the morning dew lingering in its silky folds."

"Thank you, Deborah. You must have been up early."

"Maybe we never slept. Too much to do and too excited."

The morning passed quickly as they worked together to make Rebekah's tent ready for the dinner and the wedding guests. When they were having a rest and a refreshing cup of buttermilk, a clapping came from the doorway.

"Who is it?"

"Just me, mother, Ishmael."

"Come in my son."

"You look rested, mother. I am glad you slept. Abraham paced most of the night. He is asleep now and the rest of us must get to work. I will wake him shortly and take him to the village. We will keep him busy there while his tent is made ready for the wedding."

"Where will he spend the day? You can't keep him in town all day till the wedding supper."

"He is going to spend the day with his old friend Berush. They haven't seen each other much lately and they will enjoy the day. Berush knows what is happening and he won't let father leave till he is ready for the dinner. I will take his clothes there later."

"I think it will be a long day for him."

"Perhaps he will have a nap, mother. He needs to be rested, ready for tonight."

Keturah threw a pillow at Ishmael, and he dodged it easily, then picked it up. "If you need anything, mother, just call Isaac or me."

"My son, have you decided what to do? I am not trying to send you away, but I think you are unhappy here. In Egypt, there are people whom you love and who love you. Surely, contentment lies with your family."

His eyes were black slits under his furrowed brow. "Today is your wedding day. Do not worry about me. Let us get this over with and not think about tomorrow."

And he was gone, running up the hill, without looking back.

Taking a last look around her tent, Rebekah felt that all was ready, until it was time for the flowers and lamps. Deborah headed to tend to the cooks who were preparing the feast. Everything had to be perfect, and she was determined to watch every step and taste every dish. The other two walked to Abraham's tent to prepare it for the wedding night.

At Abraham's tent, women were already at work, sweeping away the dust and cobwebs. They had baskets and were filling them with all the bits and pieces that Abraham kept lying around. Fishing gear and writing skins. Tools and sandals. Small baskets and dishes.

Keturah fussed. "Where are you going to put all this? He will never find these things when he wants them. Is this necessary?"

"We are just following his instructions. He said that we were to clean this place up. It was to look like an elegant, palatial room for his bride to come home to." As she spoke, the servant girl tossed a pile of sandals into a large bag and carried it out to a wagon.

The dust was making Rebekah sneeze. "I think we can leave these women to their work. Let's go and see what we will need to decorate the room when they are done."

Isaac poked his head into the tent. "Father ordered that great heavy trunk be brought here. He said it was filled with rugs and cushions and fabric. Who knows what is in there? I think I will go find him and we will do something useful. Perhaps we will get some beer and ponder the ways of the world."

Rebekah persuaded Keturah to leave and let the women do this for her and Abraham. "It doesn't really matter what they do, it is a gift they are offering to their beloved master and to his wife. Come, we will gather flowers for both tents."

The time passed quickly, and Deborah sensed it was time for the bride to begin to dress.

She found Rebekah and Keturah and suggested it was time to get the bride ready. They washed her hair in the river as she bathed and dried it with soft cotton towels. They brushed and combed it and perfumed it with scented oil. When finished, it shone like ebony in the fading sunlight.

Just as the sun went behind the hill in a blur of blue, red, and gold, all was ready, and Keturah waited at the open door of her tent for the guests to arrive. They came, wearing the best they had, fine linen and silk, jewels and rings, hair ribbons and combed beards. Rebekah and Deborah came, each one playing a lute, and Esther followed with a tinkling tambourine. Shortly after them, Jacob and Eliezar marched to the beat of a small drum. Their faces were flushed and their happiness uncontained.

With all the dignity they could muster, Isaac and Ishmael led Abraham to the tent. The two escorts entered, and Abraham stood and gazed through tear-filled eyes at his bride. Her eyes sparkled and her smile shone with love. They waited until all were settled on cushions placed on the floor all around the table. He took her arm, and they walked together to their places at the head of the room.

The dinner was a feast like no other Rebekah had seen. The happy couple laughed and talked while they dined. At the end of a wonderful meal, small triangular cakes were brought in. They were made of flour and ground nuts, fried in oil, and slathered in honey. Keturah brought the recipe from Egypt and had supervised the baking. The cakes were served with wine and cheese, and the guests stated they had never eaten anything so delicious.

Dancers and singers entertained till many guests were getting sleepy from the food, the wine, and the late hour. Abraham took Keturah's arm and led her from the room. They did nothing to draw attention to themselves, and very few noticed they were leaving.

Keturah took a moment to smile broadly at Rebekah and Deborah, and Abraham gave a brief bow. Then they went to Abraham's tent and the marriage bed.

Looking at the mess, Rebekah wiped her brow and arched her aching back. After much work, her tent was almost back to normal. The floor mats needed to be swept but she was ready to sit down and put her aching feet up. It was hard to know which hurt the most, her back or her feet.

She heard Isaac's voice. "Mother. You are coming with us to Esther's tent. Ishmael and I are going to get you some hot tea. Esther will treat your aches and pains. No discussion. Come along."

Deborah gave her a gentle push. "Go. I will finish up here and then go to bed."

She had no intention of arguing; it sounded wonderful. Esther was at the tent and had oil warming near the fire and a tea made of herbs to soothe and relax her. The men disappeared into the outdoors, and Esther began her ministrations. Rebekah felt the muscles relax and all the tiredness and pain drain away. She lay on the bed, almost asleep, as Esther put away her potions and tools. The quiet was interrupted by Isaac and Ishmael's return.

"Feeling better, Mother?"

"Very much so."

"Good. We need a drink, and then we can enjoy the night sky. The stars are singing a song to you."

Rebekah smiled. It was a good memory.

Esther smiled. "I will leave you now and don't talk all night. You need some rest."

"Goodnight and thank you, Esther."

With a wave, she was gone.

They went outside and stood under the trees and watched the stars wheeling across the sky.

Rebekah smiled at Ismael and invited him to sit across from her. "Tell me what you see that is different here in this land of your birth."

"I was young when I left. Memories shift and fade in time, and I have been gone for many years. But the tents of Sarah and Abraham seem bigger than I remember, and so does the central gathering place."

"They are bigger, brother. Both tents have had a room or two added, and we have cleared more space in the meadow. We have many more people than when you left. The village has grown."

"I see that. But I don't see any progress. You still live in tents. Water is still a concern. You are growing all the same things in the vineyards and fields. What have you accomplished in all this time?"

A gasp of shock hung heavy in the air. Rebekah's frown was the only sign of her feelings. *This man has learned nothing. Egypt may be advanced in many ways, but at least we are polite and kind to each other.*

Isaac's voice was steely. "We have lived in peace all these years. There is very little evil here, neighbours care for each other. Our children are strong and healthy, and they play safely in our paths and lanes." Isaac sat down and crossed his legs and arms. "The school is growing with many teachers instructing the children and youth. We are true to the laws of El Shaddai and the codes of our ancestors, and he favours us with his goodness. The mountain has been quiet for many, many seasons. I take pride in what my father has done."

Gently, Rebekah tried to change the tone of the conversation. "Perhaps you would tell us about the land of Egypt. Father does not speak of it, and we will never travel there. Tell us, help us see how you live."

"The people who have settled in Goshen live in ease and plenty. I am the magistrate of the area and prosper from my position. I walk in the halls of the great palace of the Pharaoh and eat at his table. I ride a great black stallion to visit the fields and the shops and workplaces. All bow when I come near and there is never a word of complaint."

"You have children. Tell us about them and your wife." Rebekah tried to keep her voice even and pleasant.

"I have two wives. Ayes ha and Fatima. They have given me twelve sons. All will be men of wealth and high standing in Egypt."

"And daughters?"

"I have one."

"Does she have a name?"

"Mahalath. It means lyre, but she is useless as a musician. I know little about her as she spends her time with the women."

Isaac looked distressed, and Rebekah suddenly felt exhausted and slowly rose to her feet.

"I think that we are all getting tired. It has been a long and very busy day. Thank you for your company, but it is time for me to rest. I hope you will go to sleep too and sleep well and long. Goodnight."

"I will walk with you to your tent."

"Thank you, Isaac, but I can manage quite well. You go to your rest. The moon is high in the sky, and it is time we were all asleep."

I wonder if Keturah knows how rude and self-important he is. She must. What sorrow it must cause her. She needs kindness and compassion, and she will find that in her husband. I pray that El Shaddai will give them peace and happiness till the end of their days.

She replied to the night owl that called from the top of the cedar. "Especially for Keturah. She has suffered much and needs to find contentment in her last days."

Chapter Thirty-Five

Keturah was becoming at ease with her new role. She presumed nothing and asked for advice when she was unsure. Rebekah was always ready to explain or answer questions. Abraham, as they sat together after their meal, suggested a walk to the river bench.

"I need to ask you about something important." She saw his furrowed brow and his eyes all scrunched up.

"What is it that you are concerned about?"

"You are now my wife and should be seen to be the leading woman in the village. Rebekah has been doing it since her marriage. I am not sure what to do?"

"I have been thinking about that. I believe that it would be best for everyone if Rebekah continued as she has been. She is trusted and loved, and I am a stranger among the women."

"You are wise, my dear, and I am sure that Rebekah will be happy to continue, and at times come to you for advice. I too think that is the best for all but needed to be sure you were not expecting that honour now that you are my wife. It is yours by right, but I am glad you are saying no." He linked his arm with hers. "It is not that you can't do it. You would be very good at that task, but this way you can spend your time with me and not be kept busy with the problems that the chief woman has to deal with. I am very selfish and want you all to myself."

Keturah laughed. "As long as we are both happy."

"I am, Keturah, happier than I have been for many years. Maybe ever. But I do have a problem. Ishmael. I have requested that he meet me at the river. I have spent little time with him since he came, and there is so much we need to say to each other."

Keturah sighed. "Good. He is not happy, but you know that."

"Do you wish to join us? It would be fine with me."

"No, thank you. You and he need to have some time to talk about the future. I will be busy at the tent. There are things I want to do, and you said I could change anything I wished."

"Absolutely. Enjoy yourself." After a loving kiss, he was on his way to meet his son.

Isaac was sitting on the rocks beside the water. He noticed his father approach, but stayed hidden, not wishing to intrude on his father's quiet time.

Abraham had been sitting on the bench for a little while, wondering how to begin. In the peaceful surroundings, he heard footsteps behind him, and turned to greet Ishmael. Abraham smiled broadly and held out a hand in welcome. Ishmael ignored the offered hand and stood sullenly by the bench.

"Good morning, son. Thank you for coming. We have had little time to spend together, and I want very much to spend some time with you." He patted the bench beside him.

"You have been busy and distracted by your marriage. It is good of you to take some time away from your bride to be with me." He did not sit down but towered over his father, sneering.

"Yes, the wedding. It all happened very fast. But your mother and I have a long history and we quickly came to realize that we have much in common. Growing old alone is not a happy state."

Ishmael folded his arms across his chest. His face was filled with distain. "But neither of you is alone. You have family here and mother has a good life in Goshen."

"That is true, but we didn't have a partner to share our lives with. As one ages, that becomes very important. We are both lucky to have found each other."

"If you say so."

Abraham drew back at the curt reply but pressed on. "What plans do you have for the future?"

"That depends on what there is that I can do here."

"I will give you a piece of the best land in the valley and herds to start your flock."

Ishmael bent down, his face inches from his father. "You expect me to be a herdsman! I am the chief overlord for Pharaoh. What makes you think I would stoop to be a keeper of animals?"

Abraham's jaw dropped at this outburst. Ishmael straightened up. His hands curled into fists, went to his hips. He glared into his father's wide eyes.

"I was disinherited by the birth of the insignificant son of Sarah, your dead wife. You now have a living wife, my mother. That makes me the son of your present wife and therefore, someone much more important than a goatherd."

Abraham reached toward his son; his voice thin but firm. "If you stayed you would never be just a goatherd. You are my son and would share with Isaac and me the tasks of being one of the leaders here."

Ishmael's gaze returned to his father, and he pulled his shoulders back. "In Egypt I share my power with no one. There, I am the law and I rule."

Abraham looked at his son. His voice once again firm and strong. "Do you think you would become the ruler here? I am not a ruler. I am an advisor, a helper, a guide. Have you forgotten all you learned of our customs and laws?"

Ismael waved an arm in dismissal at all he saw. "I don't give a fig for your ancient customs. This place needs someone to take charge. I have been away for years, and nothing has improved. Your paltry village will always be insignificant unless someone starts improving things."

Abraham could not believe what he was hearing. His ears burned with the insult and his heart ached. *Is this why you came back?*

A deep sigh filled the still air. "Ah. Now I think I understand. You did not come to see your aging father. You did not come to share memories of the happy times of your youth. You did not come with love and hope in your heart. You came with greed and ambition."

Ishmael turned to walk away.

Abraham barked. "Do not turn your back on me. Face me and hear my words."

Ishmael turned. His face twisted into a sneer. His eyes black pools of loathing.

"You came with malice and spite." Ishmael made a guttural sound, a snarl of disgust. "You are welcome to stay here as the son of my loins and you will be well looked after. But you can never be the heir to the blessing or the inheritance. They belong to Isaac. They always have and they always will. If you won't accept that, I don't know what else to say." Abraham bowed his head and covered his face with his trembling hands.

Ishmael snarled. "Now, you look at me, old man."

Abraham raised his head and tears traced rivers of pain down his cheeks.

"I came in expectation of change and found the same father who shamed my mother and rejected me. I don't understand her change of heart. She will regret her marriage before the sun brings its warmth again."

Abraham opened his mouth.

"No. Don't speak. Once again, I have heard your words of rejection. I am neither accepted nor wanted here. I will leave for Egypt, where I am respected for my wisdom and my power." He spat a curse on the ground and stormed off along the path.

Abraham sat motionless on the bench stunned and heart sore. He stroked the smooth wood, so lovingly shaped by Isaac. Suddenly, a chill went down his spine, and he wrapped his cloak around himself tightly. His eyes searched for the sacred mountain in the distance. Its peak white with winter snow. He raised his hands in confession.

"God of the mountain, hear me now. What Sarah and I sowed so long ago has born its fruit. Sown out of our impatience, we have reaped our harvest. The boy is not a bad seed. He is my lost child, now grown to a man. A man of false ambition. An angry man filled with bitterness. May he find peace in his soul, forgiveness in his heart, and happiness in his life in Egypt."

I am so very weary. I long for my tent where I can weep. But I must go up the mountain to the high altar and there kneel before my maker. May he have mercy on me.

He stood and looked to the mountain. Its peak veiled in a dark cloud. It was heavy with sorrow. Abraham spoke his agony.

"Ishmael is leaving. There seems to be no other solution. I hope the pain and sorrow of this visit will not touch those who remain. Keturah most of all, but also Isaac and Rebekah." He stood and with halting steps began to climb the hill.

Suddenly, Isaac was beside him. "I heard some of what my brother said, and I heard your prayer. It would be an honour if I could walk with you on this journey."

Abraham put his arm around his son and leaned heavily on him along each step of the hilly, twisting road.

Chapter Thirty-Six

The seasons rolled by, wet and cold, sunny, and hot. Winter and summer. Years went by and Rebekah's life spun past like the winter clouds and summer heat.

Once again, the rains were drenching the land. Tents and trees dripped water, paths and roads had rivulets running down them and the ground had turned to mud. The sky emerged each day heavy with clouds. They hung close to the ground and covered the hills in cloaks of grey. Rebekah knew that this season was necessary for the survival of the people. Without the rain, there would be no food, and that was unthinkable.

She and Deborah did their best to keep busy with small weaving projects, mending, and sorting and cleaning in the tent. They tried to sing as they worked, but it seemed harder to sing without the sunshine.

Another moon time came, and Rebekah passed it in the woman's tent. It hurt her when former friends would no longer sit with her, and when all talking stopped as she tried to join a group. It didn't matter to her if it was pity or scorn behind her rejection. The pain was the same. No one wanted to sleep near her, and she curled up in her misery in a dark corner.

They act as if my barren womb would contaminate them if they talked to me. I have heard their whispers. Some are planning to take my place as Isaac's wife. Their former friendship turned to bitter bile in my throat.

When she finally could leave, she walked home sadly. She didn't care that she was very wet because she didn't have her warm cloak. It would be good to be at home and have Deborah fussing over her. Deborah was there when she entered their tent. She had towels warming near the fire and a goblet of hot mint tea ready.

Rebekah sat by the fire and dried her wet hair. "I know we need rain to make the crops grow, and that we would starve without it, but it gets so dreary."

"It should be over soon. There was a glimmer of pink sky tonight as the sunset."

"It can't come too soon. There is a visit I must make, and it is impossible now. Paths are so muddy, and everything is dripping water."

They spent the evening around the fire talking about the year just past. So many things had happened. They wondered what the summer would bring. Rebekah yawned and suggested they go to bed and try to get a good night's rest.

"Maybe it will be clear in the morning, and you can make your visits. Anyway, sleep well tonight."

Deborah left one small lamp burning in the corner and curled up on her mat. The warm dark was comforting, and they were soon both sleeping calmly.

Rebekah woke early and went outside. During the night, the rain had stopped, and the winds were at work to dry out the sodden world. *Perhaps I can go today to see Abraham.*

They had their simple breakfast and soon had the tent tidy, and their things put away. Deborah looked outside and saw that Abraham was stretching at his tent door and waved at her.

"Who are you waving at?"

"Abraham is standing outside testing the weather."

Rebekah grabbed her warm cloak, and without a word, hurried outside. She waved to Abraham and began to walk slowly and carefully up the still muddy, slippery path to his tent. He waited and welcomed her.

"I was hoping you weren't going to fall, for I didn't know how I could help you. But here you are. Come in. We have hot tea ready and hope you will share a cup with us."

"Thank you, I will. If you have some time, I would like very much to stay and talk to you. It is important."

"Good. Good. We have nothing but time these days." He drew more cushions to the fire, and they sat as Keturah brought tea. As they sipped their drinks, they spoke of mundane things. The weather, who was ill, the state of the land and the fields.

Keturah gathered up the dishes. "If you wish to speak with Abraham, I will go into the far corner, and I won't intrude or hear your voices from there."

Rebekah touched Keturah's arm. "Please stay. You may well have some wisdom to offer, and I would welcome your opinion."

She sat down again, across the fire from both Abraham and Rebekah. The silence was awkward, but no one was sure how to start. Abraham gave a small cough. "I have felt that for some time now, my daughter, you have been unhappy. We will hear what you have to say with respect and love."

Rebekah looked at him, her eyes filled with tears. "This is extremely hard for me. I feel ashamed and embarrassed. But I do need your advice. I have just come from the woman's tent. Each month, it is painful for me to go there and know that I am either pitied or feared. I sit alone. Only a few will speak to me, and I am never invited to join in anything." She swallowed her tears and wiped her eyes. "Sarah must have experienced the same treatment. How did she bear it all those years?"

"I know it was difficult for her, but I did hear her say that in spite of that, she received a sense of peace and blessing by going each time." Abraham smiled weakly.

"I understand that. It is true for me too. Isaac and I have been married for a long time, and by now there should be children at my knees." She was holding a small piece of cloth in her hands and was twisting and wringing it with every word. "Isaac needs a son, and I am failing my duty. I have done all that I can. I have spent countless days and nights trying to think how I have offended the gods, but I am unable to name my wrongs. I've made burnt offerings, eaten pomegranate seeds, and drunk the juice. I have prayed to El Shaddai, the mighty one, and to the breasted one."

"And have you found the little goddess Inanna that Sarah had?"

Abraham's question surprised her. "You knew about the idol?"

"Sarah told me many years later. While I do not approve, I can understand. I am not the one to judge the way others deal with such disappointment."

"But it was no more use than all the potions that the midwives gave me to drink. They were foul."

Abraham chuckled gently. "That's what Sarah said."

Keturah raised her hand. "May I speak?"

Rebekah smiled and nodded.

"I am just a woman who has lived a long time and seen many things. I am not a priest or a leader, but I do not believe that this is your fault. Things happen in life, good things, and terrible things. Some are caused by what we do, but most just happen. The world unfolds in ways we do not understand and cannot explain. This may not make it easier, but I hope you will stop feeling guilty."

Rebekah looked at Abraham. *What will he say to this? It sounds right to me, but it is not what I have been taught.*

Abraham smiled at Keturah. "There are many mysteries in life. I have no answer to them. As Keturah suggests, at times, we just learn to live with the unknown."

"I came to ask you, Abraham, how did you and Sarah deal with this weighty unknown for so long? How did your love survive the emptiness you must have felt? And what changed? How did she finally have Isaac?"

"Do you have time for a story?"

"Of course, if you have a story to share."

"Sarah, like you, felt great pain as time passed and there was no child. And as you know, we tried to solve the matter. You have been a witness to the anguish that path brought to all of us. Then one day three visitors appeared at our tent. They told me that by the time they returned, in the following summer, we would have a son. Sarah did not take this promise very well. She raged against the messengers and against god. After she expressed her dismay, I persuaded her that if we were to have a child, we had a pleasant evening ahead of us."

Rebekah blushed and looked at her hands, and Keturah gave a jolly laugh. She stood and passed the dish of grapes. “I don’t have any pomegranates. But have some grapes.”

“Earlier, days earlier, Sarah asked to speak to me about something that was troubling her. Briefly she said that when we were in my tent, she found it difficult to relax completely as we lay together. The surroundings were just not right. She then shyly asked if we could meet in her tent. I understood that she thought she would be more comfortable in her own place.”

Rebekah’s eyes grew big and round, and she clasped her hands at her breast.

“So that day, after the strangers left, we went to Sarah’s tent. And in time, Isaac arrived.”

“But it is always in the husband’s tent.”

“It wasn’t that night, and it hasn’t always been that way for me since. He grinned at Keturah. There is no law, only custom. And when custom fails, change something.”

“Rebekah.” Keturah’s gentle voice spoke. “I see a glint of something in your eyes.”

“Isaac’s tent has animal horns, traps, arrows, bows, spears, all kinds of things. They make me think of many things, none of which are warm, soft, or loving. Do you suppose?” She let the words hang in the air.

Keturah reached for her hand. “I suppose you need to think about this, and maybe, just maybe, you need to talk to your husband.”

They sat in comfortable silence.

“If you will excuse me, I think I will go home now. Thank you.”

In a daze, she put on her cloak and walked out into a fine mist.

All day she thought about the things that Keturah and Abraham said. *It makes sense. It gives me a glimmer of the possibility of a child. This land is called Canaan. It means a place of hope. I came to this valley filled with hope for the future. I was so confident.*

Deborah got their meal ready, and they sat together and talked of little things. Rebekah struggled, wondering how much to tell her faithful companion. *If I can't talk to Deborah, how will I ever talk to Isaac?* She took a deep breath.

"I talked to father and Keturah today?"

"Am I to ask what? Do you want to tell me?"

Rebekah reached out and hugged her. As she hugged her friend, she held on to the small hope that fluttered in her breast.

"I talked about my discomfort in the moon tent and asked how Sarah dealt with it. They spoke of customs and how things need to change over time. I learned that Abraham went to Sarah's tent, and it was there that she conceived Isaac."

Deborah said nothing but leaned closer to Rebekah and took her hand. *She needs to feel my support and love.*

"For a long time, I have felt uncomfortable in the tent of my husband. I answer his lamp when he calls for me, but it isn't right for me. I think Abraham's confession may give me the answer to my unfruitful state. What if all that is wrong is my discomfort? Could a change of tent for our times together make that much difference? Can it be that simple?"

"I don't know, dear one, but if you think it could, then do it. It is simple to do, but can you ignore the customs of our people?"

"Abraham told me that he and Sarah did. Why would he say that if not to give us permission?"

"I am sure you are right. Shall I go and tell Isaac you request his presence at the late day meal?"

"That would be helpful. I'll start cleaning up here. Then we can make sure the tent is perfect."

Deborah returned in a very short time. "He seemed surprised but said he would come at sundown. Now let's get things ready, and then we can get you ready."

The sun was a ball of orange fire in the western sky as Isaac approached Rebekah's tent. She met him at the door with a hesitant smile.

"I have come as you asked. Is there anything wrong?"

"Not really, Isaac, but I do need to talk to you about something important. We will have our meal and then talk."

Deborah served them fresh fish with lemon, barley bread, and vegetables. Wine and honey cakes with cheese and dried figs soaked in wine finished the meal. Deborah cleaned up and quietly left the tent.

"That was a wonderful meal. Thank you for all the trouble you went to."

"You are welcome, Isaac. I cook for you so seldom that I wanted this to be special."

"It was. It certainly was. Now what is it that we need to talk about?"

"It is very difficult for me, so please be patient as I try to tell you my concern."

He took her hand and stroked it soothingly. "I will listen to what you have to say."

After a long pause, she spoke softly. "I have mentioned that I am not eager to go to the women's tent for my moon time. I feel both judged and scorned because I am not yet holding a baby in my arms. We have been married a long time and I am failing you."

Isaac started to speak, but Rebekah placed her finger on his lips.

"I know what you are going to say, and I am grateful that you have never mentioned my empty womb, but you must have a son. I have done everything women have suggested, herb, potions, incantations to the gods, foods to help conception, everything. It has made no difference. And so, I went to Father Abraham for advice."

"You talked to father! Did he listen with a kind heart?"

"He was wonderful. In fact, he told me the story of your beginning. Sarah had an uncomfortable feeling in his tent. She suggested her tent would be a better place for them to lie together. Soon after, she knew she was carrying a child."

"Does that have something to do with us?"

"I think so. Your tent is the place for a man to feel proud and lordly. But weapons and animal pelts are not so good for my peace of mind. For me, your tent speaks of war and killing. It is not a comfortable place for me to relax and enjoy our time together." She took a sip of wine from the goblet she held. A deep sigh followed. "Here in my tent, I feel at peace. Flowers, scented oils, and dancing flames make me feel calm and tranquil. Here, where I am relaxed and at home, perhaps I could conceive and fulfill my duty. I know it is against custom, but that is why your father told me the story. He was giving his blessing and saying sometimes custom needs to be changed."

Isaac stood and helped Rebekah to her feet. "I think I hear an invitation."

"We are alone, Isaac, and just over there is my sleeping place." He took her in his arms and held her close. Releasing her, he led her to the waiting bed.

The next morning, Isaac sat beside a freshly glowing fire. He was softly humming. Rebekah stretched languidly. She looked across the room and smiled. Isaac returned a rakish grin. "Good morning sleepy head. I have water heating but felt I didn't dare go looking for anything. Deborah would have my hide if I messed up her cooking things."

Rebekah giggled and beckoned to him. He crossed the room in two long strides and sat on the floor beside her. He placed a kiss on his finger and then touched her lips. "If I can make an observation, I would suggest that my lovely wife was most definitely at ease last night."

"I can't explain how different I felt. Please can we come here often to be together?"

"If last night is a clue to our making love here instead of my tent, we may never go to my tent again."

Rebekah giggled again. "Just think of all the oil you will save."

"True, but you will burn much, keeping a lamp by your door for me."

Rebekah blushed crimson.

"That's right. I remember how many years ago? You suggested a lamp at your door to invite me to your tent."

"You didn't take me seriously then, did you? I get what I want, my dear, and right now I think I want some food."

Isaac laughed and pulled her to her feet and held her in a sweet embrace. Neither noticed the flap at Deborah's tent open, then drop back into its place.

Chapter Thirty-Seven

Isaac left after they had a meal together. As he left, the day showed promise in the east. The sky was glowing with light against the distant hills. *The rain must be over for this season. Now comes the busy time of plowing and planting. I need to talk to father and work out my responsibilities. He needs my support, and as Rebekah said; I need to get to know him better.*

Gershom met him at his tent and a simple breakfast was waiting for him. “I trust you slept well, Isaac.”

Isaac knew he was baiting him, wanting to tease him for being away all night. “If you are thinking I wasted the night in some shady way, I did not. It is not your concern, but I spent the night with my wife. We had food together this morning. Now today we are going to clean up this tent and make it presentable.”

“Of course. I meant no harm. What do you want done in here?”

Isaac instructed him to get rid of all the trophies of war and all the animal hides that were piled about. Rugs, mats, and bedding were to be cleaned, the floor swept, and the outer tent walls brushed till all the dust and sand were gone. Gershom looked stunned but made no comment.

“I am going to see father. If you have any questions, try to figure it out or wait till I return.” He turned and walked up the path.

Gershom watched him leave and muttered. “I guess his carefree days are over. He is acting like a married man. It is time, I suppose. What brought this about, I wonder.” He set to work to do what Isaac asked.

At his father’s tent, Isaac heard voices and clapped at the doorway.

“Who is it?”

"It is I, Isaac. May I come in and talk?"

"Of course, son, enter."

They greeted each other warmly, and Keturah offered a drink. Father and son sat facing each other. There was a good feeling in the room.

Isaac broke the silence. "It looks to be a pleasant day, and I think the rain is over. It will be planting season and I know that I have not been doing my duty. We need to think about what my responsibilities will be, and I need to learn my future role. I have come to ask for your direction and your help."

Abraham and Keturah shared a smile and Abraham turned and smiled at his son.

"The last couple of seasons you have been preparing. Your writing and reading of the symbols and signs have improved a great deal, and I am pleased. But keep working at that. I have scribes, as you know, but they need to be supervised. As my sight fails, and it will, you will need to do that. Might as well start now and get the scribes used to your ways."

"I must admit it is more interesting than I thought it would be."

"That is good, but a lot of work must be done, whether one enjoys it or not. Now, what else do you need to discuss?"

"I know that I have neglected my sacred duties to El Shaddai. Today I start correcting that. I will go with you to the altars on the shoulders of the mountain and we will worship there together."

Abraham smiled from ear to ear. "I have waited a long time for those words. I hoped that marriage would help you to become a man, and I was sure Rebekah would be a good influence if you cared enough."

"Indeed, she has. I have come to love her dearly, and her happiness is all I care about. Hers and, of course, yours too. What else do you see that I need to do?"

"We will share the supervision and oversight of the flocks and the crops. But there is one more thing. It is important that you get to know the people of our clan. Know them by name, and what they do. Learn of their hopes and their cares. Not just the men, but their wives and children."

"How do I do that? There are so many."

"It will take a long time. But I think Rebekah can help. She knows the women. When she walks in the lanes and paths, and goes to the market, go with her. Listen to her as she visits the tents, and find something to ask a question about, or compliment them on. Start by learning the names of the men. The rest will follow as you talk to them."

"Will I ever be as wise a leader as you are, father?"

"As wise as I am, and much wiser. You will need new ways to do some things. Always consider new ideas, changes, and modifications. You don't need to always follow what you hear but think about the ideas and then decide your actions."

"Changes such as spending a tender night in your wife's tent?"

Abraham chucked. "I don't know what you are talking about." But his warm smile glowed with understanding and approval.

Later, Isaac found Rebekah by the river. "I've had a long talk with father about my responsibilities. He had a couple of suggestions. An important one I think was that I should get to know the people I live and work with. I was ashamed to admit that I didn't know how. He said that you could help me do that."

"I can and I will. I am going to the market soon. Why don't you come with me? You can carry the basket. I'll tell Deborah she can have a rest."

"Just tell me what to do."

"You know what to do. When I tell the merchants you are my husband, greet them, make some remarks about their wares. They will try to give you something, but politely refuse anything except an offer to taste something they sell. You can always find some excuse that does not insult them."

"How do you remember all the names?"

"We will do a few each time. And we can practise on the walk home. I am so pleased that you are doing this. It will be important later."

Rebekah spoke to Deborah, who looked skeptical, but nodded. Rebekah picked up her shopping basket and her purse with her money. "Let's go. I am ready."

They walked to the market, and Isaac followed a little behind. He was a bit overwhelmed by the noise and the press of people. He never went to the market but sent a servant. *I suppose father has been paying all these years. What a lazy good for nothing I have been.* The basket soon was filled with things Rebekah bought. Salt, some herbs, a clay dish, and some fish from the man she called David. He tried to give her the fish, but she refused, and he gave her a pretty shell, which she accepted.

On the walk home, she questioned him about the people he had met and was delighted that he remembered most of the names and what they sold.

"If you have time, you could come with me the next time I take a walk down the lanes where the people live. It is good to see them in their homes. It helps me to remember them."

"I would like that. I have so much to learn. But I have a beautiful and kind teacher."

"Your teacher would be pleased if you joined her for a meal of fresh fish later."

"I will see you at sunset and thank you for an interesting and profitable afternoon."

The sun was almost out of sight when Isaac came carrying a cornflower bud. She was surprised he found one so soon after the rain but took it with a smile. When Isaac came to the table, the shell from the fish seller was at the centre and nestled in its curves was the blue flower. With the lamp on the table and the dishes, it looked very attractive.

Isaac said the blessing, and they enjoyed the food. Deborah served them but stayed in the background. Isaac looked around the space and he liked what he saw. *I see what Rebekah meant when she said this was a gentle place. It is full of beauty and warmth. I am a lucky man and so glad that Eliezar found her.*

They sat together, enjoying the food and each other's company, until the stars filled the sky. The moon was a silver curve against the black sky.

"Isaac, tomorrow will be the dark of the moon and I will go to the woman's house to welcome the new moon."

Isaac groaned. "Oh no. I'll have to eat Jacob's cooking. After this, I can't look forward to that."

They laughed together in comfortable closeness.

Chapter Thirty-Eight

For some time, Keturah had been concerned about Abraham. During the rainy, windy, winter, he was always cold. They moved their bed close to the fire and Keturah was up many times in the night to add more fuel. It helped, but she knew that she needed her sleep and she needed a better solution.

In Egypt, we had houses, mud-brick houses. If Abraham had a house, the winds could be kept away and the heat from the fire would linger. I don't know why we still live in tents.

She walked to Rebekah's tent and asked if she could talk to her and to Isaac. Deborah went to get him while the women set out food.

As he entered the tent, he looked worried. "Is something wrong? What has happened?"

"There is no emergency. Keturah just needs to talk with us. Let's sit and hear what she needs."

Keturah smiled at the three people seated around the low table. They were now her family and she loved them dearly. Rebekah's table was adorned with a candle and some green branches. It was so like Rebekah, calm and beautiful. *But she looks sad. I hope I can find a way to help Abraham and maybe Rebekah as well.*

Deborah passed the food.

Keturah cleared her throat."You know that I love Abraham, and it is that love that brings me here. During the wet winter, he was cold and shivering much of the time. He doesn't sleep well and neither do I. All night I am up adding fuel to our fire. We have moved our bed closer to the fire, but he still suffers from the damp cold."

Heads nodded in understanding. "What do you suggest?" Rebekah's voice showed her concern for the beloved head of their clan.

"In Egypt we lived in clay brick houses. A house would be warmer than a tent. Why have no houses been built? I know you were once nomads, but you have lived here for many years."

Rebekah turned to Isaac. "I don't know, do you?"

"I can't think of a reason except habit. We were always on the move, so we needed tents.

"You can't pick up a house and drag it with you. But we are settled here, perhaps permanently." He shrugged his shoulders.

"That is what I thought. So why don't we build my husband a house?"

Isaac frowned. "I have no idea how we could persuade him."

Deborah had been quietly listening. *I have no right to speak, but I think I have a clever idea that might work.* She took a deep breath. "May I speak?"

"Of course, you may." Rebekah smiled.

She looked at Rebekah. "You have not seen your father for a long time. If you invited him for a visit, he could not be expected to stay in a tent. We would have to build him a house worthy of his stature. Later Abraham could be persuaded that it was foolish to leave a house empty for the wild animals to ruin."

They all began to talk at once.

"Wonderful idea."

"A house of stone, or a house of clay bricks?"

"Who knows how to build a house?"

The chatter died away as words turned to thoughts.

Keturah broke the silence. "There are house builders in Hebron and all the supplies we would need. They would be happy to work for Isaac, and Abraham would pay the bills. We just must decide on stone or bricks."

Isaac chuckled. "Why don't we let Abraham decide? Especially since we have decided father will pay for it all. But the big question, is who will talk to father?"

"Since this is my idea, I will talk to him. I will suggest that Rebekah seems to be missing home and then it can grow from that. He seldom refuses me anything I ask. He will probably come to you to suggest it. You, of course, will be surprised and pleased."

The conspirators celebrated their plan with hugs and smiles and went their separate ways.

As the evening glow appeared in the sky, Keturah and Abraham sat outside their tent by a pleasant fire.

"You had a visit with Rebekah today. How is she?"

"Well, Abraham, I was upset by her lack of interest in things. She seemed to be sad."

"We all know she carries the burden of her empty womb."

"I asked her if she was happy here. She said she loved it here and enjoyed her life. I sensed some hesitation and asked her to explain."

"Did she tell you anything more?"

"She sat curled up like a suffering child. When she finally spoke, she admitted she missed her father very much. She has not seen him for years and knows he is getting old. I think she would like to see him before it is too late. I wonder if she could go to visit him."

"That would be possible, but do you think he would come for a visit if we invited him?"

"That is a wonderful idea, Abraham. We will never know unless we ask. Maybe we should say that you would like to see your nephew and leave Rebekah out of the invitation."

"You aren't suggesting we surprise her, are you?"

"Oh no. I don't think that is a good idea. We will just not tell her the real reason, at least not yet."

"I did not know that the woman I married was able to contrive such plans."

She laughed and patted his arm that was wrapped around her shoulders. They sat in the comfortable silence of people who knew each other well and shared many common interests.

For a time, they talked about the improving weather, and coming months of sun and warm days. Keturah spoke into the soft darkness. "It's a good time to invite a guest. The village always looks its best when the sun lights up the hills with a rosy glow. The shadows made by the tents always look peaceful. We will have to get them all freshened up for such an important visitor."

Abraham pulled his beard as he always did when thinking.

Keturah was about to ask him what he was thinking when he spoke.

"He is an important man back in Haran. A leading ruler in the whole area. I hear he has a wonderful big house made of stone, with many rooms and windows and doors. Our tents, even mine, will seem small and crowded to him."

"I think he will understand. He knows that we are nomads. Nomads who seem to be settled for good in this wonderful valley."

Abraham stirred the fire and added another log. "We have been here for a long time. I hadn't thought about it, but maybe we are now a settled people. Our wandering days could be over. Do you suppose it is time that we thought about building houses?"

Keturah had to stop herself from laughing with delight. "You might be right, Abraham. I know it is pleasant to live in a house, as I did in Egypt. And Rebekah grew up in the house of her mother. I am sure she remembers those days and the house of her parents."

"Do you think we could build a house to welcome Bethuel?"

"I don't know. How long does it take? Do we know how? Where would we get the stone?"

"There are stone cutters in Hebron. They even sell stones all ready for building. The stone is not a problem, and they have builders too. Yes, I think we can do it. Bethuel knows nothing of this, and we won't mention it to him. It will take him many weeks of travel to get here, and we could have a house built by the time he arrives. Tomorrow I will talk to Isaac, and Rebekah. We will do this, for I will not be shamed before my brother's son."

Keturah hugged her knees and her eyes shone with happiness. They sat watching the stars peep out from their hiding places in the sky. Abraham said the prayer at the end of the day, and after kissing Keturah, retired for the night.

She sat by the fire and thought of what she had done. *I have always had to manage my husband a little, but this is trickier than anything I've done before. But I think, no I know, it is the right thing to do. For Rebekah, and for him.*

As she stood to enter the tent, she noticed Isaac looking up at his father's tent. She waved to him and then raised her hand in a show of victory.

He waved back enthusiastically. The scheme was established. Tomorrow the planning would begin.

Chapter Thirty-Nine

Early in the morning, before Keturah was awake, Abraham was outside and walking along the riverbank. He went to his left, looking for the best place for the house he was going to build. *I don't see the perfect spot. Too damp, no trees, can't see the river.* He retraced his steps and then carried on along the bank in the other direction. He came to the curve in the river where he often sat to listen to the song the river sang. He walked around the curve. *I hardly ever go farther along the bank. I am always on the road as I walk this way.* His eyes followed the flow of the water. Right in front of him was a large, open clearing. Trees sheltered the space from the busy road. The view of the river was clear and open. The river flowed happily toward the faraway sea. "There it is. The perfect spot. I'll get Isaac and show him."

He moved to the road and looked to his right. Isaac was blowing on the coals to get a fire going. He cupped his hand to his mouth and called. "Isaac, come here. I have something to tell you. I have found the place for our new house."

"What are you doing out this early, old man? And what house are you talking about?"

Isaac listened with a straight face as Abraham explained the hope for a visit from Bethuel and the need for a house for him during his stay.

Abraham laughed. "I have been walking up and down the river, looking for the ideal site for the house, and I have found it. Come, tell me what you think."

He followed Abraham to the river's edge. *I guess food will have to wait.*

Water tumbled over stones and white necklaces adorned the ripples that circled the rocks. The bank was a ribbon of sand along the water's edge. Willows dipped their leaves into the water and their branches waved a welcome. The ground was level and looked like an empty plate, waiting for something to cover it.

"Yes, this is ideal, father. It is perfect. I can see a handsome house sitting right here."

"Pace it off, son. How big can we make the dwelling? And we need room for a courtyard in the centre, open to the river, and big enough for flowers and bushes."

Isaac paced it and his father made marks on a bit of skin. "Alright. Off to Hebron to talk to a builder and the brick mason."

"Stop, father. I have not had any food, and I see Keturah waving at us from your tent. First, we will eat and then go to the city. Come to my place when you are ready."

Abraham was so excited he could hardly take the time to eat. Keturah watched him and was delighted by his enthusiasm.

"Slow down, old man. You will get a stomach-ache from eating so fast. The city will wait for you."

After the meal, Abraham walked to the house of Rebekah and, with great enthusiasm and much arm waving and pointing, explained it all to Rebekah. Later, the two women watched their husbands as they walked toward the city. Just before he disappeared beyond the small rise in the road, Abraham turned and waved to Keturah.

The women passed the day working in their gardens. The winter rains and winds had done their worst, and there was damage to repair before any seeding could be done. They worked well together and before it was time to start the fire to cook the late meal, they sat with a warm drink and rested under the canopy at Abraham's tent.

Keturah let out a deep breath. "I wonder if I have done the right thing by tricking Abraham into building a house for himself."

"Sometimes I think that husbands need a compassionate helpmate. Abraham doesn't want to admit that the years are piling up, and he needs to accept some assistance now."

"Do you think our children will need to handle us as we get older?"

Rebekah didn't answer.

"I am sorry. I didn't think. Please forgive me."

"There is nothing to forgive. I don't expect people to have to think about every word they say for fear of offending me. I am coming to terms, that like Sarah, I may wait a long time for a child."

"You are very understanding and forgiving. In many ways, you remind me of Sarah. You have the same gentle nature, kind and considerate. But there is a strong core within you. Just like the cedar tree. You bend but you do not break."

"I have learned that Sarah watched Abraham carefully. He was crafty at times and inconsiderate of her. Isaac might do well to watch me in the same way. I have been used to getting my own way ever since I was a child. Old habits stay with us, I think."

"Thinking of your parents, you must be looking forward to seeing them."

"Father yes. We were very close. Mother, no. Laban was her favourite, and I was just someone she had to take care of. We have always had a troubled relationship."

"Parent and child feelings are often hard work. When I think of the discontent I caused Ishmael, I cannot judge anyone."

"No one is perfect. Come, it is time to get our fires started for cooking. But I admit I have no idea when our men will return. They were so excited, and father seemed years younger. This will give him something to look forward to. It will be good for him."

"I agree. I think they will be late for the meal, so why don't we all eat here? We can get the meal ready together. I would like to spend time with you, and this seems a good way."

"I'd like that. Let's get busy."

All was almost ready when they saw the men coming along the path. Rebekah called to Isaac. He waved, and they came to the tent.

Both men started to talk at once. Keturah covered her ears and spoke. "Go and wash up for the meal. You can tell us when we have eaten."

They sat around the fire. The younger couple on the grass, the older ones on stools. Isaac politely asked what the women had done, and that conversation was lively and lasted until the food was gone.

Abraham could hardly contain himself during the meal. He fidgeted and squirmed. The women smiled when he helped clean up to get that chore done quickly.

Deborah passed out clay goblets of wine and then waited.

"You tell them, father. This is your plan."

Three pairs of eyes smiled around the circle. Abraham never noticed.

"We had a very successful day. We have hired a man to oversee the work, under my watchful eye, of course." Abraham grinned with delight. "The stones for the walls have been ordered and flat stones for the courtyard. The house will be one room high with a sturdy wooden beam ceiling. A room will be added on the roof for sleeping on hot days and times of celebration."

Isaac interrupted. "Not a real room, just a canvas roof over poles. And the masons persuaded us to use stones, not mud bricks. They said the bricks would not last through our rainy season."

"The first workers will come tomorrow to measure and to level the ground, ready for the building to begin."

Again, Isaac spoke, his excitement evident. "I suggested that we put a stone floor in the courtyard. The other rooms will have the usual hard earthen floors." There was a lot of talk about the merits of stone or earthen floors. But all agreed in the end.

Abraham chuckled. "I only agreed to the stone courtyard, son, because you are like your mother. You can't let an idea go. If I hadn't, we would still be there talking. But I admit, it will be something for the villagers to talk about all summer."

Rebekah declared. "I think they will talk about the house for years to come, not just this summer."

"They will gather here to watch, like bees flock to the honeycomb. father." Isaac was so delighted that even his voice smiled as he spoke.

Keturah patted her husband's arm. "It sounds wonderful, Abraham. I can't wait to see it as it grows out of the ground."

Rebekah giggled. They looked at her. "I suggest that the house needs to be tested before father arrives. The one who is looking after the work should have that honour."

Around the circle, eyes met again, and they clapped. From Abraham came words filled with pride and joy. "If you insist."

Isaac turned to Rebekah and took her hand. "I have sent a message to your father. There was a caravan of traders leaving for Haran tomorrow. Your father should know in a few weeks."

Tears filled her eyes.

Abraham's voice was filled with emotion. "It will be good for us to see Bethuel. I will welcome my nephew and his family."

Always practical, Isaac was counting on his fingers. "We will have about two moons to get the work done. We can do it. We will just have to hire extra workers. Our labourers need to get our crops in the earth, so we will need more people to get this done."

The talk continued until the moon sailed high in the sky. It was so late, when they were ready for their beds, that Rebekah and Isaac stayed and slept in the tent of Father Abraham.

Chapter Forty

Laban had gone to the market, not to buy anything but to look for some entertainment. He hoped to find a gambling game in progress as he walked up and down the little lanes, oblivious to the colours, the sounds, and the tempting aromas. He stopped, for he thought he heard his father's name. He listened more carefully and at the next stall, a dusty traveller was asking for the house of Bethuel, son of Nahor.

In his most commanding voice, Laban spoke. "Who is asking for the house of the great leader, Bethuel?"

The untidy man bowed and replied. "I am but a humble messenger, seeking Bethuel to give him a message from Hebron."

"Who sends the message?"

"The great sheik of Canaan, Abraham," and he bowed low.

"I am the son of Bethuel. Give me the message."

"My instructions are to tell it to the ear of Bethuel and no one else. Please direct me to his house." Once again, he bowed.

"I am his son; you can give it to me. I will give it to my father."

"I am but a humble servant. I must obey the orders given to me. If you cannot help me, I shall ask another."

Laban thought about teaching this insolent servant a lesson but remembered his humiliation by Eliezar, another servant of Abraham, and thought better of it. "Then follow me and see that you keep up. I am in a hurry."

Laban strode away and was surprised that the ruffian kept a few paces behind but matched his step with no trouble. *At least he knows his place.*

They entered the courtyard, and the stranger knelt in respect. Laban shouted at a servant to get Bethuel and to do it quickly. The servant scampered away and Bethuel soon appeared.

"Well, Laban, what kind of trouble are you in this time?" He stopped when he saw a man kneeling on the ground at Laban's feet.

"Father, I found this scoundrel in the market asking for you. I questioned him, but he was insolent and would not answer or give me the message he is bringing us."

"Begging your pardon, great one. The message is for the ears of Bethuel, son of Nahor."

Bethuel dismissed Laban with a wave of his hand. "You may go and continue whatever trouble you are planning to do today." To a servant he said, "We will sit on this bench. Bring our guest water to wash and then bring us wine and food."

"Laban. Why are you still here? The message is for me. Be gone."

Laban skulked away. While the stranger refreshed himself, Bethuel asked about his journey.

"My travel was safe and swift. When one travels with the great trader, Caleb, one is in good company."

"So, I have heard. I travel little myself. Now, tell me who sent you with a message for me?"

"I come from the house of Abraham, son of Terah. I bring greetings from him and from his son Isaac and his wife, Rebekah."

Bethuel leaned toward the guest, "Rebekah. My daughter. Tell me, is she well?"

"She is well and happy in her new home. Her tent is prominent in the village, and she lives comfortably, surrounded by beautiful things. She is well cared for by her faithful servant Deborah."

"And her children? Do I have many grandsons?"

"I have no news except that all is well and that you are invited to come and visit your daughter. She asks to see her father and to greet him in her new home."

"A visit. I would see my child once more before I die." He paused for a few moments and noisily blew his nose. "When you have rested, return to Caleb and inquire if we might journey with him on his return to Hebron. He will be well paid for his trouble."

In his great booming voice, he called for Ruth, his wife. At once, she came running.

As I thought, you were listening behind that great mulberry bush. I should put a stool there for you to rest your weary bones while you eavesdrop.

"What is wrong, Bethuel? Are you ill?"

As he always did, he answered in his most patient voice. "I have a message from Rebekah. She is well and happy. We are invited to visit her and her husband in Hebron. I am looking into travel plans this very moment."

"Go to see Rebekah? Travel all that way? If she is well and happy, that is all I need to know. Why would I leave my home and live like a peasant to learn what I already know?"

"Do you have no desire to see your daughter? What if she has children?"

"I suppose that if Laban was there to care for me, I might think about it."

"Laban will not be going. It is time he proved he can manage my business here. This will be a good opportunity for him to show me that he has the ability to look after things while I am away."

"If he stays here, I stay here."

"If that is what you choose, then I shall go alone with only my faithful servant, David. He and I will make the arrangements and be ready to leave with the caravan."

The next days were busy ones for Bethuel. He and David packed clothes for them to wear. They chose elegant tunics and cloaks, well made by skilled artisans, but without being too ostentatious. It would not be right to humiliate his host. "I do not know what to expect and must be careful. I want to show my importance to my uncle, but I must not offend him and his house."

There were gifts for the family in Canaan. Bolts of fine linen, delicately painted pottery, and gifts of jewelry for Rebekah and Deborah and for other women they would meet. They carefully chose the camels that would carry them and their goods. Bethuel paid for the trip and for the food and a large tent which would be provided by Caleb. A fast runner was hired to join a small company of soldiers who were going to Hebron. They would travel faster than the caravan and he would carry an acceptance of the invitation to the household of Abraham.

The evening before his departure, Ruth sought out Bethuel and reproached him. "How can you leave me without anyone to care for me and without concern for my well-being?"

This familiar litany was very tiresome to Bethuel. *I married a child, and she has never grown up. My own doing as I have given in to her every whim.* His voice was filled with frustration as he spoke. "Ruth, my child. You will not be alone; all your servants are here to look after you and Laban as well."

"You will be killed before you have gone far. How will I live when I am destitute?"

"A poor widow you will never be unless that son of ours mistreats you and robs you of all that I have worked to provide for you. I travel with a large and well armed caravan. We will go the fast, safe route through the Jezerel Valley. I will return to you in due time."

She sniffled and wiped her eyes with her hand.

"Ruth, as my wife, you can come with me. To stay is your choice. Do not pout and try to make me stay by claiming falsely that you are being abandoned. If you change your mind, you will be welcome to join me. Just be ready on time, as I cannot delay my departure."

On a lovely cool morning with just enough breeze to make travel pleasant, the trade caravan lined up near the house of Bethuel. His camels were standing in a grumbling line, ready to begin the journey.

Ruth stood forlornly and Bethuel took her in his arms. "This is just farewell, not goodbye. I need a new heavy cloak before the rains come. Perhaps you could oversee the making of a new one for me. It will pass the time for you."

The distraction worked. "I will make a cloak of deep blue wool. And it will have a hood attached to cover your hair." And she was gone to find wool and a weaver.

He turned to his son. "Laban. We have had some rough patches along the way, but you are my son and my heir. Someday all this will be yours. While I am gone, it is in your care and keeping. I place my holdings in your hands and trust you to do your best. Be cautious, be careful, but above all, be kind toward all whom you deal with. But especially toward your mother. Gentle, loving kindness will keep all running smoothy."

He reached out to shake the hand of his son and was shocked when Laban grabbed him in a bear hug. "Go in safety, father. Give my sister my warm-hearted greetings. And I will await your safe return. Thank you for your trust. I will not fail you."

Through tear-filled eyes, Bethuel mounted his camel and gave Caleb a shout that he was ready to begin.

Amid waving scarves and cheers from the staff, with a shout from the drover of the caravan, the cavalcade began the journey to the distant valleys of Canaan, the land that promised hope to all.

Chapter Forty-One

The caravan led by Caleb was moving quickly. As was the custom, they stopped only for a brief rest when the sun rode hot and high in the sky. The first meal of the day, usually at sunup, was a hearty one, for they did not eat again until the stop for the night.

By the third day, Bethuel was walking beside the camel for a change and a chance to use his legs, which tended to become stiff and sore if he rode all day. "David, good friend, now I remember why I had stopped travelling. It is a task for younger folk than I am."

"It is a long time to ride on the back of a camel, swaying to and fro, with his rocking gait. But it is also a very long way to walk and I am glad to ride in the heat."

"I am not complaining, just stating a fact."

"Well, here is another fact. We will soon be turning south and entering the river valley. The servants tell me it is a beautiful road, well travelled, smooth and easy for the camels and for the riders."

"I have heard that it is a wonderful journey, hills and mountains on the west, the river on the east and a good road all the way."

"Caleb says it is safe as well."

"There are towns where he will stop to trade. How long does he stay in each place?"

"I don't know for sure. I think it depends on how good business is. As little as one day, or as long as a week. They expect good trading as they will be the first traders after the rain. People will need many things, so there will be much talk and long discussions."

"I don't want to spend weeks on the road just to listen to traders bickering. What else could we do?"

"I will ask some questions and see if there is a way that might save precious time."

That evening when they stopped, David spent all the daylight hours with the workers, soldiers, and Caleb. Bethuel was snoring loudly when he returned to their tent. He let his master sleep.

In the morning, over their breakfast, he shared what he had learned. "It would be possible for our party to go on without the traders. But Caleb does not recommend that we do."

"Did he say why?"

"Normally the road is well travelled and safe. But things can happen. He didn't give details but suggested we would be much safer travelling with him. He has a reputation, a large party and well-trained desert fighters. He does not expect to stay more than one day in each town, so we would gain little and stand to lose everything."

"I have heard rumours of large gangs of cut-throat thieves in wait of easy prey. I guess that would be us if we went on alone."

David merely nodded.

"I want to arrive alive and with my goods. We will travel with Caleb as planned."

A huge sigh of relief was David's only answer.

"If you felt that concerned, why not try to change my mind?"

"You are the master, and I hoped you would see the wisdom in your plan. But if you had persisted, I would have objected strongly."

"When do we reach a town?"

"Laish is the first and we reach it late tomorrow."

They arrived at Laish and the traders went into the town. Bethuel stayed away from the town and made his camp at the bend of the river. As he sat by the river, he wondered if Rebekah might have stopped here. *I must remember to ask her.*

He slept well and was awake early and ready to begin the rest of the long journey. Each day was a repeat of the previous day, uneventful, and Bethuel wondered if he could have gone on alone. David spent some evenings with the troop of men that Caleb employed to travel with him. He became friends with their captain.

After talking with his new friend, David shared with Bethuel that during that day, the travelling caravan had been watched by men hiding in the woods.

"I guess we made the right decision. I have always tried to follow reason and logic, not emotion. If I had ignored my own guidelines, we could have been in trouble. David, I trust your instincts. Don't hesitate if you think I am making a poor decision."

"Thank you for your confidence. I have always felt we make a good team, you and I. I hope you are satisfied with our progress. We are in the last few days of the journey."

David retired to his rest and Bethuel stayed by the fire.

Soon I shall see my beloved daughter. I hope that all is well with her, and her marriage has been agreeable. He walked to his tent and paused to look at the stars. *It is comforting to know that Becca looks up at these same stars each night.*

He entered his tent and stretched out on the mat. He blew out his lamp and said to the smoke. "It will take a special man to deal with the strong, independent woman my daughter was raised to be. It will be good to look deep into her eyes. I hope I see only happiness there."

Chapter Forty-Two

The whole village was excited. Abraham realized at once that he was going to have to control the staring onlookers watching the workers on the house. He spoke with Isaac.

"I will put up a barrier at the east and west edges to keep people back. It could be dangerous, especially for curious children. Do you think we will need a guard or two at night?"

"I wish we didn't have to do that, but it is a good idea. We need to protect our property and the curious. Consider it done."

Isaac put up posts and strung a rope between them, and he had thorn bushes brought and made a thorny hedge between the posts and around the rope. "That should keep the nosy folk and interested watchers away. A couple of guards will take care of any who might want to steal bricks."

The men from Hebron, led by Baruch, the overseer, were there with the sun the next morning and worked till the sun slipped away in the west. Abraham was paying extra for the job to be finished quickly. Any workers who could be spared were taken from their jobs in the pastures, the vineyards, and the stables. Baruch was pleased with Abraham's men. They were diligent workers and followed orders without question. He was also happy at the time when the men took a rest time during the heat of the day, and women came with water and fruit and sometimes bread and cheese. This did not happen in other jobs. *Abraham is a man of honour. I will do the best work that I can for him. There will be no shortcuts, no poor workmanship. This will be a house that stands forever.*

The ground was levelled, and the outline of the house marked that first morning. The rest of the day was spent setting out the first layer to establish the size. This foundation was of stone cut and shaped in Hebron. It made a strong first layer. All day, donkey carts clattered back and forth from the city carrying the stones for the walls. By sunset, the outer edge of the walls could be seen. It was going to be a house fit for a great ruler.

Baruch set up a station to mix mortar. It was at the edge of the river where the clay and sand were available. Straw chopped fine was mixed in to make it stronger. Baruch requested women to cut the straw. Abraham was firm. "The women have more work than usual, carrying water and fruit to the workers. I will not ask our wives and daughters to chop straw for mortar. Hire extra workers from the city."

Many youth and children gathered at the thorn fence to watch. Isaac took time to talk to them and explain what the workers were doing. It made them feel important and a part of the project. Isaac knew he could count on them to report any suspicious activity.

At the heat of the day, Abraham went to his tent. Keturah waited with cool water to bathe his hands, face, and feet. "It is not necessary for you to rub my feet with warm oil. But it does feel good and I thank you."

I should have known he would watch every stone put in place. I never thought what a strain this would put on him. The good side of this is he is no longer bored and irritable. He has a reason to get up, and he feels he is useful once more. There is a good and a bad side to everything in life.

Rebekah watched the work with great interest. *What a wonderful thing this is. A perfect house for my father when he comes and then a safe home for Father Abraham. Keturah is wise and clever. I can learn much from her.*

In just a few weeks, the walls of the house were finished. Carpenters came to make the shelter for the roof. Stone masons arrived to pack and treat the dirt floors in the house and to lay the stone floor in the courtyard. In days, it was declared finished.

Rebekah and Keturah had furniture, carpets, cushions, and lamps ready to place in the rooms.

"I wonder if father has left Haran. When do you suppose he will arrive? I can hardly wait."

Isaac tried to reassure her. "I am sure he left as soon as he could. It is a long way, and he is not a young man anymore. If he is travelling with a caravan of traders, they will stop on the way to sell their goods."

"I know that in my head. But my heart is impatient."

"Father has spoken to me about who will sleep in the house to make sure it is acceptable. We said he should. He replied that you and I should."

"Oh, Isaac. I would love to spend a night there, but surely it is father's right."

"He says he would rather offer the blessing prayers and light the first lamp and then go to his own bed. He has never slept in a house since leaving Ur and is quite happy in his tent."

"But it has been built for him. What if he refuses to live there?"

"I think Keturah can see to that problem if it arises. Are you ready to move our sleeping mats into the house that Abraham built?"

She smiled, and overcome with emotion, could only nod. Isaac went to tell his father that Rebekah had agreed. Keturah spoke. "The people have watched with great interest. I think we should take down the fence and let our friends join us for the blessing."

The day of the blessing, workers carried away the thorn fence. They piled it in the central square and planned a celebration before the blessing time. Rebekah and Keturah had invited friends to join at the house and be a part of the ceremony. Baruch was asked to come and cut a cord tied across the door. Deborah, Rivkah, Esther, Ayla, Shira, Benjamin, Gershom, and even old Asher would be a part of the ceremony.

When they had finished their late day meal, people drifted to the central square. When the family arrived, there was a large crowd. They clapped and cheered as their leaders arrived. Baruch and Abraham took torches and lit the pile of thorn bushes. Flames danced in the twilight, sparks floated up and the wind carried them toward the sacred mountain.

The excited voice of a child called out, "Look at the mountain. The god is awake." There were hundreds of small points of light shooting into the sky from the peak of the mountain. Another cheer from the gathered crowd.

Abraham held up his hand for quiet. All turned and watched him with respect and awe. "This is a momentous event in our history. We began as a people living in a city, the great city of Ur, far away to the east. Then we were nomads wandering the earth. Now we have built our first house and we are a settled people. Never again will we wander the earth without a place to call home. We have a home, here in the land of Canaan, the land of hope."

A great cheer rose into the velvet blue sky, and the women fluttered their hands in their own special blessing. The women had carried lamps, and they lit them one by one all around the large circle. It was a spectacular sight as the people followed Abraham and Baruch to the new house. The lamps people carried, flickered along the way as Shira sang a song of blessings for a new beginning. When all were gathered outside the house, and quiet, Abraham's strong voice echoed in the gathering darkness.

"El Shaddai, your light has led us to this valley. You have favoured us with rain and sun, each in its season. This house has been built for the father of Rebekah, daughter of Bethuel and Ruth. We wait to welcome him to our village." The men clapped, and the women did their silent salute. "May all who dwell here know the god of the mountain. May they live in safety and in peace. May their sons be strong and brave, their daughters wise and beautiful. We offer thanks to you, almighty one, and tomorrow I will go to the high altar to offer a sacrifice of gratitude. So be it and amen."

Shira sang once again the song of blessing and other voices joined in softly. The special guests entered the home and lit lamps as they went. Just before he entered the house, Abraham turned to the gathered crowd. "By this time, there is wine and fresh pressed juice for everyone at the thorn bush fire. There are small cakes for all. Please enjoy the evening and then when you return to your homes sleep well."

Abraham and his guests walked around the house and exclaimed that it was the best home in all of Canaan. Flowers were in every room, cushions piled invitingly on the floor, and lamps flickered in the corners. Cedar bark burned in vessels and the powerful scent filled the home. After a cup of wine and food, the guests began to say goodnight to the host and make their way home.

Finally, only Keturah and Abraham remained with Isaac and Rebekah.

Abraham raised his hands in blessing. "This home is yours for tonight. May you find peace here, and may your love bring a blessing to this place. A new life for our people and perhaps a new life for you, my children."

Rebekah and Isaac looked deeply into each other's eyes at his words, and when they turned to speak, they were alone.

There was silence. The wind was still. The only sounds were the babbling of the river and the gentle whisper of the night wind.

"My dear wife, do you wish to sleep on the roof on this gentle night?"

"My husband. If it pleases you, I would like to sleep in this wonderful house."

Hand in hand, they walked to the corner where the sleeping mat beckoned them.

Chapter Forty-Three

The weeks passed slowly and Rebekah grew impatient. On a warm sunny evening, Rebekah was sitting at the river's edge with a spindle in her hand. She was watching the blue river flowing past more than she was tending to her spinning. Her thoughts were far away, wondering where her father was and what it would be like to see him again. Her pleasant reflections were interrupted by loud noises behind her. She became aware that someone was loudly calling her name, over and over. It was Isaac. She stood and saw him at the front of her tent. She called and waved. He came toward her, running, and she met him part way.

"A runner has come from your father. They will be here tomorrow at mid-day. All is well, and they have had a fast and uneventful journey."

"I must get everything ready. I don't have much time."

"Rebekah, it is fine. Everything is ready. The best thing for you to do is just relax, get some rest and be ready to greet your father. I am the one who should be nervous. What if he does not approve of me?"

"How could he not? You have made me very happy, Isaac. That is all a father can wish for in marriage for his daughter."

"There is a fire burning in my fire pit. Come sit there with me and tell what I need to know about your family."

They sat together until the night chill descended from the hills. They entered the tent to rest and await the important day that had come at last.

Isaac was awake with the sun. He got up and looked at his sleeping wife. *I love to look at her when she sleeps. There is such a calm about her then. Awake, she always seems to be worried about something. If only I could find a way to ease her mind. I hope this visit from Bethuel will help.* He brushed a lock of hair from her face and placed a kiss as gentle as the brush of a butterfly's wing on her cheek.

He got the fire burning and put water on to boil. Setting out dishes and fruit, he went and sat by her side. She stirred a little, and he took her hand and began to stroke her arm. Her deep brown eyes opened, and she smiled at him. Then she sat bolt upright.

"Why did you let me sleep? I have so much to do!"

"The water is boiling on the fire, there is fruit ready, and I put out the dishes. I thought that if I let you sleep a little later, it would shorten the waiting time for you."

Isaac was happy to see that she relaxed and enjoyed their breakfast.

"What will you do this morning?" she asked.

"Do you need me to help you?"

"I don't think so. As you said, everything is ready. All we need now is the guest of honour. Deborah and I will sweep the house and freshen the flowers. We will bake some fresh bread and I will make the date cakes he loved back in Haran."

"If you don't need me, I will head for the camel yard and make sure everything is ready for the animals he will bring. I will keep watch and come to you as soon as I have any news."

With a loving hug and kiss, he was off to the stables.

Rebekah walked up the hill, stopping to look back at the house. It sat surrounded by trees on this side; its stone walls were beginning to blush red as the sun shone on them. The house seemed to nestle into its grassy clearing. It looked as if it had always been there, and she was immensely proud of the work that had been done. *Keturah is a wonderful, caring person. And clever too. It will be so good to know that father will be warm and dry this coming wet season.*

Deborah was already at work getting the flour measured for the bread. They shared a smile and, in the comfortable routines practiced for a lifetime, they set to work. Deborah hummed a pleasant tune, and Rebekah concentrated on the vegetables she was washing and chopping.

Time passed quickly and as the sun shone down from a brilliant blue sky, Deborah brought a cool drink, and they sat in the shade of the canopy at their tent. As Rebekah relaxed in the warm rays of the sun, her eyes closed, and her breathing became just a whisper. Deborah didn't move but let her rest. Deborah looked up at a sound and Isaac was coming along the path. Deborah held up her hand and mimicked a sleeping posture. He came quietly to Rebekah's side and squatted down beside her.

"Becca. Wake up."

She roused and then jumped to her feet. "Is he here? Has my father come?"

"He is at the stables with father. They will come to your tent when the animals and servants are taken care of."

She didn't have time to fuss over her appearance, for at that moment, her father stood before her. He opened his arms and gathered her into a hearty embrace. When they broke, they were alone.

She signalled for him to sit on the bench that had a blanket on it for softness. They sat together and spoke of the journey, of the weather, of everything and of nothing.

"Rebekah. Enough of this. I have missed your smile, your laugh, your questions. How are you, my child?"

"I am well, father, and happy. Isaac is a good, kind, gentle husband. It was a good bargain that you made. We are a good team and balance each other's shortcomings very well."

"You make it sound good, my child. But I can read you like I read the clouds for stormy weather. There is sadness in your eyes which belies your happy tale."

"I never could put anything over on you. I could fool mother, but never you. The sadness is there are no grandsons for you to hold on your lap. I am barren, father." Her eyes filled with tears, and they spilled down her cheeks like a waterfall in the river.

He put his arm around her. "I can feel your sadness and pain. How does Isaac respond?"

"There is no reproach, no judgement, no shame. He says we are young; we have time. He reminds me that his mother waited beyond all reasonable hope for a child and then he laughs and says, 'And after all those years. Look what she got. Me!' He says it half joking and half full of pride. He carries his disappointment deep inside and does it with great compassion for my pain."

"The moment I met him; I knew you had chosen the only one who was man enough for you. I liked him from our first formal greeting at the camel pens. He is wise, and he is right. But we are men, and I am sure we can never know what this emptiness means for a woman. But trust him, he is an honourable man and a wise and compassionate one, too."

"Father Abraham knows from his own life, and he listens to me when I rail against the gods. Listens and says little. Deborah helps, she makes me work to forget and she tells tall stories about the past legends and even taller tales about the future. I live here with kind and loving people. Enough of me. How is mother?"

They sat and talked of Ruth and Laban. Bethuel told of Laban's marriages and his children. It seemed that not much had changed. Ruth still acted like a spoiled child, and Laban was a spoiled child. Bethuel said that he left her brother in charge, but that his scribe and head servant were to watch over him. "I have left a properly witnessed letter that gives them authority to take over if they are concerned. This is Laban's chance to prove himself worthy of leadership in Haran. I am not very hopeful, but I sincerely hope to be proven wrong."

They continued to talk, and Deborah came and brought food and drink. Bethuel greeted her. "I see you are treated well here. You are younger and more beautiful than you were when you left Haran. This place agrees with you."

Deborah laughed, gave a respectful bow, and left them alone. As the sun was just beginning to kiss the hills, Abraham and Isaac interrupted.

"We apologize for this intrusion, but I think it is time that Bethuel was shown his dwelling for the night."

Rebekah jumped up, grabbed Bethuel's hand, and pulled him to his feet. "Of course. Thank you, Father Abraham. Come, father. Come and see your home for as long as you stay."

And she was almost running down the road toward the river. Bethuel looked puzzled and trotted after her, as did Isaac and Abraham.

Rebekah stopped at the path that led to the house. Bethuel was looking at it with his mouth open. "This is your home, father." She reached up and laughingly closed his mouth.

"I expected a tent. This is a magnificent house, and it looks new."

Isaac spoke. "We realize it is time to give up our nomadic life and to start to build a settled town. This is our first house. It is for you to test and tell us what we have missed or done wrong. We hope you can be comfortable here, but please be honest about our work."

Rebekah led the way, and the men followed her. She went from room to room talking all the while. "We have put a few things in the house. A bed is in the far corner. If you brought your own, we would take that one away. Ask for anything we have missed, and we will be happy to get it for you."

"This dwelling is the rival of anything in Haran. The view is enchanting, and I have never been lulled to sleep by a lullaby sung by a river."

He walked to the fire in the courtyard. The coals were glowing in the gathering darkness, and he stood by the fire, looking at his daughter and her family.

"In the house of Abraham there is honour, courtesy, and much kindness. I will be comfortable here and I thank you most sincerely for your thoughtfulness. May the god of the mountain smile kindly on you and give you peace."

"Thank you for your kind words. We will go now to my tent for our evening meal." Abraham led the way, and all followed him.

The meal was a time to tell stories and share memories. When it ended with the prayers for the closing of a day, smiles were shared all around the circle and fond goodnight wishes expressed. Rebekah almost floated as she went to her tent. She was so proud and happy.

Chapter Forty-Four

The summer sun shone from a sapphire sky. Heat shimmered from the still blue water at the bend in the river. Where the water tumbled over the stones, rainbows glistened and flashed. Rebekah sat on her favourite bench and was at peace. She had seen little of her father in the first week he was there and she knew that his visit would be ending all too soon. He and Abraham spent hours on this bench as they talked of family. Wayward sons were discussed at length, and they compared the value of their wives. One evening Rebekah overheard her father say, "You have the better of me, I think, in sons and wives. But I have the joy and blessing of a daughter." Her eyes sparkled and her face glowed when she heard the reply. "Ah, but now she is my daughter too, and I thank you for letting her come to us." She tiptoed away before these men she loved, saw her.

Isaac had spent many happy hours showing Bethuel the fields with the flocks of sheep and goats. They toured the vineyards and the gardens, the pens with the milk goats and the camel barns. Isaac told Rebekah how impressed her father was. "I was surprised that he was happy that we had irrigation trenches for our fields. He was pleased that father had not forgotten what he learned in Ur and in Haran. And he even noted that father had made some improvements."

And one evening, Benjamin took Bethuel to Hebron. They came home late and Bethuel had purchased gifts for Ruth and for Laban. But today it was her turn to be with her father and she and Deborah walked to the house together. Deborah noted that Rebekah was looking pale. "Are you feeling well, Becca?"

"I have not felt myself these last days. I can't seem to get going in the mornings and my meal sits like a lump in my belly. Today I thought it was going to come back up. I guess I am just nervous about seeing father."

"I don't think so. I think it is something else."

Rebekah grabbed her hand. "What else could it be? Am I ill?"

They were at a grassy place under a willow tree. "Sit here with me. I need to talk to you."

Puzzled, Rebekah left the path and sat in the shade of the tree. She loved the patterns made by the shadows of the leaves as the sun filtered down to the ground.

Deborah was smiling and her eyes glittered with some secret knowledge. "Tell me, when did you go to the women's tent last?"

"I go every moon time. You know that."

"You and I always go there near same time, a day earlier or a day later, but always together, do we not?"

"Of course. What is the point of this?"

"You were not there for my last moon time. I missed you."

Rebekah stared at her. She paused. Her eyes opened wide, and she grabbed Deborah. "What are you saying?"

"Are your breasts tender? Are they heavy?"

"Well, yes, but I don't understand what you are thinking."

"Heavy breasts, morning illness, no moon time. What do you think?"

Silence from Rebekah. Then a loud squeal. "Do you really think so? I am going to have a child. How can that be?"

"The usual way I expect." And she laughed.

"This is wonderful news. Father will be so pleased I can't wait to tell him."

"Becca. There is someone who needs to be told before your father."

"I must find Isaac. Thank you. Will you tell father I will be a little delayed?" And off she hurried. She found him at his tent. He smiled and went to meet her. As he approached, she ran to him and threw herself into his arms, crying and laughing at the same time.

"Becca, what is this? Are you laughing or crying?"

"Both, Isaac, and with utter joy. We are going to have a child."

He held her at arm's length and saw the joy in her eyes. He let out a holler of sheer joy, picked her up, and spun around in a circle. Her scarf blew off as she whirled around with him. He stopped. He gently put her on the ground and placed his hand on her belly. “That was very, very foolish of me. Have I harmed our son?”

“No dear one. We are not that fragile. But what if our son should be a daughter?”

“If she is as beautiful and wise as her mother, all will be well. We must tell our fathers.”

“Deborah has gone to get your father and we will meet at my father’s house.”

“You told Deborah?”

“She told me. I was feeling poorly, and she pointed out to me that I had not been at the moon house lately. She is very wise in the ways of women. Come, let’s go to the new house with our news.”

They walked slowly, arms around each other, smiling and laughing at their news and their love. At the house, the others were there, waiting for them. They gathered around the low table and a wonderful meal was presented.

It was the end of Bethuel's visit. They lingered over the food and told stories until the servants lit the lamps and cleared the dishes.

Abraham spoke. “Again, I say, welcome, welcome. We all know why we are here.” Isaac gave his wife a hug, and they smiled even broader smiles. They said nothing, as they knew Abraham had a speech to make and then there would be others to follow.

“We are here to bid farewell to Bethuel. The time has passed quickly, and I wish it could be longer.”

Bethuel smiled and nodded.

Abraham continued. “It has been good to get to know my nephew. The grandfathers would be proud of this man for he has dignity and honour and has brought distinction to the house of Abraham by his presence.”

Everyone nodded and voiced agreement. Isaac spoke next.

“To the father of my beautiful wife, I offer my respect and deep affection. I was a bit afraid to meet the man Rebekah spoke of so highly. I was sure I would disappoint him, and he would return the dowry to Abraham and return to his home with my wife.” Laughter filled the room.

Bethuel looked around the room at this family. "I have been honoured to stay in this lovely home you have built. If it is a pattern for homes for you in the future, you will have a village above all others in Canaan. I have been welcomed here and honoured by your care. I have only good news to take home to Ruth about her daughter and her new family. I don't know what I will find when I get home, but if my son has ruined me, I will be back dependent on your charity for a house and for my food." Again, there was much laughter.

Rebekah spoke. "I have invited Shira to come and to sing for us. She waits outside, so please let us all stay awhile and I hope you enjoy the music."

Shira entered and bowed to Abraham and to Bethuel. Two musicians followed her in, a young woman with a lyre and a boy with a drum. The fire crackled in the fire pit and sent sparks into the air, which added to the delight of the evening. Voices blended in songs of joy, hope and blessing. After many songs, Shira bowed and indicated the music was over.

Rebekah's soft voice filled the room. "Please stay for a little longer, Shira. There is a song of thanksgiving and blessing I would like you to sing in a moment. But Isaac has something to say first."

He was on the far side of the circle and came around to sit beside his wife. They looked into each other's eyes for a long moment. "This day brings us sadness as we say our goodbyes to Bethuel. But it also brings boundless joy to the house of Abraham, and Bethuel, and to my house. By the time, the almond blooms in the spring, the cry of an infant will be heard in the house of Isaac."

There was a moment of stunned silence and then complete bedlam. Everyone was talking at once, clapping Isaac on the back and hugging Rebekah. Deborah nodded to Shira, and she spoke to her musicians. The small drum began to sound, a gentle, soft beat. Next, the lyre joined in with a joyous melody. When everyone was quiet, Shira began to hum a lilting tune. Adding the words, she offered a song of thanksgiving. She sang of new life, of hope and of the promise of a miracle in the future. Tears were in the eyes of everyone in the room as the drummer and the lyre player led the way out of the house. Shira followed and continued to sing. One by the others who were present offered a blessing to the happy couple and left.

When only the parents to be were left with Bethuel, he gathered them into an embrace. "This is the best gift I have ever had. El Shaddai is good and has heard our prayers. May the holy one of the mountain defend and protect you until we meet again."

Rebekah and Isaac walked home under a starry sky and the golden light of a huge yellow moon.

The morning dawned with a pink and gold sky. Everyone was up early to see Bethuel off to his homeland. He would meet Caleb and the caravan just beyond the border of Abraham's fields. The camels that would carry Bethuel home were ready to go, laden with gifts and provisions. The soldiers that came with Bethuel were standing guard. The sun glinted off the tips of their spears which seemed to be dancing in the morning light.

As Rebekah looked at them, she thought. *Dancing spears. That is a strange image.*

Bethuel stood and accepted the good wishes for safe travel from everyone. In a short while, they had all left except Rebekah. She stood beside her father with tear-filled eyes, but a grateful heart for his visit.

He held her close and stroked her hair. "I want you to take diligent care of yourself as you wait for the birth of your child. Take after your mother, lie around, and give orders." They smiled as they both held back tears.

"I will, father and we will try to let you know when you have a grandchild. It has been good to have this time with you. Safe travels and tell mother and Laban I miss them both."

A last tender hug, then he climbed onto his camel. Rebekah stood back as the beast came to its feet. Bethuel signalled time to go, and the line lumbered into motion. Rebekah walked back to the house and went inside. *I can't bear to watch him disappear. I will never see him again.* Isaac had been waiting for her and he enveloped her in his strong, yet tender arms and held her close while she wept.

Chapter Forty-Five

An ominous grey sky hung like a shroud over the mountain. Rebekah, unable to sleep, sat in the courtyard. Her mind filled with thoughts of her father and Abraham. She wished a safe journey for Bethuel, and she hoped that he would find everything satisfactory when he arrived at his home in Haran. Her heart was heavy as she thought of Isaac. He was worried about his father. *I pray Abraham is just weary from such a busy day.* Footsteps at the gate interrupted her thoughts.

"Who is there?"

"It's me, Talia. Keturah has sent me to get you and Isaac. Abraham is asking for you. Please come quickly."

Rebekah felt her chest squeeze tight, and it was hard to breathe. She stopped and very deliberately took a few deep breaths and then went to wake Isaac. In a short time, they were on the path to Abraham's tent. They stopped at the entrance and held each other close for a long moment, then stepped apart as Keturah came out.

"Abraham is dying, and he has asked for you." They followed her inside and went to the bed near the fire. All three sat down close to the bed.

"Father. It is Isaac and Rebekah. We are here. It will be all right."

He roused. "I need to talk to you, and I have much to say. I am very tired so please listen and don't make me say anything I haven't planned. It is good that I will die in my tent. The house we built is a good one, but I have not lived in a house since Ur. A tent has been my home, and it is fitting I die here, surrounded by my memories. When I am gone, I want you to see that Keturah goes to live in our rooms in the house. I will rest easy, knowing she is in a warm, safe place. I hope you two will move into the house when she does."

He lay back and reached for Keturah's hand. She took it and held it to her breast.

"My son, all that I have will be yours. You are ready to take over my lands, and cattle and lead our people. Trust Rebekah. She is wise and clever. Let her do the records and make all the marks. She does it better than you ever will. You know what you need to do, and I know I leave it in good hands.

He paused, and Keturah gave him sips of watered wine.

"Take care of Rebekah as she carries this child. Let her read and make the marks, but that is all she should do. She needs to rest and let the child grow strong and healthy. When he is born, teach him carefully. He will have much to learn and will have to work hard, but he needs to play with others as well. When you have another child, treat them fairly. They will be different. Let them be who they must be. Do not favour one over the other. Teach them responsibility and fairness and to be kind and just in all their dealings. Learn from my failures."

Isaac dropped his head to the light cover on the bed. He hid his grief and his tears. Abraham placed his right hand on his son's head. He asked for another pillow, and Rebekah jumped up and got one. Keturah raised him up and Rebekah slipped the pillow under him. A long, rattling breath escaped his lips.

"Bury me in the cave beside Sarah. Leave room for Keturah, for I want to sleep with the women I have loved. It has been a good life. I have made mistakes, but I tried to atone for them. I have loved and been loved, and that makes life sweet. I am ready to be at rest with Terah and the old ones."

The voice stilled and only raspy breathing gave evidence that he still clung to life. In the silence, they heard a deep groan from the back of the tent. Eliezer was sitting in the darkness.

Abraham's eyes flew open. "When I am gone, do not grieve for too long. Remember the cranky old man with love, and then let me rest gently in your hearts. Let the past be. Spend your love on each other and the future.

He lay back on the pillows and his hand relaxed and fell from Isaac's head. Eliezar rushed outside. Isaac stood. "Let him go."

Keturah groaned. "I sent for Gershom. He is waiting outside. Eliezar will not be alone."

Rebekah touched Keturah's arm. "In your grief, you are still taking care of us." They joined hands as they sat by the bed and wept together.

Many hours later, as the dawn began to show in the east, they heard someone near the tent. "It is Eliezar and Gershom. May we enter?"

Three voices replied. "Come in." They stood to face the men and Keturah motioned to seats around the fire. They gathered there in silence, which was finally broken by Gershom. "We have eaten and we bring food for Isaac. There are women gathered at the river house with food ready for you." He gestured to the two women. "We men will attend to Father Abraham and the women will help you with the rest."

Keturah nodded and went and picked up a bundle from a nearby bench. The three left the tent in silence and made their way to the river house. As they neared, they heard women's voices chanting a lament. They listened to the mournful yet healing sound until it died away. Rebekah led the way into the house.

She looked at the faces that greeted her. Talia and Deborah stood near a table with the first meal of the day set out. Candles flickered and blossoms fluttered in the breeze to welcome and console them. Seated on the benches near the fire were Ayla, Esther, and Rivkah. As they sat together and talked, plans for the day began to take shape.

In some ways, the morning flew by, as there was much to arrange. In other ways, it seemed to drag on painfully. As the sun reached its highest point, women from the settlement arrived bearing food. They came quietly, set out their offering, and with a nod or a bow, respectfully left. Someone must have alerted them for Isaac, Gershom, and Eliezar arrived at the tent.

The non-family individuals made motions to leave, but Keturah rose to her feet. "You have been an important part of this family for much longer that I. Please stay and be a part of this challenging time and conversation. They all bowed in respect and gratitude and took a seat with the others. Isaac broke the silence. "I wish to offer a prayer." All stood.

"God, of mercy, who dwells in the heights, provide a sure rest for the soul of Abraham, son of Terah. son of Nahor. To the god of the mountain, we entrust his soul, May El Shaddai protect him forever. May he rest peacefully upon his lying place and let us say: Amen."

The words reverently spoken, drifted away on the breeze. "Let me continue and tell you what we have planned. We have prepared the body and placed Abraham on a litter. It will be carried to the tomb by four of his warriors. The rest of his men will march in front of the litter. The chief mourners will follow the litter and after them anyone who wishes to may join the procession. Is this acceptable to you, Keturah?"

"It is most fitting. Will Esther have a part in the ceremony?"

"It was our hope that she would lead the prayers and offer her thoughts at the tomb."

"It would be an honour. If you will excuse me, I go to prepare." She left quietly.

A deep, mournful silence hung in the room. Isaac continued. "Soldiers are preparing the grave and will stand guard at the time of the burial. Even now, people are lining the road that leads to the mountain. I think some will choose to do that rather than make the long climb."

Rebekah nodded. "That is a wise choice for the old ones and for those with children. We women spoke of food and drink in the commons for all, when it is over. Rivkah will look after that with Ayla's help. They said that our late meal is ready for us when we signal that we wish to eat."

Deborah raised her hand. Isaac nodded to her. "Has any thought been given to Rebekah? That is a long hard climb, and she would be standing at the tomb for quite a while."

"We spoke of it and felt that you would want to walk with the family." Isaac looked at his wife.

"Thank you, Isaac." She met his gaze and a tender smile flashed between them. "Yes, I would like to walk with all of you. But a chair at the top would be good."

Gershom spoke. "That we can do easily. I suggest that someone walk close to Rebekah with a donkey, just in case."

The quiet voice of Eliezar spoke. "I would like to do that. Abraham would want me to." He shrunk back into the shadows.

Without waiting to be acknowledged, Deborah asked, "Will Shira be singing? Abraham loved her music."

"Sorry, I forgot. Thank you, Deborah. We hope that Shira and musicians and singers as she chooses will follow the family."

"Like Eliezar, I would consider it an honour."

"Unless there is anything else, it is time to get ready. But let us eat. Then we will gather at father's tent and start from there. We will meet there as the sun begins its descent toward the hills."

Rebekah had gone to her bed to rest. She was asleep when Isaac entered later in the day. He brought her a small bowl of fruit, some bread, and a glass of wine. She looked rested and began at once to fix her hair and think about what to wear. She chose her favourite deep blue tunic and added a creamy white cloak, which had golden cedar fronds embroidered on the edges. Isaac had chosen to wear the uniform of his father's guard. She had never seen him dressed as a soldier and thought he was most handsome wearing the short, dark green tunic with gold braid. He carried a matching cloak over his left arm. They stood together in a close embrace.

"I couldn't do this without you by my side. Nor could I face the future unless you were there with me. You are my strength and my shield, Rebekah."

"And you are my help in all my troubles and your strength sustains me."

He laid a hand on her belly. "And you carry the future of this great family. This valley truly is the valley of hope."

They left the river house and walked to Abraham's tent. Tears filled Rebekah's eyes as she saw the litter. It was covered in gold fabric and Abraham lay wrapped in a green burial cloth. His sword lay on his breast and at his side was a rolled-up skin with black marks.

"It is perfect, Isaac. Simply perfect. Keturah will be deeply touched."

Gershom explained. "She was overcome, and Talia took her inside for a few minutes. When they come out, we will begin. If you are wondering where Eliezar is, he stands at the bottom of the hill with the donkey."

When she saw Keturah, Shira began a chant, and the musicians joined her. The honour guard moved forward, the litter followed, and the long walk to the tomb began.

People lined both sides of the road, the old ones were seated on stools. Many children were among the mourners, and they stood in awe as the one they knew as Grandfather Abraham was carried past. There were tears, but most stood in respectful silence, bowing their heads as the litter passed near. Most had not made the climb and left the family to say goodbye to their beloved patriarch in privacy.

They stood in a close circle as prayers were said, and the singers offered a dirge that gradually evolved into a song of thanksgiving for the long successful life of this great leader. Abraham's guard laid the body in the tomb and then stood in silent salute to their leader. Isaac felt Rebekah's body tense and then, with a moan, she grasped her belly and collapsed in his arms. At once, the soldiers took the litter and removed the golden cloth. Gershom and Eliezar covered it with their cloaks. Isaac laid his wife on the litter and looked at her ashen face. Keturah took charge and beckoned to the midwife. Ayla came and knelt beside Rebekah. She watched her breathing, felt her forehead, and listened to her heart. Then she gently explored her belly, which was showing signs of her pregnancy. She stood and looked at Isaac.

"It is all right Isaac. She is exhausted and these last few days have been very emotional. She just needs to rest and then some nourishing broth would help her recover."

Keturah motioned to the soldiers who had carried Abraham up the steep path. They picked up the litter and turned to carry her home. As she was lifted, she spoke one word.

"Isaac."

He was at her side and held her hand. "It is all right, dear one, you are tired. We are taking you home to rest. Hold tight to me and we will get you home."

Step by careful step, they made their way down the hill to the sound of stones being placed at the mouth of the cave.

Hours later, the family and servants gathered in Abraham's tent. Rebekah propped up with cushions and still pale, smiled weakly at everyone. It seemed fitting that they eat their meal together in the old man's tent as they shared what the day meant to them. They all agreed it was a fitting tribute and farewell to the one who had been their father, their leader, their teacher, and their friend.

Keturah stood and looked at this gathering of those she loved. "I can't begin to thank you for this day. It has been hard, but it has been healing, and it is a day to remember. To remember with deep sorrow, but with great thanksgiving. I would like someone to end this day with a blessing prayer."

Everyone stood and waited. Isaac helped Rebekah to her feet, as it was clear that she wanted something. She took a step to a nearby shelf, reached up and took down a battered plate and a chipped cup. She turned back to the group. "You may know that these were Abraham's favourite plate and cup. They are not prefect. They are chipped and scarred. They remind me of life." She held them up high. "El Shaddai, giver of life. Bless this plate and this cup. May they always remind us of the man who shaped our lives for many, many years. He too, like these vessels, was not perfect, and neither are we. May his memory inspire us, his teachings lead us, and the warmth of his love give us peace. We loved you, Father Abraham, and we will never forget you as long as we have breath. Amen." The word echoed on every tongue, and every eye shone with sacred tears.

Chapter Forty-Six

The days were sunny and warm, the nights cool and pleasant, but a sombre cloud hung over the settlement. People went about their business in a subdued manner. Each person was dealing with the death of Abraham in a different manner. For Eliezar, it was as if his whole world had come to a dismal end.

He sought out Benjamin and shared his turmoil.

"I have no purpose left in my life. For as long as I can remember, Abraham was the centre of my being and doing. What do I do now?"

"I can't say I understand fully how you feel, nor does anyone, but we all are trying to find our way without him."

Benjamin pointed to a couple of stools that were nearby and they sat beside each other. *I feel like putting my arm around him, but he has always been such a private person. Do I dare?*

He sighed, shrugged, and put his hand on the shoulder of the broken man beside him.

Eliezar breathed a shuddering sigh. "Thank you. That gesture of sympathy means a great deal."

"Is there anything you wish to talk about? I am listening if you do."

"I don't think I can stay here without him. I have family in Haran and I am thinking about going there. Do you think I would be allowed to leave?"

"You are a free man. No one can stop you from leaving, but I know that no one would even try. What you need is what matters now."

"I know I don't have much time left, and I would like to find my family. My brother, if he is still alive, or his children. I would like to die with family nearby. Everyone here is kind and treats me like family, but the only one who truly felt like family to me is gone. With every breath I am reminded of that while I stay here."

"If finding family is important, then that is what you should do. Go to Haran and search for them. If there is no one, or you don't feel at home, then come back here."

"Thank you, Benjamin. I feel better hearing your words of comfort. I will leave tomorrow."

"Tonight, after we eat, let's go to the gathering spot and we will spend your last night there, remembering and telling Abraham stories."

They stood and Eliezar reach out his arms and gave Benjamin a bear hug. Then he was gone to his tent.

Benjamin finished his task and then hurried to find Isaac and Rebekah. He told them what he had just learned from Eliezar.

"We will miss his gentle presence, but he must do what is best for him. What can we do to say goodbye?"

Rebekah answered at once. "We will organize a farewell party. Drinks, food and stories. It will be both a farewell, a tribute to Eliezar and a promise of hope for the future." She and Isaac exchanged a loving look.

"Good idea." Isaac pointed at Benjamin. "You keep him away until the sun has set. We will light a fire and that is the signal for you to bring him to the celebration." They parted, and each one went to get the village organized for the evening. As the word spread, the mood seemed to change and the dark cloud receded into the darkening sky.

By sunset, tables were ready with sweets and drinks. Everyone worked quietly so that nothing special would seem to be happening. As many as could, had gathered to wish the faithful companion of their beloved leader a good journey and a happy future. They sat in small groups, trying to stay hidden in the gathering shadows.

Benjamin led Isaac down a path that wound through the trees. He would see nothing until he stepped into the communal area. When he walked into the undeveloped area, he stopped, eyes wide and mouth open. Shira broke the silence with a bright welcoming song and everyone joined in.

Isaac walked toward the top of the circle, away from the dumbstruck Eliezar. When the song ended, he beckoned Eliezar to follow him. He went to a newly constructed raised floor, and they climbed the steps to stand above the cheering crowd. Isaac held up his hands for silence.

"Eliezar, dear friend. Benjamin has told us of your plans, and how you pay him back because he told us you are leaving, is up to you." Laughter rippled around the circle. "We are standing on this newly built platform that will remain here in our gathering place. Father Abraham always stood on a cart, like the one beside me. I needed something besides that, for a cart will always be a symbol of father's leadership. And sad though we are, we need to find our way to continue what he has provided for us."

The women fluttered their hands in silent salute while the men bowed theirs heads for a moment.

"Eliezar has decided to leave this family and to seek his birth family in Haran. We are here to celebrate his years of service and to wish him well in his new life. Eliezar, you will be sorely missed, but we understand. The new cart that stands beside us will have two strong, obedient donkeys harnessed to it tomorrow. It is our parting gift to you to aid you on your journey."

Benjamin came to the steps and handed Eliezar a new set of reins to go with the cart. "Those obedient donkeys wouldn't leave their hay and come to the party, but here are their reins so you can make them do as you want." Laughter and applause filled the night air.

Rebekah stepped forward and gave Eliezar a big hug. Again. cheers echoed to the far-off hills. "Eliezar, do you wish to say anything?"

In response, he held his arms out wide, turned to face each and every part of the gathering, then gave a deep bow.

Rebekah smiled at him and nodded. "Well said, dear friend. It is time for the food and the farewells many of you want to speak to our honoured guest. Let the party begin."

Much later, Isaac once again mounted the steps and stood on the platform. Gradually, the crowd gathered around and became still as they waited for him to speak. "I do not wish to end your good wishes to Eliezar. But while we have been honouring and celebrating our wonderful past, I think we all wonder about our future. Rebekah and I will do our very best to lead us into the days and years ahead. We ask for your patience as we take on our new responsibilities. Now it is time for my wife to go to our home to rest. She is very tired for she carries the future heir to this great nation. Stunned silence greeted these words.

Then, as Isaac took her hand and led her toward their home, a deafening cheer arose and drifted to the far mountain. People turned to face the mountain and a shower of sparks lit up the night sky for just a moment.

Eliezar sought out Isaac and Rebekah. "My friends. Thank you for this wonderful surprise. I shall find Benjamin and thank him for sharing my plans. Thank you for the cart and the donkeys. Obedient or not, they will make my trip easier. I plan to go to Hebron and join a trade caravan which leaves at sunup." He looked at them both and his eyes glistened with diamond drops of water. "Please don't meet me in the morning to say goodbye. Let this moment be my leave taking." He looked deeply into Rebekah's eyes, then bowed low to her. She dropped to one knee in a silent salute. He turned to Isaac, his eyes misty and his voice choked with emotion. "You are the son of your father. Remember all he taught you and serve his people well. If I were younger, I would be tempted to stay and serve you as I served Abraham. But it is not to be. Thank you for tonight. I shall remember it for the rest of my life." With a deep bow to them, he walked into the night.

Chapter Forty-Seven

Isaac and Gershom walked along the river. A thousand bits of light sparkled on the dewy grass. They neared the river house and sat down on the bank of the river; Gershom looked up the little rise to study the house. "What a waste. It sits empty except for the mice and bugs that make it their home. Didn't your father want Keturah to live here?"

"You are right, Gershom. He ordered it with his last breath. Come, let's see how bad it is."

They hurried to the house and saw the gate was ajar. They burst into the open courtyard, covered in leaves, small branches, dirt, and sand. As they walked from room to room, the same signs of neglect were everywhere.

"You know Isaac. We have ignored Abraham's wish for too long. It wouldn't take very much to get it cleaned up and made liveable for Keturah."

"Yes, let's get busy. But I want to keep it a secret from Keturah until it is all ready for her. Do you think we can do that?"

"It will be easy, Isaac. You let Rebekah in on the plan, and the two of you can keep Keturah occupied. She is anxious about Rebekah and the baby anyway, so it should be easy. If she suspects anything, just tell her we are getting rid of the dirt and animals that have taken over the river house."

"I always thought you were a schemer. Now I know for sure. I'll look after my wife and Keturah. Can you get the rest started?"

"Just do your part and I will get everyone else on the job. I always wanted to be the boss of something. But that feeling will only last until Deborah is in on the plans."

The two men slapped each other on the back and were soon happily at work on their scheme.

Deborah was unsure about leaving Rebekah, but when told of the whole plan, she headed out to find Talia. In a brief time, following Deborah's instructions, she was busy in the house, singing as she worked.

Mice and other small creatures scurried away to find a quieter place to nest. Clouds of dust flew into the air, only to settle again on window openings and the floor. Once the leaves, twigs, and dirt were banished, she swept more gently and rid the floors of the sand. Then she changed brooms for mops, and washed the stone floors in all the rooms and the outdoor courtyard.

After a break at the evening meal, she returned with damp rags to dust all the windowsills and every flat area in the house. The huge table that had been created for Bethuel was polished until it gleamed in the lamplight.

By evening, she was proud of the house she made her way to her tent to rest until the morning.

Just as the sun peeped over the hills, shadowy figures came and went from the house. They brought small tables, stools and chairs, carpets and cushions and left them on the courtyard stones. Deborah arrived with her helpers, Talia, and two strong young men. She ordered them around with a happy smile and the pile disappeared into various rooms in the building. Benjamin came by and took Deborah aside. They greeted each other warmly with smiles at a private joke. "It is going to be a sweltering day, Deborah, and I want you to be careful. Take rests in the shade and drink often. It won't help if you get sick."

She brushed his hand and smiled. "I will be careful, and I will look after all my helpers."

With a brief caress to her cheek, he was gone. Isaac and Rebekah arrived. She looked flushed and was a bit out of breath but was delighted by what she saw. She carried a basket of flowers, and Isaac had a basket full of pottery vases and dishes. They arranged it all in the two most northerly rooms. Esther and Ayla came with curtains for the windows, and soon the rooms were ready to show Keturah.

Talia was jumping about with excitement. "May I go and bring Keturah here? Please. I can find an excuse."

"Go then and we will wait in the courtyard. At that moment, women arrived with little cakes and Gershom was with them, bringing a keg of wine. They stood, anticipating the arrival of Keturah. Isaac motioned for quiet when he heard steps on the stone walk.

Talia led Keturah to the courtyard. She stopped in amazement at the friends gathered there. Her sharp eyes looked around the space. "Someone has been working hard here. It looks very inviting." Smiles shone on every face. "There are refreshments on the table. What is this all about?"

Rebekah gave Isaac a push, and he stumbled to the table. "Keturah. Since you have been here, you have taken care of everything that needed your helping hand. We all have come to love and respect your kindness and compassion. Gershom reminded me that Abraham expressed his desire for you to live in this river house." He spread his arms in a gesture of welcome. "We have tried to make this place ready for you to bring your treasures and make this your home."

Keturah's eyes filled with tears, and a broad smile spread across her face and her eyes shone with wonder. "You are doing this for me?"

Rebekah put her arm around Keturah. "This is to be your home now. It was Abraham's wish, and we all agreed. We have chosen the three north rooms for you, but if you would prefer others, that can be changed."

"I would like to see what you have done there. I can't remember them very well."

They walked to the rooms and Keturah stood transfixed. "Look at the curtains and the rugs. The flowers are beautiful. I don't know what to say."

Talia clapped her hands. "Just say yes."

"Thank you for this. For reminding me of Abraham's wish, for cleaning this space, and for the wonderful things you have brought to make it look like home. I would like our sleeping mats brought, and Talia and I will spend our first night in our new home."

Talia squealed with delight. Gershom and Isaac left to get the beds and lamps. The rest of the conspirators gathered around the table. Happy chatter competed with the night bird's song as the cakes and wine were shared.

The moon sailed across the sky, mugs were returned to the table, and it was apparent the celebration was ending.

Isaac spoke. "In the morning we will be at your tent, to move what you require here to this your home. Other things can be brought as you need them. Please tell Rebekah or me of anything you need us to arrange."

"Would it be too much to ask for a small ceremony to bless this home tomorrow morning?" She looked at Esther and smiled at her.

Esther walked to Keturah and took her hand. "I would be pleased to plan a small ceremony for the morning. You decide what you want and who is to be present, and I will do the rest."

"Just a song or two, a few words of blessing and a prayer for my new home. And thank you all again. It is good to live among people of such warmth and love."

One by one, they said goodnight and made their way to their own homes for the night's rest.

Keturah and Talia stood in silent wonder at the good fortune that had brought them to this place in the valley of hope.

"Come, Talia. It is time for rest and sleep, and pleasant dreams."

Talia woke with the morning sun and heard a noise from the courtyard. She quickly slipped on yesterday's tunic and went quietly to check. Deborah was busy, and a fire glowed in the fire pit, hot water simmered over the fire, and breakfast lay ready on the table.

"Deborah, thank you, this is wonderful."

"I didn't mean to wake you, but food is ready whenever you are. I will leave you now to start this momentous day." And she was gone.

Keturah came out when she heard voices, and the two women enjoyed their simple meal. Together, they went up to the hill to their tent and dressed for the day. They both took great pains with their hair and their clothes. As they returned to the river house, they could see people were gathering already. Food had arrived and covered the table, flowers and candles added warmth and colour, and friends were there, ready for the formal beginning of this new home for Keturah.

Esther stepped forward and nodded to Shira. She stroked her lyre and sang a hymn of blessing. The song spoke of joy, and hope, and peace. Gentle words entreated good health for all who dwelt in the house. The music quietly drifted away, and the twitter of birds filled the space.

Esther lit a lamp and placed it on the table. The oil burned with an earthy scent as streamers of smoke curled skyward. Esther raised her hands in supplication.

"El Shaddai, mother and father of all. Look upon this home in love and in mercy. May the cloud of your presence be the shield and protector of all who enter here. May your light shine in the darkness, your breath blow away all evil. Let your spirit fill this home with love and kindness. Let all who dwell here know peace in their hearts and find hope in their dreams and visions. Amen and amen."

A chorus of voices replied. "Amen and amen."

After a long silence, a child's voice broke the spell. "Can we have some cake now?"

Amid the warm sound of laughter, a ribbon of well-wishers danced toward the tables laden with food and drink.

The following days were busy. Many trips were made from the former tent of Abraham to the stone house by the river. Keturah was enthusiastically arranging her new home. When all was done to her satisfaction, Keturah stood with Rebekah and surveyed her new dwelling place.

"You know, Keturah, I always felt at peace in your tent, and I was sad to see it being torn apart. But this is even more beautiful and homey. You are so clever at putting things in their own special spot. I can see it after, but have trouble thinking ahead to achieve what I want."

"Your living space is lovely Rebekah. Don't be so critical of yourself. This is me. Your space reflects who you are, and that is how it should be."

They walked together from room to room and stopped to sit side by side and enjoy the view of the river.

Rebekah uttered a small, contented sigh. "Keturah, may I say something very personal?"

"Of course, my child. We have few secrets."

"I have very mixed feelings about my mother. I respect and honour her, of course, but real affection is not in my heart. I dislike her petulant, selfish ways. She treats my father like a servant and that offends me, mostly because of what it does to him."

Keturah took Rebekah's hand and held it cradled in her work-worn hands. "Each couple works out their own way of being together. To an outsider, it may seem—" she paused as if searching for the words. "Wrong is too harsh, but no other word comes to me."

"You are telling me it is none of my business, aren't you?"

"In a way, yes. Your father is a powerful and strong leader. Having a wife who is very dependent, even spoiled, may be just what he needs. We can never know. But he didn't seem to be an unhappy man. When he spoke of his wife, there was tenderness in his voice. I sensed no resentment."

"Keturah, I need to say to you that you are more of a mother to me than Ruth ever could be, and I am grateful for your love and support."

Keturah placed a gently hand on Rebekah's cheek. "And you are the daughter I never had."

They sat together in comfortable companionship. Smiling, Keturah reached for the plate of fruit on the table nearby and offered it to Rebekah. "I have been thinking. This is much too big a space for just Talia and me. While we are in the mood, you and Isaac should move into the rooms at the south end."

"Oh, I don't know if he would do that."

"Isaac will do what you want. He will do anything for you, you know that. Wouldn't you like to live here, warm, and comfortable when the rains come? This would be a wonderful place to await the birth of your little one."

"I hadn't thought about it at all."

"Well, I think you should. And let's get it done before it becomes difficult for you and before the winter rains make it impossible. Tell Isaac and I'll talk to Gershom, and we will get it done."

And they did. Long before the chilly winter wind blew down from the hills, Isaac and Rebekah were settled in their rooms at the opposite end of the large house by the river. Gershom and Deborah had their own rooms nearby as well.

As they sat together at the large table at the end of the late day meal, Isaac gave his small cough that told everyone he had something important to say. They all turned to him, ready to listen.

"There is too much work here for Gershom to do by himself. We need another man to oversee the outside chores. All the flowers and trees and our animals, goats, sheep, and donkeys."

"I am sure, husband, that you have someone in mind."

"Maybe. But Deborah knows the workers we have, and I wonder if she knows someone who might be interested?"

Deborah's cheeks turned crimson. "Excuse me please, I need something from my room."

"That was mean, Isaac. You embarrassed her. But it is a promising idea. Would Benjamin be willing to do it?"

"I have spoken to him. He, too, blushed and tried to pretend he was pondering the idea. But as I expected, he said, 'yes' as he tried to hide his enthusiasm."

And so, their household became complete, and they settled in to live in the river house and wait for the heir to be born in the spring.

Chapter Forty-Eight

Early one morning, weeks later, Benjamin came looking for Isaac. After some friendly teasing and then a warm handshake, they made their way to the bench beside the river. They sat for a few minutes, enjoying the sounds of the water, and searching for signs of the coming weather. A chill wind from the north whipped up white caps on the waves slapping the bank.

Isaac broke the silence. "We won't have the sun much longer. The winter winds will be chilling our bones soon enough.

"And that is why I wanted to speak with you. When our soldiers return from the city, they repeat the gossip they hear in the drinking holes. And what I hear worries me."

"What do you hear? I guess you think that I need to hear these words, too."

"They have overheard unpleasant thoughts about this house. Ruffians are talking about the riches that must be here. The tales of your wealth are getting increasingly exaggerated. It worries me."

"It is a good, strong house and do you think they would attack the house of Abraham?"

"Too much talk and too much beer can make men feel brave."

"What should I do? I am no soldier. I frittered away my time when I had a chance to learn those skills. I was too young when father went to war with the kings who raided Sodom."

"I was there, just a water boy, but I am a born soldier. I watched and tried to learn everything I could. I had a good teacher in Eliezar. I watched as he set out guards on our trip and I asked many questions. He was always patient and unbelievably detailed in his answers."

Isaac picked up a stone and hurled it into the river. "There is always something. Help me, Benjamin. Be my General. Tell me what to do."

"I have thought about it, and I do have a plan."

"Tell me, please, anything you want or need, anything." There was fear and desperation in his voice.

"We can make this place safer. It will take demanding work and it must be done before the rains."

"Can we walk while you explain? I think better on my feet."

"By all means." The two men went to the village lane and began to walk in a determined way down the hill to the main road.

"First on my list is to build a stone wall around the house and re-establish the thorn hedge. It is primitive, but effective. Second, get more soldiers and start a rigorous training programme. Third, we will need weapons. The simplest way is to buy them from the next trade caravan. But that will be costly."

"I will pay to ensure the safety of my people. Caleb will be making his last trip before the rains. I will speak with him."

Benjamin held up four fingers. "We need to build guard houses at the entrances to the village and near the big house. That is number four on my list, but a priority."

"How can we do all this before the rains come?"

"It is a suitable time. Many of our men are idle. The crops are in, and the sheep and goats are in their winter pastures. With your orders, we can start tomorrow."

"You have my orders to make this your main job. I will go to Hebron and engage Baruch. He is the best man I know to get a job done in a hurry, but still well constructed."

"I know it will alarm the women, but I think you need to make an announcement in the square."

"I will not speak of any details, just what we need to do. Do we need to keep this secret from Hebron?

"No. I think if word gets out that we are prepared, it will discourage those who are looking for an easy target. A determined thief is another matter. We will hire no one that you do not know from the city. Details must remain secret, but the idea that we have weapons, and a trained army is a start to a good defense."

"Is that all you need?"

"There is one more thing. The soldiers need a barracks more central to the village and because of the coming rains, they need a protected training area."

Isaac stopped walking and thought for a moment. Then he clapped his hands. "The tents of Rebekah and of Abraham are empty. Will they do?"

"They will be perfect. I had thought of them but wasn't sure I dared to ask. I thought they might have become symbols of our great leaders. Sacred almost."

"What is sacred is the well-being of our people, my wife, and our children. I am glad you have moved in with us"

"I have been thinking about that, as well. I am not sure it is the right thing to do, for several reasons. The most important one being I should live with the men I will lead. That is the best way to build the trust that we will need. I hope you understand.

"Anything that is in my power to give you is yours. But know that you have my complete trust and confidence."

"Thank you. You make decisions quickly and that is what is needed at this time."

Isaac chuckled. "Unlike my father, I don't need to go to the altars for permission. But I will go to ask for guidance and for our safety."

"Good. Then I go to make known the gathering tonight and to get things underway." He saluted Isaac and was on his way, running back to the village.

Isaac sat on a stump at the edge of the road. "He saluted me. Me. Isaac the shepherd. Things are changing. Can I manage all this? I must. But first, I will talk to Rebekah and then go to the high altar. If only the god of the mountain would speak to me as he did to father." He stood and made his way up the hill to find Rebekah.

Rebekah was mixing dough to make bread. Isaac looked at her and felt a wave of gratitude wash over him. Tria was standing nearby.

"I need Rebekah. Take over the bread making if you please." He smiled at the young woman. "And do it even if you don't want to please me. But do it for Rebekah."

He took his wife's hand and led her to the bench by the river. He took her in his arms and held her close.

She looked at him. Worry lines creased her forehead. "What is it, Isaac? Is something wrong?"

He rubbed her back as he told her of the rumours in Hebron. As gently as he could, he explained the need to re-build his father's small army. "We need a place for the soldiers to live and a place for them to train. The two large empty tents would be perfect. Will that be all right with you?"

"You don't need my permission. You are the chief. But thank you for consulting me. I hope there won't be a need for them to defend us, but I can see the need to be prepared."

"I think if the hot-heads in the city learn that we are prepared to defend what is ours, the talk will die, and we can live in peace as we have for as long as many can remember."

"Will you be leading the soldiers?"

"No. I am not a soldier. But Benjamin will be the head of our little army. He is knowledgeable about these things and has offered to be my general."

"Will you tell Deborah? She hates fighting as much as I do. This will change things for her, and she needs to be informed."

"Can we do it together? It must be soon as I am to inform the people tonight in the gathering circle."

Isaac stood. "I will find her right now. Sit still, we will come here to you." He kissed her tenderly and headed off to find Deborah.

When Benjamin left Isaac, he went to the soldiers' rooms and found two seasoned fighters there. In a few short words, he told them of the plans. "There is talk in Hebron that alarms me. We may be at risk. Get ready to train harder than you ever have. There will also be heavy work here to fortify the village. Also, the two big tents need to be made ready. The smaller one, Rebekah's, will be the new barracks, and Abraham's will become a protected training space. Spread the word among the men and gather here before the evening meal. I will explain more then."

He left them and, at a steady jog, went looking for Deborah, as was Isaac. When Isaac, at last, found her, he realized he would not need to talk to her. She and Benjamin were sitting under a tree, his arm was around her and she was looking intensely at him. He quietly turned away and went to inspect the two tents. While looking at them and planning how to get everyone ready for their new purpose, he was also thinking about the meeting later in the evening.

As Isaac made his way to the square, he passed the food table. There was no food there. Nothing but jugs of water. Someone touched his sleeve. It was Rebekah. "I talked to Keturah, and we decided we would offer no food. This is not a celebration; this is a serious matter. I do not think we will be here long, so water is enough."

"It was a surprise, but you are right. I see the crowd has gathered. Come and stand with me on the platform if you are able."

She took his arm, and they walked to the stairs and climbed up the few steps to the raised floor. Isaac held up his hands for silence. Gershom was there at once, with a stool for Rebekah. She smiled at him and sat. He draped a shawl around her shoulders and left.

"People of Abraham. Followers of El Shaddai. Tonight, is not an occasion for food and good times. I come with serious, even grim news. We have reason to suspect that there are those who covet the life we have here." A low murmur ran around the circle. "There is no present danger, but preparations are soon to be underway to make our village more secure for the safety of all, but especially for the old ones, and for the women and the children of our great family. You will be asked to work hard to complete our plans, extra work on top of what you do each day. If each does his part, we can be ready before the rains begin." He paused to let the news sink in. "Thank you for coming and thank you for the way I know you will all do what you can. Please do not spread rumours. Do not gossip or listen to idle tales. Do not add to the concern we all feel." He turned to Rebekah and motioned for her to stand beside him. As she did, he again asked for silence. "We will bow before the great spirit of the mountain." Many knelt on the ground, and all bowed their heads. "Great god of the fiery mountain, hear my prayer. Protect your children, give us courage and strength. Turn the hearts of our neighbours away from thoughts of envy and greed. May we continue to live in peace and harmony and good-will. So be it and amen."

Shira began to beat her drum as she led Isaac and Rebekah down from the platform and across the grass toward their river home. The stars and the moon continued their silent journey across the heavens.

Chapter Forty-Nine

The entire settlement was alive with the sounds of hammers, chisels, saws, and the noise of shouted commands. The work was going well, and the wind had not yet gained in strength.

It was a good omen, and everyone was encouraged and hopeful.

Rebekah stayed in the river house, away from the dirt, the noise, and the confusion. Deborah was thrilled for Rebekah. The years of grief because of her empty womb would soon be a faded memory. No more would Becca sit alone in the tent of women. No more would she listen to the whispers behind her back.

"She is a dried-up old fig."

"What can she have done to anger the goddess of life?"

"It is an insult to our tradition that Isaac has taken no other wife or concubine."

"Do you think you would be the one?"

"Why not? I am young and beautiful. Even the great leader Abraham did that to gain an heir."

"And how did that turn out? Trouble and grief. Trouble and grief."

Rebekah was not having an easy time in this pregnancy. The mornings were difficult, and she kept little food down all day. Even at night, she was restless and felt sick. The usual herbs and potions did little to ease her misery.

Esther had tried all the things that worked for many women. Potions to drink and fragrant oil to rub on her growing belly. Scented oil burning in the lamps only made it worse. Esther and Deborah changed the straw on her bed every day and added bits of fresh cedar to it. Nothing helped. Isaac came every day, and she would find the courage to smile for him and tell him she was fine and very happy.

But he was not fooled. He was very worried about Rebekah. He questioned Ayla, and she tried to reassure him. “It is not unusual for women to have a difficult time in the first few months. Comfort her, bring her little treats and try to get her to take shorts walks with you.”

That evening, as they sat while Deborah cleaned up after the meal, Isaac suggested a walk. “Let’s go to the river. A short walk would be good for us. You always like to sit by the water, and the rippling sound is very soothing.”

Rebekah reached for a bowl. “Just remembering the waves and ripples makes my stomach churn.” She grabbed her belly and rubbed it in small, gentle circles. They sat together in the warmth of the fire.

As the weeks passed Deborah worried as her beloved Becca grew pale and drawn. One of the few times she showed any joy was when she told repeatedly the story of her night here in the new house Abraham built. She spoke of the flowers, the wine, the wonderful food, and the joy she and Isaac had shared. She knew that was the night of love that created this longed-for child.

One windy day, Deborah returned from the well to find Rebekah crying, all curled up in a ball of misery. “What is wrong, child?”

“I don’t know, but it feels like a worm or beetle is in my belly crawling about.”

Deborah had to turn away to hide the laughter she felt.

“Oh Becca. That is the baby. You are feeling the first flutter of movement. He is stretching his legs or wriggling his hands. This is wonderful.”

“Are you sure?”

“Of course. But take a walk and find Esther. Let her feel your belly. She will know and you trust her, even if you don’t believe me.”

Without even pausing to get a scarf in case she met a man, Rebekah was gone. Deborah smiled and started to hum for the first time in months.

Rebekah clapped at Esther’s tent and was invited to enter. Esther hugged her visitor in delight. “So good to see you out for a walk. I am glad you came to visit me. Sit here across from me so that I can look at you."

Seated on her cushion, Rebekah tried to think of a way to ask her question.

Esther continued to chatter. "I know from Deborah that you are doing better in the morning. That is a good thing. The sickness rarely continues after the baby starts to move a bit. I assume that is why you came; to tell me that good news."

Surprised by Esther's insight, Rebekah thought before she answered. "Yes, I felt little fluttering twinges this morning. I came to be sure that was what was happening." *Deborah will understand this little lie.*

"The time is about right from your first sick mornings. Are you feeling well now?"

"Yes. All is well. Isaac is spoiling me, and he is so pleased that I am better in the mornings. We plan to walk by the river each day now that it won't make me feel so sick."

"Do you know where he is right now?"

"He is in his tent. Why?"

"I would like to talk to you both. Stay here while I get him."

And she was gone. *Why would she want to talk to Isaac? What can be wrong now?* While she waited, she twisted the pillow in her arms. She tried to think of the river and pleasant walks with Isaac to keep the panic she was feeling under control.

In just a few minutes, Esther returned and entered the tent with Isaac. He sat beside Rebekah and held her hands. He looked as concerned as she felt.

"I know that this has both of you worried. There is nothing to be too worried about, but I do need to talk to you both. Rebekah, your belly is getting very large, very quickly."

They both looked at her stomach, and Rebekah pressed her hands against her belly.

"That usually means one thing. And it is not a bad thing. You are carrying two babies. You are going to have twins."

The air left both with a sudden swoosh. They turned to each other in shock.

Isaac shrieked. "No babies and now two. Two at once. What does that mean? Is Rebekah in danger? What should we do?" The questions tumbled from their lips, both talking at once.

Esther smiled. "Twin babies do make for complications. You will tire more easily, Rebekah, and near the end, may need to rest a great deal. No heavy work at all and as little stress on your body or you spirit as is possible."

They sat numb, trying to grasp what this meant.

"You need all your energy to help those babies grow strong and be ready for the world. The labour may be more difficult, but that is not always true. Just do all the things I told you before. Get your rest, eat well, take gentle walks, and enjoy these middle months. They will be the most pleasant for you both."

They sat, staring into each other's faces. Esther simply left her tent to give them time to think about the news she had just given them. As she walked, she voiced her excitement. "What a blessing. I will do my best to help them and to assure them as they wait for their babies.

Keturah and Ayla walked together as they came home from the market. They were both worried about the mother-to-be. As the weeks passed, she was listless, and she seemed worried and sad. But when asked, Rebekah said that all was well. Her friends sensed that this was not the whole truth. They wanted to help but didn't know how.

Ayla sighed. "I know from Esther she is carrying twins, and that is a great worry."

"Twins. Thank you for telling me. No wonder she is exhausted. We must get her to rest more. But I think something more is troubling her. Deborah tells me she walks about at night when she should be resting. Even when she is sleeping, she tosses and turns most of the night."

"As her midwife, I have suggested all the usual things. She is trying to do as I ask. I have told Isaac what I believe, and he is following her about and being very bossy. But she knows why and is doing her best.

"So, we need to find something different. How many twin pregnancies have you cared for?"

"Not very many, and I must confess that they have not gone well. I have lost mothers and babies or both, and it worries me."

"But Rebekah can be in no better hands. We all know of your skill and how much you care."

Ayla stopped. "Thank you, Keturah. She will need all of us to help her through the next few months."

"I know I have had only one quite easy baby, but I think I will try to talk with her. Do you think that would be helpful?"

"Honestly, Keturah, it cannot hurt. She loves and respects you, and perhaps she will confide in you. It is about the only hope we have."

"The name of this area is Canaan, and that means hope. Let's hope we can find some in this situation, for us, but especially for Rebekah."

The next morning, Keturah told Gershom of her concern and asked him to keep Isaac away for most of the day. "I will need time to earn her trust if she is to talk to me, and we must have no interruptions. Please see that Isaac is kept busy, too."

"I will do the best I can, but he too is worried, as am I. If I must, I will tell him what you need and he will co-operate, I am sure. We are having trouble with the irrigation troughs and that should keep us busy most of the day. May the holy one give you words of kindness and wisdom."

With a warm hug, he was gone.

Keturah put things in order in the tent, then got food ready for later. She picked up a cover for her hair and went to find Rebekah. She was in her room, sitting in a dark shadow and just staring at nothing.

"I hate to bother you, Rebekah, but you know what a terrible job I do of mending woven things. I have a shawl from Egypt that I like very much, and I caught it in some brambles on a windy day. I wonder if you could come to my room and help me to repair it? I have matching threads in my sewing basket. I know it is an imposition, but I want to wear it to the meeting that is to be held soon."

Rebekah looked up at Keturah, her eyes dull and dark. She shuddered and then reached for a shawl.

"If it doesn't look too bad, I will see if I can fix it. I might as well. Sitting here in the dark does not help my mood. Who knows, I might even find peace with you in your beautiful rooms." She paused. "Are you enjoying living in the house?"

"Yes, I feel safe there, and it helps to know it was Abraham's wish."

They walked slowly down the hall to the room of Keturah. Inside, Rebekah looked around. "I have not been here for awhile. It is so beautiful, Keturah. I don't know what it is, but peace just enfolds me here in this place."

"You are welcome to come here as much as you like. I always enjoy your company. We can have the entire day together. The men are out looking for damage to the water system and will be gone all day."

"It sounds awful when I say it, but sometimes Isaac is a bit of a burden. He fusses over me all the time. There are times I just need to be alone. But he looks so hurt when I tell him that."

"I think it must be difficult for husbands. They worry and they want to make everything better, but they are so helpless. They know nothing of the discomfort of carrying a child and have little idea of how to help. They hear all the sad stories and take them to heart. Isaac would be lost if anything happened to you. And this pregnancy is the hope for the future of this tribe."

"You understand so well, Keturah. Deborah and Esther are good to me, but they have never born a child. You have, and so you know."

Keturah laughed softly. "I bore one child and at times that was a burden. I can remember what it was like but can only imagine what you are feeling. And here I stand, keeping you on your feet. Come, sit while I get my sewing basket." As they went to her room, Keturah thought. *A good start. She is at least talking to me about this trouble she is carrying. And I do mean carrying.* Another small chuckle from Keturah.

Rebekah smiled. “It is good to hear you laugh. No one laughs around me anymore. And your laughter is so rich and comforting. Thank you.”

Rebekah settled on a pile of cushions and was surprised how well they supported her. “This is what I mean. Deborah piles up cushions, but they don’t support me. You must show her how to make this nest for mother bird.” They both smiled.

Keturah handed a lovely intricately woven shawl with beautiful, radiant flowers woven into the pattern. The shawl was the colour of warm sand, but flowers of every hue made a garden of colour. “This is lovely. I can almost smell the scent of the leaves and flowers.”

Another ripple of laughter. “What you smell are lavender petals and cedar wood. I have stored it for years, and I wanted to keep the bugs out of it.”

Rebekah held it up to her face and inhaled deeply. A look of peace softened the pain lines on her forehead. When she looked up at Keturah, there was a hint of the familiar sparkle in her warm brown eyes. “Show me where you have damaged it.”

For the next few hours, their heads were bent and almost touching as they worked to fix the snag and a small tear on the edge. Rebekah didn’t do the work, she taught Keturah, who was a ready pupil and learned quickly. If Rebekah had a suspicious nature, she might have wondered at her skill, but she was just relaxing and enjoying the time together. When the shawl was mended, Keturah stretched.

“It is time for a change. Would you like to take a short walk with me? To the river.”

“I don’t think so, but we could sit outside and listen to the birds and the wind.”

“Let’s do that.”

They moved out to the bench overlooking the valley. Keturah arranged cushions around Rebekah and gave her a stool to support her feet. “You know exactly what I need. Thank you.”

“I can help with cushions and stools, but you need something more. You seem troubled. I am a good listener if you would like to talk about it.”

Rebekah wrung her hands and grabbed a small pillow. She hugged it to her breast.

"I would like to tell someone how scared I am. I know that many women die giving birth and it is more likely with twins. That worries me, but it is not the real cause of my fear. There is something wrong with my babies."

She stopped speaking and took deep, slow breaths. Keturah patted her hand and then held it gently.

"When I walk in the lanes and paths, a very strange thing happens. If I walk past a house that I know worships El Shaddai, my belly is quiet, and I am content. When I pass a house that worships another god, something strange happens. I have pain, and cramps and I get all sweaty. My hands tremble and my vision blurs. I have almost fallen twice when this happens. That is why I don't walk outside much anymore. So, I pace for hours in the halls and my mood drives Deborah away. At times, it is as if my babies are fighting in my womb. I don't understand what is happening and I am frightened. What is wrong, Keturah?"

"Oh, my dear child. I don't know, I really don't know. This must be very upsetting for you, and for your babies."

They sat in silence and listened to the sounds of nature that bleated, chirped, and croaked all around them.

Keturah reached out and took both Rebekah's hands in her soft, warm ones. "But I have heard of a wonderful place where the people there would know how to help you."

"What place? Where? Who is there to help me?"

"Not far from here, in the north at the large waterfall, there is a yeshiva. A school and a place of healing. There are teachers of our faith there and the healers and midwives are known and respected as far away as Egypt."

"Could they help me to understand?"

"I can't promise, but they might be able to give you some peace of mind."

"But how can I travel to that place? Would it be safe?"

"You still have time before you come to the delivery and if you go soon, you can be home before the rains come. If you wish, I can talk to Esther and Ayla, and even Rivkah. They could help you decide. And I am sure we can figure out how to make the travel safe. It is only a long day's journey."

"I know I need help. This might be the answer. Please make it happen for me if you can."

"I will talk to everyone, and we will take you there."

They sat in comfortable silence until Rebekah whispered. "I would like to go home now."

"You do that, and I will get everyone together and we will come to your room and make a plan."

Rebekah smiled, held her friend in a long embrace. Rebekah turned and made her way to her rooms. Keturah got busy. She found Esther and told her. Esther went to get Ayla and Rivkah and then Isaac.

While Keturah waited for Isaac, she made up a basket of fruit, cheese, and bread, Isaac arrived, and she gave him water and towels. As he cleaned up, she told them of the events of the day.

Isaac looked stricken. "Why wouldn't she say something to me?"

"She is a proud woman," explained Keturah. "Pregnancy is supposed to be a happy time. How would she know she would be understood? And I am sure she didn't want to cause you any worry."

Benjamin spoke. "My friend, that is in the past. It is gone. We must do what is needed to help her now. Keturah, tell us what to do."

"I spoke to her of a place that might be able to help. We women are going to meet her tent and work out a plan together. Join us in a short while."

In her tooms, Rebekah told the women her plight. There were murmurs around the circle.

Deborah wiped a tear from Becca's cheek. "What can we do, dear one? What can I do to help?"

"Keturah spoke of a place near the big waterfall where there are people who might be able to help."

Ayla groaned. "I know it well. I should have thought of it. But I didn't know you were suffering so."

"No one did. You were all concerned, and Keturah coaxed me to talk. I hear the other men coming."

Rivkah smiled at them all and asked Keturah to take charge, since it was her wisdom that saw the problem and a solution. Ideas flew back and forth until they agreed on a plan.

With the rising sun, they would set out for the yeshiva of Shem and Ever.

Isaac grinned. "If father were here, he would say in that important voice he used, 'I am descended from the line of Shem, so Ever is a distant relative. The yeshiva, the school, traces its name back to Noah, the father of Shem.'" Smiles and small laughter filled the space at his mimicry of Abraham.

And Rivkah responded. "And Sarah would have scolded, a story for another time, Abraham." The tension in the room dissipated with the memories of these much-loved family members.

Ayla smiled and nodded. "The school is known for its teaching of the law, and its dedication to obedience. Healing the spirit, mind, and body is the core of its purpose. I think it will be a good place for Rebekah to visit." All agreed to put their trust in this beautiful place by the bend in the river.

Keturah was satisfied that they had done the best they could for their dear daughter, wife, and friend. She offered a prayer to El Shaddai as they parted.

"As you travel, may goodwill surround you, love keep you strong, and hope fill your heart. May music and song shorten the journey, and may you return to us refreshed and renewed. Go in peace."

Late into the night, Benjamin was at work preparing a cart where Rebekah could rest comfortably. An ox that was steady in its gait, gentle and quiet, would pull the cart. Isaac was to go with her to care for her. Benjamin chose four warriors to accompany the ox cart and one of them was a skilled player of the lute and had a good singing voice. Hours later, he went to his bed and satisfied with his work, he fell asleep under the watchful eye of the pale half-moon.

Chapter Fifty

Just after sunrise Rebekah settled in the oxcart and Isaac took up the reins to start their journey to the yeshiva. It was a misty morning, but the clouds wore golden cloaks and so the day promised to be pleasant.

The faithful ox plodded along the road, Isaac walked beside him, and kept a watchful eye on his sleeping wife. She stirred and gave a soft moan when a stone jarred the cart, but at once relaxed into her soft slumbers.

They came to a shady meadow, with a small pond, just as the sun rose to its highest point in the sky. Isaac led the ox off the road and stopped by the great cedar tree. Rebekah woke and sat up. “Are we there already?”

“No, dear one, this is just a rest stop. I will help you out of the cart so you can walk a bit and stretch your legs. The ox needs water and a time to browse on this lush grass.”

Rebekah stepped down and held tightly to Isaac. He helped her stand, as she gained her balance. Together they took a few steps. “Thank you. I am fine to walk now. Tend to our ox and I will get cheese and grapes for us.”

Isaac took the animal to the pond, and it drank noisily at the water’s edge. Isaac checked his legs and hooves and then let him graze in the grass. He spread out a blanket and he and Rebekah sat in the shade of the tree and ate their food.

“I am glad you stopped here. Just smell the cedar. So rich and earthy. So calming and restful.” She leaned against the tree and breathed deeply. “Are you tired, Isaac? You walked and I have slept.”

“No. I am used to walking about the vineyards and the fields. This is much more pleasant. I loved watching you as you slept. I look forward to spending time with you when we are at the school.”

"I do too. I hope that we will have time to be together, alone. That sounds strange but you know what I mean."

"This is most peaceful, but we cannot stay. We must get moving again as we need to arrive before the sun sets."

"I would like to walk for a while. I promise I will stop before I tire too much."

Hand in hand they walked along beside the old ox, enjoying the view and each other's close company. After a good walk, she squeezed Isaac's hand. "I will ride again. There is room in the cart, couldn't you join me?"

"Good idea. I will do that."

In the cart they sat, his arm around her shoulder as she hummed a gentle tune. The time passed pleasantly and at the bottom of a long hill they saw a flowering hedge and two stone pillars. They turned and passed between the sturdy gates.

Rebekah and Isaac walked down the long lane. Ahead were several low brick buildings, glowing red in the last rays of the sun. They stopped in front of large oak doors at the end of the road. Rebekah looked around. The only sounds were the splashing water of the river as it tumbled over the rocks and the buzz of insects hiding among the flowers that grew in abundance around the front door. She looked for someone, but there was no one in sight. Isaac noticed a gong near the door.

He walked toward it and hit it firmly with the attached small hammer. It rang with a beautiful musical tone and echoed back from the rocky hill in the distance. The door opened, and a woman stood in the entrance.

"Welcome travellers. Enter and we will see how we can help you."

Isaac put his arm around Rebekah and led her into a spacious hallway. She sat on a bench and the woman at the door brought cushions to support her back and raise her feet.

"If you are looking for rest and help for your wife, you are welcome. We have a room where you can stay. There is a stable for the ox at the back. Someone will be there to help you. Are you able to walk, my child?"

"Yes, I can walk. Thank you."

She led them to a room just doors along the narrow hallway. Windows high up in the wall let in the last rays of the sun, which made patterns of light and shadow on the smoothly polished dirt floor. "My name is Abigail, and this will be your room. A gong will sound in a little while, and at the far end of the hall is the room where we eat. Join us there, please."

"Thank you. We are tired and hungry. Your hospitality is very welcome."

"I leave you to settle in then."

She closed the door quietly and her slippers scuffed along the floor as she hurried away.

Rebekah and Isaac exchanged a smile. There were two raised beds in the room, not mats on the floor. The raised platform looked inviting, and she easily stretched out on it. "This is a clever idea, Isaac. So easy for me to lay down and I expect also easy to stand up."

"I shall make one for you as soon as we are home. It is a clever way to make rest comfortable. Are you very tired? I could bring food to you here."

"I am quite all right. It would be rude to these kind and generous people not to meet them at the meal."

Isaac left to deal with their ox. He was back very soon and sat on one of the chairs. He stretched his legs out in front of him, laid his head back against the wall, and closed his eyes. Rebekah watched him. His breathing slowed and his arm dropped limply to his side. "You poor dear. You watched me all day while you walked in the hot sun. You are the one who is exhausted."

Rebekah was just starting to enter the land of dreams when the gong rang out from the end of the hall. Isaac jumped. Rebekah laughed. "Wake up, sleepy head. It is time to go for the meal."

They walked along the hall and past several doors just like theirs. There were no sounds but the patter of their sandals. As they approached the door, it swung open, and Abigail welcomed them.

The room had a long table across the end and chairs placed all around it. A snowy white cloth covered it and candles glowed all along its length, one beside each plate. “So many chairs,” Rebekah whispered.

“Do not be concerned with all the places at the table. We are few here tonight and I will introduce you to the others. But first I must know your names.”

“I am Isaac, son of Abraham and this is my wife, Rebekah, daughter of Bethuel and Ruth. We come from Hebron. We come because my wife is troubled, and we seek guidance.”

“This is the place to come if you wish to find peace. Ah, here are the others.”

Isaac looked up and saw his four guards enter and sit at the far end of the table. Two men, dressed in plain sand-coloured tunics, entered, and bowed slightly. Two women followed them and nodded to the strangers. They were dressed in pale yellow tunics, exactly like the one Abigail wore. Abigail pointed to chairs for Isaac and Rebekah, and she went and sat opposite them. The others filled in chairs on both sides of the table and one woman sat at the head. Without a word, they joined hands around the table and invited their guests to join, but only if they wished.

The woman at the head, in a beautiful rich but warm voice, offered the evening blessing at a meal. There was silence for a long moment and the voice spoke again. “Abigail, tell us who has joined us.”

“This is Isaac, son of Abraham and his wife Rebekah, daughter of Bethuel. They have come from Hebron.”

“Welcome to you both. Be assured they will be treated well. In this place we all eat the same food, and sleep in comfortable beds. Tomorrow all will be told of what is expected. It is not much., but each person is asked to do chores to keep the school in good condition.Two men will be in each room.”

“The men at the end of the table are labourers on their way north. They asked for shelter and rest for two or three days. Their names are Gideon, Micah, Abner and Matan.” As his name was said, the owner stood and nodded. Isaac and Rebekah shared a wee secret smile.

The older woman at the end of the table passed the first bowl of food and signalled that they were all to take what they needed. “I am

Edna, and I am the spiritual leader here for women who come. The other woman is Gabriella, and you have met Abigail. They are the midwives and healers in this place. The two men are the teachers of the law and the ones who hear the word of the almighty and interpret it for us and teach us the way of righteousness. They follow in the footsteps of the great ones, Seth and Ever. While we have special gifts, training, and duties, here all are equal."

Abigail held up her hand. "At this table, we wish to be aware of the food before us and to be grateful to the ones who provide it, from the great creator to the humble gardener. To do that, we remain silent during the meal except for necessary requests for food or drink. Please enjoy the meal that is ready for you."

Rebekah felt the quiet atmosphere very calming, and she could easily feel gratitude filling her heart. Isaac was not so comfortable. He almost spoke two or three times. Rebekah heard him shuffle his feet and clear his throat. Softly she whispered… "Shhh."

At the end of the meal, Edna said the closing prayer, then stood. "Abigail will tell you the routine and we ask that you do your best to follow our pattern. Good night, rest in peace."

When the others had taken their leave, Abigail walked with them to their room. "May I come in for a few minutes?"

She followed them inside. Rebekah lay on the bed and at once Abigail brought two pillows and supported her back. She motioned Isaac to sit and then she sat beside the bed on a low stool.

"You will hear the gong again for the morning meal. The gong tells us the time that we need to change what we are doing. After the meal, there is a quiet time to rest, to bathe, to ponder the day. At the next gong, Gabriella and I will join Rebekah here and we will talk with her. You, Isaac, will go to the back of the house where you will be given work to do. Later, we may ask you to join us to talk. Mid-afternoon Edna will come and speak with both of you. Then you will have free time to talk with each other, to walk along the river or to rest. The next gong will once again be sounded for the evening meal. Do you have any questions?"

"What do we do now?" asked Rebekah.

"This time is your own to do as you please. In a small room next to the dining area is a room with water and towels and soap. Use that space whenever it is not occupied. If the door is shut, someone is there. Anything else?"

Isaac stood. "I think that is what we need to know for now. Can we ask more questions if we have them tomorrow?"

"Of course. We want you to feel that this is your home, and you are free to do as you wish if you respect the rules. You are welcome to stay as long as you need to."

"I didn't ask. What is the cost to be here, for food and lodging and for the teaching and for the help we receive?"

"There is no charge for anything. That is why you are expected to work. But of course, not you Rebekah. The labour pays for your stay. Some choose to make a gift of some kind, but it is not expected."

"I can sew and mend, and I do both very well. I would like to help too."

"Thank you, Rebekah. I am sure we can find something for you to offer. And now I will say good night. I hope you will be comfortable, and that sleep comes easily and is peaceful."

They said good night all around and Abigail left. The two weary travellers looked at each other in both surprise and wonder and in thankfulness for the peace and calm they experienced since their arrival.

"I am very tired, Isaac. I see that someone has carried in our bundles. If you don't mind, I will just go to the washing place and then to bed."

"Good night, dear one. I may be asleep before you get back. Don't wake me till the morning gong."

When she had tided herself, Rebekah crept into the room. Isaac was gently snoring, and Rebekah lay on the bed. Despite the busy day and all she had seen and heard, her heavy eyelids closed, and she joined her husband in peaceful slumbers.

Chapter Fifty-One

Abigail was waiting for the other women to join her in the courtyard. She noted what a pleasant day it was; the flowers were in full bloom. Bees buzzed around them and the hum as they hovered over the flowers was a gentle song that soothed and comforted. Edna and Gabriella joined her.

"I have invited Rebekah to join us. She will be here shortly. I sense that she is very troubled but am not sure why. We will talk with her and see if we can ease her mind and heart."

Gabriella voiced her thoughts. "She is well along in her pregnancy. Has she come here to deliver?"

"I had just a brief word with her, and she is only in the last months of her term. She thinks she is carrying twins. So, delivery may still be weeks away. Here she comes."

The three women greeted Rebekah and expressed their happiness at meeting her.

Rebekah looked around the courtyard and then at the table in the centre of four chairs. "How lovely. Candles and cedar bark. The cedar is my spirit symbol. Did Isaac tell you that?"

"No. I have not spoken to Isaac." Edna invited them all to be seated. "I sensed that you were a strong woman who could bend with the winds of life and so cedar just seemed right. Tell us about yourself if you would like to do that."

"It would be helpful if I knew a bit about you and this place."

"Of course." Edna smiled. "I am the spiritual leader of the women who come here. Levi is the leader of the male priests, and he is ready to speak with us if we choose to ask him. Gabriella is the head midwife, and there are others who help her and are learning from her. Abigail is our healer and a wise counsel in all matters of our well-being, physical, spiritual and things of the mind and heart. We have been here since we were young and were all trained by the wise grandmothers who were here before us."

"Why the school of Shem and Ever?"

"Good question. Shem was the son of Noah, and Ever the son of Shem. This place is named after those ancient leaders. If they were ever here, I do not know. But it is good to honour those who made the path we follow. No one can remember when or how this began as a yeshiva, but it has been here for many, many years."

"Thank you. I am Rebekah, daughter of Ruth, daughter of Zera. I was born in Haran and lived there until my marriage to Isaac years ago. We grieved we had no child, and I had given up all hope of a son to continue with the family line. Isaac is the son of the great leader, Abraham."

Gabriella interrupted. "The wife of Abraham was Sarah, was it not?" Rebekah nodded. "Her story is told around the campfires at our ceremonies. We honour her wisdom and faithfulness."

"I never met her and often wish I had. We too tell her story at the new moon ceremonies."

Edna took Rebekah's hand. "How did you learn about this place, and why have you come?"

"Back in our small village, the women who cared about me were concerned about my well-being. Keturah, the wife of my father-in-law, came from Egypt. In that faraway place, she had heard of this healing house here in Canaan. She found out from me what was troubling me and suggested I come here. They all worked together and made it possible, and here I am."

Rebekah felt the warmth of the hand holding hers. Edna nodded. "That is part of your story, but can you tell us what exactly was troubling you? Take all the time you need. There is no hurry."

Abigail offered her cool water in a very pretty pottery cup. "We all understand that facing the dangers of childbirth can be daunting, and in your case, even more so. We agree that you are carrying twins."

"Ayla, the midwife at home, suspected I was. I am sure that she is right because I know that I am getting big too quickly. I am worried about the birth, of course, but that is not the real cause of my worries."

She paused and looked at the sky for a long time. The other women sat with her in a comfortable, warm silence, respecting her need to gather her thoughts.

"When I walk in our village and pass houses where I know the people are followers of El Shaddai, I am comfortable and barely notice. But as I pass by a house that has idols on the roof, or in the yard, it is very disturbing. There are pains in my belly, and I feel that it is all tied up in knots. The babies are highly active. It feels as if they are fighting. Fighting for space in my womb and even for space in my thoughts. My head aches, my legs go weak and once or twice I had to sit by the road when I felt faint. Getting to my feet again was a sight to behold, and I hope no one saw me." Rebekah managed a weak smile.

Gabriella waited while Rebekah nibbled on cheese and bread.

She looked up and added. "I don't sleep well at night, terrible dreams, and much discomfort. I am then very tired during the day. Last night was the best rest I have had in months. The sickness that comes in the morning did not go away for about four moons."

"As the midwife here, I would like to examine you. I will need to see your belly to touch and feel it and to listen to any sounds I might hear. Will you permit that kind of intimacy from a stranger?"

"I have only known you a short while, but a think of you as friends, not strangers. I will accept whatever you need to do. You only wish to help me, of that, I am sure."

"Then come inside with us."

They walked down the long hall to the end of the building, opposite the eating room. The room they entered was large. It reminded Rebekah of the moon room back home. The windows were high up on the walls. No one could look in. They were covered with a light airy fabric that shone and seemed to give off its own light as it fluttered in the flower-scented air. The walls were decorated with pictures of flowers, trees, birds, and butterflies. Cushions were everywhere and there were long, low seats, just waiting for someone to rest on them. Lamps and candles sat on tables and on low stools.

"We use this room for ceremonies and gatherings. But right now, it has become my examining room. The tall table at the far end is for you to lie on while I examine you. The others will help you get ready while I get the things I need."

When Rebekah was comfortable on the strange table, that felt more like a bed, Gabriella returned. She rubbed Rebekah's extended belly with warm scented oil. At times, pressing more heavily than others. She put her head right down against the skin as if she were listening. All the while, Abigail was humming a light and happy tune. Rebekah was so comfortable she thought she could easily fall asleep.

From far away, she heard her name gently spoken, as if someone were calling her. With a start, she realized she had been asleep. Before she could apologize, Edna took her hand to help her stand. "You are a wonderful patient. Because you trusted so fully that you fell asleep, a good examination was accomplished. We have had time to talk over what we have learned, and we have some suggestions for you in the days ahead. We have sent for Isaac, as he must be wondering what we are doing to you, and he needs to hear what we have to say. When you are ready, we will gather again in the courtyard. There is a washing-up room through that door, with warm scented water and plenty of towels. Go there and cleanse your belly and whatever else you need. Can you manage by yourself, and can you find the courtyard again?"

"I shall manage fine. Thank you. I will join you in a little while."

The room was small, but large enough. Again, there were flowers and pictures and wonderful aromas. *This is all so lovely. No animal bones or spears, just beauty. I wonder what the room where the men meet is like? I suspect I will never know.*

She returned to the courtyard to find Isaac pacing up and down. No one else was there.

"Isaac."

He turned and opened his arms; she entered the circle of his love and laid her head on his chest. "I am fine, dear husband. I am totally at peace in this place. They have treated me with love and respect. How are you and what have you been doing all day?"

"We can talk about me later. I need to know what they say about our future."

At those words, the three women returned. "Please, let us sit around the table."

When everyone was comfortable, Edna spoke. "It is important that we begin this time with a blessing." She held out her hands, and they all joined in a circle filled with warmth and peace.

"Holy mother, from the mountain top, you see our struggles.

You hear our laughter. You wipe our tears.

I ask for your patient love to enfold all within this circle.

May Rebekah and Isaac know your healing touch and feel your strong arms holding and blessing them.

In the shadow of the holy mountain, we pray."

Gabriella then spoke of what she had learned. "There are two strong babies growing under your heart. They are active and, from what I can tell, healthy and doing well. It seems that they are going to be vastly different men. They struggle together now; I think about space. However, that could mean supremacy. Perhaps that struggle will follow them all their lives."

Rebekah and Isaac sat motionless; their hands tightly clasped.

"You have done well Rebekah; you are strong, and all is going just fine. I hope that knowing this, you can relax. Let the little ones push and stretch. It will make them more hardy and ready for life. Eat good food, sleep long and rest easy."

"Now it is my turn," and all looked at Edna. "Rebekah, I wonder if the struggle between the worship of El Shaddai and other gods might be your struggle? It is something that many people in this time deal with. It may be that your babies will struggle with this too, as they grow into adults. A lot of people do and each must find their own peace in the path they walk in the search for truth. If you have questions, we will try to answer them. But I suggest you now spend time together, thinking about what we have said. If you desire, we can meet again after the last meal of the day."

The two parents were so intent on each other they didn't notice as the three women crept away.

Chapter Fifty-Two

With the dawning of the sun, Isaac was ready for the day. He had a quick but hearty meal and went into the yard. He was going to work with Enoch, the man in charge of the gardens and vineyards. Rebekah was spending the early part of the day with her guides and teachers here at the Yeshiva. Isaac knew he needed to keep busy, and he also needed to work to pay for their time at this healing place.

"Good morning, Isaac. I have a question and I hope you can give me the answer I want to hear. Do you know anything about irrigation channels?"

"I am quite familiar with the kind we have at home. We irrigate our gardens and vineyards."

"Good. Very good. Years ago, a guest spent many weeks here and put in a system of canals to water our gardens. He left when he finished and never told us how to maintain them. They are not working very well, and I can use any help you can offer."

"I will look at them and we can make a plan for repairs if needed."

"What do you need?"

"How many channels are there? Can we inspect them all or should we have workers? I will also need sticks to mark the places that need work done."

"There are many, many channels. We cannot walk them all in the time I expect we have. I will get workers and you can teach us what we need to know and then how to fix the problems."

He walked away and when he returned, he had a group of young men with him and a bundle of sturdy sticks. He also brought balls of coloured yarn. "I thought if there were different problems, we could mark the sticks with different colours."

"That is a good plan. There often are different things that need to be fixed. Lead the way and we can begin."

"I have told the lads who all work in the gardens that you will teach us what to do and how to do it. They are eager to learn, as they are tired of carrying water to the vines."

They set out to inspect the miles of canals. Isaac saw one problem at once.

"The water cannot flow well as the channels are blocked with dirt and sticks and other things. All that needs to be cleared away. And then regularly keep a watch for such buildup of blockages." He saw that everyone was nodding.

As they walked, Isaac pointed out the gates that controlled the water flow. He explained how they worked and the need to control how much water travelled along the paths. Too much and the plants died, too little, and the plants died. He told them what to look for to tell the difference.

One of the men spoke up. "It looks like the gates are in poor shape as well."

"Exactly. That was my next point. A woodworker needs to make all new gates. These are old, waterlogged, and rotten. Do you understand how they work?"

"Yes, I can see the way they should work. We can look after it now, I think." Enoch looked at his workers and they were smiling and nodding.

"It seems as if you can begin to work at clearing the garbage and removing the gates. Enoch and I will go to the beginning and close the main entrance gates. We will walk the rest of it, and Enoch can point out and mark any trouble spots. Any questions?"

There were none, and the group split up. Isaac saw at once that Enoch had a good understanding of the task, and his mind began to wander as they walked, and Enoch put sticks in the ground.

What has Rebekah been doing all day? Those women helped her a great deal. I don't know what more she needs, but they wanted us to stay another day. Perhaps it was so that I could do this and pay for our time here. That is fine, but I want to return as soon as we can.

He realized Enoch was talking to him. "I'm sorry, my attention wandered. What were you saying?"

"I said I think I can finish this. Why don't you return to the house and be ready if they want to talk to you? If you want to keep busy, there are tools that are dull. It would be an immense help if you could sharpen them."

"Thank you. I am anxious about Rebekah. I will do as you suggest." He waved as he trotted back to the buildings at the back of the main house. Once there, he settled on a bench and began to sharpen axes and saws. It seemed like hours later that a man came looking for him and invited him to come to the courtyard.

He entered the courtyard and saw Rebekah sitting by the fountain. She was beautiful in a tunic of pale blue, her hair braided and hanging over one shoulder in the front. A blue ribbon was woven into the braid. *She hasn't cared about how she looked for weeks. I see peace in her face, not fear. This is so good.* "Good morning, beautiful one. How are you?"

She turned and held out her hands. He took them in his and raised them to his lips.

She shivered in delight at his greeting."What have you been doing all day?"

"I have been teaching the men about irrigation trenches. Someone built them years ago, but no one knew how to look after them. I have been showing them what to do and they are going to look after them now."

"A good day's work."

"And you? What have you been doing?"

"The women have been teaching me. I have been listening and mending linens. I am good at that, and they needed serious mending."

"Are you going to tell me what they were teaching you?"

"They reminded me that I need to take care of myself. That's the best way to care for our children right now. Any distress I am feeling can be passed on to the babies. They get upset, then that makes the pregnancy more difficult and more dangerous."

"What can I do?"

"I need to rest. Two babies make more stress on my body. So, no heavy work, and I am not sure what that means."

"Easy to decide. No lifting; not water, or wood, bags of flour, heavy stools. Need I continue the list?"

"But that is what I do most of the day."

"From now on, you let Deborah do it, and I will get a girl to help her. You give orders and lift a needle and thread. I will be with you as much as I can and I am sure when I explain it to everyone they will understand."

She grinned at him. "And you are sad that you don't have to practise making the marks or figuring out the numbers of grain bags in storage. I know how you loved that work."

They laughed together.

"When will we return home, Rebekah?"

"At first light tomorrow. But we must take it slow and easy. I know I am going to be restless and jumpy at all these rules. But I will do my best because it is for a good reason. I can walk when the road is smooth and if I am not too tired. They said walking was good and I should do as much as I can."

"Then let's take a gentle walk around the gardens while it is still light. I haven't seen much of them and would like to." He handed her the shawl and helped to drape it around her shoulders. Then he took her arm, and they walked together along the paths. Rebekah could name most of the flowers and plants in the gardens, and Isaac knew the trees. Between walking and resting on the benches, the afternoon passed. When the gong for supper rang, they went to join the others for the meal.

It was a pleasant time and later in the gardens, Isaac and Rebekah answered questions about their lives in Haran. They talked about herb and medicinal plants and the treatment of illness. After the meal, they moved to the fire in the courtyard and sang songs and told stories until they saw the moon rising over the hills.

When there was a quiet moment, Isaac spoke. "We will leave at first light in the morning. Both of us will always remember your kindness and your wise and peaceful way of living. We will remember what we have learned and will try to live in this gentle way when we are at home."

"Your life will be busy with two babies, but we hope they will be healthy and strong. We will always remember you as we eat from our gardens and use the mended linens.

In turn, each of the women offered a blessing as they said goodbye.

In their room, Isaac said the evening blessing and Rebekah blew out the tiny flame from the oil lamp. The golden moon shone through the window and the warm, soft light eased their tired bodies and minds into the land of sleep.

Chapter Fifty-Three

The day began with a glorious pink and gold sky. As Rebekah stood on the stone floor of the shared area, every bird in the universe seemed to be singing a song of joy. After they had eaten, Isaac went to the stables to get their cart and ox ready for the journey home. Isaac spoke to Abner, the captain of his men.

"How have you spent your days?"

"We have been working in the stables, repairing pens, and caring for the animals. It has been a positive change. How is Rebekah?"

"She is much improved, quite well again. We will leave after we eat and will meet you at the place where we left our things. Can you manage to get away?"

"That will not be a problem. It will be good to be on the way home."

"Yes, we will see you then."

Goodbyes had been said the night before and after the morning meal there was a pleasant time of appreciation and good wishes. Rebekah had packed their few possessions and waited with bundles for Isaac to bring the cart around.

Home. How good that word sounds. It has been a very satisfying visit to this wonderful place, but I need to see Keturah and Deborah and tell them how my world has been changed by the women I met here.

Isaac was smiling broadly as he came around with the cart. He placed the bundle in it and left space for the soldiers' parcels. The bed was as it had been before, and it pleased her that Isaac had remembered every detail.

Abigail came through the kitchen door. "I will not delay you, but here is a basket of herbs for you. They are the ones you did not have.

Take them and stay well." She turned and disappeared into the open doorway.

"How kind and thoughtful," Rebekah murmured. Isaac was ready to help her into the cart. "I would like to walk for a little while. I want to take the first steps on the way home, with my own two feet."

Isaac took her hand, clucked to the ox and the journey home began. It was a grand morning for a journey. The breeze was gentle, and Rebekah felt the cool air as she took the first steps. *I am glad we have an ox. They move slowly and I can keep up the pace.*

Their men were waiting and had the weapons ready to stow away in the cart. They nodded and smiled at Rebekah. Isaac prodded the ox, and their journey began.

They followed the winding path, enjoying the countryside. Sheep and goats grazed on the hills, small white and grey walking balls of wool. Rebekah smiled at the image. High in the sky, a hawk soared on invisible winds that carried him in great circles as he hunted. They were passing a large stand of cedars, and Rebekah turned aside to pluck two small sprigs.

"I could have picked those for you. You should stay on the road where it is safer."

"I am fine Isaac. I just wanted a bit of cedar from this place. I will dry it when I get home and keep it as a reminder."

"I don't think we will ever forget these few days, but if you wish some cedar to help you recall this blessing, that is fine."

"But that is enough walking for now. Help me into the cart, please."

He stopped the ox and held out his hand. At the cart, he lifted down a small stool and Rebekah stepped up into the cart. "I don't remember that stool."

"I bought it from the carver. It helped him and I was sure it would make it safer for you, in and out of the cart."

"You take such loving care of us, Isaac. I am sure nothing can go wrong."

For the following hours, she rode, dozing at times, but looking with pleasure at the passing view when awake. The landscape looked like home, and yet she knew it wasn't. It just didn't feel quite right.

Hours later, they came to a spot where the river was close to the road. Isaac called a halt. He laid a piece of carpet on the grass and with a large soft pillow at her back and a smaller one under her knees, Rebekah sat and leaned up against a tall, stately oak. The ox was taken out of the harness and led to the river to drink. He walked right into the water till it reached his belly. There he stood and lowed at the water. "Listen Isaac. He is thankful for the cool water on his legs and feet. I wish I could do the same."

"Absolutely not. I will bring you a bowl of water and you can bathe your feet if you wish. The men and I will take turns in the water to refresh ourselves. We will have a drink and fruit, cheese, and bread. It will be late before we arrive home to have our meal."

As she soaked her feet in the cool water, Rebekah hummed a gay melody. After a few minutes, she stopped the song and began to chant a hymn of thanksgiving she learned from her mother. *I am surprised I remember this. Mother didn't chant her praises very often. Now that I remember it, I shall sing it every morning when I awaken to a new day.*

She watched Isaac and the soldiers as they stood waist deep in the river. They splashed water over their arms and necks. It ran down their faces, leaving streaks where the dust washed away. When she laughed aloud, Isaac made a face at her and plunged his head into the water. She laughed even louder as he stood there, bent over and headless. All too soon, it was time to get on the road again.

For a while she walked beside the ox and stroked his warm back and rubbed his ears. The ox made soft, little noises in its throat. "Careful," said one of the soldiers. "You will spoil him with all this petting."

"Besides you Abner, I don't remember your names and you have left your families to take us in safety on this journey. Thank you for helping us."

"You are welcome. That one is Gideon, the tall one is Micah, and the ugly one over there is Matan." The men smiled and Rebekah joined in their fun. For the next hour, she walked with them, and learned where they came from, and about their families and their children. Isaac listened and marvelled at the ease with which she could get people to talk to her.

The air was beginning to cool as the sun was riding just above the hills far to the west. She got back into the cart, and Isaac wrapped his cloak around her. Warm and revelling in the familiar smell of her husband, she once again fell under the spell of the rocking motion of the cart and drifted into sleep.

The cart came to a stop and jolted Rebekah wake. "Hello, sleepy head. We are at the bottom of the hill that overlooks the camp. We can freshen up a bit here, have a drink and then climb that hill, and run down the other side to greet our families."

They giggled together at the image of Rebekah running down the hill. After a brief pause, they started once more along the road. At Isaac's insistence, Rebekah rode in the cart.

From the top of the hill, the camp looked so wonderful. *Home, we are home.*

"Look Isaac, there is a fire at your father's house. And people, many people. Do you think they are waiting for us?"

"I am sure. Let's get closer so they can spot us. Maybe if we all sang?"

And that is how they came home. Singing a song of praise.

Keturah ran to meet them, and Rebekah got down out of the cart and walked toward her. Rebekah hurried into Keturah's open arms. After a warm hug, Keturah stepped back and looked at Rebekah. "You are different. You look wonderful. Calm at peace. Relaxed."

"Thank you for telling us about that place. It was exactly what I needed."

"Come along, you two. Others are waiting to greet the travellers. Keturah is waving at us to keep moving."

At the top of the hill, there were hugs and kisses and handshakes. Everyone was asking questions and talking all at once.

Isaac held up his hand and asked for quiet. "Let me say this. We had a safe and pleasant travel. The time spent at the yeshiva was helpful and healing. Rebekah is well and is carrying two babies."

When the hubbub died down, Isaac continued. "I am sure you understand that we have been on the road since sunup. Rebekah is tired, as we all are. But she needs to get to her room and rest. We have not eaten, so please bring food to the house for us. Look after our soldiers, for they have been faithful all through this travel. So has the steady ox. We will tell you all the news in the morning. Thank you for understanding that what we need now is food and then rest."

There were soft sounds of agreement, as Rebekah climbed into the cart, and they turned and went down the hill. Later, Deborah left food at the house with a word of welcome and blessing. Someone came and took the ox away with a clatter of wooden wheels and the clop of tired hooves.

After they had eaten, Isaac settled his tired wife in her bed. "You have been a strong and brave woman these last few days. Now it is time to rest. With your permission, I will sleep in your room tonight. I know you are doing fine, but I will stay to ease my mind and yours as well."

He knelt by her pallet, stroked her cheek, kissed her forehead, and covered her with a light blanket. "Good night, my beloved. Until the morning."

He sat beside her until her eyes were still and her breathing slow and gentle. Then he went to his pallet and dropped down on it. Asleep almost before he hit the bed.

Chapter Fifty-Four

Isaac walked along the lanes in the village. It was sunrise and the morning was quiet, even the birds were still in their nests. He was pleased with what he observed. The stone fence around the river house was completed and the thorn hedge along its walls was growing new roots and shoots. Benjamin had a small but elite army trained and well prepared. The men of the village were proficient in the use of spears and the bow. The tent of Abraham was busy from dawn to dusk. The clang of swords and knives mingled with the hum of arrows as they left the bow. He paused to look at the river. Thinking aloud, he muttered. "I will insist that Benjamin move into my empty tent. It will give him privacy and we can set it up for meetings with his staff. It is close enough to be in touch with the barracks and far enough away to give him peace and quiet." He turned and walked back to the river house. Smoke was curling lazily toward the clouds, dark and heavy with rain.

He was deep in thought as he approached the gate to the house. The soft voice of Ayla startled him. "Good day Isaac. May I have a word with you?"

"Certainly. We can sit on the bench under the oak tree. Is Rebekah all right?"

She laid a hand on his arm. "She is fine. There is nothing wrong. But I need to speak of her care. The rains are upon us, and the wind rises each afternoon. Mud makes walking dangerous even for the strong and nimble."

"I know, I see many slipping and almost falling. If you are thinking of Rebekah, she never leaves the grounds around the house and never walks alone."

"But she will need to go to the moon tent when the babies come. I think it would be wise to make that move before her time. It would be much safer."

"Is it soon?"

"Yes, I believe so. I have been counting the moon phases and it can be any time now. Babies come when they are ready, and we need to be prepared to welcome them. With twins, it is often earlier than expected."

"You and I may agree, but my wife may have other ideas."

"I know, so it is up to us to persuade her. I think the suggestion should come from me as her midwife, but you must be ready to use all your charm to get her agreement."

Isaac gave a deep chuckle. "I have been accused of many things, but never before has the word charm been used to describe me."

They laughed together. "I will come by later and we can talk to her about this. If you have a chance, you might mention it to Deborah."

"Yes, yes. I will do that. Thank you, and I'll be ready when you come by later."

She smiled and waved as she carefully made her way to the road.

It was mid-afternoon when Ayla entered the house. Deborah was waiting for her. "I am pleased that we will be taking Becca to the moon house soon. I am not a midwife, but her time is near."

"I do too. Do you think she will agree?

"She must. I will threaten to tie her to a camel and make her go. That image has a memory for us, and I think it will make her laugh when she thinks of it."

Deborah led the way to the courtyard where the parents-to-be were resting.

Rebekah roused and smiled. "Good morning, Ayla. It is good of you to come out in the rain to visit. Please sit and have tea with us."

Ayla decided to get right to the point. "Thank you. Tea will be lovely. I have come, but this is an official midwife visit, not just a teatime chat."

Isaac took Rebekah's hand. "There is nothing wrong, dear one. Ayla just needs to talk to us."

Rebekah looked at her husband, then turned to stare at Ayla Rebekah's brow creased with worry lines and her dark eyes held a hint of suspicion.

Ayla smiled. "He is right, my dear. All is well with those babies of yours. But it is time for you to move to the moon house to be ready to welcome them."

"But I have no pains, no signs. Why should I move away from my home and my husband now?"

Isaac spoke up. "No signs are good, dearest one. But the footing is treacherous between us and the women's tent. If you should slip and fall, it could be dangerous to you and to our precious babies."

"A fall would be bad for all of you. And that chilly wind driving the rain. You mustn't get a chill."

"Please, I am not ready to move there yet. I am content here, and warm and safe."

Deborah moved closer and knelt beside her mistress.

"I agree with these two who love you as I do. I say you should go now, while you can walk with a little help. Before long, we would have to get the cart or a litter. I think you would rather walk than ride in a cart."

Ayla nodded. "To make the journey after your labour starts would be difficult. You will soon learn that as a mother, your little ones come first. This is the time to show that you understand the safety of your babies is most important."

Isaac looked into Rebekah's eyes. "Please, Rebekah, for me, your well-being is my greatest concern. I could not bear it if anything happened to you." Concern was in every word Isaac spoke.

Deborah stood. "Becca, do I have to threaten to tie you to a camel before you agree?"

In spite of herself, Rebekah laughed. "The ultimate threat. First Eliezar and now you. I can see that I am quite outnumbered. Much as I disagree, I will bow to the wishes of my jailers. I mean my friends."

Deborah and Isaac each gave a deep sigh of relief. Ayla patted Rebekah's hand. "Good. Good. We will make the move at dawn tomorrow. The cold night air makes the mud solid and often the rains are softer than later in the day. I will meet you there. I go now to get the space ready for our most important guest."

Deborah walked with her to the road. "Well done, Ayla. My mind is at ease. Is it correct for me to assume that I will be allowed so stay with her?"

"Of course. She will rely on you as she always has."

Deborah returned to the courtyard to do what she did so well. She started giving orders and bossing everyone.

Chapter Fifty-Five

Deborah was up before the sun and had the meal ready. After a last look at the table, set with candles and cedar boughs, she went to call Isaac, and met him at the door.

Isaac greeted her with a warm smile. "Rebekah is awake and almost ready for breakfast. What can I do to help?"

"It is ready. Just bring Rebekah down to the eating room, and we can have our meal.

"Thank you, Deborah. I should have known you would be ready for us. We will be there soon."

Deborah returned to the room where they ate and stirred the porridge one more time. She heard them coming along the hall and got the cushions ready for Rebekah.

"Good morning. Deborah. I don't think I have ever been able to get out of bed in the morning before you."

"I enjoy the dawn, so it is easy for me. Come, sit, and eat."

Isaac settled her in her place and took the steaming bowl from Deborah. He handed it to Rebekah with the comment that it smelled wonderful.

Deborah smiled her appreciation. "As this is a special day, I added some cinnamon to the gruel for a celebration meal."

Rebekah held the bowl to her face. "It does smell wonderful, but I am not very hungry. Don't make that face at me. I will try to eat something."

While she took a dainty spoon full, Isaac was enjoying each bite from his bowl. "I think I will make a rule. Cinnamon for breakfast every day."

The three companions shared a smile around the table.

Isaac took another great mouthful and started to speak. Deborah held up a hand. "I am sure Sarah must have told you not to speak with your mouth full."

Isaac put down the bowl. "I have everything ready; I think. You will look after personal things for both of you, won't you Deborah?" She nodded. "Good. I have made arrangements to have the bed moved, and it should be there shortly after we arrive."

Rebekah groaned, "It seems a lot of bother, moving the bed and everything. So much trouble." She put down her spoon.

"It is no trouble. You need to be as comfortable as possible. Good for you, the bowl is empty. I think you agree with my new cinnamon rule."

The meal over Deborah stood. "Keturah will clean all this away. We can just go. I checked outside, and it is not raining now. Where is your warmest shawl?"

"I left it in my room."

Isaac ran to get it. "Here it is. Now we can begin the move as I heard Gershom at the gate."

"Why have you bothered Gershom? I can walk. Such a fuss, Isaac."

"We all know you can walk, and you will. But I insist on a strong pair of arms on each side of you in case you slip. We cannot have you falling and knocking us all down like sticks in the wind."

They slowly made their way out to the path, and then through the gate to the roadway. The ground was still hard, and the wisdom of the early start was apparent.

They walked in silence, each one intent on the task and the need for care. As they neared the tent, Ayla and Esther were standing at the door.

Rebekah pointed at the bed just disappearing into the tent. "They carried that bed the long way around, and still beat us. But no matter, I did it. I walked to the women's tent. I am ready to go inside and wait for my little ones to arrive."

Isaac stopped at the doorway. Esther motioned for him to enter. "This is a special time, and for today only, you may help your wife settle in her space. If we have forgotten anything, Rebekah, just ask."

It took time to get Rebekah settled in her corner. It contained three chairs and a couple of stools. Flowers graced the table, and a cedar branch hung over the bed. There was a small chest for her clothes and another for whatever else she would be bringing. A sky-blue curtain gave her privacy. Suddenly, there was the sound of rain pounding the roof of the tent and a blast of wind shook the walls.

Isaac shook his head. "We need to build a gathering place for the women. I must think about that. Now I leave you. If the weather permits and you feel up to it, perhaps we can meet outside sometime." Isaac looked around and he and Rebekah were alone. After a tender kiss, he strode from the sacred space.

Deborah met him outside. "I will keep you informed of how she is. Every day I will come and tell you what I can. Please do not worry. We will care for her. It will be all right Isaac."

Isaac nodded, wiped his face with his sleeve, and disappeared into the silver sheets of rain.

The next morning Deborah and Rebekah were alone in the birthing room. Rebekah looked at her lifelong companion. "I know you well, Deborah. Something is on your mind. What is troubling you?"

"I can't hide anything from you, can I?" They shared a warm and tender smile. "I am thinking ahead to when your babies come. Two will make a great deal more work. A few weeks ago, I found a young woman, crying at the side of the house of Fiefel."

"That is the house of evil that enslaves girls and women, is it not?"

"Yes. When I saw her, I talked to her. She has been here, helping me ever since. She is a good, worker and a gentle soul. Could we find a permanent place for her here?"

"If you want her as a helper, it is done."

"Thank you, Becca. I would like you to meet her and hear her story. Are you feeling well enough today?"

"Bring her here for the evening meal, and we will talk."

At the time of the meal, Deborah led a young woman to Rebekah's bed. "This is Miri."

"Welcome, Miri. Let us enjoy our meal and when you are ready, tell me about yourself."

Miri looked at Rebekah and met her eyes with a steady, earnest gaze. "My mother was Miriam. I never knew my father. Just days ago, mother took me to Fiefel. She was to be married and I was an embarrassment. She left me there to be a kitchen worker. Very soon, I sensed that I would soon be going to the rooms to be used by the men who came with their coins." Miri's voice broke.

Rebekah touched her arm. "Take all the time you need and share just as much as you wish. I understand why you were hiding from Fiefel."

"When Deborah took me home with her, I felt safe and valued for the first time in my life. If I can stay with her, I will be your slave and do whatever you command. I know that I will be safe here and not in any danger."

"Welcome to our house. This will be your home, and you are not a slave, but a worker and learner in the care of Deborah. Where will she stay, Deborah? I am sure you have it all thought out."

"Thank you, Becca. For now, she will stay with me. I will take her to meet Talia, and we will see how they like each other. Then we will see what happens."

Miri fell to her knees beside the bed. She took Rebekah's hand and placed it against her forehead.

Rebekah gently withdrew her hand. "Please, stand Miri. Do not kneel to me. I am a woman, like Deborah, like you, and like all other women. At times, our roads are grim and so we share each other's burdens. You are one of this great family of women. Here you can find peace. We live in this valley called hope. May it be so for you."

Deborah and Miri walked from the room, and Rebekah smiled through tears of joy as she watched them leave.

Chapter Fifty-Six

Ever since the move from her room to the moon house, Rebekah lay listlessly on her bed. Deborah did everything she could to rouse Rebekah, but she insisted she was simply very tired and lay with her face to the tent wall. On the third day, first thing in the morning, Deborah sent for Ayla. She came after a long delay, or so it seemed to Deborah.

Ayla entered the room and took in the scene with the eyes of experience. She went to Rebekah and asked permission to examine her. "I think some broth is needed for our sleepy mother-to-be." Deborah went at once to prepare it. Ayla brought a basin of very warm water and one of cold water. She alternated the compresses on Rebekah's forehead. And offered sips of the broth. After a few minutes of such treatment, Rebekah was getting annoyed. "Let me be. I am fine." And she swatted at Ayla's hands.

"I am not going away, and you are going to get up and walk for some exercise. Laying here is only going to make the delivery more difficult. Deborah and I will support you and you will do as you are told."

"You are not my mother, and I will do as I please. And I please to stay here."

"I am not your mother, but I am your midwife. It is my duty to deliver these babies and to keep you alive. You need to move about. Warm and cold cloths are the pleasantest thing I have planned if you will not co-operate. So, let us get on with it, and get you off this bed and gently walking about the room."

Rebekah glared at her, and tears began to leak from her closed eyes.

"Tears won't work. Pleading won't work. Here are your sandals. Let's get them on those swollen feet."

Rebekah did little to help, but in a brief time, despite her lack of interest, she was on her feet. Deborah held her firmly on one side, Ayla on the other. The two women began to take tiny steps, and Rebekah shuffled along with them. They made a few small circles around the bed, then Ayla nodded to the doorway, and they headed toward it. Ayla held Rebekah and Deborah pulled back the flap.

Deborah saw Isaac and smiled at Ayla.

He stood there and held out his hands to Rebekah. She almost fell into his arms. He held her in a warm embrace and spoke to her, crooning soft and soothing words. They were swaying side to side in a gentle dance of love and hope. After a few minutes, she let out a piercing cry and grabbed her belly. Isaac held her and still crooned to her until the pain subsided.

"Good." Ayla motioned to Isaac to pick her up and carry her into the tent. Rebekah's arms were a stranglehold on him as they entered the sacred space. Isaac was too intent on his burden to even look around. He laid her on her bed, covered her with a soft blanket, kissed her forehead and moved away when Ayla poked him. Deborah pointed to the door and as he backed out, his eyes never left the contorted face of his beloved.

While she felt Rebekah's belly, Ayla spoke to Deborah. "Go and get the midwives. I have warned them, so they are ready." And the labour began.

Isaac returned to the house and told Keturah that Rebekah was in labour. All three tried to keep busy, but their hearts and minds were on the tent where new life was struggling to be free of its cradle in Rebekah's body.

As the daylight faded, Isaac walked to the tent. He carried blankets and water and spread one blanket on the ground at the base of a great cedar tree. He sat down with his back against the tree and prepared to wait. Every time he heard Rebekah's heart-rending cry, he struggled to stay at his self-appointed watch post. *Why is it taking so long? She has been there for hours. What can I do to help?* And then it started to rain. He covered himself with the blanket and tried to shut out the cries coming every few minutes. A hand touched his shoulder. Keturah stood beside him, offering him a dry blanket of woven camel hair.

"Thank you. This will keep me dry and warm for as long as this takes."

She handed him a bowl of steaming hot stew.

"How can I sit in comfort and eat while she is suffering?" Isaac's voice trembled.

"I know it is hard. But she will need you to be strong when this is over. No matter what the outcome, she will need you."

He looked at Keturah, with eyes that were weary from the hours of waiting, but also showing gratitude for her kindness. She saw that he was holding a small cedar branch. "Would you like me to give the cedar to her? I will tell her it is from you." He nodded and gave her a grateful smile.

She walked to the tent and said Rebekah's name. The flap opened, and she entered. She was gone for only a few minutes. When Ketuuah returned, she sat beside him on the blanket, and he shared the camel hair covering. "I spoke with Rebekah for a moment. She said thank you for the cedar and she clutched it in her hand. 'Tell Isaac I am doing very well, and it will soon be over. Our children will soon be in our arms.' I held her hand for a moment while she rested, and then I left."

"Thank you. I wish I could be with her, but I know that it is not possible. You have eased my mind, and I am grateful."

They sat quietly, side by side. Keturah heard his ragged breathing slow down, and she realized he had fallen asleep. "So, father-to-be, a full belly and a warm blanket were what you needed to get you to rest." She covered him completely and walked away on soft cat feet.

In the birthing place, Ayla was encouraging Rebekah with dreams of a son who would rule in his father's place. "Your first-born son will make the people of Terah, Abraham, and Isaac greater than ever. His name will be known from Egypt to the far east and you will be honoured as his mother."

Rebekah took her place, standing on the bricks, and a midwife stood on each side, supporting her weight. They rubbed her back, wiped her brow, and offered her sips of soothing herbal teas. The first baby arrived soon after she stood on the bricks. He was cared for by Ayla, and she bathed him with warm water. She massaged him with salt, and then wrapped him in a swaddling cloth.

A loud cry from Rebekah, and the second son was born. He was cared for in the same manner. Ayla took the first born and Deborah the second baby, and they wrapped the infants in soft woolen blankets and held them close to their warm bodies. The tent flap was drawn aside, and they walked out to find Isaac.

Isaac woke at the first touch on his arm. “It is time to meet your sons.”

He jumped to his feet; blankets fell to the wet ground. He gazed in awe at the two small bundles. Ayla loosened the wrappings, and Isaac looked for the first time at his sons. As required, he reached out and laid his large, rough hand on a baby’s tiny head. “This is my first-born son. His name is Esau, for he will do important things.” He looked at the baby and asked, “Is his hair red? It looks so to me. Esau is a good name for a boy with red hair and complexion.”

Deborah stepped forward and presented the second child. Isaac looked at this baby. “This son is Jacob, a follower, for he followed his brother into this world. He entered life on the heels of his brother. I wonder if he will always follow. The younger following the older.” He briefly touched his hand to the head of the infant. The women wrapped the babies up again and stood holding them, protecting them from the icy rain.

Isaac raised his hands and offered a blessing. "May El Shaddai bless the father and the mother of these children. May we be worthy to teach them our laws and the ways of our people and to worship our god of the fiery mountain. May El Shaddai grant them wisdom and courage. May the Almighty be with them always.”

The women took the babies back into the tent to give them to their mother. Isaac and Keturah went to the river house to share the news of the birth of two sons with the house of Isaac.

Isaac could not sleep. He paced the house until Gershom came and ordered him to go to sleep and let others sleep as well. Isaac nodded his agreement. As soon as Gershom went to his room, Isaac picked up the camel cloak and walked out of the house. He climbed the small hill and stood by the cedar tree. There was no flickering of lamps from the tent and there was not a sound. With the greatest of care, he made his way to the entrance to the forbidden house of women. The flap was not tied securely, and he carefully opened it. No one moved.

As his eyes adjusted to the darkness, he saw Rebekah lying on her bed, and beside her, the two babies. He saw no one else but knew others were present.

I will just look at her to make sure she is well. At her side, he tenderly touched her hand. She stirred and gave a little moan. Deborah came out of the shadows. She shook her head in dismay at Isaac but took three steps back and said nothing.

Rebekah opened her eyes. "Isaac. You should not be here. But I am glad to see you."

Isaac took her hand. "We have two fine sons, my beloved. Are you well?"

"Very tired and sore. But I am going to be fine and so are our boys. Now go before you are discovered."

He turned to leave, but his eyes met Deborah's stare. He bowed to her and whispered, "thank you" and disappeared into the night.

Deborah gave Rebekah a sip of water and covered her with the blanket.

"Isaac came."

"You have had a lovely dream."

"He came to me. It was real."

"If you are wise, it was a pleasant dream. Now sleep and maybe you will have another dream."

Chapter Fifty-Seven

In just a few days, Rebekah was pressing to go home. "But Ayla, you say I am doing well, and the babies are healthy and strong. At home, there will be Deborah, Keturah, Talia and Miri. They will look after everything. I won't have to do anything but feed my boys. Why can't I go to my home?"

"Women stay here for many days after a birth. What is your hurry?"

"The rains are still falling from the sky and the wind is damp and cold. The river house is warm and dry. No wind can enter and chill me or the babies the way it does here. I will agree to travelling in a cart, covered by a camel hair blanket. You know they keep out the rain very well. The babies, snuggled in my arms, will be safe and dry."

"It is unheard of. Women stay here for almost a moon time."

"Isaac is a new leader. Many things are changing at his bidding. That is just one small change, and it harms no one. Only me, Isaac and our sons are affected. You said yourself, I need to be happy and content to give the babies the best start in their young lives. Well, I am not happy or content here."

Ayla turned to Deborah. "Help me, Deborah. Tell her she must stay."

"I have served Becca loyally for all her adult life. I know that once her mind is made up, she will not back down. And I believe that she knows what is best for her and the little ones. I cannot help you."

Ayla shook her head. "I do not approve, and you do this against my advice. But go if you must. Will you permit me to come to the river house each day to check on you and the boys?"

"Of course. I would be lonely for you and your smile and advice if you didn't."

Deborah let out a sigh of relief. “Thank you, Ayla. You will see it will be better for everyone. Send for Isaac at once, please.”

Isaac arrived in a very short time with an oxcart. A warm nest of pillows and blankets and a very large camel hair blanket.

“Will you send someone for her bed?”

“There is no need. I am sure you can use it here, and a new and better one has been made for her. It is in her room at the house.”

Ayla just shook her head and packed up the few things Rebekah needed to take with her. Deborah carried a baby on each arm, and Rebekah leaned on Isaac. The beaming trio made their way to the cart, waiting just outside the door.

“Look Isaac. There is a break in the clouds. There is no rain, and a golden sunbeam shines on us in blessing.”

Ayla and Isaac settled her in the cart and when Ayla was satisfied, she stepped back and Deborah handed the babies to Rebekah. Isaac stood, smiling so broadly, Deborah teased that his face might break. He covered the wagon with the blanket, peeked in to make sure all was well, then cracked the whip over the head of the ox and the trip home began.

Everyone was waiting at the gate. They were smiling and waving to welcome the family home. Rebekah went straight to her bedroom and there was the new bed. Its sturdy legs were carved in a pattern that swirled around like gnarled cedar branches. And beside the bed were two cradles, with the same pattern carved into the sides. “Who did this Isaac? They are beautiful and look and smell like cedar. How wonderful.”

“The old wood carver in Hebron made them. When I asked him, he kept repeating, ‘two babies at once’ as if he couldn’t believe it.”

They settled Rebekah in her new bed, and she looked wonderful, lying there holding her babies. “They will need to be fed again soon. I would like something warm to drink if it isn’t too much bother.”

Deborah went to the cooking area and came back with a cup of ginger tea. “This is said to help you make more milk. With two babies, you will need this.”

Rebekah sipped the tea while Deborah rocked the cradle where Jacob was beginning to fuss. "He always gets hungry before Esau. Perhaps because he is smaller. At least we can tell them apart. There is no mistaking which baby is Esau."

Talia and Miri crept into the room and stood by the cradles. "Are all babies that small?" asked Talia.

Deborah giggled. "Actually, Esau is a very big baby for one just a few days old. He is going to be a giant of a man someday. Now everybody out, we have babies to look after and feed.

The weeks went by in a blur of happiness. Esau soon showed himself to be impatient and demanding. As soon as he woke, he began to howl and only Rebekah could quiet him with a feeding. Jacob mewed like a kitten and, as soon as he was picked up, he snuggled down into his mother's arms.

Deborah had to remind Rebekah that when the babies slept, she should at least lie down, even if she couldn't sleep. Isaac was very attentive and brought Rebekah treats and little gifts. He kept fresh cedar boughs in her room and changed them often. He stood by the cradles and watched his sleeping sons. Rebekah tried to get him to pick them up and hold them. He almost ran away at the thought. It troubled Rebekah.

Keturah was present one day and as he started to leave, she stopped him. "Isaac, I have seen you cradle a tiny lamb in your arms. These little ones are tougher than they look. You can hold them, and you should. They need to hear your heart's sounds and smell your man's smell. They need to get to know their father." She picked Esau up and motioned for Isaac to sit on the stool near Rebekah.

Gingerly, he held out his arms and she placed the infant in the cradle they formed. He held the sleeping baby, and his eyes filled with tears. "My first-born son. Esau, you are heir to all that I own. Someday you will receive the blessing and the birthright that is yours."

"See, you can do it. Tomorrow it will be Jacob."

"But he is so tiny."

Rebekah looked at her husband. "And he, too, is your son and needs to know his father. Remember what Abraham said. Treat the children fairly with no favouring one over the other."

Isaac never looked up and Rebekah wondered if he heard her, or if he remembered the words of his father.

Young as the boys were, she could see they each had their own personality. Jacob settled into his mother's arms when she held him. He seemed to stare deeply into her eyes, with his tiny forehead all wrinkled. "Are you trying to figure out this strange world, my little one? Time enough for worries. They will come soon enough."

When she held Esau, he was rarely still. Even when held to her breast, his little legs pushed against her and his arms twitched and jerked. "What drives one so young? You strained in the womb and you still push against anything that confines you. I think life will be one long struggle for you if you can't learn to bend with the winds."

As the warm summer breezes drifted through the house, the boys kept everyone busy. They were growing each day, and their cries filled the air. Esau was loud and demanding. When he cried, his face bloomed red and his eyes were tearless. He continued to wail and thrash his arms and legs even when picked up. Jacob's tears streamed down his cheeks while he sobbed as if his little heart was broken. As soon as soft arms cradled him, he quieted and snuggled into the warmth of his mother's arms.

Both were now sleeping through the night, and Rebekah was once more well rested and taking back her responsibilities. Isaac sat with her and the boys on a blanket laid out on the grassy slope to the river. The boys were on their tummies, lifting their head to look around. They had to be watched carefully as they were both rolling over to their backs.

"I would like to talk to you, Rebekah. I have a plan and want to see what you think."

"I am listening. What is your idea?"

"I noticed how you felt the cold and damp in the women's tent. I think it is time we built a house for the women to meet in. What do you think about that?"

"It is a lovely idea Isaac, and so like you to think of what I was feeling. But it is not my decision to make. I will talk to Rivkah, Esther,

Ayla and Shira. We will make a decision. I will let you know what we decide."

That afternoon, she met with the women in the tent and told them of Isaac's idea. They all agreed to think about it. Each went to a space apart from the other. They sat in silence and pondered the implications. When they gathered again, Rivkah had five coloured ribbons in her hand and a small woven basket. It had a lid that had a slit in the centre. "I suggest that we each take a ribbon. If we agree, we will each place ours in the box as it is. If we need to talk about it together, we tie a knot in the ribbon. Just put it through the hole and we will agree not to peek. One by on, they went to the box. Rivkah was the last. Then they gathered near the sacred fire pit and Rivkah lit a lamp and put it in the centre. This will do to represent the sacred fire." She removed the lid and lifted the ribbons out one by one. All five had a knot in the centre.

Ayla laughed. "At least we all agree we need to talk about this. Who goes first?"

"I will, since it was my husband's idea. It is true that it is cold and damp, and that is not the best for babies, their mothers, or for those who are ill or dying in the tent."

"I agree with that." Rivkah replied. "But there is a lot of tradition, memories and history in this space. I would not like us to lose that connection with the past and with our mothers and grandmothers."

"That is true. A building would be more comfortable for many reasons. I wondered if there might be a compromise, where we could keep the past with us, but make it safer for all." Esther spoke in her gentle strong voice.

They all looked at her with questions in their eyes and in their hearts.

"I know very little about buildings, but this is what I wonder. Could we keep the earthen floor where we have buried so many of our painful memories and we symbolically buried them in the sand?"

"I don't see why not. The floor isn't the real problem. We sit on carpets and cushions, and with walls the air would be warm and dry." Ayla sat, hands folded, but seemed to have something to say. The others waited, respecting her silence. When she looked at them, her eyes were dancing. “The walls are the problem, I think. What if we had brick walls and kept the floor and the canvas roof? Wouldn’t that be the best of both ways?”

Rivkah clapped in glee. “I think that would be perfect. We could decorate the walls, and the images would stay in place and stay dry. They would last much longer. The roof could still be opened to the night sky when we wished and the smoke drift away to the mountain as it always has.”

They were all talking at once and laughing. Into the noise, the sweet voice of Shira threaded a gentle song. The noise died away, and everyone began to hum or sing with Shira. Gradually the song faded away with the smoke from the lamp.

Rebekah stood and held out her hands. They joined a circle. Esther picked up the lamp and placed it in the midst of them. Rebekah spoke. “We have agreed on a new place, and I will tell Isaac of our hope and we will have to trust that it can be done. Thank you for your wisdom.”

Rivkah plopped down onto the floor. “I am glad that didn’t take too long. I tire so quickly. Please tell Isaac how grateful we are for his concern. He is a good and just leader as he walks the path Abraham set before us.”

They broke up to return to their homes. Esther and Ayla walked close to Rivkah; their arms ready to support her if she needed it.

Shira stood and watched with Rebekah. The sigh from Shira came from a place deep inside of her. “I only hope we can have the new house finished in time to embrace Rivkah as she faces her last journey.”

Chapter Fifty-Eight

It was almost dawn when Rebekah left the moon house and walked to Ayla's tent. She called softly, and Ayla answered at once. Rebekah entered. "I have just come from the moon house. Rivkah said her final goodbye a few minutes ago. She spent a quiet night and just roused long enough to say farewell."

"You stayed with her all night? I am glad for her sake, but you must be tired."

"I am sure I dozed off a little, but yes, I am going home to sleep. I leave Rivkah's care in your hands. I have told no one else."

The two women held each other close, murmuring words of comfort.

"I will sleep for a while, then join you again to hear what you have planned."

She left Ayla's tent and walked to the river house. She stood at the gate for a minute and watched the sky begin to glow pink and gold. As she entered, she bumped into a clay pot, and it shattered at her feet. Deborah was at her side in an instant.

"I have been waiting for you. Come, let's get you to your bed and rest."

"Have you been here all night?"

"It is a comfortable place to rest, and I have slept more than you have, I think. I presume Rivkah has entered the long sleep."

"Yes. I have let Ayla know and she will look after it while I get some rest. Are the boys sleeping?"

"All three of your men folk have slept the night away." Deborah urged Rebekah toward her room."

"I will tell Isaac then I will go to my bed. Should I wake Keturah and tell her?"

"Yes, she will need to know. Let me do that. I will put light food out and make tea while you wake them."

"Of course."

At the door to their room, Rebekah paused. She took deep breaths to calm herself for the task that awaited her. She coughed two or three times, and as she expected, Isaac was holding her in his arms before she could call him.

"At last, you are home. You must be very tired."

"Yes, I am exhausted, but I must speak with you, and I have a request. Grab your cloak and meet me by the fire."

She turned and walked away, too weary to explain. She sat by the fire and Deborah brought bread and cheese, tea, and wine. She said nothing and left as soon as Isaac appeared.

He sat and took Rebekah's hand in his. "Did she die peacefully? I hope so."

"Yes, she quietly slipped away in my arms. With her last breath she asked for a favour."

"Anything, dear one, just ask."

"Be careful what you promise. I will understand if you must refuse." She sipped the tea and looked at the floor. "With her last breath, Rivkah asked to be buried in a special place. She did not want to be in the cave at Machpelah. It was her wish to be laid to rest in Sarah's grove." She raised her tear-filled eyes to meet Isaac's gaze.

He hesitated only for a moment. "It shall be done as she asked. For her to lie in Sarah's grove is most fitting. Sarah was her teacher, friend, and lifelong companion. I will get Gershom and at first light we will go and choose the spot. Or do you want to do that?"

"No. I need to sleep, and you will choose the perfect place, I am sure."

They held each other in a tender embrace and then went their separate ways.

Much later the bright golden sun was high overhead when Rebekah came out of her room. Talia and Miri were amusing the boys, and they quickly brought Rebekah a plate of food and a cup of tea.

"Thank you."

The boys ran to her and climbed up into her lap. Jacob settled, quietly sucking his thumb. Esau babbled and shook a rattle he held. Their mother smiled at her boys and tousled their hair. Esau swatted her hand away and slid down from her lap to toddle away, still talking in his baby way. She finished her meal and her tea. Talia took Jacob and held him on her hip.

"I think they are all gathered at the woman's house, Rebekah. Can we do anything to help?"

"Where is Isaac?"

"He is with the men, preparing the burial place for Rivkah."

Rebekah thanked the girls and walked out into the glaring sunlit afternoon.

"Rivkah loved the light. She must be happy now to see it shining in a warm, comforting way."

The women at the moon house welcomed her. Esther, Alya and Keturah had been busy. Rivkah was dressed in a much loved and well-worn tunic of yellow silk. Her silver hair was braided and tied with a golden cord. On a small woven pillow, tucked in her arm, the symbols of her life as a healer, and her copper woman's bracelet were fastened. A cluster of the berries of a myrrh plant, and a vial of spikenard were in her hands.

Ayla stood nearby. "If there is anything you wish to change or to add, please let us know."

"You have done well to honour our sister. What plans have been made for the ceremony?"

Esther offered Rebekah a chair. "The women will be arriving shortly. Ayla and I will say a few words, and we assume you will as well. Shira will, of course, lead the singing."

Keturah brought tea to Rebekah. "She will be carried to the grave side on the litter. Six young women have been chosen to carry her up the hill. Isaac and Gershom will walk behind the litter just in case they are needed at any time."

"She is not to be laid to rest in the caves at Machpelah. She will be buried in Sarah's sacred grove. It was her last request."

There was a prolonged silence. Esther wiped the tears from her cheeks. "How perfect. That is exactly where she should rest."

"Yes. And Isaac agreed at once. What happens after the burial?"

"The women are right now, busy in their kitchens, making food and drinks. Any who wishes will gather in the common area to share a meal, and to remember Rivkah and share stories. We know there will be tears, but we expect they will be smiles and laughter as well."

"You have done well. It is a fitting tribute and goodbye to our dear sister and friend. With the flowers and the soft glow of the lamps, this space looks very peaceful, and Rivkah would be pleased."

The rich voice of Shira rang out as she chanted a lament. It drew ever closer and at the door of the house, she stopped and stood, still chanting. One by one, the women reverently entered. Most were gently weeping and wiping tears from their cheeks. Shira was the last to enter, and the song grew softer until it just floated away into silence. The women formed a large circle, and Rebekah held up her hands in a gesture of blessing.

If any were surprised at the choice of her resting place, no one showed it. At the entrance, Isaac announced that the space inside was small and only the people who had been given a palm leaf would enter. "But please stay and listen to the words and the songs that will be offered."

Rebekah stooped to enter and looked for the place. Against the western row of trees there was a mound of earth piled up and many flowers were placed on it. Beside it was the cavity, dug to receive the body. At one end, there was a large pile of heavy stones.

Those invited stood near the stones. Shira sang a song about leaving and it gradually turned into a lament. At the end, Ayla spoke about Rivkah, named her and her family roots, and told of her strength, courage, knowledge, and compassion. Isaac, Gershom, and the women who had carried the litter gently lowered the body into the earth.

Esther held her hands high in blessing. "To the earth she loved and tended with care, we return our healer and beloved leader. She loved the sun, and it is fitting that each morning the light of the new day will warm the earth where she lies." She bent and placed her palm on the shawl that covered Rivkah. Then she walked out of the grove. One by one the others followed her example.

As Esther exited the grove, she invited any who wished to enter and say their own goodbye to do so, and then gather in the central circle for a time to visit and to share in a light meal.

Most of the village gathered in a circle. Their voices were filled with both joy and hope as they spoke of the one who had been such a part of their lives for so many years. The glowing sun was just slipping behind the hills when people began to leave and return to their tents. Isaac took Rebekah's hand. "Come, dear one, it is time for you to go home. We will continue to pay our tribute as we light the lamps in our house.

Rebekah smiled a wan smile. "Yes. I am tired and it is time for me to leave. Once again, our world has shifted and changed. It is always unsettling, but life goes on. Rivkah would not want us to mourn unduly."

And hand in hand, they walked toward the river house.

Chapter Fifty-Nine

Sunny warm days, followed by cold rains, marked the passing of the years. The twins were now active, busy boys, learning the ways of their parents. Rebekah and Isaac stood side by side and looked at the breakfast table. The cushions were all fluffed and spaced around the low table. Cedar branches lay along its length and lamps nestled in the greenery glowed cheerfully.

Rebekah took Isaac's hand. "I can't believe our sons are ten years old. I remember the day they were born, and it seems such a brief time ago."

"I know, and yet they seem to have been part of our lives for a very long time. Oh, I hear Esau coming along the hall."

He burst into the room with all the energy he always showed, and Jacob walked behind him, in his own far-off world.

"I'm hungry. Let's eat." Esau's voice rang off the stone walls.

"We will wait for all the others to gather, but you may sit at the head of the table."

He bounced to his place and flopped onto the cushion. Jacob sat beside him and settled cross-legged on his cushion.

The rest gathered. Keturah looked lovely in a deep blue tunic. Gershom wore the short girdle of his uniform and carried his dagger in his belt.

Rebekah stared. Isaac offered an explanation. "I asked him to dress in uniform to lend a more serious tone to the day. I hoped that Esau might sense how important this day is."

Talia, Miri, and Deborah arrived balancing trays heavy with food. They placed them on the table. Keturah was startled at Esau's voice.

"Good, the food is here. Let's eat."

Isaac groaned. "Esau. You know that no one eats until the morning blessing has been said."

Esau whined. “But it is my birthday. Why do we need long prayers on my birthday?”

Isaac gruffly cleared his throat. “Birthday or not, you know we say prayers before we eat.” He held his arms high as he faced the mountain. “Blessed are You, Lord God, King of the Universe, who brings forth bread from the earth.”

A small voice stated, “Amen.”

Isaac frowned and Jacob poked Esau.

Isaac spoke again. “Blessed are You, Lord God, King of the Universe, who brings forth the fruit of the trees.”

Another amen, slightly louder came from Esau. Jacob whispered, but not very softly. “He will keep praying until you stop saying amen. Sh.” Smiles passed across the faces at the table.

“Blessed are You, Lord God, King of the Universe, by Whose word all things came to be.”

There was a long pause while Jacob glared at his brother.

Then from Isaac, one word, “Amen.”

Esau grabbed some bread and a few olives and began stuffing them into his mouth.

“Esau.” Isaac spoke firmly but not unkindly. “Eat politely because there is no hurry. You will stay at the table until you are allowed to leave.”

The meal progressed without any more incidents and at the end, Isaac thanked those who had prepared the food and El Shaddai for another day of life.

Isaac turned to his sons. “Today we are thankful that god has given us two sons to continue our name and our traditions. We have things planned to celebrate, and later we will gather in the fallow field behind the stables. But now, birthday or not, we all have chores that need to be done. I will blow the small horn when it is time to meet in the field.

Everyone went their way to complete the morning tasks. Isaac and Rebekah sat and finished their tea. Isaac looked at his wife, who seemed to be far away. “What are you thinking, Rebekah?”

“I just wonder when Esau will begin to settle down and think more seriously about our customs.”

“He is still young. Give him time. He will grow up, I am sure.”

"I can't help looking at them and thinking about Ishmael. Esau has many of his ways and we know how unfitted he was to be the heir to the birthright."

"Don't borrow trouble Rebekah. There is plenty for each day."

The sun was high in the sky when the boys heard the sound of the horn. They jumped up from playing with their toys and ran to the field. Their parents and Keturah were there, and the servants as well. There were two donkey colts tied to the fence. The boys both shrieked with delight and ran to the animals.

"My sons," said Isaac. "These two colts are the gifts we have for you to mark your birthing day. The one with the red bridle is yours, Esau, and the blue bridle is Jacob's colt. They do not have names and you can choose their names when you are ready. The two stable boys, Nathan, and Uri, will be your teachers as you learn how to care for these fine animals."

"Help me up on mine. I want to ride as fast as the wind." The excitement in Esau's voice was clear.

Gershom walked to the colts. "This is a joyful day, and I know you are eager to ride your donkeys. But slow down, Esau. You must learn many things before you can ride like the wind. You are not to take the donkeys out of their stalls unless one of the stable boys, or your father or I, is with you."

That same voice from breakfast muttered, "I hate rules. Why are there rules about everything, even presents?"

Gershom ignored the boy. "The first thing is to get to know them and let them learn your smell and the sound of your voice. They must have names so they can learn to come when called. Now take the reins and walk them around the field."

The women and the servants left the field and went back to the endless chores that awaited them. Isaac stayed and watched for a short while.

All were gathered for the evening meal. After the blessing, Isaac asked about the boy's afternoon. "Do the donkeys have names?"

"I called mine boots because he has two white patches on his legs." Jacob answered.

"Mine will be called speed because we will go very fast together. But why did I have to brush him when we were done?"

"Didn't the stable boys tell you?"

"They said something about healthy coats and burrs and bugs, father, but he looked fine to me, and I was tired."

"You don't have to brush him." Isaac smiled as he spoke. "But no brushings, no rides. It is quite simple."

To change the subject as Esau was getting sulky, Isaac turned to Rebekah. "What did you do today? Not too much, I hope."

With exasperation in her voice, Rebekah replied. "I accomplished very little." She frowned at Esau. "I managed, in spite of interruptions to bake a special cake for tonight in honour of our sons' birthday celebration."

They enjoyed the cake, and the grown-ups had an extra glass of wine.

Keturah stood and asked to be excused. "I am quite tired and will go to my room."

Wishes for a restful night were offered around the table. Miri and Talia took the boys, Esau objecting all the way down the hall on their way to bed.

"Is Keturah all right? I noticed she didn't keep up as we walked back to the house."

Deborah asked Rebekah.

"She is only tired, I think. After all these years we still miss Rivkah and she and Keturah were close. Please excuse me, I will make sure she settles soon and goes to bed. Thank you for your concern and good night."

Isaac waited for Rebekah to come to their bedroom. "Is she resting?"

"Yes. She was just weary. I think the boys exhaust her, as they do me at times."

"You mean Esau, don't you?"

"Mostly yes. I hope you are right about him, but it worries me."

"Don't worry, I will take him in hand before it is time for the inheritance blessing."

"Don't wait too long. Remember how quickly these past ten years have flown by. It is only three more till he becomes a man, old enough for the blessing."

Isaac patted her hand and lay down to sleep.

"Remember the last words that your father said. 'Train the heir for his duties and responsibilities'."

"Enough woman. It is time to sleep."

But Rebekah lay wide awake for a long time before her eyes closed and she fell into a troubled sleep.

Chapter Sixty

The many years since the birthday of the twins had not been kind to Isaac. Gershom had finished getting Isaac up, dressed, and fed his morning meal. His eyesight was failing and seemed worse day by day, and his energy was limited.

Gershom sat on a bench and leaned against a tall oak tree. He opened his eyes and sat up as he realized that someone was standing nearby. It was Rebekah.

"Good morning, Gershom. I didn't mean to disturb you."

"Not at all Rebekah. I was just resting after the morning routine. It seems to take longer each morning to get Isaac ready for another day."

"I know, and I am so grateful that you are there to care for him. He seems to resent anything I try to do for him."

"He is still a proud man. It is hard for him to be so dependent. It is easier I think to accept help from a man than from his wife."

"I am grateful that he sits in the afternoon and talks to me about what needs to be done regarding the animals and the vineyard."

"Rebekah, we both know that you are totally managing things around here. Since he has been almost blind, you have done it all. And done it well, I might add."

"We both do what needs to be done. It is good for me to know that you are there when I need advice and help to make some hard decisions."

"Together, we will keep things running. What a blessing that you can read and write."

"Yes, and I must return to the house and take care of the records. Enjoy the rest of this lovely day."

He watched her walk away. *What a great choice Eliezar made all those years ago. She has kept the holdings of Abraham safe and has done it with quiet grace, letting Isaac take all the credit.*

As he looked about the camp, he spotted Jacob tending a fire near his tent. The breeze carried the scent of lentils and onions cooking in the pot suspended over the coals. He stood to go and speak to him when he saw Esau stumbling up to the fire. He flopped down and spoke in a surly manner to his brother. Gershom sat back down.

"Busy at the cooking fires again? What a way for a man to live. I have been hunting game. That is a chore for a man, not stirring lentils."

"I don't see any game. Did you not have any luck hunting?"

"It is skill, not luck, that finds the game. Today I was mostly scouting for trails. That smells good and I am hungry." He grabbed a bowl and shoved it at Jacob. "Give me some, before I die from hunger."

"Perhaps you will admit that my time has not been wasted."

"Never mind that. Fill my bowl."

"I made this for mother and me. What is it worth to you to eat your fill?"

"I am so hungry, I don't care. Anything you want."

"The birthright."

"My birthright?"

"Yes. That is what I want."

"What does a starving man care about a birthright? I need food, not ancient dreams."

Jacob filled the bowl, then looked at Nathan and Uri, who were standing nearby.

"Nathan, Uri. You have heard these words. You are witnesses to what has just taken place."

They both nodded, and Jacob turned to his brother. "This is a legal binding contract between us. I am now the heir to the birthright that you so casually sold for a bowl of stew. Agreed?"

"Yeah, yeah. The birthright is yours. More stew, I am still hungry. Uri, get me some wine to make this tastier."

Gershom could hardly believe what he had just witnessed. He sat very quietly until Esau left. He walked to the fire and Jacob looked up. "Hello Gershom. Will you have some stew?"

"And what will you charge me for a bowl full?"

Jacob was shocked.

"I didn't mean to listen, but you were both speaking loudly, and I couldn't help but overhear every word. I am another witness if those lads are not believed at some future time. I suggest that you inform your mother of what has just taken place. Good day to you." He walked away without looking back.

As the day was turning to dusk, Jacob went to his mother. "I have something I need to tell you, mother."

His eyes on the ground, not looking at the face of his mother, he related what had happened. She sat, unmoving. Jacob became increasingly uncomfortable. "Say something, mother, please. Say something, anything."

She looked at her son. Thoughts whirled in her head. When she understood what had happened, she spoke quietly, calmly, and purposefully.

"This is more than I could ever have hoped for. I have seen over the years that Esau was not the one to take over from Isaac. You are the one to lead us in the future. Esau pays no need to our laws or customs. Nor does he follow the faith of Father Abraham. He only cares about his own pleasure." She paced up and down the room, chewing on a fingernail.

Jacob sat speechless as he watched his mother.

"That is the first part accomplished. Now you must also get the blessing. Let me think about this tonight and we will speak again in the morning."

Immediately after the first meal of the day, Rebekah went to Jacob's room. "Meet me at the bench by the river. Don't let anyone see you." And she left, heading toward the river bench.

Jacob joined her in a few minutes.

"No one saw me, mother. I was careful."

"Good. Now listen to me. I have a plan. Esau will hunt today. Your father mentioned a few days ago, that you both are young men now. This morning, he mentioned he had asked Esau to make him a venison stew for his late meal. Before Esau returns from the hunt, you will feed your father a stew that I will make, and you will receive the blessing."

"But father will know it is I, not Esau."

"I will make a lamb stew and flavour it so that it tastes like game. You will wear a cloak and tunic that belong to Esau, so you smell like him. Speak in a harsh, guttural voice, and say as little as possible. He won't be able to see you, so this will work. Just do it quickly and be confident in our plan."

"But his hairy hands and arms?"

"Esau's sleeves will be too long for you. Let them cover your arms and hands. Permit your father to touch you as little as possible, not at all if you can manage that."

"What will they do when it is discovered?"

Rebekah paced again. "Esau will be very angry, filled with hate and seeking vengeance. You must be ready to go as soon as all is done."

"Leave you mother? Where will I go? How will I live?"

"All sons grow up and make their own lives. They leave their mother and they do just fine. I must think of what to do. Just be ready to go when I have it planned. Now let's get on with our plan." She stood, tousled his hair as she did when he was a boy, and walked back to the house.

Jacob sat by the river. "What is happening? I had no plans to take over when I bartered the stew with Esau. I was just trying to teach him a lesson for all the mean things he has said and done. All my life, he has tormented and bullied me."

He left the calm of the river's edge and went to his tent. Rebekah came with the clothing, and he hid it. To keep busy until the stew was ready, he packed a bag of clothing and the few possessions he would take with him. He tucked it out of sight behind some baskets and lay on his bed to get some sleep. *I will be on the run tonight and for many nights. Better sleep while I can.*

Jacob awoke with a start to find his mother standing by his bed. "The stew is in this pot. Get dressed and go to your father. Gershom will be waiting for you by the great cedar tree at the bend in the road at the top of the hill. Go there when you have finished in your father's room. He is there now and resting. No one else is in the house, I have taken care of that." She took him in her arms and held him tightly. "Gershom has the rest of the plan. He will tell you where to go. God go with you until we meet again." She turned and walked away.

Jacob stood stunned by how quickly all this had transpired. He forced himself to get dressed in his brother's clothing. It was much too large for his slender frame. *I must be careful not to trip on this cloak.* He placed the bundle of his clothes by the door and grabbed the stew. Not looking left or right, head down, he marched to his father's house and to the room where Isaac waited for his evening meal. He knocked and then entered.

"I smell my meal. I must admit, I am hungry for a change. I don't feel like eating much these days but fresh venison stew temps me."

Jacob placed the food near his father, then took his hand and guided it to the bowl and spoon. Isaac said the blessing, then asked. "Where is the cloth that covers my tunic to try to keep it clean?"

Jacob looked around and saw a large piece of cloth on the table beside the bed. He snatched it up and handed it to his father. "You know I need help to put it around my chin. What is the matter with you?"

In a voice as gruff and growly as he could manage, he answered. "Just tired from the hunt, father."

His father gave a small chuckle as he took the first spoonful. "You must be tired. You sound like Jacob, but you smell like Esau. The stew is different tonight, but good. I will eat two bowls, I think."

Jacob gave a small chuckle. "This is good, father." When Isaac had eaten two bowls of the stew and drank a large cup of wine, he laid back on his cushions and gave a loud belch. "Well done, father."

"You still sound like Jacob."

Jacob cleared his throat. "Mother said this was the night of the blessing. Are you ready?"

"You have done well, Esau. When I am gone, you will take over from me. Stay true to the faith of Father Abraham. Be fair and honest in all your dealings. Work hard and take care of this great trust left to you."

"Yes, father. I will."

"Kiss me, my son. First-born son of my loins."

Jacob knelt close to his father's bed and gave a quick kiss to the old man's cheek.

"I can smell the clean smell of the fields, the wind, and the trees. It is good." He placed his hand on Jacob's headdress. "May God give you heaven's dew and earth's richness—an abundance of grain and new wine. Let the people serve you and bow down before you. Be lord over your brother and the son of your mother will bow down to you."

Jacob muttered his thanks and bolted. He ran to his tent, grabbed his bundle, a short sword, and a shield. Running for his life, he went to the cedar tree his mother named. Gershom was waiting as she promised with one of the warrior camels.

Gershom helped him into the saddle and fastened his bundle to the saddle blanket. "The other bundle is food your mother prepared. Here is a bag of money. You are to go to your uncle Laban in Haran. Tell him nothing except that your brother is angry, and you are escaping his wrath, and Rebekah sent you to her esteemed brother. The camel is a gift to Laban. Just follow the great road north. Join a caravan if you can for your safety. Send a message to your mother when you can and as often as you can. She will let you know when it is safe to return. Now be off and may you arrive safely." He ordered the camel to stand, and Jacob grabbed the reins as the beast broke into a gallop and headed down the road.

He was only a few miles away when Esau appeared at Isaac's door bearing a savoury venison stew. "Get up, father. I have brought you your favourite stew and come for the blessing."

Isaac sat up. "Who are you?"

"I am Esau, your firstborn son."

Isaac shrieked. “Then who brought me a meal which I ate?” He shook uncontrollably as he sat in his bed. “I ate his food, drank his wine and gave him the blessing for the firstborn.”

Esau howled like a wounded beast. “My brother has tricked me twice. He stole my birthright and now he has taken my blessing.” With his head on his father’s breast, he cried with great heaving sobs. “Have you no blessing for me?”

“I have made Jacob your master and have declared you will be his servant. I have guaranteed him an abundance of grain and wine—what is left for me to give you, my son?”

Esau pleaded, “But do you have only one blessing? Surely you can, bless me, too!”

With a heavy heart, Isaac spoke. “You will live without the richness of the earth, and away from the dew of the heavens. You will live by the sword, and you will serve your brother. But one day you will throw off your anger and reconcile with your brother.”

Esau stormed out and raged around the common area. Keturah came and quietly sat, waiting till his anger abated. Finally, exhausted, he sat on the floor with his head in his hands.

“I know you don’t want a lot of words from me right now. Just know that I was once rejected and cast aside, and I can understand your anger. But I also know anger eats away at one’s soul and robs every scrap of joy from daily life. If you ever want to talk, I will listen with patient understanding. Go in peace, Esau, son of Isaac, son of Abraham, son of Terah. But before and forever, beloved of God.”

It was a long, tense evening. Clouds hid the moon and the stars, and the inky night sky reflected the darkness that filled the hearts of the tribe of Abraham. Rebekah sat in the gloomy house and waited for the morning. Waited for the sun to bring light once more to her people.

Rebekah was awake with the first rays of the sun. She dressed quickly, saw that Isaac was still sleeping soundly, and silently walked out and went to the river bench. She picked up a stone and tossed it into the calm water. The ripples spread out in ever larger circles. She watched them until they disappeared. “If only the river could carry away my troubles, like the ripples that disappear into nothing. I did what I believe to be the right thing and here I sit, alone and wondering." She forced her hands into her lap. She had chewed her nails until her fingers were raw and sore. "I may never see Jacob again, and Isaac may be so outraged at my interference that I will have lost him too. It is done, but it is also just beginning."

She turned to the house. All was quiet. *If everyone is gone, I will go and speak with my husband.* With slow, heavy steps, she walked to the gate and entered the courtyard. There was not a sound. She walked softly to Isaac's room and saw that he had not moved. *Good. I will prepare some food and then wake him.*

Soon the table was set with a bright yellow cloth to echo the sunlight streaming in the windows. Cups, plates, and spoons were set out beside the two plates. In the centre, she placed bread, cheese, fruit, olives, and cups of wine. She heard Isaac stirring in his room and began to hum a gentle melody.

He came into the room, walking with his cane and holding one hand against the wall.

Rebekah touched his arm. "Good morning, Isaac. I have food prepared. Come to my voice and I will get a low stool for you."

When he was seated, she sat close to him. "What will you have to eat?"

"I can smell fresh warm bread, cheese, and olives. That and some watered wine will be just the thing to start this lovely warm day."

She prepared a plate for each of them and sat quietly while he said the morning prayer.

They ate in silence and when finished, she quickly cleaned the table and returned to her seat beside him. She held his hand as she spoke. "Do you want to talk about the events of yesterday?"

In a trembling voice Isaac replied. "Let me speak my thoughts. You may respond, and then we will be done with it." He retrieved his hand and crossed his arms against his chest. He turned to face her, and she felt tears on her cheeks. She wiped them away in a quick motion.

"I know you had a hand in the things that happened yesterday. What is done is done. As I thought about it last night, I remembered words of my father from his death bed. He cautioned us to be careful of the way we raised our children. We both knew that Esau did not have the character needed to lead our people. I realized it, long after you did, I suspect." He reached for his cup, and Rebekah put it in his hand. "Thank you. You must do many things that I cannot do any more. Yesterday, you took care of the problem of our unfit eldest son. I do not worry about the running of our great fortune, for you have been doing it for years and I know you can and will continue. What Esau and Jacob do is their own decision. They are men and must choose their own path." He reached for her hand, and she cradled it in both of hers. He looked at his feet and she had to lean very close to hear his words. "I hope that Jacob has gone far away and that he will be safe from his brother's wrath. Will you tell me where he is?"

"He has gone to Haran to his uncle Laban. Gershom sent him on one of the prize camels and he will give it to Laban as a gift. I hope you approve."

"It is good. Where is Esau? I do not know but heard that he went to the city late last night."

"That is what I would expect him to do."

Isaac shrugged. "The past is gone. What is done is done. And I will say this only once. You have done what needed to be done. What I could never do. Thank you. Now we turn to the unknown future."

"Thank you for your understanding. I felt it best that you did not know and could not be implicated in the events. You said we face an unknown future. That is always true. The things of tomorrow are always shrouded in mystery. Only the mountain knows and guides our steps."

They looked to the mountain. "Tell me what you see, Rebekah."

"The mountain stands firm and proud against the sky. El Shaddai sleeps today. Peace is in her heart, and strength is in his arm. Blessed be the one with no name."

Chapter Sixty-One

The seasons spun out year by year, and once again the rains were turning the world into a morass of mud. Rebekah was grateful for the house, which kept her dry and warm. She seldom left the safety of her home, and her thoughts were often on her absent son. Traders occasionally brought word and for that, she was grateful. Just yesterday, Keturah had talked with a caravan worker who brought a message from Haran. Tea and cakes were ready to serve when Keturah came to the central meeting space. Rebekah lay on cushions and waited.

Keturah entered, and they held each other close. "I am sorry that I am so late in coming. Everything takes so much longer to do these days. Joints ache, bones creak and I forget what I am doing."

"I know. It is a blessing to live so long, but also a burden."

"Tell me how Deborah is faring. I know she is not able to walk far, and she cannot get her breath when she is up and fussing over you."

"I can bear my own failings easier than to watch her struggle with every movement. Talia and Miri are wonderful. They look after her without making her feel useless."

"They look after the three of us and still leave us our dignity. They have been a blessing all these years. And so many years have passed."

"Please, what have you heard from Haran, lately?"

"As you know, Jacob was welcomed by Laban and has been a member of the household all these years. The news of this trip is that he has married two women."

"My boy has two wives. Who are they? What do we know about them? Are they good, god-fearing women?"

"One question at a time, please. Jacob married Leah, the eldest daughter of Laban, and then later married her younger sister, Rachel.

The camel boy said that Laban made Jacob work for seven years for each woman. It was the bride price he demanded."

Rebekah snorted. "Laban has not changed in all these years. It was his right, I suppose, but he never did have any compassion for others. But Jacob is married, and that is good. Tell me about the women."

"A young camel drover cares little about the things you want to know. He said they were hardworking and loyal. Rachel is beautiful and Leah is strong."

"What about their faith? Do they worship as we do?"

"I do not know. What do you know of Laban's habits?"

"That is why I ask. When we were young, so long ago, he had little respect for the holy one of the mountain. My father did not give a lot of importance to the gods. He mumbled prayers before meals, and on the holy days, but without any meaning. We were not taught reverence or even respect for the holy one. I had so much to learn when I came here."

They sat together, each deep in her own thoughts. Keturah broke the silence.

"You are fortunate. You have four daughters-in-law now."

Rebekah spat on the floor. "Two are only names, and I know little about them. And the two I know; Esau's wives are not a blessing. Adal and Judith are idol worshippers. They stink of incense. I have tried to help them understand our worship and our faith. They sneer and laugh." Rebekah sighed deeply and twisted her hair around her finger. "Isaac weeps whenever he is reminded of the failure that Esau has become."

"Parents are not to blame when children go their own way. You and Isaac have had many troubles to bear, but also many blessings for which to be thankful."

"My greatest blessings have been the women in my daily life. Rivkah—" and Rebekah's voice broke as she said the name. She paused and sipped her tea and wiped her eyes. "And Esther and Ayla have been faithful companions. But you have been my closest and dearest friend. Your experience and what you have learned by your trials have given me courage and hope."

"I, too, have been blessed by the time I have lived here in Abraham's valley. Who would have thought when I left in disgrace that I would return to a welcome beyond my expectations?"

Keturah reached for their small looms, and they sat together weaving cloth along with their memories.

After the evening meal, Isaac suggested that he and Rebekah needed to talk in private. The others scattered to tend to their chores in the other rooms of the house.

"What is it you wish to talk about, Isaac?"

"What have you heard from Jacob?"

She related to him what Keturah had learned.

"I am saddened by the lives my sons live. I feel like a failure. Who will continue after we are gone?"

"We know little of Jacob as a man. He was faithful to the worship of El Shaddai when he lived here. I am sure that he will have kept his faith, even living with idol worshippers. He was a pious and devout lad, and I must believe that he is a man of honour now."

"All of this work is too much for us now, too much for you. It is time that Jacob returned. I have talked to Esau, and he understands and is even grateful that the burden of the inheritance was not on his shoulders. He is ready to welcome Jacob home."

The radiant smile on Rebekah's face lit the gloomy room. "Can it be true?"

"Whatever else he may be, I have never known Esau to be a liar. I sent a runner to Jacob to beg him to return. I would see my son again before I die."

"And so would I, Isaac. But will he come? Perhaps he is too content with his new life."

"You said he would still be the honourable youth we once knew, but now grown to a man. I am sure he will return to fulfill his duty as the heir to these lands."

"I had almost lost the promise that this really was a valley of hope. Dare I believe again in the goodness of the holy one?"

"We will hope together." He sighed and touched her hand. "Is there any wine on the table?"

"I will fill our cups."

They helped each other to stand and, with their arms linked in love, and for support, they raised their cups and spoke the words of hope and blessing. "L'chaim."

Weeks later, the runner returned. He had travelled with a trade caravan and arrived unannounced. He went straight to the house and met with Isaac and Rebekah. They sent for Esau, and he arrived dusty and grimy from a day of hunting.

"You sent for me? I hope it is important."

Isaac shook his head. "Of course, it is important." He turned to Rebekah. "I have little patience. Would you please explain to our son the immediate plans I have set in motion?"

Rebekah nodded and looked at Esau with a solemn frown. "Your father has decided that the tribe has not had strong male leadership for many seasons. Things are not as they should be. The soldiers are lazy, the field workers need a strong hand, and no one is counting the herds. And those are just the obvious matters that need attention."

Esau squirmed and looked very uncomfortable. "Father, I—" but Isaac held up his hand. "Do not interrupt. Listen, for once."

"Esau, your father recognizes that he cannot go to the fields, walk the water ditches, or keep track of the skins. I have done what I can, but I am a mere woman, and am not obeyed. Isaac has sent for Jacob."

Esau choked on his next breath.

Isaac scowled at Esau. "Word has come from your brother that he is returning. According to the messenger, he will camp near the river, and you can meet him there. He is concerned about the threat to end his life you made years ago. Now you may speak."

"When my brother took my birthright and my blessing, of course, I was angry. But I have learned a lot about myself since then. I would not be happy counting sheep or reading marks on skins. I am a hunter, a great hunter. That is what I was born to do. Jacob was born for other tasks. It is better that my brother becomes the chief of our village."

Rebekah and Isaac both gave an immense sigh of relief.

Isaac clapped his son on the back. "Well said, Esau. Your grandfather said on his death bed that we, your mother, and I, should let our children be who they need to be and let them find their own path in life. It is good."

Esau stood. "Is he coming alone?"

"No, my son." Rebekah's gentle voice answered. "We have been told that he comes with a great company, wives, concubines, and many children. He is bringing servants, flocks, and herds. He has prospered in the land of Haran."

Isaac struggled to his feet, refusing the hand that Rebekah offered. "I have prepared gifts for him, and they are loaded, ready for you to take to your brother. You will leave tomorrow to meet him and welcome him home."

Esau walked to the door, then turned. "This has been a momentous day. When the sun rises tomorrow, things will change here. I hope it will be a good change. I will continue to live as I have, hunting for my family and for the village. Goodnight." He nodded to his parents and slipped out into the velvet night.

Chapter Sixty-Two

The morning air hung like a cloud over the village. Esau had gone north to meet his brother. There was great apprehension. Would this meeting lead to a battle? Had Jacob really been forgiven for his trickery? Would the brothers live in peace?

Rebekah could scarcely contain her excitement. Esau said he had accepted Jacob's role as the heir. "I must believe it, Keturah. Abraham's sons, Isaac and Ishmael, had finally reached a place of mutual respect. Surely my sons can do the same."

Keturah smiled. "Of course. You must believe it. Esau has no reason to lie about such an important matter. I am sure they can live in peace. As you said, the sons of Abraham have reached an understanding. There is no need to borrow tomorrow's troubles. Each day has enough of its own."

"Will he return impoverished or able to look after his wives and children?"

"Jacob is a clever man, and one driven to succeed. He will not return a beggar; of that you can be sure."

The two women stirred the fire and sat completely at ease with each other.

It had been days since Esau left and the brothers were expected back at any moment. Isaac had spoken to Gershom, Rebekah, and others, and they had talked about land that would be given to Jacob. He would need good pastures, fresh water, and space to plant and grow fruit, vegetables, and grain. They talked but settled nothing. Tents were set up in some vacant space near the river house if they were needed.

The next day, a rider came to the camp saying that the brothers had met near Bethel, and Jacob's great company was going to camp there. Jacob would come with Esau to be re-united with the family. They would arrive when the sun was high in the sky in two more days.

Isaac and Rebekah gave the messenger food and drink in their home. When he had refreshed himself, they asked about the meeting of their sons.

"When they met, Jacob knelt before his brother. Esau raised him up and kissed him. They hugged, laughed, and danced around in circles. They stayed up all night talking together. There appears to be no more animosity between them. All is well."

The old ones could no longer dance in circles, but their hearts swelled with happiness and their smiles were broad and their eyes glistened with tears of joy.

"Prepare a feast. Kill the fatted calf. Bring the best wine. Light a welcome fire on every hilltop. Beat the drum. Sound the horn. My son is coming home."

Rebekah laughed. "It will be done as you ask. Everything except the fire on the hilltops. That could alarm the city and other villages. But fires will burn in our central square."

For the next two days, the village was alive with activity. When the day arrived, all was prepared. Isaac and Rebekah sat under a canopy beside the road to wait. Gershom was ready to blow the ram's horn when the travellers were sighted.

Just before the sun reached its highest point, the small company of travellers crested the hill. The horn sounded. A cheer went up from the village, and Isaac and Rebekah waited impatiently.

When they came near, the two brothers broke from the rest and ran into their parents' arms. Gershom withdrew a little way off to give them privacy. Soon, the rest of the company caught up.

"Father, mother, this is my family." Jacob nodded and three women stepped forward. He took the hand of one. "This is Leah, first wife, mother of seven sons and my daughter Dinah." She gave a deep bow but stood with her eyes cast down. "Beside her is her handmaiden, Zilpha, mother of my sons, Gad and Asher." She too, bowed and kept her eyes on the ground. Isaac and Rebekah smiled, nodded, and repeated their names as they offered a greeting to them.

Jacob motioned them to move back, and the other woman stepped forward. Jacob's face became solemn, full of sadness. "My beloved wife Rachel is buried in a tomb by the roadside, north of here, near Bethel. She is the mother of my sons, Joseph, and Benjamin. She died shortly after the birth of Benjamin." Rebekah reached out to touch her son, but Isaac held her back with a frown.

"This woman is her handmaiden, Bilhah, the mother of my sons Dan and Naphtali." She bowed low and did not meet the look of the dazed elderly couple. "The rest are our servants."

Jacob's sad countenance changed, and he smiled. "My sons have stayed at Bethel. I will bring them to meet you two or three at a time. I have been blessed with strong sons and a sweet young daughter, but they can be overwhelming all at once. Bethel is a place that is particularly important to me. A story for a night by the fire, not now. I will settle there where there is good land and fresh water. It is only a short distance to travel to see each other."

Rebekah shook her head to help her think. She remembered her role as the wife of the clan's head and bowed briefly. "Welcome to the land of your birth, Jacob. Welcome home, my son. A welcome also to the mothers of your sons and Dinah, your only daughter." She pointed to the village. "Come, there is cool water to wash dusty feet and food and drink for all. We will have a celebration to welcome our son and his family."

As they walked, Jacob questioned his mother. "Where is Deborah? She was so good to me and taught me so much. I looked forward to seeing her."

"Deborah is, as you must know, old. The years have taken their toll. She is not strong enough to greet you here but will welcome you to her room. A quiet visit there will be good for her. We are all living in the stone house by the river now."

"Who is all?"

"Your father and me, Keturah, Deborah, Gershom. Talia and Miri. There would be room for you and your wives to stay as well if that is your wish. The rest can stay in tents we have prepared on the near-by hills."

"I will give it some thought."

They arrived at the river house, where Jacob offered greetings and introductions.

Isaac stood, leaning on Gershom. "We will all meet here for our evening meal and then move to the gathering circle for the welcome home party. I go to my room to rest. Make yourselves at home. We will meet here at sundown."

They gathered for their first meal together in a long time. Esau joined them to welcome his brother home. Isaac offered the blessing, and Jacob noted how his voice was not the strong, commanding one he remembered. But the sacred words were familiar and comforting. *I am glad I kept the rituals of my family. They were a great comfort in my time of exile. We must continue them in this land.*

The talk around the table was lively and animated. There was a lifetime of news to share. When she felt the time was right, Rebekah signalled to the servants that they were finished their meal and they could clear the table.

She smiled at everyone. "We need to begin our walk to the celebration. The leaders of our women will accompany your wives and daughter, Isaac." She turned to the women. Please ask any questions you have of your guides. They will be happy to answer them.

Esther, Ayla, Talia, and Miri joined the group and Rebekah introduced everyone. Jacob looked surprised and pleased that his mother had remembered all the names.

"Well done, mother. I wonder if you can do as well with my sons. Maybe I well bring them all at once to test you." There was a comfortable chuckle around the table.

Gershom helped Isaac to his feet, and they set out for the common area. The women sorted themselves into groups, and they left, all talking at once, it seemed to Jacob. He put his arm around his mother. "I am glad we get to walk together. There is so much I need to hear."

"While I finish clearing all this mess away, why don't you go and see Deborah? She is waiting for you, I am sure. You will find cakes and wine in her room that you can share with her. Meet me here when you are done."

"Thank you for reminding me. I had forgotten in all the excitement."

She pointed the way to the room, and he walked down the hallway.

Rebekah sighed. *I wonder if I should have warned him. Too late now, and he is a grown man and must have seen old people in these passing years. He knows how long he has been gone. I cannot count the years, but it has been a lifetime in many ways.*

A silent and sombre Jacob returned shortly. "I think it is good I came home now. Deborah is extremely ill, isn't she, mother?"

"She is old, Jacob. She is seasons older than I am if you remember. But yes, it is good you are home. I think she will be leaving us before very long."

He offered his mother his arm, and they left the house to join the party.

When they arrived, Jacob looked at the square in wonder. There were more people than he had expected. Three flaming fires lit the whole grassy area, and an enormous table stood at each end, laden with food and drinks. His father rested comfortably in a large chair, well-padded with colourful cushions. Keturah sat beside him, looking lovely in a gown of soft blue fabric that reflected the light.

"How grand it all looks, mother. So much larger and more impressive than I remember."

"You weren't much more than a youth when you left. You were more interested in rough games with your friends, than how things looked."

"There are many more people, too."

"The village is vastly enlarged. The family of Father Abraham, your family, is one of importance in the area. We are prosperous, and our goods are traded in many places."

"This will one day be my responsibility. It is a great burden for me to take on. Not too soon, I hope."

Rebekah looked at her son. "You took that burden on years ago. A bowl of pottage and a plate of stew sealed your future life. And that is true whether you realized it then or not."

"I understood it in a hazy sort of way, far into the future. But my future is right before my eyes now."

Rebekah rubbed his hair, as she did when he was a child. "Tonight, just enjoy your welcome home party. Tomorrow we can begin to plan."

Jacob kissed his mother. "Still as wise as ever. I will speak to father and then see who else I might know." He walked to join his father and sat on the grass at his feet.

As the night went on, Rebekah watched her sons carefully. Esau, as she expected, drank too much wine, and was soon in the company of a woman who had arrived, uninvited from Hebron. She shook her head in dismay. Jacob was moving around the crowd, speaking to anyone who stopped him for a word. His face was full of happiness and his hearty laughter rang out over the noise of the crowd.

She walked over and sat with Isaac and Keturah.

"Can I get you some food?" asked Keturah.

"Thank you, but I am fine. Miri has been taking loving care of me. She and Talia are such fine women, and they are so good to me."

Isaac grunted. "They take good care of all of us. Including the ancient ones, like Deborah and me."

"Yes indeed. I just came to speak with you and shortly I will go and see how she is and get her settled for the night."

Rebekah paused at the door to Deborah's room. She took a deep breath and then entered the room. Miri sat by the bed in a chair. Her eyes were closed, and her head nodded slightly. Rebekah touched her gently. "Miri. It is Rebekah. I can sit with Deborah now."

Miri sat up and stared. "I was asleep. I am sorry about that."

"Nothing to be sorry about. You are here with our dear friend, and you would have heard her if she awoke. How has she been?"

"Sleeping most of the time. She rouses sometimes and tries to speak, but I cannot make out what she is saying."

"It is all right. I am here now. You get a good sleep unless you want to join the celebration. It is still going strong."

"I think I will, just for a little while. Good night, Rebekah." And she crept away without a sound.

Rebekah sank wearily into the chair beside the bed. She took Deborah's hand and held it gently. With her other hand, she felt the old one's cheeks and forehead. She leaned down and put her ear on the barley moving chest and listened. Rebekah tucked the blanket around the still frame and tenderly stroked the cool hands and arms.

"All my life, you have been by my side. Now, in your last hours, I am here at your bedside. How can I go on without you?" A tear trailed down her cheek and added to the others soaking the blanket. "I know you would tell me I have much to live for. The return of my son, his wives, and my grandchildren. But who will scold me when I am selfish? Who will weep with me for lost opportunities? Who will remind me of my blessings and my duties?"

The sounds from the celebration were growing quiet. A voice at the door asked for permission to enter and Keturah came in. She carried a basket. "I have brought bread, soup, and tea. I can stay and have some with you or leave as you wish."

"Stay. Please."

All during the long night, the two women sat on cushions at the bedside of Deborah. Her breathing was irregular and shallow. Her skin drawn tightly across cheekbones that defined the crepey skin. She stirred once and seemed to want to say something. Rebekah leaned over her and put her ear close the Deborah's dry lips. She could barely hear the words.

"I do not want to lie in a cave. Bury me under the great oak tree near Bethel."

It was her last breath. Rebekah and Keturah held each other and wept.

Chapter Sixty-Three

Rebekah roused at the gentle voice of Keturah speaking her name. "What is it, Keturah?"

"Miri and Talia. May they come in?"

"Of course." Rebekah stepped away from the bed. Talia and Miri came in, weeping.

"Deborah has gone to the land of eternal rest gently in her sleep."

The two young women sat on the bed and rocked back and forth. Dry-eyed, and silent now. Grief too deep to reveal. Rebekah and Keturah waited until at last a wail of pain filled the room. Keturah and Rebekah formed a circle of grief with the weeping young women.

They heard Isaac call out, "Rebekah." He repeated it over and over. Gershom was soon with him, trying to calm his fear.

Rebekah withdrew from the circle. "I must go to him. He will not calm down until he hears my voice." She went to her husband and Gershom stepped back into the shadows. The women, in Deborah's room, stood respectfully as the soothing voice of Rebekah drifted to where they were. When Isaac was calm, knowing Rebekah was nearby, she returned and took control. "Miri, you fetch Ayla. Talia, get Esther."

Gershom entered the room. He paused and bowed his head at the still form of Deborah. "With your permission, I will get help to carry her to the woman's house."

Rebekah nodded. "Thank you, Gershom." She turned to Keturah. "We will get properly dressed and go to the moon house."

"Can I get you anything to eat before we go?"

"Thank you, no. We can do that later." And she left the room.

The women had gathered and stood, waiting for Deborah. Men's steps clattered on the stones. The noise seemed like thunder to the women, who stood solemnly in their grief. Talia opened the door, and the men entered. Ever since the death of Sarah, the presence of men, while not encouraged, no longer caused anxiety. They did what they needed to do, stood for a moment by Deborah's body, bowed to the women, and slipped away into the night. The first streamers of gold were fluttering over the hills.

The women began their sacred task of preparing Deborah for her final rest. Rebekah had chosen the burial clothes for Deborah and handed them to Esther. As they worked, Gilla, a singer of songs, hummed a lament.

Word spread quickly and soon a circle of women stood in the room and joined Gilla in the wordless song of grief. Others came and spread food and drink on the table. Rebekah lit the sacred fire, which would burn until the ceremony ended, and Deborah was laid to rest. Rebekah returned to her room to gather her strength for the hours ahead. As she entered her room, Jacob was waiting. He held out his arms, and Rebekah fell into them, and the tears flowed. He held her until the sobbing stopped, then he took her to her favourite seat.

"Mother, you have lost the woman who loved you all your life. But she did not just belong to you. She raised me to be the man I am, as surely as you. She was like the tree of life to me, and I loved her fiercely. All the years I was in exile, she managed to get word to me, that you were well. She kept me informed of this family I had been forced to leave. She has been my nurse, my teacher, and my grandmother."

"You were the son she never had. She loved you as she would her own child. I wonder how we can honour her properly."

"We must do that. The whole of our people respected and loved her. She had time for the old and the young, the strong and the weak, the wise and the foolish."

"Have there been any decisions about her burial place?"

"Not yet. Do you have any thoughts, Jacob."

"Yes, I do. I said she was a tree of life for me, strong, dependable, a place of rest and calm. We are camped just south of Bethel. It is a place that has great meaning for me. There is a great oak there, and if she were to be buried beneath its branches, I would be honoured to take care of it. "

"The thought of that pleases me, and I remember Deborah spoke of it. Thank you. Now I must return and make the arrangements."

Jacob helped her to stand and put his arm around her. He walked with her to the place of mourning. At the door, he held her tenderly, kissed her cheek and watched as she entered.

The space was pulsing with grief. Rebekah smiled a brief smile, as she saw the bee that Mia and Talia had made, lying at Deborah's feet. Shira's rich voice, called Rebekah to the present. She nodded to Esther to begin.

The comforting voice of the spiritual leader wafted on the breeze that carried the scent of flowers that filled the room with colour.

"El Shaddai, mother of mercy, who dwells in the high mountain, today we bring our sister Deborah to her final resting place. As she brought comfort and peace to us in her life, may she rest in the peaceful valleys of your mountain, in her final long sleep. Protect her in her lying place, provide a sure rest to our sister Deborah. Amen."

Women who wished to tell a story had been given a candle. They flickered in the dim light of the room and their light danced in hope on the walls. As each woman shared her story, she blew out her candle. Hands of blessing and farewell, fluttered around the circle.

The stories ended and Rebekah stood. On unsteady feet, she walked to the litter where Deborah lay. Beside the body of her lifelong companion, she placed a candle and a small round stone.

"The candles are a way we remember and honour the grandmothers. This stone I place is to remember Sarah, foremother of our people." Beside the stone she rested a waxy piece of honeycomb. "The honeycomb will help us remember the sweetness Deborah brought to our village and all its people. Goodbye, friend, companion, and guide. El Shaddai, mother of all awaits you."

She stumbled back to her place, blinded by tears. The open arms of Ayla were waiting for her. Shira hummed a lament as the women filed out of the room. No one went to the central gathering place for food and drink. They joined the children and men who lined the road for as far as one could see. They stood, in silent tribute, as Deborah was carried north, to her resting place under the great oak, the oak of weeping.

Chapter Sixty-Four

There was great concern for the well-being of Rebekah. She went through the motions each day, but there was no joy in her step, no smile on her face and no sparkle in her eyes. Keturah tried to reach her, but with little success. She spoke with the others, Isaac, Jacob, Esther, and Ayla. They were worried and shared their concern.

"She looks but doesn't see."

"I don't think she really listens to me when I talk to her."

"We have lost our Rebekah. How can we help her?"

No one had an answer.

One evening, Rebekah and Isaac were sitting near the river. Isaac sat close to her with his arm around her waist. "The river sings a pleasant song tonight, don't you think?"

There was no response. He wondered what he could do to draw her back to him.

She heaved a great shuddering sigh and turned to look at him.

"The wind has turned. The rains will be here soon. Isaac, I need to go away for a while."

"Where would you like to go?"

"To the healing place, the school where I went before."

"The school of Shem and Ever?'

Her voice lightened. "Yes. That is the healing place I need to go to. I would like to go tomorrow, before the rains come."

"Gershom will take us there. I will ask him to prepare a cart for you to ride. Keturah can help with all the rest. It will be good for us to return to that place of healing."

"I am glad you agree I need to go there, but I feel I must stay there alone. Gershom can take me and return in a week to bring me back."

Isaac tightened his arm around her. "You do not want me to stay?"

"It isn't that I don't want you, dear one. I don't want anyone. I need to be by myself and let my spirit heal. They can help me there. I know they can." She twisted around and took his face in her hands. "I love you, Isaac. I want to be whole again for you. But I need to walk this hard journey alone. Please understand."

"Of course, my beloved. If that is your wish, your need, it shall be as you ask."

"I have one more request. Please come to my room and spend the night with me. Your warmth would be a great comfort."

He leaned toward her and kissed her with great tenderness. She drew him closer and responded with an urgency he had not felt from her for a long time. Her head rested on his shoulder, and they sat in comfortable silence as the moon made a golden path on the water.

In the morning as they gathered for the first meal of the day, Isaac told them that Rebekah was going away for a few days. "She is returning to the yeshiva. They helped her before and she is sure they can again. She chooses to stay there alone."

Jacob looked up. "I am returning to my family. I will take her with me to the school. It is only a short distance out of my way."

Keturah looked relieved. "That is a wonderful plan. We women will get the food and clothes ready. You men get the cart and an ox."

"When is she returning here?" Jacob spoke about what everyone was thinking.

Rebekah joined the circle. "I plan on staying about seven or eight days."

"I will take you there, mother, and can return to get you when you tell me to. A few days will be perfect. When I return, I will bring my eldest sons to meet their family."

All agreed and while Rebekah ate her meal, they scattered to do what needed to be done. The first thing Keturah did was inform Esther and Ayla. They hurried to the river house.

In a brief time, they piled the oxcart with cushions, blankets, a bundle of clothes and food and water for the journey. Esther offered a prayer for a safe journey, and Rebekah received hugs and blessings from the small gathering. Jacob and his party waited at the bottom of the hill. They had gathered on the road north and were eager to get underway. Gershom led the ox cart down the hill as Rebekah said goodbye to those she was leaving behind. They stood silently, each hoping that this would prove to be what Rebekah needed. No one moved until the travellers disappeared beyond the hill.

Keturah took Isaac's arm. "Do not worry, old one. She will be back soon, and you will have your beloved companion with you again." She led him to the river house and settled him for the morning. She brought the skins he asked for and she left him to his work and his thoughts.

Chapter Sixty-Five

Rebekah soon learned that Jacob was an excellent travelling companion. He kept up a lively conversation as they journeyed, pointing out interesting landmarks. Rebekah walked beside him. The action of walking eased her troubled mind, and the time passed quickly. They stopped every little while, to rest and to have some nourishment. After the second break, Rebekah climbed into the cart and the rocking soon put her to sleep. As soon as he sensed her deep breathing, Jacob snapped his whip over the ox's head, and he began to trot. The miles slipped by quickly. At a bend in the road, Jacob saw a small river. He guided the cart off the road and the bumping woke Rebekah.

"Hello. I hope you have had a good rest. We have come a long way while you dozed. Our faithful ox needs a drink and a bit of a rest, and we can take a break as well."

"You have most certainly earned a break, and I need to walk a bit." She climbed out of the cart, stretched her arms, and walked to the riverbank. Jacob joined her when he had tethered the ox near the water and within reach of tender shoots. With a bowl, he scooped water from the river and offered Rebekah a drink. She grasped it. "There is nothing as refreshing as cool, fresh water."

"Especially when we have been eating dust since early morning." Jacob stretched out on the grass and cradled his head in his hands.

"How much further do we have to go?"

"Not far. We should be there well before sunset. Will that be in time for a meal?"

"I am sure that they will feed us when we arrive. Hospitality is especially important to our hosts. You will stay the night, I hope."

"If I will be welcome. I would rather not travel at night."

Jacob closed his eyes as he had fallen asleep. Rebekah walked to the grazing ox and rubbed his ears. "Are you tired too? I am feeling better just being in this quiet place." She sat on a rock and listened to the sounds around her. The wind in the trees, the splashing waves, and the birds singing their songs to the evening sky. She was startled to hear Jacob calling her name.

"Time to get moving again. The sky is beginning to fade into grey."

They made their way back to the road to finish their journey.

Jacob touched Rebekah's sleeve. "Can you tell me what to expect when we get there?"

"Of course. There will be tasty food, comfortable beds and people who can help me. The meals are always on time and there is no talking, except to ask for food or drink. I think there will not be many guests as the harvest is completed by now. We may be the only guests there."

They walked in silence until Rebekah spotted the trees that stood guard at the gate to the school. "We are here. We are here."

They turned into the lane and walked to the long, low building. Rebekah went directly to the bell and pulled its cord. In just a moment, the door opened. "Welcome travellers. Have you come for the night?"

"I am Jacob, and I need a place to spend the night. This is Rebekah, and she needs to stay longer for a rest."

"We welcome you to our place of peace. A worker will put your things in rooms for you and take care of the beast and the cart. Follow me to the dining room, please. We are about to have our evening meal. Do not be concerned, there is always enough food and plenty to share with others."

Rebekah remembered it all, and the memory was a pleasant one. The host pointed out the door to the dining room and the rooms where they could wash the dust of the road from their hands and faces.

"When you are ready, just enter the room. We will wait for you."

When Rebekah left her room, Jacob was waiting in the hall. At the door, he took a deep breath and held the door open for Rebekah to enter. The room was exactly as she remembered. Dishes neatly laid on the table, candles and flowers made it colourful and friendly, and the staff stood waiting for them.

They heard a gasp. A voice that she remembered said, "Rebekah. Welcome back." She looked along the table and recognized Abigail. She was much older, with silver hair and a map of wrinkles on her smiling face. "May I offer introductions?" The man at the end of the table nodded.

"Friends, this is Rebekah. She was here years ago and returns now to a warm welcome. Edna is still here, Rebekah, but is confined to her bed. You may visit her tomorrow. Sadly, Gabriella has gone to her long and peaceful rest. All the rest are new to you, and names will be spoken later. Who is with you?"

Rebekah bowed, and so did Jacob. "This is Jacob, the son of my husband Isaac and me. Alas, Isaac is too ill to make the journey and so Jacob has brought me here and will return to take me home."

The tall, distinguished man at the end of the table said. "I am Samuel. When I have finished the blessing, we can sit and have our meal."

"Blessed are You, Lord God, King of the Universe, who brings forth bread from the earth.

Blessed are You, Lord God, King of the Universe, who brings forth the fruit of the trees, and by his word everything came to be, Blessed are you, Lord God Almighty."

The familiar words were a comfort to Jacob in this strange place. The food was tasty and there was ample for everyone. At the end of the meal, another offered the blessing, and all prepared to go to their rooms.

Abigail led the way to their rooms and bid them a good night. "We will meet in the morning to break bread together." With a slight bow and a broad smile, she turned and walked away.

Jacob paused at the door. "I will not see you in the morning, mother. I shall be up with the sun and on my way at once. Be at peace, I will see you in five days' time. Goodnight."

Rebekah entered her room and lay on the bed. "This is where I need to be. Blessed are you, El Shaddai. Watch over me and guide me each day." She blew out the little lamp and closed her eyes.

Chapter Sixty-Six

The ringing of a bell woke Rebekah from a deep sleep. For a moment, she wondered where she was. Then she remembered; she smiled and stretched. She carefully stood and looked out the small window. "I am at the end of the house. That is the garden on the east side. How lovely the flowers look with the dew glistening on the leaves and petals." She slipped off her night tunic and chose a clean blue tunic to wear at breakfast. The hall was empty as she walked to the dining room. Soft voices came from the open door.

A woman stood there as if waiting for someone. She smiled in greeting. "Good morning. I am Elan, the spiritual leader. I hope you slept well."

"Good morning. I am Rebekah, and I slept very well, thank you."

"Come and I will introduce you to the others." Together they entered the room. "Good morning, everyone. This is Rebekah. She is here for a visit with us." The people around the table smiled and nodded. Abigail smiled the broadest. "I know Rebekah from her last visit here. Welcome. May I introduce her?"

Elan nodded in agreement. Abigail introduced Moshe, the men's spiritual leader, and the head of the school. Beside him stood Nathan, his pupil, and Yoah, the overseer of all the outside work and the animals. Next to Abigail stood a tall, stately woman, named Gilla, who was a midwife and healer, and next to her, Emuna, her pupil. Each smiled and bowed. Rebekah responded with a smile and a bow.

Moshe said the morning blessing, and they all sat. The breakfast was ample and delicious, eaten in silence as Rebekah remembered. As they rose at the end of the meal, Elan invited Rebekah to the central courtyard when she was ready to begin her time at the school. Back in her room, Rebekah brushed her hair and re-did the braid. She slipped a light shawl around her shoulders and went to the courtyard.

It was exactly as she remembered it. Benches and chairs formed a circle around the fire pit, and all had cushions and a soft blanket on them. The chairs were light and could easily be moved around the space. There were lamps and bowls placed within easy reach of the seats. As she breathed in the air, scented with the perfume of the trees and flowers, Abigail and Elan came into the space.

Elan walked to the fountain in one corner. "Let's sit here. I love the sound of the tinkling water." They gathered in a small circle and the music of the water calmed any feeling of unease Rebekah had.

Elan gestured to Abigail. "Since you know our guest, why don't you tell us about her?"

"Rebekah came here many years ago. We were both much younger then." A grin spread across all the faces. "She was pregnant with twins. Tell us about your babies if you would like to."

"I have two sons. Esau, the eldest, is a shepherd and a hunter, a man of the outdoors. He has two wives, and eight sons, but alas, no daughters. Jacob, the younger, lived for many years with my brother in Haran. Jacob lives a gentler life and is a man of the land, and a scholar. He has recently returned home with his wife and two concubines, twelve sons and one daughter. One wife died giving birth to his youngest son."

Elan exhaled. "You have a large family and that is a gift from the great mother of all."

Abigail continued. "Rebekah is the daughter of Ruth, daughter of Zera. Her father is Bethuel. She is married to Isaac, son of the great tribal chief Abraham. The mother of Isaac was Sarah, and we tell her story as we sit around our evening fires."

Elan clasped her hands in delight. "Perhaps you can tell us more stories about Sarah."

"I did not meet her. She had died before Isaac took me as his wife. But we can talk, and I may have fresh stories to tell you."

A servant from the kitchen came and brought a pitcher of water and a tray of fruit. She placed them on the central table and left without a word.

"Thank you," said Elan. Let's get some refreshment and then we will tell you about the routine and what we expect of you while you are here."

They returned to their chairs and Abigale spoke. "Is there anything you need to know, Rebekah, before you tell us why you came to this place of healing?"

"I think I have all I need to know now, but it will be helpful to hear what you expect of me. I came because I am still grieving the loss of my lifelong friend and dear companion, Deborah. Grief follows me like a dark cloud, and I hoped that the peace of this wonderful place would help me heal, as I listen to the teachings of the wise ones who live here."

Elan patted Rebekah's hand. "We will do our best to help you. We have songs, stories, and rituals. Along with our healing herbs and fragrant oils, fresh air and good food, I am sure we can help you remember your friend with gratitude, and ease the pain of the grief."

"What do you need in return?"

Abigale teased. "We expect a lot. A lot of your time and a lot of co-operation".

"But I must pay you for my food and my room."

Elan stood. "There are many chores that need to be done. Chores in the kitchen, in the gardens, in the dining room, and in the house. When you feel able, just show up in one of those places in the morning and someone will give you a task. Now excuse me please. I must meet with Moshe." She waved as she walked to the house.

"Is it still that simple? Just as it was before?" asked Rebekah.

"Yes. It is that simple. There are flower beds and herbal gardens to tend as well as the food garden. And there is cooking and cleaning, washing clothes and bedding; water jugs need to be filled and—well, you get the idea.

"And the afternoons"

"We gather here, and Elan will have a plan for our time together. Evenings are free. You might do some mending or weaving, go for a walk, or just come here and see what is happening. If you wish, we can do something together in the evenings."

"It all sounds too good to be true, but it is what I hoped for when I came here. Now I will go to the gardens and see what I can accomplish before we meet here again. If I remember, there is a bell in the early afternoon to call us?"

"You remember well, and it has been a very long time since you were here. I look forward to hearing more about your sons and all those grandchildren."

The days passed quickly. Each morning, Rebekah worked in the gardens, weeding, watering, and picking flowers for the rooms. She spent the afternoons with one or more of the teachers at the school, learning to let go of the past and turning to the future with renewed hope. In the evenings, there were many ways for her to spend her time. Most evenings, she talked with Abigail, but twice they gathered with the others to tell stories and sing songs. When she went to her room and prepared for sleep, she was at ease with the changes she felt in her heart, her soul, and in her body as well. Tense muscles felt relaxed, her breathing was regular and calm, and her heart sang a song of peace. She stood at her window and the moon bathed her in silver.

"Great mother, spirit of El Shaddai, gratitude fills my heart. Thank you for this sacred place and for the people who make it a refuge for the weary and the ones who feel lost. I pray I can keep this peace in my mind and heart as I journey home tomorrow."

With thanksgiving in her heart, she lay on her bed and settled into the arms of sleep.

Chapter Sixty-Seven

Rebekah woke to the musical twittering of the birds in the garden. She hugged herself and replied to the birds. "Today I go home. I heard Jacob when he arrived last night and I am ready for our journey home. She ate quickly and went looking for Jacob. He was waiting with the ox and he had loaded her bags.

She greeted him, and he hugged for close. "I hope your time here has been good for you."

"It has my son, and I am ready to return home."

"Will you walk or ride in the cart?"

"I will walk, and you can tell me more about your family."

They walked side by side, and Jacob told stories of his boisterous sons, his beautiful wife."

Rebekah was silent for some time then with some worry asked him about Zilpah and Bilhah.

"They have been wonderful friends and companions to Adinah. Her life has been difficult and that is a story for another time. Those two women, friends, not servants, have been a great help in raising the two girls. Leah was quite a challenge as a young girl. But she grew into a fine woman. And her sister Rachel was a wonderful person. Zilpah and Bilhah have born four of my sons."

"It seems strange to me, wives and concubines. I don't think I could have lived that way. I am very glad that Isaac was like his father and only wanted one wife."

"Times and places and events, change things mother. We have all been very happy, most of the time."

They walked in silence for many miles. Rebekah broke the lull by asking for help to get into the cart. She was soon asleep, and Jacob urged the old ox to hurry along.

The miles passed quickly, and the sun was reaching the highest point in its journey when Jacob pulled off the road and onto the grassy riverbank.

"Time to give this old ox a bit of a rest and a drink. We can enjoy water and fruit and dabble a bit in the river."

When Jacob signaled the break was over the miles and the hours flew by as Rebekah told Jacob about the family he was now part of. She was surprised that he seemed to know little of Abraham or Isaac. She asked about her brother, and soon sensed that he was going to say only a few words about him. *Things must be difficult. I had hoped Laban might have changed.*

The sun was just starting its descent when they stopped at the bottom of the hill, leading to the settlement. They stopped for a breather then began the climb.

There was a crowd gathered on the hilltop. Someone had been watching for the return of Rebekah and spread the word. They cheered and clapped as the weary travelers climbed the hill. Rebekah smiled at the happy gathering. "Thank you for this welcome. It is good to be home." She searched for Isaac and saw him seated at the gate to the house.

Happy voices called out a welcome and continued to clap as they made their way to the river house. Isaac stood to meet them as they approached. He welcomed Jacob with a hearty handshake and a clap on the back. He kissed Rebekah on both cheeks and held her close to his heart.

They gathered around the fire, and Isaac said the prayer before meals and added words to thank the mountain god for the return of his beloved Rebekah. The conversation was loud and lively, filled with questions, answers, and laughter.

After a time, Rebekah stood. "This has been a long and tiring day for me. It is time I retired to my room for the night. We will talk more in the morning."

Isaac joined her and they walked arm in arm to their rooms, bathed in moonlight, they were unaware of the loving eyes that followed their departure.

Chapter Sixty-Eight

Winter was once again casting its grey pall over the world. The skies, the rain, the mist, the clouds, and the mood of the people were grey. Rebekah had always reacted badly to the cold, wet weather. One evening, when there was only a light mist, Isaac and Jacob bundled Rebekah into warmed blankets and a heavy woolen coat and the three went down to the river to listen to the water.

The women were ready and gathered in the common room at the river house. They were all present out of their love and concern for Rebekah. Keturah, Talia, and Miri had hot tea and fresh almond bread ready to welcome their guests. Alya and Esther arrived and shook their heads to get rid of the dampness, and they gathered around the cheery fire.

Keturah spoke first. “Thank you for coming. We all know why we are here. It is because of our concern for Rebekah.”

In her quiet way, Miri asked, “Has she always had this deep sadness in the rainy season?”

Esther nodded. “Some years are worse than others. But we are all aware that she is not the Rebekah we once knew.”

With a catch in her voice and tears in her eyes, Miri whispered. “It makes me sad to see her so unhappy. When she came back from the school, she was so alive and now—.”

Ayla took a piece of bread and dipped it in the honey. “I can only say a little. Rebekah is a private person, as we all know and understand. She is not well, and she knows her days are few on this earth. I am doing all I can to keep her comfortable and ease her pain, but she grows weaker each day.”

All eyes turned to Keturah as she held out her hands in a gesture of peace. “She has spoken to me of her death and has told me what she wants to happen. As expected, she wishes to die in the woman’s tent surrounded by those she loves." Talia gave a muffled sob and Dinah went to her and held her in a warm embrace.

Keturah smiled and continued. "She has asked that, like Sarah at her death, the men who were closest to her will stay with her in the woman's house. That will be Isaac, of course, and her two sons. Jacob and Esau. Jacob has sent a messenger to inform Esau. She asked for flowers, music and many lamps to light her way."

Together, they planned a fitting ceremony for the leader of the women.

The men with Rebekah by the river sat close to her to hear her feeble voice. "Isaac, it is time to name the way the work will get done when I am not here. Gershom has been working at my side, and he can take over the books and the records. The rest is up to you."

"My dearest one. Must we talk about this now? Let us hear the song of the river."

"I need to know what will happen. Jacob, what will you do?"

"I am glad to leave the records to Gershom. I have little interest in the marks and what they mean. He will keep Isaac informed, as you have. There are overseers in all the vineyards, gardens, and pastures. They do good work and can continue under Isaac's oversight.

I will live mostly with my family and visit here often enough to keep things running well."

"And your brother, Esau?"

"He will do as he has always done. Hunt game for everyone and live near the city which he loves."

Isaac nodded in agreement. "I am getting cold and tired. I am sure Rebekah is too. We will return to the house. While we warm around our fire, you may continue this discussion."

Rebekah waved her hand toward the women's house. "I will go there now. It is time. Get the women to come and care for me."

Word flew on secret wings around the camp. Soon fires and lamps glowed in the sacred space. Flowers and cedar boughs, in colourful jars and clusters, brightened every corner and filled the air with an earthy fragrance. The bed was ready and waiting for Rebekah. Jacob asked for permission to enter, and he and his brother carried their mother to her bed. Gershom led Isaac to the head of the bed and helped him to sit on the ground, supported by many cushions. He sat ready to cradle the head of his beloved in his arms. Her sons gently placed her on the bed and covered her with a soft blanket. They sat one on each side, holding her hands and stroking her arms. Shira and her musicians hummed quietly near the fire. The women formed a comforting circle and began their sombre watch.

From the outside, the sounds of morning began just as Rebekah breathed her last breath. The stillness in the room was all-embracing. Jacob stood and touched his father's shoulder. "It is done, father. Mother is at rest from all her labours." The old man reached out and touched the face of his beloved, then leaned forward and kissed her forehead. Jacob helped him to sit up and his sons helped him stand. They almost carried his frail form from the tent.

All day the preparations went on. Mostly in silence, only an occasional gentle sob told of the sorrow that each one carried. The space smelled of cedar, candles glowed in every corner, and colourful cushions softened the space. The sacred fire burned, and its smoke carried the memories of the ones who mourned out to the sky. In the women's space, friends told stories, the women sang songs, and Esther and Ayla offered prayers. Talia and Miri stayed close to Dinah and held her as she rocked and moaned. In her hand she clutched a fragrant branch of cedar.

The ceremony ended and the chief mourners came out into the warm sun. Four sons of Jacob entered the tent and lifted the litter and carried it out of the room. Rebekah began her final journey. The people lined the steep path to the Cave of Machpelah. They stood shoulder to shoulder all the way to the top. Four more sons carried their grandfather Isaac on a litter beside his beloved Rebekah. It had taken all the skill and tact Gershom had to persuade the old man not to try the arduous climb. Jacob, and the rest of his sons walked behind the litters. Following them was Esau, his wives and children. The women, clung to each other as they stumbled, blinded by tears up the rugged path. The men walked with slow and halting steps.

At the tomb of Sarah and Abraham, Rebekah was laid to rest.

Isaac stood leaning on the entrance stones. He raised one feeble hand in prayer.

"At the blueness of the sky and the warmth of summer,
We will remember Rebekah.
When the suns rises, and when the sun sets,
We will remember Rebekah.
As long as we live, she too will live.
For we will remember Rebekah."

The sun broke through the clouds and bathed the valley of hope in its summer warmth.

List of Characters: Biblical

Abraham- Patriarch of the Hebrew people

Sarah -wife of Abraham

Hagar -slave of Sarah later known as Keturah

Isaac – son of Abraham and Sarah

Ishmael – son of Abraham and Hagar

Eliezar – servant to Abraham

Rebekah – wife of Isaac

Esau- son of Isaac and Rebekah

Jacob- son of Isaac and Rebekah, twin to Esau

Bethuel –nephew of Abraham,

Laban-son of Bethuel

Adinah-wife of Laban

Dinah-daughter of Jacob

Fictional Characters

In the village

Rivkah -companion to Sarah, leader of women

Deborah -nurse and companion to Rebekah

Ayla – head midwife

Shira – singer

Esther – spiritual leader and healer

Talia – maid to Keturah

Miri – servant to Deborah

Gershom - servant to Isaac

Baruch – builder

Benjamin – servant to Isaac

At The School

Jessi – spiritual leader, Leah's teacher

Nava – midwife and healer, Rachel's teacher

Zahava – leader of women, Adinah's teacher

Amos – male leader

Ruth and Dafna – workers

Questions

1. Name the matriarchs whose stories are told in the Book of Genesis.
2. What do you know about these women of the Hebrew Scriptures?
3. How would you describe Rebekah as portrayed in *The Valley of Hope* story?
4. Give examples of the attitudes and treatment of women by the society of that ancient time.
5. How has that changed over the centuries?
6. What events on a global scale might have caused the changing of attitudes toward women?
7. In what ways can you draw similarities to the life of Rebekah and your life?
8. Are there events in your life that help you connect with Rebekah's life?
9. Can you make any comparisons between her growing sense of the divine and your own spiritual journey?
10. Where do you find hope in the valleys of your life?

Acknowledgements

A book is the end result of unnumbered encounters with wisdom gleaned from books read, stories shared, and life's lessons learned along the way.

To all who helped me be who I am, and who I am still becoming, a heartfelt thank you.

To my daughters, Deb, my live-in IT person, ready to help when the computer gremlin attacks, and Kathy, first reader and gentle, wise critic.

To those who read the manuscript and offered their wisdom, Kathy, Gloria, Pat and Paul.

Erin, whose cover design reflects so beautifully the light we all follow.

And my patient, skillful, editor, Gloria, always there with great advice, and support in all the tasks of publishing a book

Manufactured by Amazon.ca
Bolton, ON

35025251R00197